THE FAMILY

The Sean Rooney Psychosleuth Series

Tom O. Keenan

M^cNIDDER | &
GRACE
CRIME

Published by McNidder & Grace
21 Bridge Street
Carmarthen
SA31 3JS
UK

www.mcnidderandgrace.co.uk

Original paperback first published 2019
© Tom O. Keenan

A catalogue record for this work is available from the British Library.

ISBN: 9780857161970
Ebook: 9780857161987

Designed by JS Typesetting Ltd, Porthcawl
Cover design: Lara Peralta

Printed and bound in the UK by Gomer Press Ltd, Wales

ABOUT THE AUTHOR

Tom O. Keenan lived in Glasgow for many years before moving to Morar in the North West coast of Scotland. This is Tom's follow-up to his critically acclaimed debut novel *The Father* which was shortlisted for the CWA Debut Dagger in 2014. His experience as an independent social worker in the mental health field informs and underpins his writing.

DEDICATION

To Maggie, Gemma and Claire,
and all the wonderful people in my life.

CHAPTER ONE

It's Friday night and Jackie lies wounded and flat out on the road, outside an obliterated taxi on Glasgow's Sauchiehall Street. A stunned silence has replaced the drunken banter at the rank, the sing-song with the auld busker, the tapping of feet to Johnny the fiddler.

Next to her broken body, a mobile is in bits on the ground, the one with a device triggered by a call answered by her minutes before. And there am I, Sean Rooney, standing over her saying, "In the name of the Father," with tears in my voice.

An old lady asks, "Is she dying son?"

"I think so. I was blessing her."

"Aw, last rights, get it. Do you know her name?"

"Aye, DCI Jacqueline Kaminski… she used to be my wife."

I turn to see shocked faces, hands over mouths, shaking of heads. A cacophony of questions arrives. "What happened to her?" "Why's he standing over her, blessing her?" "Where's the polis when you need them?" I look past them to see Jean Dempsie, MI5, looking on from a doorway. Why was she there? I turn back to Jackie. I want to help her, but I have to get out of there fast, disappear, go somewhere no one would find me; especially her dad, Hubert, the Chief Constable of Strathclyde Police.

A bomb attack on a DCI while travelling in a private taxi confirms Glasgow has moved on from the chibbing after the clubs spill out, the female spats, the muggings. This is a much more cynical and scary climate of crime in No Mean City. An attack on Jackie, in charge of the investigation into The Father, the infamous and recently deceased leader of The Family, a collective of the most feared crime families in the country, breaks the code of the traditional mob not to involve the police nor the public in their turf wars. This is a real game changer; even more so as she's Hubert Kaminski's daughter, a man who doesn't take prisoners.

I turn away, pull my hood over my head and scurry along Sauchiehall Street; just another disturbed man in Glasgow that night. *In the name of sweet Jesus, what happened back there?* I ask myself, as I splash through the puddles on the pedestrian precinct in Buchanan Street.

Jackie, left close to death on a Glasgow street, and you standing over her like a vulture on carrion.

Jesus, the unholy voice in my head is back. It has a habit of turning up in times of stress, or when my mania or depression opens the door into my mind to let it out. "Go away," I tell it, then sit down on one of those black marble seats to think back. "Why was Jean Dempsie there, what did she, they, have to do with it? I wanted to help Jackie; but I couldn't, I was frozen to the spot."

Well, you made the call.

I rest my head in my hands. "Christ, it was her or me." I had succumbed to another bloody double bind, I make the call, lose Jackie; don't, I'm a dead man. Don't make the call, save Jackie; do, I lose Jackie. I need to make another call.

Hubert is on the warpath. His daughter is now in a hospital bed in the GRI. He's a hard man with a harder reputation and he wants answers, he wants arrests. The teams have been active on the streets and a DCI, his DCI, has been attacked. He needs to get those who did this and he seldom fails.

At his desk, bedecked with pictures of his family, his new wife, one of Jackie as a child on holiday, he pulls out his "crook book", as he calls it. His first call is to Davy McGing, the boss of the McGing firm, only the most powerful team in Glasgow. Is this a mob hit? If anyone knows, he will.

"Davy, it's me."

Hubert doesn't need to introduce himself, Davy is expecting this call. "Aye, how's it goin' big man, you on about Jackie?"

"Don't suppose you'd know anything about it?"

"Blown up in a taxi?"

"Gold star; what do you know?"

There's one thing Davy knows; his telephone is tapped, not by Hubert but most likely MI5, given his prominence in the Glasgow underworld and his days gun running to Northern Ireland.

"Hitting a DCI in a taxi on a Glasgow street, who the fuck would be daft enough to do that?"

Hubert draws enough breath to deliver a blast. "Look, son," he says, even although Davy is only two years younger than his sixty-three, "I don't give a fuck how many of each of you fuckers kill each other, no member of the public nor police officer gets caught up, injured or harmed, in your fucking wars. You know the score; you got that?"

Davy puts the phone back to his ear. "Aye, no problem, big man. Hubert?"

"What?"

"You know Jackie ran with the bad boys."

Hubert isn't sure whether to applaud his daughter's courage or condemn her stupidity. His daughter's relationship – good or bad – with the Glasgow teams is known and understood, as is his: it paid dividends.

"You taking over, Davy?"

"Eh?"

'The Father in waiting?"

'Suicide that, Chief."

"You keep me posted if you hear anything."

"Aye, sure, Hubert. Hear she's in a bad way."

"Aye, but she'll survive. She's a fighter."

"Just like her dad?"

"Mind, Davy."

Hubert's 'mind' always meant something. Those who knew him knew exactly what he meant by it.

"I'll get back tae ye' if I hear anything; watch yourself."

"Always do wee man."

Hubert ends the call and Davy waits for the usual 'click' before replacing the receiver. He nearly says "Cheerio arsehole, I know you are there." Davy would never reveal anything by telephone; both he and Hubert understood this. If Davy knew anything, he'd contact Hubert personally, directly.

"Next, the spooks," Hubert says, calling Jean Dempsie, section head, MI5, Glasgow Office.

Jean's phone buzzes. "It's the Chief," Margaret Johnston, her admin, informs.

"I told you, no calls." Jean slams her phone down.

"Just one minute, sir."

Dempsie paces her office floor, not because she is agitated, which she is normally; it's part of her exercise regime: don't sit at your desk, keep on your feet, walk up and down your office, burn the calories, kill the stress. Running intelligence services in a place like Glasgow had its obvious demands. "Glasgow is a bloody tinderbox and I'm the bloody smoke alarm," she'd spell out, word by word, step by step, as she walked the floor.

Margaret gets fed up with her boss's keep-them-waiting games. "Ma'am, it's Hubert, you know what he's like."

Dempsie takes the call standing up. "Hubert, you OK?"

"As well as could be expected, Jean."

"Jackie?"

"I believe you were there."

"Yes, indeed, official business, matters of national security, you know I can't –"

"Oh, you can't say; 'political immunity in the interests of the state', but she's *my* fuckin' daughter, Jean, my fuckin' daughter."

"Hubert –"

"Aw, fuck off." Hubert loses the rag and crashes the phone down. He's in no mood to discuss MI5 and Police protocol, but he'll find out soon enough why she was involved.

For the meantime, he'll return to his official duties, soon to be the first Chief Constable of Police Scotland, charged with leading Strathclyde Police into the new national police force.

"Bloody cheek," Dempsie says, puffing. "That's it." She's done her thirty breadths of the office. "That'll do." She drops onto her office sofa. "Police Chief or not, no bloody way does he get classified information." Her phone buzzes again. "Fucks sake, Margaret can you no –"

"It's Rooney, ma'am."

"Jesus, Hubert first, then Rooney. Tell him –"

"He says he's about to talk to the papers."

"Put him through." She wipes the sweat from her arms. "Where did he go? Headed off, not part of the plan. No problem, Hubert'll pick him up." She presses hands-free and strips off her top to the delight of the office letches leering through the internal office windows. "Well, Rooney?" She dries her armpits and rolls on antiperspirant.

"Why were you there, Jean?"

"Just enjoying the show, Rooney."

I coory into a doorway next to Buchanan Street Subway. "Jackie, she's –"

"No, Rooney, she's in the GRI, she survived."

I thank the gods.

"But?" she says, then "fuck," she adds, chastising herself. 'But' was the word she was thinking, but not the one she should have used. "Watch what you say," I hear her say to herself. "She could have been killed."

"You said I was –"

"You were at risk, Rooney."

"What do I do now?"

In asking this, I know there'll be no answer.

"I am not in the business of giving advice to mentally ill criminals, Rooney." She ends the call and dons a fresh shirt taken from her desk. The letches go back to their intelligence inquiries.

It *is* time to panic.

I move onto George Square at a pace. I have to get away, out of sight, to hide, to think. Where could I go, where Hubert wouldn't find me?

Where would a bad man go?

"To hell, that's where I deserve to be."

I find a seat in the middle of the Square. There I'll watch and sit for a while, take stock, try to make sense of it all. People speed through the square, to get home, to get out of the rain, but that's not the main reason to get out of Glasgow, for them to get home this night. Only a fool, a drunk or a madman would be sitting in a wet but packed George Square this night.

They'll find you there.

"I'll go… underground."

They'll dig you up.

I look around. Our chat draws looks from passers-by. However, a man on a bench in Glasgow's George Square talking to himself doesn't draw too much attention. "Poor man, he needs a doctor," combines with a few shaking heads.

"It is OK, God loves you." I say, raising my hand in a show of peace. "God is good."

You have to hide, numpty.

"Yes, somewhere to keep my head down."

Gartnavel Royal, you'll be safe there, you'll get some treatment.

"People know me there."

I worked there as a forensic psychologist in a time when I was sane and the world was mad. Now, in Glasgow, everything is mad, including me.

Somewhere you're not known. Hairmyres Hospital.

"Will I get in?"

You, an expert in admissions to psychiatric hospitals, you'll get in.

"It's not that easy."

You'll know what to do.

"Remind me."

First you go to A&E.

"Yes."

Convince them you're mad, that won't be hard, then tell them you won't leave, that MI5, Strathclyde Police, and the Glasgow underworld are all out to kill you.

"I tell them the truth?"

You got it.

I walk all the way to Hairmyres Hospital in East Kilbride, almost twelve miles away, but I am as high as a kite and move like the last train out of Glasgow on a Friday night. I get there and present myself at the reception in A&E. I tell this woman behind the glass, the receptionist, that I need to see a doctor.

"Name?"

I push my chest out. "God… The Father."

"Address?"

"The promised land."

"Don't be cheeky, son." She looks over her glasses. "I've had a day full of smart arses, druggies, alkies, paranoids, hypochondriacs, cut fingers, colds, flus, and those out to entertain me. Now, why are *you* here?"

"*Mea culpa.* I just killed a man."

"Put a gun right to his head, pulled the trigger now he's dead," she sings. "Right, sit down there." She points to a seat at the front of the waiting room.

I hear her calling the police as a busy medic arrives to take the next patient. "Yes, officer, he said he has just killed a man; yes, yes, yes."

"Hold on, Denise." The medic is talking to her, but looking at me, becoming interested at my talking aloud. He comes over. "You're talking to yourself."

"I'm talking to… Jesus."

"Who are you?"

"I'm The Father."

"And why are you here?"

"The police and MI5 want to kill me."

He looks at me, no he studies me for a few seconds, maybe because I look like I've been in a crime scene, which I have. I say I won't leave. He moves behind the glass and talks into a phone. A few minutes later, a burly male nurse arrives with a female sidekick. This man kneels down close. "You need to come into hospital," he says. I tell him I am in hospital. "A different hospital," he says. I tell him I need safety and I am staying put.

"You can't stay here," the doctor says, coming out of his glass tank.

The nurse adds, "We want you to come into the mental health unit for assessment,"

That's it, I grab him by the neck. "I am God, and I will destroy you all," I scream into his face.

Then these two polis arrive, pin me to the seat and handcuff me. Next thing, I'm being "escorted" along these long barren corridors out of the main hospital and into the mental health unit.

Going to the big hoose, Rooney?

"Going to the happy hoose, bastard."

"How to make friends and endear oneself," the male nurse says, pointing the way.

Jackie knows nothing of this. She's in a limbo, in A&E, between the living and the dead. From the surface of her mind, she hears, "In the name of the Father…," then, "Ms Kaminski, do you hear me?" For her, it could have been seconds between these two sets of words, yet it was hours. Her oblivion, shattered by the latter voice, is only eclipsed by a sharp sensation of light. "Ms Kaminski, can you hear me?" The light from Dr Sumita Mukherjee's pen torch pierces her eyes.

The combination of sensations collide in her head, bringing her around as she coughs up her first words since the incident. "Where the fuck?"

"It's OK, you're safe," Mukherjee says. "You're in hospital." He is a busy surgeon with a list of patients lining up pre-op, but he'll talk to this one.

"Will I live?"

"You'll live, Inspector, but it'll be a while before you're on your legs, and even then, the left pretty much untreatable. You'll never be without a support, but you'll survive."

"Thanks a bunch, Doctor," she says, as she succumbs to the anaesthesia. Then, with the sensitivity of an IED disposal operative, Liz Clark, the attending nurse, lifts her bandaged arms, lacerated by the explosion, and, one at a time, places them close to each of her sides.

Hubert wants to see her and her colleagues from Strathclyde Police HQ at Pitt Street need to interview her. Dr Mukherjee will protect her as long as he can, to recover the strength she needs to deal with the reality of this.

PC John McCourt is on traffic duty on Sauchiehall Street, near to the scene of Jackie's attack on Holland Street. Following the incident, all leave is cancelled and double shifts are mandatory. Main routes in and out of the city are cordoned off, including right there where the attack happened. Traffic control is creating traffic chaos. The only consolation is this is a Saturday. Had it been a weekday, Glasgow would be gridlocked.

"Turn off... aye you, you," John bellows at a cabby, gesturing to a diversion sign with a large black arrow on a white background pointing down Elmbank Street. "Aye, that way, you fucker." *Jesus Christ, is this why I became a polis?* he asks himself. In a hard place of hard people, he knows why he became a polis. A philosopher mind and a boxer body, he had opportunities daily to exercise both.

"Aye, so I will. When the fuck will you be done here?" the cabby calls, window down, cig in fingers, hand hanging down deep over the side of his taxi. He takes another massive draw to finish the sentence. "Fuckin' terrible – fuckin' ridiculous – fuckin' war zone."

McCourt slaps the top of the black car. "Everyone in this city has an opinion. Shut the fuck up and get the fuck off the street."

The cabby snatches at the steering wheel, creating a screech reminiscent of a New York cab as he does a three-point-turn. "Fuckin' war zone," he repeats.

How many more times would this happen today before he finishes his shift, before he packs the uniform in his locker and hurries out of the station to be a normal punter? Then he'll do some cursing of his own as he heads home through the diversions and the build ups on the alternative roads, adding another twenty minutes onto a long and weary shift.

He empathises with the taxi driver, though, and he'll be back in the morning for more of the same. The forensic team won't give the scene the all-clear until it's happy; until they have photographed, measured, dusted, swabbed and analysed. They're under no pressure from anyone: whether it's the Council, who gets the complaints, the Roads Department, who want to repair the road, or the public, who are sick of the disruption. They'll do their job well, as will he. This is a particularly sensitive one, though; it involves Jackie Kaminski, a cop like himself.

"I had to go somewhere for safety, security."

Heaven?

"I needed —"

Sectioned?

People talking to themselves is acceptable in Hairmyres Hospital mental health unit. George Smith, staff nurse, pays scant attention as he mingles with the patients. I am talking into my tea. "I got myself detained, by my own hand. *They* said I was mentally ill. *They* said I was 'at risk to others and noncompliant with treatment…'."

You were delusional, my friend, and hearing voices.

"Just you."

God?

"I was…"

Off it?

"I was – I am – in control."

Leave, then.

"I will, when I am ready —"

When?

"When the time is right —"

When they let you out, you mean.

"I'll go back and Glasgow will look after its faither as it does its weans."

George sidles up, taking up position behind me. I hear his

breath and feel his eyes boring into the back of my head. "You want some more tea, Sean? It'll be lunch before you get more."

"No, I'm fine, George, this is good."

"Looks cold to me, but suit yourself."

"Where was I?"

George gets close. "You hearing something, Rooney?"

I look heavenly. "God will rain down burning sulphur on the unrighteous ones."

George takes out his notepad, talking as he writes. "Delusional material of a religious nature and oral hallucinations still prevalent."

"Jackie, my Jackie. Did I –"

Make that call?

George leans over me. "What, Rooney? What did you do?"

"I wasn't –"

"What, Rooney?"

Responsible?

"I will atone for my sins. In here, I will make amends. Please exact the punishment I deserve, warder." I strip off my shirt and await his whip. "Please do it now, I am ready."

George turns to me as he dishes out the oral medication. "I'm afraid you're away again, son. All the religious stuff." I stand up and face him. "You need a tablet?" He hands me a pill.

"No, none for me, Angel Gabriel. I get mine, Haldol, by injection every two weeks. *That* is a sign of getting better."

"You sure?"

"I'm fine."

In safe hands.

"That's good, my man. I don't want to zonk you out. You were doing so well."

"My son, in forty days I will leave this place and I will lead my children through the gates of righteousness." I make sure my voice carries through the ward.

"Sure, Rooney." George takes a mental note to inform Doctor Melville. "The gates of righteousness," he says and writes.

Sixteen hours from his 4 a.m. departure, John McCourt arrives home. It's ten past nine and he'll be up at three the next morning to do it all again.

"Hi, hon," Mary says, as he enters and drops his jacket over the back of the dining room chair. His dinner is ready. Monday is pasta night and she makes the perfect bolognaise sauce to go with fresh spaghetti. She puts a glass of red in his hand. This is a dinner he'll enjoy. She's seen this exhausted and strained face many times. This time, however, it's a tired, lined face. Though fit as a flea, he looks older than his forty-five years and, although he won't admit it, retirement at fifty seems a long way away. They were divorcees before they met and married, and Jamie came along in their late thirties. At six, he's a real handful. It is late though and he's tucked up in bed. John is relieved; although he would have liked to spend time with him, an hour of après dinner reading, two glasses of wine, his nightly meditation, and a crash into bed, are as much as he can deal with this night. He sits on the edge of his bed and digs his head into his Descartes' meditations. "I think, therefore, I am," he murmurs to himself. "But, what am I?"

Mary picks this up. "You are a good cop, darlin', and a fine husband and father, that's what you are," she says, from the other side of the bed.

"Thanks, sweetie."

"Tell me, hon, the chief inspector?"

"She's a DCI."

"So she is. How is she?"

"She'll get there."

"Who did it?"

She knows better than that, but she wants to draw it out, to get him talking, to debrief in the way she and other polis wives well understand.

"Who knows, the mob? But it's unusual."

"Do you know her?"

"Aye, everybody knows Jackie."

It's ten o'clock and he's about ready for bed, but he can't resist the news. Although national, it's about Glasgow.

"It's always about here," Mary confirms.

They both move closer to the screen, not wanting to turn the sound up for fear of disturbing Jamie.

"Highlighted by an attack on a Strathclyde Police detective," the presenter reports, "Glasgow is hit by a succession of shootings, the like not seen since the Glasgow turf wars. Then, mob violence claimed the lives of over sixty people."

"Now the Father's gone there's a vacuum. A war, the like of not known before, is happening on the streets of Glasgow. The crime lords are out to claim the throne, and the turf."

"More late nights for you, hon."

"Par for the course, darlin', since Arthur Johnston's demise."

"Any ideas who killed him?"

"The Father had his enemies, but none has come forward to claim his throne. Anyway, the overtime money'll come in handy." He pulls her across the bed. "I have to keep you in a custom you have become accustomed to."

"No-one keeps me, polisman." She pushes him off. "But, I'm worried about you. I don't like you being out there. People are getting hurt."

"Don't worry about me. I'm too streetwise to be caught out by those jumped-up street neds. We take precautions. You know that."

"Aye, sure, but watch yourself."

"I will darlin', don't you worry about that."

She tucks him in as a mother would. There will be no sex this night, nor much sleep for either of them. She's preoccupied, worrying about her man, and he'll re-run the scenes of Glasgow that day, knowing more bloodletting is inevitable.

The Father's death preceded Jackie's attack and now the Family has fallen apart, creating a void that individual gang leaders will try to fill. Murders will occur, and some of them will be police officers. Notwithstanding the double shifts, late nights and early mornings, which will be the norm for her husband for some time to come, Mary has a good reason to be worried.

CHAPTER TWO

"This is heaven compared to the Bar-L, Rooney," Ben says, entering the mental health unit. He hands me a pair of WRVS slippers. "I thought you may need these."

"I knew you'd turn up, Bensallah." I drop the slippers back into the plastic bag. "Go away, social controller, go and find some child abusers."

Ben looks around. Some patients have heard some familiar words. "Ward 19, Hairmyres Hospital," he says. "Keep your voice down, you wanting an increase in your meds?"

"Here's not for sinners, here's for saints." First, I look upwards for some divine intervention that doesn't come, then I scan the ward, observing the locked entrance and the nurses overseeing everything, the other patients; some detained, some for years.

Ben is my friend and long-term colleague, but today he is my named person under the Mental Health Act. He feels it necessary to confirm my status. "Criminally insane, Rooney, at the time of the act, diminished responsibility, mental disorder, lacking ability to make decisions, at risk, delusional?"

"I *am* the Father." I remind him of my *proper* status.

A bad man.

"Shush, bastard."

"I know that doesn't refer to me, Rooney. You still hearing voices?"

"A voice."

You tell him.

Ben puts his social worker voice on. "You're on a twenty-eight-day short-term detention, then it'll be a six-month order?"

"I'll be here for forty days, just like Jesus. Then, I'll get a smart lawyer and appeal it. I'll go to the mental health tribunal. I'll be lucid and appropriate. I'll say I have never felt better in my life. I'll thank everyone for their kindness, sterling professionalism and fantastic care, and good food."

Careful.

"Aye, and they'll believe you."

"I'll tell them I'll take their treatment and I'll be a good boy. I'll stay on my meds and keep out of trouble."

"And you'll tell them you're God?"

"I'll tell them I do God's work, as many people do."

"And you'll be out?"

"Not quite."

"Sorry?"

"They'll need something to confirm I am well. They'll ask if I have any voices. I'll say not anymore."

That's me fucked.

"They'll ask if I think MI5, the police, and the mob are after me. I'll say not anymore."

"You'll lie."

"I'll forgive myself."

"Aye, ten Hail Marys and you'll be out?"

"I'll be out."

"Into the big bad city?"

"To pursue earthly pursuits."

"Where will you go? You can't go back to your flat."

"I'll go to Davy."

"Oh, a made man there."

"Doing bad?"

"Bad, doing good."

Bad, mad man, Rooney?

"Where will you live?"

"Where else, a church."

George makes a casual pass, casts a look at me, listens in; some more monitoring before the next review. Ben shakes his head and leaves, taking the slippers with him.

Hubert's cough wakens Jackie. "Oh, hello, Dad," she moans from below her sheets. "You on your own?"

"Aye, your mother –"

"She's no' my mother."

"She's your stepmother, Jackie, and she's worried about you."

The mention of Hubert's new wife, Deirdre Hamilton-Brown, is hardly commensurate with Jackie's recovery. She tries to pull herself up. Hubert reaches in to try to help her. "No thanks, I'll manage." She wrestles with the sides of the bed. 'The woman wouldn't even take your name *and* she's younger than me."

"Just by a year, Jackie."

"Aye, by a year. What do you want Dad?"

"I wanted to see you."

"No flowers?"

"I don't do flowers."

She groans. "Get on with it Dad, I know why you're here."

"I've been here three times, Jackie, but you weren't… your doctor didn't –"

"I know, I hadn't to see anyone."

"You know how important it is to –"

"Aye, I know, get the info, an investigation after all. Not sure why *you're* doing it though."

"Millar has been allocated the investigation."

Martin Millar, smarmy, brownnose Millar, is doing the investigation into her attack.

"Fuck him. I hate the man."

"He'll stay away. I just wanted to –"

"Hear it from the horse's mouth?"

"Talk to you."

"Where do you want me to start: lying on the road, the shattered bone of my thigh sticking through my skin, my nether regions turned into mincemeat, me bleeding to bloody death?"

"They tried to kill you, Jackie."

"I would bloody well say so."

"Just as well you wore the bulletproof vest."

"That you bloody-well ordered."

"Well, Johnston, the mob. You were at risk. We expected an attack."

"Saved my miserable life, what's fucking left of it, for a cripple."

"I'm going to put some uniforms around you, day and night."

Hubert is reminded of Jackie's independent streak. "You'll do nothing of the sort, I look after myself."

"Why did you decide to take a taxi after leaving work, Jackie? What was happening that day and the day before? What you were working on? Were there any indications of anything about to happen? Did you –"

"Wow, give us a bloody break."

Dr Mukherjee comes into the room and picks up the medical notes at the end of her bed. "You OK, Jackie? I don't want you stressed."

"I'm OK, Doctor."

Hubert gets up to leave. "I'll be back, darlin'."

"Just let's get this said, Dad." Jackie pulls herself up. Hubert reaches to help. "No, don't, I can do it. And no, I fucking don't know who did it, no indications, nothing, totally unexpected."

"Can you remember what happened?"

"Oh, sweet Jesus, do we really have to go through this?"

"I need to, Jackie."

She thinks for a minute or two. "OK, I got a taxi because I had a drink, there I said it, and –"

"The mobile. How…"

She starts crying. He moves to comfort her. "I don't know," she says. "It was stolen. I got it back. I opened it, in the taxi. I heard this voice."

"Whose voice?"

"I can't tell you."

"You won't tell me, you mean." She doesn't answer, which confirms this. "But I'll find out, you know I will." Again, she doesn't answer. "Rooney, why was he there, Jackie?"

"So was Jean, Dad, MI5. Why was she there, Dad?"

'That, I will establish, darlin'; and we will find Rooney."

"Just leave him, Dad. I want you to leave him alone, do you hear me?" She slides under the sheets. "Just leave him Dad, for me."

"You are *my* daughter."

She looks up from under the sheets. "Dad, you bring Rooney in and you'll never see me again."

He studies her. Never before has she put such an ultimatum to him. "OK, enough, Jackie. You need to rest."

CHAPTER THREE

For forty days and forty nights, I plan my crusade. Then, securing my discharge, I arrive at Gracelands, Davy McGing's mansion on Aytoun Road, a road of large mansions in Glasgow's Southside, so called after his love of Elvis Presley,

The twenty-eight-day short-term detention is over and the application for a six-month hospital detention is denied by the Mental Health Tribunal, but it is converted to a community based compulsory treatment order, a CCTO. That's fine, it gets me out. I argue that my psychosis was to do with DTs, having come off years of alcohol abuse, and now, as a recovered alcoholic, I was symptom free. Ben, as my named person, says that the order is necessary to ensure I don't relapse. My friend!

"It's Rooney, Davy." My voice is shaking as much as my thumb on the gate intercom.

I'm just out of Hairmyres Psychiatric Unit. I need supported accommodation.

"Fuck off, bastard."

"See your language hasn't improved, Rooney," Davy growls through the intercom. "And what the fuck can I do for you – bastard?"

"Sorry, Davy, Tourette's. I'm here for… to help you."

"Well then, suppose you'd better come in," he says, like he's answering the minister on his annual visit.

The gates part like the Red Sea and I walk through into the courtyard, where I am frisked from head to toe by two of Davy's heavies before being taken in to see him.

"You need help or you offering help, Rooney?" Davy's head is in a pile of papers at his desk. "What is it?"

"I need help, but I can help you too,"

"I helped you before, we're quits."

"You said I was a made man with you."

"I did."

"Let me work for you."

"Work for me?"

"I'll do all of that." I point to the paperwork.

He lifts his head. "Jesus, Rooney, you look… weird."

"I am recovered, reformed." I look down on my black pinstripe demob suit, obtained from Oxfam on Byres Road on the way. I wanted to create the right impression.

"Sinner or murderer, Rooney?"

"There's a war on, Davy."

"Oh, there is that son, for sure. And one we'll win. No firm is big enough to fuck us in Glasgow, you know that." I have no intention or strength to argue this.

"Where you been hiding, Rooney?"

"In a safe place, Davy, three meals a day and drugs on tap."

"Barlinnie?"

'Something like that."

"And now you're here."

"I can't go back."

"It's been a bloodbath after the Family disintegrated, a turf war's erupted."

"I can do it."

"You can do what?"

"If you could give me –"

'Sanctuary, support, Rooney; food and board, money?"

"Anything, you said, after Thomas."

"I did and I keep my word, but you'll no' stay here. It wouldn't work; I couldn't cope with your suit."

"I'll find somewhere."

"Good." He pulls out a wad of notes from his desk drawer. "Here, take this." I take his money and stuff it into my inside pocket. "You gave me the correct story of how my son died, how the SAS murdered him, and how –"

"Jean, Davy?"

"Aye, but mind, trust no one."

'Sure, Davy. We know all about that, don't we?"

"Where will you stay?"

"Somewhere secure."

"Safe as a church, Rooney?"

"In a church, Davy."

He phones me a taxi. I say cheerio and tell him that I'll be back the next day to start work. "Good, you'll start on this stuff." Relieved, he pushes the pile of papers on the desk aside then sits back.

The taxi arrives. "To Saint Andrew's Cathedral," I inform the cabby. "Down on Clyde Street, along from the Clutha Vaults."

"It's OK, pal, I'm a Tim," he says, referencing the infamous Tim Malloys of the 1920s. "I know the Cathedral." I had half hoped Davy would take me in, but he was right; I wouldn't have fitted in there, in his home, suit or no suit.

We arrive and I peel off one of Davy's twenties. I say "God bless you," and tell him to keep the change.

The driver looks at me strangely through the mirror. "Aye, God bless you too, Father," he says. How did he know?

Something to do with the suit and the dog collar.

I arrive, by then late Monday afternoon. The front door is open and I go in. The place is empty, apart from a couple of women fussing around the altar. It is the day after Easter Sunday and they are tidying up and preparing for mass at 5 p.m. I pass the eight-foot-high painting of Saint John Ogilvie, Jesuit priest and martyr, by Peter Howson. I go up to the ladies and ask to see the priest. "Monsignor McElroy," they inform me, then tell me he's out, but that he's taking confession at four forty-five; he'll be back then.

"Perfect."

I wait until confession and, seeing an older, distinguished looking man enter the priest's side, I go into the confessional. "In the name of the Father, and of the Son, and of the Holy Spirit," I say into my hands. "My last confession was…"

He peers through the grid. "It is OK, my son, no need."

"Thank you, Father."

"You may begin."

"I killed a man and severely injured a police officer, my ex-wife, and I –"

"Sorry, what did you say?"

"I said I killed a man, and –"

"I have to stop you there my son and advise you of my… obligations to the public. Have you really… killed someone?"

"Yes, Father, for I have sinned."

"Indeed, son, but…"

"I need forgiveness, and I need –"

"You need…"

'Sanctuary."

"You need sanctuary."

"And I am just out of Hairmyres psychiatric unit and I have nowhere to stay."

"Oh, just out of… nowhere to stay."

"I am sorry for these and all the sins of my past life."

"Go outside and say the rosary, my son, wait for me there."

I do what he says. I remember the rosary from a child. I had been an altar boy and knew it by heart. Around ten minutes or so later, he approached me and asked me to accompany him through to the Cathedral House, passing the magnificent Italian Cloister Garden on the way. We arrive in the house and into his office study. He invites me to sit and asks me about being in hospital, how well I think I am, and where I will sleep that night.

I tell him I was in hospital to repent, that I had returned to lead my flock through the gates of righteousness, and I would sleep in George Square.

"You'll stay here, my son. What's your name?"

"Sean Rooney, Father."

He takes me to a room upstairs, one used by visiting clergy. "You'll stay here, at least until I can find something better for you." I thank him and tell him I had been an altar boy and I know the mass; I would be happy to assist him. "Not to worry, just make yourself comfortable," he says.

I impress him with my knowledge of the old hospital that used to stand there before the cathedral was built in the early 19th century, the "hospital over the brig" where people were detained by the water sergeant. He says he hopes that will not happen to me. I bless him and tell him I would not inconvenience him unduly, but would he mind if I lock the door.

My driver drops me at Tennent's Bar, on Byres Road. It's Friday night and six weeks since my discharge. Monsignor Christopher McElroy, or Chris as I've come to know him, had provided me with accommodation while I worked by day for Davy McGing. In the business of crime by day, repenting my sins in St Andrew's Cathedral by night.

I'll go in, but not for alcohol, not this time. I've to meet Ben, and here is as good a place as anywhere, the site of many debriefing occasions when we were in the major incident counselling team together. I reach the bar and scan the place like a beam from a lighthouse for any known faces. I'm known in this pub, but not to talk to. I come here to think. Though, like in any pub in Glasgow, there'll be those who'll sidle up and say, "How you doin'? What you been up to? How's business?" I avoid any eye contact that'll invoke discussion. I pull up the collar on my overcoat, order a glass of ginger ale, and place it square in sight. The bar light passes through it like a prism, giving it a golden glow in my hand. I study it for a few seconds.

I'm aware of a large guy to the right of me, standing square on, looking ahead expressionless. He's there for a pint, not for chat, just like me. He's gay, I guess. The haircut and the crown henna tattoo on his face ID him. To the left, there's an old man holding on to the brass rail surrounding the bar, his Zimmer frame around his hips, with a plastic Iceland bag hanging over it. His tea, I think, or maybe a pizza from Little Italy. He keeps it in the Iceland bag to protect his street cred.

Just then, however, "Well, hello stranger," comes from across the corner of the bar. I don't lift my head; I know this is Ben. "You receiving guests?" He squeezes in beside me before I have the chance to tell him to fuck off, but my face says it for me. "Cheer up Rooney. I'm your friend, mind."

"My conscience, more like."

"I'm also your named person. You appointed me, mind, when you were detained."

"I was resting, recovering."

"Aye, Rooney, and now you're on a community order."

I stare into his eyes. "Just a precaution, they said, in case I… kill someone."

He looks up to see if anyone had heard this. Relieved, he says, "I see you've gone up in the world, Rooney," he feels my coat, "since Davy took you under his wing."

"I survive."

"You sure do. Now the high profile adviser –"

"Facilitator."

"Sorry, facilitator."

"Just say it, Ben."

"What, that everyone's saying that you're Davy's man?"

"I am God's man."

"Aye, in God's house."

"No longer, Ben. Got a rented flat in Ruthven Street, off the Byres Road. I am, though, looking for something more… substantial."

"Evicted?"

"Chris said he couldn't allow… unnatural practices in the Cathedral house."

"You still masturbating to holy pictures?"

How did he know that, unless he was fishing, or someone was watching me?

"The room was full of them, I couldn't help myself. I am getting better, though, that way."

"That's good, Rooney."

"I am –"

"Doing good?"

"I'm trying."

"Daniel in the lion's den, pal?" I don't respond. "Why didn't you call me? You know, when you got out. You know I have to –"

"Monitor me? I was busy."

"Are you better?"

"I'm good."

For Ben "good" is fine. It'll allow him to report back to Dr Melville and offer a few minutes of shoulder-to-shoulder, not saying anything, contact. We gaze on to the gantry, sharing the same space, the same place we had shared when we were counsellors together.

"We did good back then, Rooney."

I stare into the golden glow in the palm of my hand. "*In nomine…*"

He hears the remark, but ignores it, rightly. "What are you going to do?"

"When?"

"Now."

"Stop a war."

"You'll be busy then. Lots to do there." I turn to leave. "You've changed, Rooney."

"We all change, Ben, or we die as men."

He studies me. "You *were* a good man."

I smile. "A good man who does bad, Ben?" I sweep my coat over my shoulders. "Or a bad man who does good?"

"Rooney?"

"What?"

"You always said if I saw you losing insight, acting bizarre, to keep an eye on you."

He's hearing voices. He thinks he's God.

I am in control, I have to convince him. "Well, that was then and this is now. As you can see, I'm doing very well, thank you. Now stay well out of my way. Go and save some children from the paedophiles. Gomorrah is full of them." That'll do it.

"I've seen you go the other way pal, going down, down."

My final stare precedes a sign of the cross as I bless him. I finish the ginger ale in one slow gulp and place it carefully on the bar, all the while holding the stare. The barman collects the glass, relieved to see the bouncers stand aside almost in deference as I pass between them. They had been street players, these security men, recruited by the publicans to protect them from the very mob organisations that provide them. I know them and they know my influence in Glasgow's underworld. A nod from me could mean promotion to lieutenants or a shake of the head could mean they would be back selling crack to junkies. "Thank you, my children," I say, as I pass between them.

Little do Ben or I know that Hubert and Martin Millar are in the Belle Bar this night, on Great Western Road, only five minutes' walk from us. I might not have been so relaxed had I known this. Millar, poached from the Metropolitan Police, had risen to become Assistant Chief Constable, Local Policing West, at Police Scotland. At fifty-three, he should have been looking forward to retirement, happy to cruise to it through meetings rather than direct operational work, but he had greater ambitions than that.

The Belle is Hubert's favourite watering hole, just across from the Glasgow flat he uses when working late and just as often to escape the society parties of his wife in their Hamilton home.

Millar, being his usual ingratiating self, gets the pints of Sagres in, then sits to open his jacket to let his rotund belly almost flop out on the table. Hubert finds them a seat by the open fire, slightly incongruous for June, but this is Glasgow. He passes Hubert a pint. "I believe they say 'Get that doon your thrapple' up here, boss."

Hubert warms his hands. "Crap Sco'ish, Martin."

"Sorry, twenty years up here and I still can't get it. The gangs in Glasgow, boss?"

"Businessmen."

"Indeed, businessmen."

"Hoods in suits."

"Tit for tat killings, on the streets."

"It is managed."

"Sure, managed, boss. I'm too old to fight the bastards."

"How's the investigation going, into Jackie's attack?"

"Still conducting enquiries, Chief, interviews with everyone who was there."

"Jean?"

Hearing his wife's name disconcerts Millar, especially in the context of an investigation, but he knows Hubert "doesn't give a fuck for the spooks".

"I talked to her."

Millar had been married to Jean Dempsie, MI5 Glasgow, for twenty years. She had been in Thames House, London MI5 headquarters, before being transferred to Glasgow. He'd met her while he was a Commander at the Met.

"A wee bit uncomfortable that one, Martin? Did she give you a kicking when she got you home?"

"Interesting night that, boss."

"And Rooney?"

"You said to leave him just now."

"Aye, leave Rooney to me."

Millar hears the raw ruthlessness in Hubert's voice. He knows not to mix it with him over Rooney. He heads off like a poodle to collect a toy, to the bar to replace the empty glasses. Hubert allows him; he never buys.

Millar returns with the pints. "Boss?"

Hubert moves back from him. He sees no point in telling Millar of his serious body odour; he'd explain that by his actions. "What?" Hubert slides along the seat.

"Jackie. Do you think she'll ever be the same?"

"Stupid thing to say, son."

"I know, but –" Hubert was now sixty-three and way past his retirement age. Should Millar have any chance of Hubert's recommendation for promotion, he had to be more diplomatic than that, especially when discussing his daughter.

"You just wondered."

"Sorry, boss."

"She got the job, Martin, not you."

"I know, ACC, organised crime and counter terrorism and safe communities. Great job that, boss."

"You got the operational lead, Martin. ACC, Local Policing West, more than you deserve."

"I'm happy about that, boss. I hear she's coming out."

"She'll be back in two weeks."

"Two Weeks, no way."

"Like I say, she's determined."

"She's to get the Queen's Police Medal."

"She deserves it."

"Her attack and injuries, no doubt."

"Her work on the Father case, Martin!"

"Aye, of course, boss." Millar knows not to cross the line. "Back off now" flashes in his mind. "How's the new wife, boss?" This is also not the right thing to say. That's it, Hubert is up; coat snatched from the seat and he's out of the door. He'll pick up a curry from Little India a few doors away on the way home.

CHAPTER FOUR

I hesitate before I enter the Hotel Central in Glasgow. "Today, God willing, I'll make them stop."

And how will you do that?

"I'll… talk to them, persuade them."

Manipulate, exploit and control others to do your will?

I take off my coat, straighten my jacket and head in. I hand the doorman a ten-pound note as he opens the door for me – he'll remember me the next time. I understand money is power: money buys people and power both makes and destroys people, and both float the boats of these gang leaders. This is the way of the moneylenders in the temple. This will help me do God's work here.

I'll explain to them how futile their war is. I practise it in my mind, *No one can prevail and everyone will lose if it continues.* Turf war costs money and time, and time for a gang leader is limited. They could fight and hold their own against one, two, or even three teams at any given time, but a dozen gangs at any given time was impossible, a set of circumstances they know they cannot sustain. They'll not know, though, how to withdraw from this fight with pride, how to keep their heads held high, their status preserved. This is where I come in, and I know it.

I move into the foyer, this grand space, presumably held up by girders forged in Glasgow Iron mills. Completely apt, I think: hard and strong, like the men there that day. I need to be strong. God give me strength. I had arranged the meeting and got them together with payments of a grand. Davy offered these so he could host the meeting, if only to establish his right to control the event with the pursuit of ascribed power. He also agreed to fund my gifts to the bosses. I reach the corridor leading to the Grandroom. "This time I will deliver them from evil," I say, contrary to the last time when I arrived to deliver the Family terms. "No cap in hand this time, pals."

Watch what you say. They'll think you're off it.

"Off it? I'm on it." I prompt a waiter to spin on his tracks.

I had advised the events manager that we are a group of businessmen having an EGM, which in a sense we are. He is waiting as I arrive. I nod and he escorts me into the Champagne Lounge, where many of the teams' leaders have assembled. They are standing there looking around at each other like an estranged family getting together for a funeral. They are Charlie Campbell of the Campbells, Ian Simpson of the Sighthill Mafia, Geordie Montgomery of the Monty, and the McStay twins; all suspicious of every boss arriving there.

Alan Taylor arrives with Davy McGing. The Taylors and the McGings go back a long way. Alan's father, George Taylor, is now serving life in Shotts Prison after he hit the Grosvenor Hotel in a bomb attack, and he and Davy were in the Cumbie Gang together in the late sixties.

The events manager invites us all through to the Grandroom. Loud chattering accompanies us taking up prearranged placings around the table, indicated by place cards. I had chosen the seating arrangement carefully. The wrong mix would be like gunpowder, explosive. Arch-enemies sitting next to each other may lead to violence, even death. Magically, they all sit down and say nothing, most sitting back on their chairs in a relaxed concentration. They had agreed on one lieutenant each, sitting behind each of them in hardback chairs.

I give them a few minutes more than they're used to. They're less relaxed now, fidgeting in their chairs, reading the menu. Perfect; I don't like complacency. Their lieutenants are even less relaxed, however, which is less than perfect, panning the room, anticipating the possibility of anyone taking a pop at their respective boss's. All were frisked, though, with guns removed at the door, only agreed because this is universally applied. Not to say that the players would not have a weapon secreted somewhere: a pistol in a leg holster, a blade in a lapel, a pile of marbles in a sock, or a deadly look.

Davy is the last to arrive in to the room, as is his demand. This is a show of power and he deserves it. He's the biggest player there and he sanctioned the meeting. He not only agreed it, he is paying for it too. Apart from the grand a head, for around fifteen players, it includes the cost of the event and some sweeteners he had sent to their homes, a Gucci G-Chrono Collection men's watch for them and an iPhone for their oldest child, for their… support. All told, around 30K. I had convinced him it would be worth it. He takes his seat, nearest the door; again, as is his demand.

Everyone knows it is for me to open the meeting. I had arranged it after all, and I'm the weakest one there, the least threatening one in the room, the most vulnerable in the middle of this group of hard men. I'm not hard, but I'm emboldened, God has put me there to convert these sinners and to save their souls. I stand up and a nervous hush descends the room. I deliberately scan the table, looking each of these men in the eye.

I look at them one by one. I had researched them and I know their "portfolios" intimately. Davy, to the left of me at the centre of the table, as head of the McGings, is the heaviest leader there. To his right, Bill Bingham of the Binghams, possibly only second to Davy by way of authority. They bookend me which gives me a slight but uneasy sense of security. The fact that no one would get by them if they tried to attack me gives me some comfort. To the left of Davy is Jim McGraw of the McGraw clan, then Alex Frame, of the Frames, or the Torturers, known for pulling the teeth of those not paying extortion debts, Charlie Campbell of the Campbell Clan, Patrick Devlin of the Devlins, and Paul Moffat, of the Moffats, nicknamed "the Bunnet" due to his insistence in wearing a tartan bunnet hat on any occasion.

Then next, my eyes stop on Ian Simpson, only a sadistic killer, heading the Simpsons; then Andy Hamilton of the Hammie, and John Fullerton of the Fullerton; then Geordie Montgomery, of the Monty and the McStay twins, Robert and Peter. To Bingham's immediate right, Alan Taylor of the Taylors, only the same Taylors, previously headed by his father George Taylor now serving life. A circle of chairs behind each of them holds their lieutenants, and behind them their bodyguards. This is a formidable display of power. Only Mick McGing stands behind his father, displaying contempt for the integrity of the group.

I clear my throat as I pull out my notes, not that they would help me here; this calls for calm but spontaneous engagement rather than a speech. I pour water from a jug on the table into a glass and take a drink. "Thank you all for coming," I start, like a condemned man greeting a firing squad, "to what I believe will be a… momentous meeting."

I can see their thoughts in their faces: "This had better be good. We don't meet with these people unless either our lives or our families' lives depend on it, or there's money to be made." The grand in cash helps, alongside the sweeteners I sent to their homes, to secure their cooperation.

No one answers. Most are looking through their hands passively at the no man's land of the table that separates them. It provides some safety from attack. The lieutenants do their looking for them. I notice that some of them are wearing my gift, which is encouraging.

"I..." I look at Davy for support, which he doesn't give. I carry on. "We have a proposal to make." Again no response. "It is this." I pour some more water. "You will be a collective..." I take a drink. No-one reacts. Is this a good sign? "Whatever you want to call it, a syndicate, an organisation..."

"A Family?" says Bill Bingham. "We tried that before, Rooney; Arthur Johnston and the Family shit, it didn't work." I always knew that the syndicate would disintegrate, the individual interests of the constituent firms would be too strong and create an implosion, creating the turf war now raging.

"It got too big, Mr Bingham. This time *you* will be in control."
That's it, give them a sense of ownership.
"You have more to gain together."
Rein them in, corral them, brand them.
"Consolidate your businesses. Multiply your strength. You have more to gain together than apart."

Togetherness, however, is yet to be found here. "That bastard there chibbed my son," Charlie Campbell stabs orally towards Alan Taylor, who ignores him.
Squirming like a bunch of mackerel on your hooks.
"That cunt there torched my house." Campbell turns to Ian Simpson, three places from him to his left. "And *he* fucked my daughter," he shouts at Bill Bingham, sitting adjacent to him.

Here we go!
"And you're a lying, grassing bastard, up the arse of the bizzis," comes from the latter of the trio.

This isn't going to be easy. I had established that all of the top team bosses had older sons, all of whom could be in line to take over leadership in years to come.
Information is power.

I'm armed with information that empowers. "Unless you stop killing each other, within five years each and every one of you and all of your oldest sons will have been killed, along with other members of your immediate family."

While most of them think this will be inevitable, that they will go, the thought that their sons would not be there to continue their family is inconceivable to them. Through my enquiries on each of them, I know that they have had enough anyway. Weeks of fighting multiple enemies has left them battle weary: this is back up, if needed.

"*We* will protect our sons, and our families, Rooney," Bingham snaps. "Don't you worry about that."

Moans of agreement resound around the table like the House of Lords at a late sitting.

"You can't protect them. You know that," I say. "They'll all go the same way as you will." I turn toward Davy. "It's the life, Davy, you told me that. That's what you buy into when you come in."

Davy looks at me through fingers, resting his head. "Our sons *will* be safe, Rooney," he says, in a slow growl.

"I will prove to you they are not." I whack my knuckles off the table for effect.

There's more movement now, much fidgeting in seats.

"You touch a hair –"

"Steady, McGraw," says Davy. "Your sons will be fine." He turns to cast a look at Mick, his son and lieutenant, standing behind him, before pointing at me. "Rooney, just stop fucking about."

It's time to make an impact. "I have placed a device on all of them," I say. Amid the inevitable silence, I bring up my own mobile. I know I'm flying by the seat of my pants with no ejector seat or parachute. "I just need to send a call to all of them and they will be blown to bits."

I gird myself for the inevitable response. Some reach for their mobiles to check on their sons. Some get to their feet while staring intently at me in the eye. Most are ready to spring across the table, knock me to the floor, rip me with a blade, pound me into mincemeat with their fists.

"Rooney," Davy roars, "get a fucking grip."

I look around. Although they hear Davy's words, their eyes are on me. What will happen next? They could shoot me dead or they could wait to see what happens. I need to ensure they choose the latter.

"Cool it," I say. "I'll not do anything, but they're there just the same. On every one of them is the same device."

This did little to quell the raging mob.

Mick moves intently towards me. "You are a fucking nutjob man, and I'll be the first to fucking do you."

"Mick, mind the new iPhone I gave you recently." This stops him in his tracks. "The same one I sent to all the bosses' oldest. A gift from me, remember? You got it on you?"

Mick reaches into his pocket. "Aye man, it's a great wee phone." He brings it out and shows it around. "And a great camera for selfies – look man." He takes a picture of himself.

I ring his number, pre-set in my phone.

"Fuck sake man, the phone's getting warm." Mick drops it clattering to the table. I reach for it, open the back, and pull out the battery unit.

"It's warm because there's a filament in there, and if I hadn't pulled out the battery it would have ignited this." I crack open the phone to reveal a device. "That's a small smart bomb, big enough to kill anyone in close contact with it."

I look to Davy. I see his eyes. He knows this is the –

Same as Jackie's?

There's two reactions: first, they are on their phones and second, I am on my way to being a dead man.

"Don't worry, your sons are safe." I hope this will stave off the inevitable. "Just tell them to dispose of the phone in the way you would normally deal with any explosive device."

"Down the fucking toilet," Taylor says.

"Whatever," I say.

"You bastard," Mick says, making an inevitable lunge at me. Davy stands and blocks his way. "You! Back off, now. Now!" he says to Mick. "You, you are seriously fucking close to being shot," he says to me.

"And I'll send the second shot into his fucking head," says Bill Bingham.

"And I'll do the third," says Geordie Montgomery.

"Cool it," I say. "It's just to show you how easy it is to kill your boys. If I can do it, anyone can do it."

They lean back on their chairs instructing their lieutenants. "Get to our sons, make sure they are OK, and ditch the phones."

I really need to do my stuff; my apprenticeship has to become time-served. "You have to work together, to trust each other."

"Aye, like a cat would a fucking fox," says Alan Taylor.

"Well, carry on killing each other then."

"Fucking right."

"And then the public and the authorities will destroy you."

"And we'll fuck them proper."

"And you won't win."

A helpful and healthy pause happens, some thinking going on. Time to move things along; see if I've made the point. "There are new threats."

"The new crews." Peter and Robert McStay talk in unison, they always do. "The Albanians, the Romanians, the Russians? We need to hit them, but they're too fucking heavy."

I respond, pleased with the opportunity. "Aye, how will you fight them as they move in to your turf, while you're kicking the shit out of each other?"

"We kick with both boots," Alan Taylor says.

"That's what we fucking do," growls Mick.

"What all of you do is spend all your time and resources fighting each other and you don't see anything outside your own domains." Another thinking pause. "You have no collective strategy to deal with the threats to your turf, your businesses." I reach into my pocket. A few of the players reel back as their lieutenants move forward. "Don't worry, you know I don't carry a weapon." I pull out a handful of pound coins I had been gathering for this occasion, and with a clatter I smash the coins on the glass-topped table, the glass increasing the sound and the effect, the coins scattering down the table. "This is what it is about: money, money, money. The war is costing you money. You are losing a fortune, each of you. Get together, invest in your businesses, bring them together under a collective. Police... sorry, wrong word... *manage* them across your teams and multiply your income. And more importantly get together to deal with developing corporate risks."

Cast out the money-changers.

"He sounds like a corporate fucking banker," John Fullerton says. "Talk fucking English, man?"

Do not make my father's house a house of trade?

"He's *my* adviser," says Davy, somewhat incongruously. "You all got that?"

The silence returns, to be shattered by Charlie Campbell. "Fucking rubbish. I'm not giving up the payday loans, the tanning parlours, the laundries."

Davy is determined to control the discussion. "Aye, the Campbells were always good at laundering… money from drugs, prostitution, racketeering."

There's a muffled collective snigger, but not in his direction.

"Well, you bastards grabbed the casinos," Campbell says. "Upmarket cunts." Davy holds him in a steady stare. This man's card is marked.

"We're keeping the taxis," Alan Taylor says, "and the multiple occupancies."

"And what about the gun running? You cunts'll take money from any cunt." Campbell talks for many of the teams there.

"And any cunts that intrude into our security business are dead cunts," the McStays add.

Time to intervene. "Well, each of you take the lead on a particular business line."

They look around at each other.

"Aye, I'll build my property portfolio to include seven-star hotels in the East End," John Fullerton laughs.

"And I'll do renewables," Campbell adds. "An onshore windfarm in Garthamlock run by the wind fae your arse."

All laugh; peace is regained.

I sense accord.

"I'll leave it with you."

Davy gets to his feet. "What he says is right. For years we've fought each other. This time we do it right and proper. We'll control the Glesca turf and every deal done here will have oor stamp on it, and we'll stop the Russians, the Romanians, the Poles, and any other fucker that tries to muscle in. I'll take the helm and if I fail you'll boot me out and put someone else in. I know that and you know that. You know I'm the only wan here that has a relationship with all of you. You know I speak my word and I'll be fair… and sound."

The silence descends on the room, until one hand slaps the table. Another follows, until there is a cacophony of hands slapping the mahogany table. Davy is now the Father and they will have a Family, a syndicate, a collective.

Davy sidles over and takes my hand like a politician, one hand over the other, these hands that had ripped, throttled and pounded people to death. "The war is over and *you* did it Rooney." I smile and nod. "But don't cross the line, son."

I know what he means: don't push too much or it will rebound and crush me. But there's more to these words. He knows it and I know it. Although I respect this man, there is a sinister side to him, a total mindless ruthlessness. I know what he is capable of. He leaves the room, followed by all the bosses who acknowledge me as they leave the room. Davy is the new Father, but now I have power in the biggest crime syndicate in Glasgow. *Your grandiosity knows no bounds.* "God reigns," I whisper, putting my notes into my attaché case.

In nomine patris!

"We would have preferred you to stay with us a bit longer, Jackie." Dr Mukherjee reviews Jackie's charts on the clipboard. "Although your wounds are on the mend, there's the pain programme, the physio, the OT assessment of your house, the aids and adaptations you'll need before you go home."

"All fine, Doctor, they can be done at home. I've been here for over three months. I need to get out of here. It's doing my head in. I have things to do."

Mukherjee knows she'll not be persuaded, but he has to advise her of his main concern. "Jackie," he says, writing.

"Doctor?"

"Your loss will re-emerge in different ways, emotionally I mean."

"Sorry?"

"Don't be surprised; the flashbacks, the depression, the sense that your life is irreparably changed, the damage to –"

"Damage?"

"Your ability to lead a normal life, have babies, have sex, run marathons, has regrettably changed for you, Jackie. Stay in touch."

My new Jaguar XJ draws up to the gates of Gracelands. The driver drops the window with a powered smoothness. He reaches out to a button on a control panel that says *Press*.

"Hello," comes from inside, via a small speaker. Then the voice demands an ID, to be presented to the small camera above the speaker.

"I've got Rooney, Mick," my driver says. "Do we need to go through this every time?"

"Just fuckin' do it, right!" A growl comes from the speaker.

"Just do it," I echo. I've been going through these gates every day for weeks, sometimes two or three times a day and Mick makes me do this every time. A show of authority I know, but it is done and the gates part in the middle, sliding behind eight-feet walls and revealing a courtyard that already holds two black Range Rovers. The car moves through like a barge would a canal lock, just as Mick arrives backed by two men in long black coats. The coats are misshapen, holding heavy armaments inside. Mick holds out an open palm to stop the car.

"Sorry, I didn't recognise the car, Rooney." Mick's lying, he'd seen it before.

"Let him through, Michael." Davy wanders into the car park holding an umbrella. He is the Father, and what he says goes.

I understand this game that occurs every time I or anyone arrives: a demonstration of Family power; ensure everyone knows who is in charge, and a reminder that no one is to relax security. It doesn't matter who they are, me included, they will go through the same process, no easing up in keeping anyone out, anyone with an interest in doing harm.

I observe Davy through the car window. Framed by his palatial mansion, this could have been a staged photo-shoot for a glossy advert in Time magazine, a portrait of a lord framed by his stately house somewhere in the home counties; but this is Glasgow and, albeit a mansion ala Alexander "Greek" Thomson, this house is a fortress first, business premises second, and a home last.

Davy is no lord, though. He is a lord in his own terms, but not in the way of aristocracy, nor is he a gentleman.

My driver arrives at my side to open the door. Not that I need this, I can do this for myself, but it adds to the stature I am trying to present. Davy, however, with an outstretched hand, steps forward to open the door and welcome me. "Typical summer weather, son." The rain pelts off the umbrella.

No one needs reminding that this man has complete power in Glasgow, where power reigns and losers perish, where dog eat dog isn't only left to the public parks, where man rules man and man kills man. That is not to say no one would threaten the Father; the man who leads the collective of firms, mobs, teams. Davy is not invincible and he knows that. He knows he'll go the same way as those he had killed to get there.

"Good to see you, Davy."

He takes my hand in his, and puts the other on my shoulder, as he guides me into the house. The touch feels gentle, genuine – like a velvet glove around a throat. Mick follows us in.

We arrive in a large sitting room. It's dim, the windows covered by thick curtains, the room lit by standard lamps. This is an extravagant room, bedecked by the trappings of wealth. Heavy art works by Mutter and Howson adorn the walls.

"Here, sit by the fire." Davy guides me towards a chesterfield adjacent to the spitting fire. "Logs; I like the smell. Take off your coat. Mick?"

I pass my coat, scarf and gloves to Mick. "Some summer, bloody miserable," I say. No answer, only 'I'm no' the fuckin' butler pal,' in his eyes. I shift to the end of the sofa to avoid the fire. This is not a place to doze off.

Mick takes a seat at the window looking outward through the side of the curtains, like a settler awaiting an attack.

Davy fills a cup of freshly brewed coffee, an Americana from a coffee machine. "I enjoy our meetings, Rooney." He hands me a cup. Since becoming teetotal, I love my freshly ground coffee. "They're… interesting."

"Hope so." The coffee mixes with the words in my mouth.

"I hope we can relax, son." He casts a fleeting glance towards Mick, who turns away like a petulant teenager, feigning disinterest.

"Thanks, you really have been like a –"

"Father, Rooney?" Davy says. "I'm the Father, but I'm not your father." He looks towards Mick, ensuring he hears that.

"No, not my father, but I am grateful."

"Mind that day you arrived here, terrified Hubert and the whole of Strathclyde Police Department were after your guts?"

"I had… done things."

"Aye," he says, with a worrying hesitation. "We all did… things." I can see by his eyes he knows my meaning. "But nothing that concerns me. You are a made man with us."

This emboldens me. "A made man," is one no one would dare touch, or the McGings would whack them good. I recall the discussion that led to this badge of honour, the one I had with him the day I explained how Thomas, his son died. Thomas didn't need to die, I informed him. He had a bomb, Davy pointed out. The SAS had him in a clinch, no way could he have detonated it, I explained. "They executed him," I said at the time, revealing something he needed to know. "Those were difficult days, Davy."

"Aye son, dangerous times." Although his words are for me, his eyes are on Mick. "You impressed me then. I didn't think you had it in you to deal with Johnston."

"I had... changed."

"Aye, you changed." He moves to a table filled with a connoisseur's range of malts. "Drink?" He holds up a crystal decanter.

"No. Thanks."

"No' something you use these days, son?"

"No."

Mick smirks.

"You impress me even more now. The way you took on the bosses."

"You've been a good teacher."

"Johnston was an even better one, son. You learned from him and you remind me of him."

"Thanks." I hesitate, uncomfortable with being compared to Johnston.

"He impressed me. He always said information equals power, and the right information on the right people is real power. He knew how to –"

"Use it?"

"Aye, but there's one thing son, and I wouldn't be much of a mentor to you if I didn't say this."

I place my case on the sofa. "Go on."

"When you chose the life of a gangster, there is nowhere else to go. You live and you die within the Family."

"I understand that."

"I don't know if you do, Rooney. You will go the way we all go: me, everyone involved in this business. You will die too, son."

Mick turns away, disgusted in his father's reference to me as son.

"I understand that." I nearly add 'Father'.

"They will kill you, eventually. You need to know power never lasts forever."

"*Septuagint*, a man has not strength and power forever." I draw on my newly found understanding of the good book. There wasn't much else to read in the Cathedral House.

"Aye right, son," he says, hesitating. "Now, to business."

I open my case and take out a leather folder. It holds ten sections: one for each file, for each matter to be discussed. "OK." I am pleased to retreat to a more comfortable place. "We have a meet, next Wednesday evening, venue to be confirmed."

A meeting venue was only revealed one hour before, to prevent a hit being planned.

"I know, anything interesting?"

"We are moving into nursing homes, nurseries, and tanning parlours."

"Boring; any more on the Albanian crew?"

"Moving into sex trafficking, immigrant smuggling, heroin –"

"Not good."

"We can't let them get a foothold," Mick says, from behind the curtain. "We can't let them take too much."

"Don't worry son, if they get above themselves, we'll do them, like the last time."

The last time the Albanians pushed it, the McGings put a bullet into the heads of all their lieutenants in Glasgow, leaving them leaderless. "Then Police Scotland locked up ten players, Davy."

"Aye, got off lightly. You inviting Hubert this time?"

"He'll be there. It's part of the… agreement."

"Aye, the deal, keep the public out of it. To hit each other is OK. Keep Glasgow's citizens out of the hospital and the morgue."

"It ensures we can do our business, without… interference."

"You still worried son?" I remain quiet. "I doubt if Hubert atribu… holds the bomb attack on Jackie… to you."

"Well, there were more likely –"

"Jackie fell out of favour with some heavy players and –"

"I made the call to you, Davy."

"You did son, but that doesn't mean you were… attrib… utable."

I enjoy hearing him seeking multisyllabic words. He allows me the privilege of pointing out new ones. His rows of classic books had grown under my tutelage.

"I made the call to you, Davy."

He gets up and towers over me. "Now, know where the line is, son, and how not to cross it." I stay shtum. "Anyway, you're in safe hands."

"Thanks."

Davy scans my new Kiton K50 suit. From a Crombie to the finest cashmere, from an off-the-peg to a Saville Row, from a psychiatric patient to consigliore, I had come a long way.

"Aye, with success comes reward, son."

Beats being a mad shrink.

"Beats being a mad shrink," I repeat out loud.

He gives me a telling look. "Aye, son."

I recall my "previous circumstances": a forty-nine-year-old, divorced, used-to-be professional man, living in a shitty Partick pied-à-terre, talking to himself.

"Things have changed, Davy."

"Nothing stays the same."

He moves forward with a tray of coffee and scones. "Now you look after us and we look after you." He offers me a plate.

"You gave me this chance... this job and all." I accept a scone.

"You do a good job son, you got respect."

True respect is gained.

Praise indeed. Davy disrespects any man who falls short of his own standards. Disrespect means disenfranchisement, disenfranchisement means isolation, isolation in Family terms generally means death.

"I try, Davy. But I know the only thing that keeps me safe is what I know –"

"Aye, information, son, dangerous thing." He laughs. "You were always one step ahead. That's why we appointed you. You give us an edge. You know what's goin' on."

"We need to confirm our relations... with Police Scotland, from a collective point of view."

Davy nods Mick's way. "Usual crates. Haig Club for Hubert and Jackie's favourite champers; you'll know it Rooney."

"I mean –"

"I know what you mean. We don't shoot the public or the polis."

"More than that, Davy. We manage organised crime and they leave us alone."

"Anything else?"

"MI5?"

"And Jackie?" He completes the sentence, giving me something he thinks I should have. A gift from a man who doesn't normally give anything away.

"MI5," I repeat.

"The spooks, they're watching us." He feigns a ghostly voice and tries to divert or make light of what he is saying to me.

"They're more than watching, Davy, they're breathing down our necks."

"You worry too much, Rooney." He rises and moves towards me. "Always the worrier. You give a fuck you die, you don't give a fuck you also die." He laughs. "Do I give a fuck?"

I smile at him: this man, going on seventy and fit as a flea, not a worry line on his face. Head of the country's biggest crime syndicate and nothing appears to concern him; nothing he would show. "Right, enough for today. I've my swim to get. Anything more, we'll do on the day."

Then, cup in hand, he is off like a whippet out of a trap through the house. It's clear the meeting is over. The other items in the folder will have to wait until the next meeting. Nothing that important, although reigning back some of the individual team bosses is up next. Old feuds were never far away from the surface, always in danger of reigniting.

I know I tread a fine line in maintaining order with these men: sometime the lion tamer, sometime the referee, sometime the diplomat. I need to know how to manage, *manage* these men. These are businessmen and I have to treat them like an executive team. Money and power motivate them. Everything that needs to has to be predicated on these two objectives; nothing else is important, apart from revenge, that is. They all know they'll achieve more together, however, on all of these fronts; this is economy of scale and the proceeds of collective power. During the turf wars, tit for tat killings did nothing but deplete their individual strength. Yet, I know from their ranks would emerge a man that would want it all, who would be prepared to go to war with all of them for total power in Glasgow. Since Johnston's death, that man had yet to appear. The leaders, individually, however, have learned from their battles and have secured stability, but there are some hothead young guns set to knock them from their thrones. I turn to look at Mick and he's one of them right enough.

"Time to go, Rooney." Mick hands me my coat.

For this former psychologist, maintaining homeostasis was never easy. My training as a forensic psychologist plays its part. I understand conflict in individuals and groups, and know, with dangerous men, unless conflict is harnessed it will erupt like a volcano over a densely populated area.

I accept my coat from Mick. "Thanks."

"On your way," he says, turning away.

I retreat down the stairs, looking over my shoulder as I always do when I leave this house.

Watch your back... son.

CHAPTER FIVE

Jackie is back at work and, driven by Euan Baird, her detective sergeant, she travels to the monthly Executive Team meeting at Police Scotland HQ in Tulliallan Castle, a large baronial house in Kincardine, and the site of Hubert's office. Her disability doesn't allow her to drive and this is a long way from Glasgow. This is the early days of Police Scotland and before the opening of Gartcosh, the SCC, the Scottish Crime Campus. She operates from French Street, the new Glasgow divisional HQ in Dalmarnock, but, daughter or not, Hubert expects her to attend executive team meetings in Tulliallan: she'd to be there. It is two weeks since her discharge from hospital and her disability and the pain in her leg doesn't make traveling easily, but she "has to go".

Her promotion to Assistant Chief Constable demands much, but provides more, like a new Porsche Boxster automatic and a new townhouse in Park Quadrant overlooking Kelvingrove Park in the West End. These assets add to the kudos from taking the credit of ending Glasgow's proxy killer, the Father, and his campaign of terror. While, most of the time while she was in hospital, like an armour piercing shell, in less than three months, she blasted through the police establishment glass ceiling, shattering it for all-time: the first female DCI to do so, as she always said she would. First, there was the promotion to Area Detective Superintendent, then to Chief Superintendent, and then to Temporary Deputy Chief Constable of Strathclyde Police. When Police Scotland was created, with a clear out of the old guard, and a political emphasis towards gender balance, she was in the right place at the right time. Not to say Hubert, her father, moving from Chief Constable of Strathclyde Police to be the first Chief Constable of Police Scotland, had anything to do with it; however, her being awarded the Queen's Police Medal sealed it.

Each day is full of meetings. This one is the Executive Team meeting, and her father chairs.

She observes him going through "strategic plans for tougher community policing", and, being her brief, she knows she has to concentrate, but the pain in her right leg just won't let her. She wishes her mobile would buzz. "Operational crisis, sorry chaps, have to go right away."

She looks down at her stick, resting on her twisted right leg, an outward sign of the attack that day on Sauchiehall Street. She recalls regaining consciousness in the GRI and dwells on how lucky she was to survive.

This time it is Hubert's gruff voice that wakes her. "ACC, are you with us?" He stirs her from her dwam.

"Eh, yes, sorry sir. Late night at the office." She knows it would be best to admit her vulnerabilities, but that would be admitting she is weak, and at this table of Police Tsars that would not be the right thing to do.

She casts a glance towards Hubert at the other end of the table. She remembers his pushing her for information when she was in hospital. He knew there was more to her assassination attempt. He returns her look and she turns away. To reveal too much of their relationship with this testosterone-fuelled group wouldn't do.

"Stability!" Hubert grabs everyone's attention. "We are informed that Davy McGing has re-established the collective family fraternity in Glasgow. The heavy teams in Glasgow are now under one banner once more and no longer fight each other. Stability... has been... consolidated."

This is generally welcomed. Although, Martin Millar, who likes to court controversy because he had read somewhere that this gets you noticed, has to say, "Ah, but at a cost, Chief." He is positioned next to Jackie, just too close for comfort for Jackie, partially because he is big, fat and reeks like a cross between an ashtray and an east end fish and chip shop, but more probably because he is a smarmy, self-promotional bastard.

Hubert prompts. "Tell us, Martin?"

"Happy to, sir. We have had twenty-three gangs members killed and, more importantly sir, twelve police officers have been seriously injured... boss."

"There's been... collateral damage."

"Indeed, collateral damage, boss." Millar looks around for support. "The public... the gun battles?"

"The public are not at risk, not directly, Martin; you know that."

"Yes, boss, but our forces are bearing the brunt." Millar knows just how much to edge it.

"It has hit Glasgow bad, sir," says Deputy Chief Constable Cheryl Kirkpatrick, nicknamed 'Cher' by the team. "Roads are blocked, public transport is disrupted, services are affected across the city."

"Sure, Cher, but Glasgow *is* open for business." Hubert reveals the politics of his post.

Jackie straightens herself in her chair, trying to gain some perspective over Millar's domineering presence, knowing she needs to get into the discussion. "And the mob makes a tidy profit, sir," she says. "Crime pays. Kill people, create chaos, get a return."

Hubert looks up. "The… renewed relationship with the firms is paying dividends, Jackie. They now talk through Davy McGing, with one voice."

"With the help of your man," Millar whispers in Jackie's ear.

"Used to be, bastard," Jackie whispers back.

"I know, you're kind of… on your own, now."

"Rooney has brought order from chaos," she says, outward, while looking Millar in the face, then adding, "arsehole," but trying to preserve some distance from the smell exuding from his armpits.

"We must… exploit the new arrangement." Hubert's voice bellows over them.

"Must we turn a blind eye to their activities, sir?" Millar asks. "While they act legit and are uncontrolled, we turn them into multimillionaires."

"And what is the alternative, Martin, more turf wars?"

"It's hard to tell what the real cost is, boss."

"Check that with the insurance companies and the health board." Jackie's murmurs are heard by all. "I can tell you about both these things."

Hubert allows a pause. "Further matters," he says, happy to move on. "You'll be aware the Home Secretary has announced a new Terrorism Bill set to go through the UK parliament."

Jackie's attention is piqued. Already briefed on this, she wants the Executive Team's take on it.

Hubert continues. "We are to be given new powers to seize passports, travel documents, and there will be exclusion orders."

Positive mutterings ring out around the table. "I need someone to lead the implementation group?"

"*I'll* do it," Jackie says. More mutterings, but less positive this time. Many there believe Jackie, just in the job and still traumatised from her injuries, is hardly ready to take on such an important role. "It is *my* brief." She knows this is her opportunity to demonstrate her abilities and to show them all she can overcome her frailties. However, even she knows the extent of this responsibility.

"Chief," says Millar. "I am happy to relieve ACC Kaminski and do the implementation group; it is operational after all, at least while she is… recuperating." Hubert acknowledges the nods around the table. "However, I believe a civil liberties board is to be set up."

The nods cease. Many there are sceptical of laws where civil liberties – the human rights of those who would harm the public – inhibit officers in the exercise of their duties.

"Indeed, Martin. Do you want to convene that too?"

Jackie looks askance at Hubert.

"No way, Chief, but ACC Kaminski has good experience in… community relations. I suggest she is appointed to do it." Millar turns to Jackie who is in her bag to spray some perfume in a hankie to put to her nose.

"The civil rights lawyers will bite your arse off," says DCC, Bill Grant.

"And I'll bite their bloody heads off." Jackie realises she is talking herself into the role and out of the implementation committee. "I'll ensure our officers balance security with rights."

"And what rights did the poor bastards on Flight 103 that came down on Lockerbie have?" says Grant.

"The rights that the people of Glasgow expect," Jackie replies. "Protection from the bad guys. Will that do?"

Grant nods, knowing Hubert is ready to wade in.

"It's agreed then." Hubert stops any further debate on that matter. "Martin leads on the implementation team and Jackie does the civil liberties board."

Millar leans over and whispers in Jackie's ear, "Should be fun, love. I fuck the terrorists and you fuck their lawyers." He makes sure he's well out of Hubert's earshot. "And maybe we can have some fun… fucking together."

Jackie digs her nose into the perfume sodden hankie. "In your dreams, Martin; have a bath." Millar lets out a snort of a laugh. "And, anyway, what would your wife say?"

"Oh, Jean's OK about things like that."

"Aye, I'm sure she is. Likes the men, herself, I hear."

Millar snorts again.

"And now!" Hubert's bark offers Jackie some respite from Millar's miscreant sexist talk. "A most important item."

All fall silent. They know this one is coming. They gird themselves for it.

"We have received information," Hubert looks up to a hushed room, "that ISIS extremists have threatened to kidnap and murder a Glasgow police officer."

"That's all we need, boss," Millar says.

"What information, sir?" Jackie asks.

"Came in on Monday. A threat to uniformed staff. Not unlike similar threats in our cities nationwide."

"Over my dead body," Millar says.

"Could be arranged, Martin." Millar knows it is time to zip it. "Give the officers extra security briefings. And they're not to wear the uniform travelling to and from work. And they'll take appropriate measures to safeguard themselves."

"The public, sir?" Jackie enquires.

"Threat level severe, ACC. Full and total preparation for terrorist attack. You've all been briefed. You know what to do." For a few seconds Hubert feels like he's convening a council of war.

"Public information, boss?" Millar knows there would be a demand for it.

"Nothing, at this time. The meeting is over. Go about your business, but with care, and… with vigilance."

"*Semper Vigilo*, always vigilant," Millar murmurs in Jackie's ear.

"Excuse me," she whispers back, "while I am sick."

"Jackie?" Hubert asks.

"Yes, sir."

"The Justice Secretary says we have to… liaise with the intelligence service, and that's your remit."

"Fantastic."

"And direct from John Maclean, First Minister. 'The ISIS killers will not tell us how to live our lives and we will not bow to their prophet,' he says."

"Ouch," Jackie says, quietly.

"Our instructions are to work closely with our security partners and to remain alert to all terrorist threats that may manifest here, or where individuals overseas seek to direct or inspire others to commit attacks in and against the UK."

"Got it."

"Good. So talk to Dempsie."

"I'll look forward to it… sir." Jackie turns to Millar. "Can't wait to talk to your wife about your behaviour, arsehole," she whispers.

Jean Dempsie, senior spook, MI5, paces as she awaits Jackie's arrival. "Ten steps from one wall to the other, three hundred times a day, three thousand steps, twelve hundred calories, high protein foods, all equals increase in overall muscle mass. Yes!"

This is their first meeting since Jackie's incident and she is unsure of how it will go. She stops occasionally to gaze down the Clyde from her office window in the Criminal Justice Information Services, a department of the Scottish Police Services Authority in Pacific Quay in Glasgow. There is no nameplate on her door, nor is there a sign to say this is MI5 Glasgow. Covert operations require a covert address. MI5, Military Intelligence 5, or the Secret Service, and none of this is on display to say it is there.

She looks out at the scene and imagines the great panoply of sea-going vessels that plied their trade on the Clyde, travelling everywhere MI5 doesn't go, but SIS, the new title for MI6, does. One day, she'll get that job. "One day, I'll get to fuck out of this place and get to those places those ships visit," she says, at the twenty-first length. She is held in the job, however. "No one leaves MI5, unless in a fucking box." She gasps for breath.

MI5 Glasgow had been a busy – albeit discreet – office for many years, since the late 60s, with the rise of the CND and the threat to the nuclear submarine base in the Clyde, and the links between the major gangs in Glasgow with the Krays, the London firms, and their association with the Belfast paramilitary organisations. Davy McGing and George Taylor were close associates then. Gunrunners for the UDA, they were a useful source of intelligence. MI5 feared growing violence in Belfast that would spread to Glasgow, which had the same sectarian forces and a source of arms and soldiers for both the UDA and the IRA.

Dempsie is more concerned, however, about what is happening these days.

Two British Muslim converts got life for hacking a soldier to death on a London street in broad daylight, Islamist terrorists killed twelve people in the Paris offices of Charlie Hebdo, and Glasgow, having had a bomb attack at Glasgow Airport, remained an imminent and definite target. Current threat level from international terrorism is severe, meaning a terrorist attack is likely. Now, extremists have threatened to kidnap and murder a Glasgow police officer. Tensions are high, and none more so arising from her anticipated meeting with Jackie Kaminski.

"Good to see you Jackie." Jean welcomes her in, swiping the sweat from her brow with a towel. "Or should I say, Assistant Chief Constable. I suppose congratulations are in order." She spins a swivel office chair, adjacent to her desk, inviting Jackie to sit.

"No, you're alright." Jackie takes a hard back seat at the window. "Thanks." Jean doesn't reply. "Good view."

"I know." Jean tucks the towel in her neck as she moves there. "Unusual, you know –"

"What, being a woman, the Chief's daughter, disabled?"

"Amazing how people get promoted."

"What, like being a woman, the Assistant Chief Constable's wife, and being fucked in the heid?"

"Good, Jackie. Martin said he had talked to you."

"He gave my regards, did he?"

"He mentioned Rooney is doing well in the criminal fraternity."

"I know, nothing surprises me these days."

"Well, beats the alcohol, and the mental fraternity."

"And you'll know all about that, Jean."

"Get it out, Jackie, you know you want to."

Jackie swings round to face her square on.

"Why were you there, Jean?"

"Where, Jackie?"

"You fucking know where, at the scene of my attack. Just happened to be walking past at the time, eh? Shopping on Sauchie, Jean, designer trainers?"

"Confidential, Jackie, you know we don't disclose… sensitive intelligence."

"What did you have to do with it, Jean?"

Jean moves fast and forcibly towards Jackie. She looks every inch the compact kick-boxer; Jackie knows Jean could easily spin and whack her head from where she stands. Jackie grips her stick, bringing it into her two hands on her lap. I'll fuck her hard if she gets any closer, she thinks.

"Jackie, you are close to making serious allegations; do you really want a high level directive from our Director General to Police Scotland, with a copy to the Justice Minister?"

"Oh just lovely. Alasdair Charlton would just love that at a time of major threat."

"Well, you started it, Jackie."

"I know there was something, Jean. I just don't know yet what, but I'll find out."

"We've to talk about Daesh."

"Daesh? ISIS, you mean?"

"Daesh. Barack Obama calls it ISIL. David Cameron does the same. Others refer to ISIS or IS."

"Fine, we'll call it ISIS.".

"OK, although ISIS is the Islamic State in Iraq and Syria. ISIL is the Islamic State in Iraq and the Levant. It's not a state."

"Fuck, what does it matter, we've to talk about *it*."

Jean returns to window gazing, turning her back on Jackie, clearly to gain greater emphasis. "Opponents of the term say it is neither Islamic nor a state. The French government adopts Daesh. It is the Arabic acronym for Al Dawla al-Islamiya fil Iraq wa'al Sham, or Da'ish. It is also viewed as derogatory by ISIS."

"Give me strength." Jackie digs out her mobile to check her texts. "What the fuck am I doing here?"

"I say Daesh. We have to demean these people."

Jackie's had enough. "You say tomato, I say… Can we talk about *them*?"

"Yes, let's do that." Jean sends some spray from her mouth in Jackie's direction. "Charlton has given a three-line-whip from SGoRR. They are here already."

"Unconfirmed, I believe."

"Jackie, they are here." Jean sends her a cold stare, her eyes almost out of their sockets.

"They are here?" Jackie repeats. "And you're sure about that?"

"We have it from MI6 and Interpol; they've tracked them, and social media. They've moved through Europe and are in the UK. They are here, believe me."

"You give us the details and we bring them in. That's how it works. You know that. We'll stop them before they do any damage."

"Don't be naïve, Jackie; you'll stop those who want to be stopped. There are those we know nothing about and will never know about until they hit us. Some have come home after a holiday in Syria and Jihadist militants are coming into Europe disguised as refugees. They're crossing the border into Turkey; then, using fake passports, they're travelling into European countries. They've entered established Islamic communities in London, Birmingham, and here in Glasgow. We are aware of at least one operational cell here in Glasgow; and that's where you and I come in."

"Our Islamic… communities aren't radicalised to the extent that they would accept… ISIS."

"Daesh soldiers are groomed in the Islamic communities in the UK, Jackie. You know that." Jackie remembers Rooney always referring to Jean as the woman who knows everything. *Living up to her reputation*, Jackie thinks. "We've foiled thirty-four terrorist plots since the 7/7 bombings," Jean says. "ISIS is consolidating itself in the Islamic gangs of UK cities. There they'll multiply, organise, ready themselves, and increase the threat tenfold."

"Glasgow has been quiet since the Glasgow Airport attack, terrorism wise."

"Oh, and what about your bomb attack, Jackie?"

Jackie gets to her feet and whacks her stick flat on Jean's desk. "We don't know who is behind that, do we Ms Dempsie?"

Jean steps back out of range. "Jackie!"

"You were fucking there. I was hit."

"Jackie."

"What?"

"Calm down, you're –"

"I'm out of order, pushing it, going to get whacked by a kick-boxer?"

"You are out of order, Mrs. Are you up for all this… Daesh and everything else that's going on?"

"I'll do what is necessary, Ms Dempsie." Jackie moves back to her seat. "Don't you worry about that." Jean moves back to the desk and starts to read some files, ignoring Jackie. "And you, Jean; you're happy to move away from it?"

"Eh?"

"You saw what happened to me. Are you really happy to move on, in your life, in your job, in your fucking mind?"

"I explained myself to the Inquiry, Jackie. I have nothing further to say on the matter."

"No, well I want to fucking well know why you were there." Jackie gets on her feet and positions herself above Jean. "What was going on there with you and Rooney? What was the MI5 role in the whole Johnston fiasco, and my… attack?"

"It is all explained in the report. Read it, you have a copy." Jean doesn't lift her head from her files.

Jackie rounds the desk. "You'll say nothing, Miss spook, Miss spy."

"Talk to your ex-husband. He was there."

"My *ex*."

"Why don't you pursue *him*, Jackie?" Jean lifts her eyes until she is line with Jackie's, without raising her head, a slight smile on her face.

Jackie could have said more, asked more about Jean and Rooney, but she knows it is best not to pursue it.

"Daesh?"

"Yes, Daesh, Jackie. I believe we've to talk."

"Talk, fuck-all, Jean. Just tell us, what do you want us to do?"

Jackie sits down, which allows both of them time to draw breath.

"We need information, direct from the street, the communities, the –"

"No more than that, Jean, information? Are you fucking with me?"

The smile returns to Jean's lips. "No more, not yet, Jackie."

"Not yet?"

"First, we have to poke this hive of bees."

Jackie turns to gaze through the glass of the office and into the open space beyond where dozens of operatives were busy milling around computers, in discussions, standing around in groups. "The hive of bees," she says, before turning to Jean. "What then, Queen Bee?" It is her time to smile.

"The soldiers first, Jackie. Now, if you will excuse me, I have a lot to do."

"I'm sure you have, get those abs working."

"Margaret?" Jean presses a button on her phone console. "Escort Ms Kaminski to her car."

Jackie grabs her satchel and stick. "Not fucking necessary." She heads to the door. "I can manage to get to my car, on my own."

"You know it's protocol. You have to be escorted off the premises, Jackie, you know that."

Margaret arrives in the room. Jackie looks up at her towering above her. "I know you know something about me, Miss Spook, you and I both know that. But I know something about you too, and don't you forget about that."

"Goodbye, Jackie, safe home." Jean returns her head to within her files.

"Fucking hive of fucking bees, Miss fucking queen bee." Jackie mutters as she moves through the desks, accompanied by Margaret at her back, applying policy that all 'non-operatives' leave the building, sign out, and hand in official temporary name badges at the reception desk on the way out.

"You happy being that bitch's lackey?" Jackie points in Margaret's direction as she opens the outside door for her.

"It's a job, Jackie," Margaret says, but from her tone Jackie knows it's not one she enjoys.

I'm in my bathroom looking at the man in the mirror, as I have done since I came out of hospital, something I seem to do more often these days.

What have you become?

"Well, bastard." I nearly applied cognitive behavioural therapy, stopping a lapse into both a delusional and hallucinatory episode, but I let it go; better out than in. "First there is the child, the good child. He goes to chapel, to school, runs the shopping for everyone. He is an honest child. Then the father bears down on the child, and the child is no longer a child. He has lost his innocence. Then he is a young man, a good young man; but he cannot heal the child who lives within him. He drinks. Then he is a man, a good man who helps others; but the child has become a demon, seeking to destroy him from inside. "Why did you let him do that to me?" He becomes a broken man, an ill man, so he becomes a bad man; it is the only way to survive, he understands. Then, he becomes God's man, and he learns the ways of persuasion, conversion –"

Exploitation?

"They *will* fear God."

The real deal. The sum of all the responses to every life experience you ever had, that's you: a fuck up, pal.

"And you are just a noise, an ear worm, a mind worm."

Ask yourself why you think you are God, that you have divine powers, that Police Scotland and MI5 are after you, that you tried to kill your ex-wife, and why you have no insight into your condition. Oh, and why do you hear a voice in your head, and call it bastard? Mental illness it is called, my friend.

"You sound like Dr Melville, my consultant psychiatrist."

You never listened to him either.

The mobile buzzes in the pocket of my robe. I draw it out to see "Jackie" on the screen. I only have one Jackie in my contacts. This is the phone I used to make *that call*, the trigger to the attack on Jackie. It refuses to give up.

It's the call you dread, Rooney, but the call you desire.

"Hello. Is that you, Jackie?"

"Aye, it's me, Rooney, Jackie."

Those words go to my soul. I always knew she would be in touch. If anything, to establish my role in her attack, the bombing; to tell me she had made it, to confirm I would keep her secret, as she would mine.

"Well, well, a blast from the past."

"Not funny, Rooney."

"Sorry, unintentional."

"I hope so. I suppose I should ask how you are."

"I am well. God is good. How are you?"

"I am… OK." Having kept up with our respective lives, we both know how we are. It's a way of breaking the ice. "Are you well, Rooney; really… well?"

"I take my tablets, Jackie, I don't drink, and I don't hang around with dangerous women."

"You'll be fine then, God willing."

"Absolutely."

"I need to talk to you."

"That'll be good, I think."

"Stay cool, Rooney. I'll keep the handcuffs in my bag."

"Boring."

"Curlers, today, one thirty. I'll see you there."

"OK, I look forward to it."

Should I do this? Am I able to face this woman, who represents my past, who roots me there, who will stop me becoming what I need to be?

I had been dreading this meeting with Jackie, but looking forward to it just the same. The questions would come, notably "Were you involved in my attack?" She had never had me taken in though, not even for questioning, but she would know I had some part in it, not that she or Police Scotland knew where I lived. I made sure of that. She knew my patterns, though, she could have found me, if she wanted to.

There will be more to this meeting, I know it. She's not going to say she had missed me, or be pleased I am on my feet, or I'm taking my medication, or I'm staying off the booze.

Time to prepare.

Prayers, self-flagellation with your trouser belt, or pack a bag for a holiday at Her Majesty's pleasure?

I head to Curlers bar and restaurant on the Byres Road. I get a taxi, no firm car this time. I get there fifteen minutes before she arrives, to check the place out. The words 'trust no one' enter my mind.

Trust no one. Mind that? Where did trust get you the last time?

I could have sent in a team to check it out, but this was a meeting that couldn't get back to Davy. I check the lane at the back; no dark cars with inauspicious occupants. I loiter outside for a few minutes, to see if there is any unusual activity, like men taking up positions in shop doorways. I'm happy and go in. I find a seat by the toilet, to survey the place. I move to the bar and ask the barman if there's a table for two for lunch. He tells me to sit where I want. I select a table next to the side wall, taking a seat facing outwards and wait, nervously drumming my fingers on the table. How would she look? She always was a doll: tall, slim, great clothes. We had been divorced two years and I had never stopped wanting her. The games we played while pursing Johnston, those power games, came to mind. She would sex-bomb me, flash her legs to the thigh, show a massive cleavage, tease me with those eyes – all part of the need to command me, though. Someone had to, I suppose. I had always hoped it would be for other, more basic, reasons – like wanting me. Those days are long past now; these days she has real power.

I'm anxious. I pace up and down from my seat to the outside door. Then I see a taxi pull up outside and there she is. I rush back to my seat like a wee boy heading for bed to wait for Santa Claus, and there she is coming through the door. She's wearing a rabbit fur jacket, fluffy scarf, and a white fur Russian trooper hat. She struggles with the door. A man exiting it holds it open for her. She comes in and looks around. I wave. She sees me and walks my way. It is only then I notice the limp and the stick, and I get an instant and vivid flashback of her on the ground, her thighbone revealed through her torn flesh, her blood pouring into the gutter.

She approaches the table. I don't expect anything, like a hand held out or a hug. That would be too much to expect. There's nothing. She empties her glasses, mobile, hankies from her bag onto the table, while taking her jacket off and pulling the chair out at the same time. I get up to help. She puts one finger up as if she is about to bless me. I half hear "In the name of the Father," in my head, the last thing I said to her on Sauchiehall Street as I looked down upon her, but instead I hear, "No, Rooney, there's no need." She sits down, taking time to settle, folding her jacket, placing her scarf, hat, gloves inside and placing them on an adjacent chair. She gives a rough shake of her hair, her fingers passing through it, tidying it. All of this gives me an opportunity to look at her, observe her.

There's more grey than I remember. The makeup mirror comes out. The makeup is checked, lipstick replenished, lips shaped, eyeliner relined. A hankie cleans some mascara from under both eyes. She looks tired. She always worked too hard, but this is a weary face. I catch the perfume: Prada, the same as always: strong, feminine, sexy.

"Well, long time no see." The words seem incongruous, but correct, and someone has to break the ice.

"You're a sight for sore eyes." The words don't fit, but what would, a lie?

Looking fantastic, darling?

"Suppose I am." She brings her hands up, palm to palm, in

front of her face like she was about to pray. Her manicured nails shine from the light above the table.

I'm mesmerised and don't respond. I just stare at her.

"Cat got your tongue, Rooney?"

I'm about to say something, like "I'm sorry". I am sorry, but I know she'll ask "Sorry, about what?" "Foul weather," comes out instead.

"Aye, foul weather."

"You wanted to see me." I cut to the chase, knowing she'll get annoyed at any procrastination on my part. She's not into small talk, never was.

"I did."

"You want to reconcile?" I know it is shit as soon as it comes out of my mouth – typical. She'd heard stupid things from my mouth many times before. Rightly, she ignores me and folds her arms on the table, looking down at the menu. "Want something to eat, drink?"

Picking this up, the waiter appears.

"Croissant, butter, jam, cappuccino, thanks," she says to the waiter. "You?"

"Bagel and cheese, double espresso. Thanks."

She engages my eyes. "Changed days without the booze, Rooney?"

"You… you wanted to see me."

"Aye, don't worry, I don't intend going over it all. I just don't have the strength." I'm also relieved, I also don't have the strength. "I know you were involved Rooney, but I just don't know how, why, or by how much; but I content myself by believing you wouldn't have harmed me, not wittingly."

"I wasn't well, Jackie, things were going on all around me."

"Shush, Rooney, don't say anything that might incriminate yourself. Why didn't you come to see me in hospital?"

"I was –"

"Scared, fair enough."

"Otherwise detained."

In Hairmyres Hospital.

"Oh, I see."

"Also scared."

A real shite.

"Rooney, you know things about me and you haven't blabbed.

I know things about you and I haven't blabbed, less so had you arrested. So, we share secrets about each other. We are cool."

"Guess so."

She pauses. "So, we know where we are?"

"Mmm."

"Good."

"Is that it?"

"I hear you are a big man in the Family?"

"I… pastor things."

"Oh, you do. I need you to do something for me."

"Oh?"

"I need your help."

"I mind the last time you asked for my help. Look where that got me?"

"This is different, Rooney. Then you were in your hole. Swimming in your alcohol induced urine. I needed to get you out of it."

"I think you had your own reasons for that, Jackie."

She sits back, waiting for the argument. Not this time, no more, never again, too tired to go through all that old crap. "I did, Rooney. Our secret, mind?"

"I mind."

Your secret, mind!

"You need to help me, Rooney."

"And what do you want… this time?"

She leans forward. "I want you –" Just then, the waiter arrives with the order. I wonder if this is an old type pass. She always used sexual innuendos and I would always respond to them, leading to extended sex chat games. This time her whole demeanour says the opposite and my whole take on it is against it; she has found reality and I have found God. She moves back as he places the plates on the table. "Thank you." She uses a spoon to scoop the froth from the top of her cappuccino into a paper napkin. She doesn't look up. "I want you… to get me… some information." She slips the spoon into her mouth between the "get me" and "some information".

Provocative, Rooney? Forget it.

"Some information?"

"We believe there is about to be a… campaign. The Islamic State. ISIS, ISIL, or IS, whatever. We believe they are here, planning something, preparing to act. You know what they can do."

"Jackie, you know our turf."

"You're into organised crime, Rooney. The migrant gangs are taking advantage of the… positive climate here in Glasgow. There'll be ISIS followers among them, no doubt. They'll know something. They'll have to. They'll have a supportive role."

"Supportive role?"

"Where else would ISIS get its information, find safe houses, direct assistance even?"

"The migrants know better. They're developing empires here, not to be destroyed by siding with… ISIS."

"They'll support it. ISIS are paying big cash. Rooney, this is extremely big shit."

I look into her eyes and see the fiery determination I remember well. "Big shit" has brought us together once more; not recrimination, nor love nor need, sex nor power; nor whatever else would have brought her to me in the past.

"Why don't *you* investigate the migrant gangs, Jackie? Call them in? You know who and where they are."

"Aye, sure. We bring people in and we are accused of racism. Mind the Macpherson Report, Stephen Lawrence, and the backlash that followed. We don't like investigating ethnic crime for fear of being called racists."

"Well, no change there."

"We have our community relations to consider. It's my brief."

"Some communities are being terrorised by Asian gangs."

"We can only do so much."

"Ethnic gangs operate with impunity."

"Only if the Family allow it, you could do it… on our behalf."

The words "on our behalf" have clear relevance for me. Doing for, acting for, proxy killing, were all part of my life in the Johnston era. Immediately, however, I realise this would only strengthen the Family's relationship with the authorities, and bring rewards. But I also realise Davy, a traditional Glasgow gangster, won't agree to it. "Davy won't do it."

"Davy'll protect our… agreement." She leans across the table pointing that spoon right into my face. "We need this. You tell him."

"What do you want him to do?"

"A, determine their strength. B –"

"B?"

"Tell us where they are."

"C?"

"I didn't give a C."

"C, destroy them, on your behalf?" I get to my feet. "You've got your new Terrorism Act. That'll give you powers to."

"I didn't give a C, Rooney."

"I know you didn't, but I know how it works."

"We are held bound by conventions, protocol, rights, and every human rights lawyer in the country. It'd take us years to… infiltrate."

"They're a threat."

"They'll inveigle themselves with the communities. Look at the Glasgow Airport bombers. One of them worked at the Royal Alexandra Hospital in Paisley. *He* had links with radical Islamic groups."

"It's still not our business, Jackie."

"Rooney?"

"What?"

"You owe me, hon. You have to help me." I hear the emphasis on the "have to".

With that, she places her right hand on my left hand. I nearly turn my hand around to grasp hers, but decide against it. I'm not sure what this is: care or love, manipulation or exploitation? Then she pulls out a ten-pound note from her pocket, drops it on the table, picks up her jacket and hat, and she's off towards the toilet, dragging her right leg. She appears a few minutes later bedecked for the cold evening. She walks straight past me on the way to the door. I think about calling to her, to ask if she would like to meet again, but it just won't come out.

"Thank you for seeing me, Davy," I say, arriving at Gracelands. Davy is having breakfast before he goes for his daily swim.

"They want us to do what?" Davy nearly chokes on his toast. He isn't a man to have his breakfast interrupted, but I had insisted on seeing him.

It is the Family meeting later that day and I have an important item under any further matters to add. "The Muslims," I say, also explaining Jackie's request.

"Bring them to book? Get to fuck Rooney."

"Have you heard of the Islamic State?"

"Don't insult my intelligence son, or try my patience. You know my position with the Muslims. Anyway, they're stupid young men."

"They're into human-trafficking, passport forgery, kidnapping and murder, Davy, muscling in on international heroin trafficking. Fundamentalism is producing young men who'd commit mass murder. Look at Glasgow Airport, Paris. They're killing Christians!"

He looks me full in the face. "Look, John Paul the fucking second, I don't give a fuck who they kill as long as it's not us. We control their activities because if we didn't, it would damage our business and they'd take over key markets. They are anyway, but only those businesses we don't want."

"This is our business, Davy. Believe me, it's in the Family's interests. You are the new Father..."

He looks at me intently, with those eyes that say everything. "Aye, and business will be done on *my* terms." I know not to argue with him. "And the Family's interests? What about the Muslims, what would they say about us getting involved with their *interests*?"

"We would be protecting their interests too. Their young men are becoming radicalised, going to Syria, some are –"

"Coming back?"

"You got it."

"The Glasgow Muslims are no' daft. They're no' into terrorism. It would destroy them. They know that."

"They have new hot-heads who intend making... political statements."

"Political statements? Anyway, it'd create instability. So, no fucking way. Terrorism is nothing to do with us."

"Northern Ireland, Davy?" I know this is dangerous territory to enter with this man.

"Just don't go there son. I give you a lot of rope in this business, don't let it hang you."

"I just wanted to –"

"I know what you wanted to do. Just don't."

"Don't what?" A groggy looking Mick enters the kitchen.

"Do the Muslims."

"The Pakis."

"Asians, son."

"Not the Asians, Davy," I say. "The Islamic State."

"Is that the fuckers that killed the soldier in London?" Mick asks. "Hacked him to fucking death in public?"

"They were British Muslims," I say.

"Muslims, Islamic, Asians, Pakis, they're all the fucking same man," Mick says.

"They're becoming radicalised."

"Fucking radicalised? Mad bastards."

"And they are here."

"If they give us trouble we'll fuck them," Davy says. "Right? But, we're not playing polis for no cunt."

Davy won't trigger the Family for this. He is a traditional leader. He does what he knows best: straightforward drugs, loan sharks, money laundering. He knows that radicalised Asian groups are a bad thing for business, though, and this would increase their strength, create chaos, but he is not going to act on a diktat from Police Scotland or MI5.

"Davy, we need to cut off this snake's head before it bites."

"Look son, I respect your opinion. It's just different from mine. You got it?" He returns to his toast and tea. To push it beyond this point will lead to him losing it. I had been there before, one time coming close to losing an eye when he hurled a heavy glass ashtray at me in a meeting.

"Have you got it pal?" Mick echoes his father, as he pours him tea. "Time you were going." Mick shows me out. "You always were a stupid cunt, Rooney." He opens the door. "From that time Jean brought you to us in Gardner Street." I feel my finger, the end cut off by a chopper as an example of power by Thomas, Mick's dead brother. I was to "go underground" to get into the Family network. Jean Dempsie set it up.

"I mind it." I rub the end of my finger.

"You got his back up, Rooney," Mick says. "Not a good idea. Go back to your bible thumping and give us all peace." He heads back to bed.

I know too well that Mick will be happy about this. There is no love lost here. Mick is heir apparent for Davy's throne, and I threaten that.

Later that evening, I call Jackie.

"You've not to phone me anymore, Rooney, you know that. We

don't do that no more." Not to mention MI5 tapping his line, she thinks.

"I need to talk to you." I put the phone on hands-free. I am at my desk in the study, a replenished espresso in front of me. I scan the photographs in frames that cover the desk: my mother, us together when I was a boy, and my dog, Trix; another of Jackie and I in happier times, right after our marriage when we travelled to Corfu. This is a happy memory, partly why I keep it. Sharing a bottle of Greek wine, overlooking the Adriatic, the sun setting to the west, we were young, happy, trouble free.

"It had better be important, Rooney. I've a… an engagement tonight."

"A society do, Jackie?" It is not lost on me that Jackie is mixing with the nobs since her elevation to the echelons of Police Scotland.

"It's none of your business, Rooney. Dad says I've got to do it. It's… community relations."

"Some community!"

"Get on with it, Rooney. I don't have the time."

"He won't do it."

"Oh, right. That's a shame. Can he be… persuaded?"

Jackie knows Davy could normally be persuaded. Cash payments, charges dropped on players, turning a blind eye to his activities, generally worked.

"Not this time. No' his business, he said."

She understands this. Davy knows his boundaries and he won't deviate from them.

"That's too bad. We'll just have to think about something else."

"Jackie…"

"What?"

"God bless."

The line goes dead.

I get another espresso and ponder the "something else", which could be a range of things, all of which would involve unknown subversive activity by Police Scotland or MI5. I didn't like not knowing what was going on out on the streets. It is bad for business, bad for me. I also know that the special relationship the Family has with the authorities is under threat and that is even worse for business; and even more so for me.

CHAPTER SIX

Small chat isn't welcome in Jean's office. Jackie knows this. "Does everything to do with MI5 need a bloody meeting? What about the telephone these days?"

"Protocol expects no such communications, Jackie." Jean is reading from her laptop. "You know that."

"Yes, protocol." Jackie takes her jacket off and places it over the back of the chair. "I hear from the media that MI6 is encouraging Jihadi fighters to come home." She hovers over the seat. "Where the fuck does that fit with protecting the homeland? Jesus, Jean, we have threats of kidnapping here."

"Just sit down, Jackie. Richard Barrett doesn't speak for us; *he* is a former director of MI6 counter-terrorism."

"Great." Jackie sits down. "At the same time as we are given new powers to seize passports of terror suspects, stopping British extremists from returning to the UK your guy says this. A bit of a fucking contradiction, don't you think?"

"If you say so."

"I say MI5 and MI6 speak with forked fucking tongues."

"SIS."

"SIS?"

"The new name for MI6, the Secret Intelligence Service."

"Just fantastic, SIS and ISIS. Amazingly similar, funny that."

"Get on with it, Jackie." Jean's mind is strictly on her computer.

"You want them back so we'll have to deal with them here. So much safer than leaving them loose in the world like rogue sharks to kill tourists."

"Well, we'll have a better idea who we are dealing with; don't you think, Jackie? The way things are just now we don't know who they are. Where they are? Some are here already." There's a pause for breath from both sides. "And how are you getting on with the information?"

"What information?"

"You know what information, Jackie, don't be obtuse."

"Obtuse, good one." Jackie opens her mobile. "We are doing everything we can… within our resources."

"That's good. If these guys disappear into the Islamic communities, they'll be impossible to find. Then they'll attack us."

"The communities won't accept them." Jackie has her head down also, checking her texts. "Our liaison officers are working with them to identify any radicals."

"Yeah, just like 7/7, Glasgow Airport, Woolwich, Paris. What about the Asian gangs?"

"I've taken steps… to reach in there."

"Rooney back on your radar, given his influence these days with the criminal fraternity?"

Jackie clicks away on her mobile. "We have a working relationship with the Family."

'Relationship' with the criminal fraternity incites Jean to her feet. She goes behind Jackie and spins her chair, bringing her around to face her. "Cosy. Not too cosy, Jackie?"

Jackie is startled and puts her mobile away. "We cooperate, as you would expect, spook. And if you –"

"Scratch my back –"

"Do that again and I'll stuff my stick up your arse."

"Cooperation, Jackie. Cool it."

"Christ, Jean, you know how it works. It maintains order."

"Oh, Davy won't sanction it then?" Jackie doesn't answer. "He wouldn't, but would Rooney?"

Again, Jackie doesn't answer and goes back to her texts until the towering Margaret appears over her. "Time to go, I guess. Interview over?"

"You got it." Jackie gets up. "Why do you hate me, Jean?"

It is Jean's turn not to answer. Jackie wonders how she would do against the kick-boxer *and* Margaret, the Hulk. *I need to get another stick*, she thinks.

Malky Fraser has this name for two reasons. First, his name is Malcolm Fraser and second, "Malky Fraser" is known in Glasgow as rhyming slang for an "open razor", the preferred one time weapon of many Glasgow hard men. Malky, a famed proponent of the "tool", had drawn it down the side of many faces, those either unable or unwilling to pay loan sharks. "Give them the Malky," was a common term used in Glasgow. Though the razor gangs were long gone, he is still associated with the term. Then, he was also known to favour six-inch nails, nailing unfortunate men to the floor in front of their families in mock crucifixion, through the palms of the hands and the feet into the living room floor of their tenement flats. These days, however, this street fighter and survivor of the gang wars is a cold-blooded assassin, his trademark known as the "Glasgow send-off", where, after giving his victim a severe kicking, he would put a shotgun up his back passage and pull the trigger, sending shot up through the stomach and into the heart; always lethal that one. This man would kill if the money and reason were right. This time they were. The cash was substantial: ten bags: ten thousand, in used bills. The reason: hit a heavyweight player and previous gunrunner to the UDA. Malky had killed for the IRA in Glasgow during the troubles, but this man had evaded him. For him, this was unfinished business. This one was unusual, however. He was not to know the name of the customer, only the target.

Davy enjoys his daily swim in Woodside Baths, an old Victorian swimming baths near Charing Cross in Glasgow. His usual bodyguards – two street players elevated to the position based on their ability to keep their heads while seeing off some serious attacks – at his side. He is a creature of habit, same place and same time, which just happens to be the key feature in most hits. Most gangsters survive by avoiding this rule. Davy isn't stupid, though, he thinks he's untouchable. He doesn't believe anyone in Glasgow would have the balls to threaten him or his family.

He loves the old baths, which he had attended since he was at school, not far from there in Maryhill. They had seen better days, however, the wall windows and roof skylight were painted over with bitumen to stop leaks and save the cost of major repairs. It gave an eerie and gloomy effect in the water, the arc lights casting shadows of the swimmers on the floor of the pool. As he swims, he doesn't notice a man with goggles doing the rotational route up and down the side of the pool. This man had been here for the past three days, same time as Davy. Nor would he have noticed him observing the bodyguards as they hung over the banister looking down on the pool, watching their movements, as he also had for the past three days.

Malky had noticed they took turns to go outside for a smoke, leaving one of them to guard Davy. Each day, Davy would do his normal fifty lengths, get out, rinse himself in the communal showers, and move to the same cubicle he always used to dry and dress; another routine. He enjoyed this cubicle just off the corridor upstairs. There were cubicles on the main drag, but he likes this one in particular. It is tucked out of sight, however, which is a vulnerability. All the time he's watched by the bodyguards. They were aware, however, that any assailant approaching him would also be in trunks and in a hand to hand, even if he had a small knife hidden in his trunks, they knew Davy, a hard battler, would have no trouble dealing with him until they reached there.

This day, one bodyguard is caught up in a chat outside with an attractive young woman. He isn't there as Davy leaves the pool. The chat and the young woman was set-up with the promise of a bag of cocaine. The remaining bodyguard is in his usual place, not perturbed by this change in routine. All is quiet and calm. The pool is empty, apart from two men who have since left it to return to their cubicles. Davy finishes his fifty lengths, has his shower and moves to his cubicle. All appears well.

All is not well, however, and the bodyguard doesn't hear the pop of Malky's Beretta 92, silencer fitted, as he stands on the bench of his cubicle, pulling himself up until he's balanced, elbows into Davy's cubicle, where he fires a true bullet into the middle of Davy's head. Davy crumples to the floor. He makes no sound or groan as he goes down, such is the accuracy of the shot. Malky would have been happy to dispense with his trademark on this occasion. He has done what he had gone there to do, but Davy's body has crumpled to the floor with his backside adjacent to his cubicle. Never one to miss a chance, Malky gets on the floor on his side and pushes his gun into Davy's anus and fires. There's a deeper sounding pop this time, as the bullet explodes into Davy. The job's done well and he has left his mark. A success.

He expects the bodyguard's arrival and he'd shoot him dead too if he has to. Moving outside, he sees him standing where he was, chatting to a female pool attendant. Malky squeezes the gun into his shoulder bag, finger on the trigger, muzzle pointing forward in case he needs to use it. He leaves his cubicle and makes his way toward the bodyguard, and has the cheek to check his hair in the mirror to the side of the bodyguard. Walking out, he passes the other bodyguard arriving from outside. He gives Malky a glance as if he recognises him from somewhere. Later he would remember they had been on a job together as young men, some twenty years earlier on a protection racket visit on an East End butcher who didn't pay, when they emptied his shop of beef.

The bodyguards become concerned when Davy overstretches his normal fifteen minutes getting dressed. They move towards the cubicle. There panic erupts, as halfway there they see blood flowing into the pool from the cubicle area. A shove opens the door and there lies the crumpled body of Davy, blood pouring from his head and anus. Once outside, Malky ditches the unmarked gun down a drain, steps into a waiting car ready to disappear into the back streets, and away from the scene before the police or any members of the Family arrive.

The bodyguard calls Mick almost at the same time the pool attendant calls the police. Mick arrives at the same time as he sees his father's body being loaded into an ambulance, to be taken to Stewart Street for the Procurator Fiscal and forensics. Police are arriving en masse and he can't wait around to be interviewed or detained.

By this time, Malky is on the way to the airport, soon to be on a flight to New York. He doesn't think for one minute that, between Mick who recognised the trademark and knows the one man who would have done the job on his father and the bodyguard who recognised him afterwards, he had been identified. Mick knows more than anyone that the mind of a hitman would be on getting out of the country for a while, if not for good. He would now be the quarry. Where Malky was going, though, in upstate New York, no one would find him. Malky had to get on that plane. His timing is meticulous. Hit Davy, half an hour to the airport, through security, KLM flight 1476 leaving Glasgow for New York, ETD 1.30 p.m., within an hour. Many a son would have followed his father's body, but not Mick; he knows where Malky is heading.

To get through security is uppermost on Malky's mind; safer there and one-step away from getting on the plane being readied on the tarmac at Gate 34. Check in is easy, done on line, nothing more than a shoulder bag to take into the cabin. Damn, boarding had not been announced, or the gate, he thinks. He would get through security and hang around duty-free until it was. Security was tight since the car bombers' failed attempt. Taking a car close to the terminal was impossible, not even to rush in with a pretext of delivering a forgotten passport.

Mick dumps his car at drop-off. It will be viewed suspicious after a short while which will bring in the airport police. He'll take a taxi back and say it was stolen; he has a job to do first. He gets into the terminal, has a glance at the departure screen; where's he going, he asks himself. No doubt as far away as possible, though there were only a few international flights leaving that afternoon. Paris is too close; Europe would be within the EU and Interpol jurisdiction. Dubai was possible, so was Florida, and so was New York. All departures went the same route through security. He knows where he's heading.

Malky is nervous as he waits in line, more than the normal nervous traveller. In a few minutes, he'll be through. He scans the TV screens to see if any news has broken, but he doubts if SKY or FOX would broadcast the demise of Davy McGing. BBC Scotland would, however, have it on the six thirty news. He watched the faces of the army officers checking passports and boarding passes ahead of the x-ray and security checks. He looks into their eyes; they look into his. They are briefed on all major threats. He is getting out of Glasgow to escape, as many of these passengers are doing. Though his escape is to escape impending death. He is confident he would not be on their radar, though. The person who commissioned him had said all would be OK. He would have no problem getting on that plane and away. He feels assured by this. He just needs to get through security.

A wee boy turns to him in the queue and says he is going to Disneyland in Florida. Malky doesn't answer. The wee boy's mother pulls her son to her. This man isn't in any mood for small talk. Just then, there's a tap on his back.

"Hello, Mr Fraser, I thought I recognised you in the queue."

Malky knows the voice. He turns to see Mick standing by his side, his hand inside his jacket, grasping a hidden handgun, the shape of it clearly identified by Malky. He could cry out, bring security; but what would that do, he has no weapon. Mick would kill him there and then and spend his time in prison, something he was used to and happy to do if he had killed the murderer of his father. He could fight him: same outcome.

"Fancy a coffee? We've got plenty of time before the flight is called."

Malky understands he has to go with him. There is a chance, if he does. He'll think of something, he has to. Malky nods and moves away from the queue, Mick behind him.

"To the toilets," Mick says in his ear.

Malky knows this is where Mick intends doing him. He could run, but Mick would kill him there and then, same as at security. His only chance is in the toilets. There, he'll muster every skill he has to stay alive. He moves into the toilets, where there's a young man washing his hands. Both of them move to the urinals and piss. This might be his last, Malky thinks. Mick's hands are busy doing up his belt and trousers. This is Malky's chance. Whether the man was there or not he had to take it. He lifts his arms in a fake stretch and swings his right elbow into Mick's face. Mick sees it coming and is keen. He knows this is a vulnerable movement and he's prepared. He dances aside, avoiding the swipe, digging his hand inside, and in a flash has his hand on his gun bringing it to bear on Malky. The unsuspecting man is stunned, rooted to the spot.

Malky looks at him. "He's going to kill me."

Mick knows the man will bring the house down if he leaves the toilets. "I won't harm you if you stand there and say nothing."

The man nods.

Malky wonders if Mick has the stupidity to do him there in front of the man. He knows Mick has a dilemma: should he take the chance and shoot him there or get out and away? A gunshot would ring out through the terminal like a school dinner bell. He might have one last chance. He makes to reach the man, to pull him to him, to cover him. A stronger man, Mick grabs Malky by the neck, spins him onto the floor, sits on him, his hand across his mouth, his knife at his throat.

"Before I kill you Malky, I'll give you one chance to say who commissioned you."

Malky spits on his face. Mick, in a second, digs the knife deep into Malky's right eye, then cuts his neck, putting all his weight on the knife as it just about slices Malky's head off. Malky is dead in seconds. All the while, Mick is watching the terrified young man.

What would he do? Mick cleans his knife and gets off Malky. He moves towards the young man, putting his knife away.

"It's OK, son, this doesn't concern you. I'll just walk out that door and you'll give me five minutes before you call someone in here."

The young man nods. He's shaking in his shoes. Then, as Mick is about to leave, as is he is about to shake his hand, he reaches for the man. He looks at Mick's outstretched hand and brings out his own. Mick grabs it and pulls him to him, thrusts his knife deep into the man's middle, then covers the man's mouth to muffle his groans as he allows his limp body to drop to the floor. Mick knows he is lucky. This is a busy toilet and no one had come in. If anyone had, he would have had to do them in the same way – no alternative – but best to get out when he has the chance. He washes the knife in running water in the sink, washes his hands, pulls his jacket over his blood sodden shirt, and tidies himself, before leaving behind a scene which will terrify the next occupant of the toilet. He rushes out of the terminal and steps onto the first bus out of the airport. Luckily, it's the airport shuttle that will take him back into Glasgow. He pays the driver £6.50 and takes a seat at the back. It pulls away and, as it heads out onto the M8, he turns to see an ambulance racing into the airport, klaxon sounding. The toilets will now be a crime scene, but security would be first priority, the safety of passengers there. Lockdown of the airport would be immediate. All attention will be on inside. He is well away and arrives in Glasgow in twenty-five minutes to get off at Buchanan Bus Station. He'd used his mobile to summon a car and it's waiting for him as he gets off the bus. He would now get back to dealing with his father's body. He would be a prime suspect in Malky's killing, the CCTV catching Malky and him going into the toilet, his car discovered in drop off; but he'll get the Beltrami solicitors firm on the case – no direct evidence. But, he had to do Malky, he had to. If he hadn't, the message would have gone out to every hostile player in Glasgow that the McGings were finished. He did what was expected and he would do the same to anyone who tried to take advantage of the Father's death.

I get the inevitable call and race to Gracelands, arriving almost at the same time as Mick returns from the airport. The place is surrounded by armed men. Davy's wife Rosemary and his daughter Anne are inside sobbing their hearts out. Mick appears in the sitting room as I arrive. Mick has showered, changed and disposed of all clothes, shoes and weapons. They would never be found for DNA.

I put out my hand to Mick, a gesture of solidarity that is rejected as I expect. "I'm sorry Mick, your father was –"

"Don't, Rooney, just fucking don't. Things were fine until you came into this… family."

"Where is he, Mick?" Rosemary asks.

"Fuck knows, Mam. The hospital or the morgue, we'll find out soon enough."

"And where were you?" Mick doesn't answer.

"We need a conference," I say, understanding the implications of this for the Family. "Davy would have wanted an immediate response."

"It's dealt with," Mick says. This isn't what I mean or what I want to hear. I need to organise a crisis response, to make sure everyone is safe; this could be part of an overall attack. I also have to maintain business. Again, Davy would have wanted that. "Dealt with, you got it?" I look into Mick's eyes. From his lack of response, it's clear to me that Mick really has dealt with the attacker. I'll not push this line.

"OK, but we need to meet. We need to agree a response, to find out what, who was behind it."

"I'll sort it," says a tight-lipped Mick. "*I'll* sort it."

CHAPTER SEVEN

Davy's memorial dinner takes place in Cameron House, a large baronial hotel on the west side of Loch Lomond. This is an escape for rich Glaswegians who like to get out of the city, away from the violence and the threat of terrorism. Although Mick says this should not be a wake for his father, he sanctions a sumptuous meal, an all-drinks-provided golf, private seaplane launches on the loch; a full weekend for the heads of the families that make up the syndicate that is the Family. Through me, he arranges this grand send-off for his father. I make some important phone calls to London, Manchester, New York, and written invites follow. This is to be a gangland showcase of strength the like never seen for many a year in the UK. It's clear Mick intends making a case for supremacy, taking his father's place at the table of the most feared players known. He'll slip envelopes in many pockets that day, an appreciation of their attendance; most with at least a bag in cash, some much more, an old custom he intends continuing.

The real funeral has been conducted in private in Gracelands. Davy is laid to rest in Glasgow's Western Necropolis, with only his family, close associates and friends there. He is not given a stone for fear it would become a target for the enemies he had made in his career.

A cavalcade of large black cars, full of heavyset men, rolls up at the door of Cameron House. I step out to meet each one of these men. Most have scars and grim presentations. The hotel has been taken over for the event and heavy players police the grounds and ensure only cars of invited guests enter the entrance road.

The dinner is a full five course with wine liberally topped up all the way through. There's a hearty throng in the room, until Mick picks up a crystal glass and a knife, and gives the usual three tings to gain attention and to start the formal proceedings. "I'd like to thank you all for being here today," he says, "for two reasons: one, to honour a great man, my father, Davy McGing." All around the table rise, lift their glasses, and toast Davy. "Thank you." They all sit down expecting a eulogy to Davy, but instead, "And two, to maintain business." Muttering abounds around the table, like "Who gave him authority for this? Why's he taking the lead?" This doesn't stop Mick, though. This is his moment. "I've gathered the heads and members of the Family and close friends from across the land."

The men look at each other around the table.

I've been placed at the side of Mick as I had with Davy. Many look to me to acknowledge a tacit approval. I was often Davy's voice after all. Why would I not continue to be this, in this meeting?

Alan Taylor starts the commiserations. "George, my father, sends his sincere condolences to you and your family, Mick." There was a strong friendship between George and Davy that went back to the razor gangs. Now with their shared drugs, casinos, taxis, and property portfolio, these families cling together. I know the Taylors from the Johnston days, when George Taylor was head of the clan, now currently in Shotts prison serving a full life sentence for his bringing the roof down in the Grosvenor Hotel in a bomb attack. Although George Taylor is in prison, he runs his family through his son, Alan, who acts as proxy leader on his behalf.

"Thanks Alan," Mick replies. "I know if your father could have been here, he would have been here. Give him my best and tell him we look forward to the day he leaves the jail to join us as the head of the Taylors."

"I'll tell him," Alan says. "My father is ragin' at the death of his friend. He's going to find and destroy the bastards behind it."

"Alan, you tell George, thanks all the same, but the McGings'll deal with their own business." Alan nods. "Now, to this… business."

The team bosses believe this is to open the discussion over what had happened to Davy. A hubbub erupts around the table. "We are all at risk here; we have agreed to be collective in these matters. Davy was our leader," rings through the room.

Mick trumps the murmurs. "On the sad departure of my father, which as you will know has been resolved, we must move to appoint a new chairman." Wittering abounds. Is this the time and the place to agree a successor to the leader of the Family? Many think not. Mick continues. "This is what my father would have preferred." Is it? "My father was always one to ensure stability and I, as his son, will ensure that. I will offer continuity in a time of instability and ensure business continues as it did under his hand."

The men look across the table at each other. Mick is assuming control. 'Continuity and stability', Mick? Continuity maybe, but he's hardly the man to ensure stability.

There's a pause. Mick waits for a reaction. Just in case, in addition to his knife, which never leaves the holder in his back pocket, unless he is going to use it on someone, he's armed himself with a Rossi five-shot revolver tucked into his belt at the back of his trousers, which he can whip out should there be a violent reaction; and his lieutenants had been briefed to 'take serious action' against anyone who looked as though they would reach inside their jackets.

Mick looks into the faces of these men, as his father did. He is stepping into illustrious shoes. Davy was heir apparent to the previous Father, being the biggest and hardest player in the group. Mick, however, had no such influence or standing. Davy had taken me on board and I rose in these ranks to be the consigliore. I was good at it, though, and all there understand this. But, do I have it in me to lead these hard men? Managing business, arranging things, dealing with issues, ensuring the smooth running of the Family, is one thing, but to lead it and them is a very different matter.

The silence is deafening, forcing Mick to be more assertive. "I need your approval. My father would expect it of you." There's more palpable silence.

It is clear no one is going to speak first on this matter. No one will be the first to give approval. I could let Mick sink before these men; but this would lead to a situation where they would ignore him and strike up their own conversations around the table, giving him the deaf ear. Others could get up and leave, and others might react more forcibly. I had too much respect for Davy to allow this, but this isn't the motivating force behind my decision to stand up. It is because it had to be done. Someone had to hold this group together in everyone's best interests, in the interests of the Family.

I get to my feet. "I would like to address the meeting." I don't need to raise my voice; everyone hears the words. Mick turns to face me. I could tell him to sit down, I could try to talk over him, or I could let him say what he was going to say. I chose the latter, correctly. He sits down. "Our Father, who –"

"Just don't fucking go there Rooney, you religious cunt," Mick bellows out.

"Sorry, I was referring to Davy."

"Aye, we fucking know, get on with it."

"Who accepted me, after my…" Many there knew me and their respect of me allowed me in, to become the consigliore, where Davy was clearly the boss. "You understand the value in maintaining our… cooperation, our collective. There are many threats to our business and we must stay strong, vigilant, determined. This is not the time to split ranks. Forces from Eastern Europe, China, Russia are taking advantage of our business environment. They are here in numbers and growing by the day and significantly there are threats arriving from the Middle East."

There are more mutterings. They understand this threat; they are dealing with aspects of it daily. Taxi businesses, once the domain of indigenous families, are now in the hands of the Asians; money lending with the Chinese; drugs and trafficking with the Romanians; extortion with the Albanians. All of this, however, is insignificant relative to the threat of blood on the streets, of suicide bombers, terrorists, gunrunners, radicalising and recruiting local players. Their nightclubs, casinos and bars at risk, they have to stay together and act together in the face of this menace.

"I suggest Mick assumes control, for the meantime." I mean *pro tem* until they confirm either me or one in their midst as leader.

Getting above yourself, Rooney?

I am acutely aware of the possibility that at this point Mick is ready to push his knife into my side and let me bleed to death on the table. He would be a dead man himself if he did; there are many there who would have been happy to shoot Mick dead there and then. He was not Davy McGing; he was Mick McGing. But more, they know Mick can only accept this. He would get no more than that this day. He will have to earn it and this is a platform to his doing that very thing.

Their respect for me, thankfully, carries the motion and there's a show of hands; a majority, some abstentions, and some against, but it is carried. Mick is caretaker Father.

Over the next few weeks, I try to form a working relationship with Mick, to have meetings, to agree a Family agenda. He is having none of it. He is enjoying the power, the glamour, the direct debits paid by the Glasgow families and the high life this produces, like playing the tables in Monte Carlo and Las Vegas, extended stays in Los Angeles and Dubai, where he has homes. He is loving it. The McGings keep him busy though. He takes the Family more into drugs, low-grade Heroin laced with talcum powder, pay day lending and loan sharking. The McGings are developing a reputation not known in Davy's time, and Mick wields his power with a brutality seldom known even in a hard city such as Glasgow. He makes examples. Some, not meeting their dues, are knee capped; others, disappear. Mick's security company cover the new M74 link and have access to the construction with its cement columns, quick drying, within which people would never be found. Mick thinks if he can show real brutality as head of the Family, his place at the helm will be secure. He is wrong. Conversely, I try hard to conduct the Family's business with a shrewd and sharp mind.

Only affected by the ravages of mental illness?

Mick gives me a free hand, while setting his face against the customary meetings with Police Scotland and local politicians. He hates the police after being brutally arrested as a teenager for a range of offences, and he has a hatred of the local councillors, whom he views to be hoods in the City Chambers. The only difference between them and him is, he thinks, while they steal their money from the pockets of the citizens of Glasgow through their Council tax to fund their expensive junkets abroad, he steals from them face-to-face.

It is Sunday 7th of July, and it has been a day for Hubert of his wife Deirdre Hamilton-Brown's family, her stuck-up children, Mellissa and Mathew: 'the two Ms', Hubert calls them, 'Mayhem and Murder', who were raving about their holidays in the Caribbean. He escapes to his Glasgow flat. "Early meeting in Glasgow tomorrow, darling, need to be there early, best to miss the morning traffic." He'll meet Millar in the Belle. Drinks on the creep, curry, then home in time for Homeland, that'll do.

"An update, Boss, on... matters." Millar delivers the pints.

"For work." Hubert takes the pint and consumes around a third of it in one gulp.

"Enjoy, boss, guess you need it." Hubert doesn't answer as he checks the beer. "I needed to talk to you, boss. Jackie's attack, Davy's murder, Mick becoming bossman." Millar knows work is work and drinking is drinking, and best not to mix both, but this is an opportunity he wouldn't get at work. "Jackie's attack?"

"Your brief, Martin."

"I know, but…" Millar leans farther over the table to ensure he isn't overheard. "Jackie had enemies, boss."

"We all have." Hubert moves back from the smell. "Now, please."

"She had links with Davy and the mob, boss."

"Careful with the word links, Martin." Hubert looks around.

"She had a… working relationship, contacts."

"Stick to links."

"Links."

"I spoke to Davy. I am confident they weren't involved."

"I did too, boss. He said nothing. Do you think he knows anything?"

"If he did, he didn't tell me."

"He was killed, boss."

"A life with the mob, it was inevitable."

"Jackie was in a mob taxi."

"Half of the taxis in Glasgow are owned by the mob, you know that. Why would the mob hit Jackie?"

"She hit the Taylors, after they attacked Owen at the Grosvenor."

"I know that."

"Maybe she knew too much."

"Too much?"

"About them, the mob, and all that."

"Hubert moves closer to Millar. "And what about the MI5, Martin? Jean? Your wife was at the scene with Rooney. The bomb was triggered by a remote device."

"Jean wasn't –"

"Involved in the whole Johnston thing; come on, get real, she's a spook."

"She was tailing Rooney, boss." Millar hesitates. "She just happened to be with him at the time. She wouldn't –"

Hubert doesn't like to get too close to Millar, but on this occasion he feels he has to. "Listen, son, the device was the kind Johnston… piloted. It was triggered by a call. By that time, Johnston was dead. So, who do you think triggered it?"

"Rooney?"

"Why? What did he have to gain?"

"Power?

"Jackie was his... ex-wife."

"Revenge?"

"Just stop it, son – get the pints in."

"Self-preservation?"

"Maybe, the beers?"

Martin ambles away through the tables to the bar. Hubert turns to the Sunday newspapers.

"Do we bring him in?" Millar returns, two pints in hand.

"No, I told you, leave him." Hubert looks up from the newspaper while pushing his glasses back up the bridge of his nose. "Anyway, there's other... advantages."

"Sorry?"

"If we arrest him, we lose him from where we need him just now, with the Family."

Millar gazes at Hubert as he digs his head back into the newspaper. He is talking about his own daughter for god's sake, he thinks, and wonders if Hubert is prepared to limit the investigation on her attack for the benefits of the service or if there was there something else.

"Rooney knows more than he is saying, boss. He was at the scene."

Hubert gets up and rounds the table heading to the toilet. "Listen son, we leave him," he says, into Martin's ear. "That's it, have you got it?" Millar knows he shouldn't continue this. To do so he would be risking both his relationship with the Chief and his job. "However, Jean's place in all of this needs –"

Now it is Millar's turn to get defensive. "Chief, Jean is MI5, she's above police investigation. She works for the... state."

"Two pints of Sagres, Martin. There's a good man." Hubert heads for the toilet, to return just as Martin delivers two fresh pints. "Listen, son, I've known you for many years, but if I want to investigate Jean, I will do it and neither you or the state will have fuck all to say about it. You got that?" Millar doesn't answer. "Now, Davy is dead and Mick's a fucking nutcase. We need Rooney. We need to work with him, and the Family. It will pay dividends."

Millar is flabbergasted. "Dividends? They are criminals, Chief, bloody criminals."

"We need to work with them and him. Do you understand that? Martin?"

Millar observes the solemnity of Hubert's eyes. He suddenly realises that retirement may arrive sooner than he would like, and any chance of the big job will retire too. He also realises that the friendship he has with the Chief only goes so far. He understands, though, that he is a clever cop and, Jackie, his daughter or not, he will still be a clever cop. Knowing Hubert, he knows policeman or no policeman, no crook, colleague or crackpot, or even his daughter's threats, will stop him getting her attacker.

"Any more on the ISIS threat, son?" Hubert switches the subject.

"No, boss. Jean doesn't tell me everything."

Hubert takes a large gulp of lager. "No, why would she?"

CHAPTER EIGHT

"I thought we don't do that anymore, Jackie." I answer Jackie's call, though I was enjoying Gregorian *Pie Jesu*, which is crashing through my mind like waves on a Hebridean beach. "One minute, Jackie, I'll turn this down."

"Merciful Jesus."

"You got it."

"Rooney, I need to talk to you, about this Mick thing."

"Okay, when?"

There's a pause as she consults her diary. "I've got a range of… appointments through the week, what about Sunday?"

"Sunday; a Sunday, Jackie?"

He doesn't do Sundays.

"Oh, I forgot, you don't do crime on a Sunday."

"I'll make an exception for you. Sunday's good. Lunch?"

"Lunch'll do, but don't get any ideas this is social. It's business, you got it?"

"Aye, got it Jackie; as if."

Chancer!

We meet upstairs in the Chip on Ashton Lane. I order haggis, turnip, and mashed potatoes. Jackie orders venison, or 'deer' as the 'attendant' advises.

"Wine?" I ask her.

I assume her determination to ensure this is business would be challenged by the range of wines there. "OK, but I choose. I don't like Buckie."

When did Jackie ever drink Buckie? What about you?

"Neither do I Jackie, been a while since –"

"The last time you had the DTs, Rooney?"

When you woke up covered in your own shit?

"Easy Jackie, I'm known in here." I look along the bar. "I'm recovered."

"Well, I'm no'." She places her stick along the seat to her side and hovers the bottle of Italian Rioja white over my glass. "Some?"

I cover it with my hand. "No, I'll stick to water."

"Water! He drinks water these days." I manage to steer her away from talking about anything important, until the food arrives, as she finishes her third glass. "Business, Rooney. I'm here to talk about business."

"Well?" I tuck into the haggis, mixing it well with the neeps and tatties.

"Mick, and the Family?"

"Aye."

"We're losing touch with what is happening."

"The Family won't support you with the migrants, Jackie. We covered that with Davy. Mick is even less likely to agree it."

"Rooney, we need... this relationship."

Relationship.

It is clear she is referring to the meetings Davy had with Hubert and her: the Family and Police Scotland relationship.

"Mick doesn't like the polis, Jackie."

"No, and we don't like him, but we need the Family's... cooperation."

"I agree, but he won't allow me to do it. If he thought I was meeting you here today, I would be toast."

"Don't tell him."

"And what about the bar staff, Jackie? The admin man of the Family and the Assistant Chief Constable, organised crime and counter terrorism, meeting for lunch in a public place?"

"Consigliore, Rooney; a Mafia counsellor. Anyway, we used to be married."

"We used to be lots of things, Jackie, doesn't mean someone won't take a sneaky picture with their mobile phone and sell it to the Daily Record. I prefer administrator; this isn't New York Jackie, and I'm not Robert Duvall."

"No, you aren't, Rooney. He was a handsome man, in the movie at least."

Ouch!

"Thanks Jackie."

"Don't mention it, hon."

She applies herself to the wine.

"Another bottle?" I notice the empty one.

"I thought you were tee-totaled?"

"I mean for you."

I order it on the way to the toilet. On the way, I pass the amazing mural by Nelson Gray, the artist and my great friend and mentor. Then I go into the toilet and think about the times I had in here, looking forward to going back to Jackie's place, or our place when we were together, to make love.

Fancy her, Rooney? Sure you do. Think you can still fuck her? No alcohol though, this time. You've never fucked her sober. Different matter that, eh?

"Christ, can I not even have a piss without you bothering me?"

"Excuse me!" I turn to see an effeminate man throw his head back in disgust as he heads out the toilet door.

Jackie is on her mobile as I return. "Yes, Dad, Rooney, mind him, the booze bag of an ex-husband," I hear her say, loud enough to ensure I hear it. "The man who –"

"Hubert?"

"Bye, Dad," she says, finishing the call.

"Jackie, I didn't mean to –"

"I know you didn't. We've had that conversation, but you had a hand in it, Rooney. I put it down to your state at the time, mental illness and alcoholism." She takes a breath. "Sorry, I need to go a place."

She is away longer than she needs. I am just about to investigate as she staggers through the door into the bar. She's clearly drunk, but she's more than drunk.

"You OK?" I ask.

"I'm fine. Were you worried about me? Just doing what ladies do, Rooney, the make-up, and sorting the panty liner stuff."

I notice a white substance on her nostrils.

"Make-up, Jackie?"

"Yes, make-up, Rooney. Any problems with that?"

"No."

"You were saying."

"I was ill."

"Mad."

"Bad."

"I don't want to play that old tune."

"What is it they say in the AA, Rooney? God grant me –"

"God helps."

"And you certainly have had some "godly" experiences, Rooney."

"You don't need to punish me Jackie. I can do that very well myself."

She helps herself to a large glass. I can see that the alcohol is starting to affect her decorum; she would normally wait to be served by the man she dines with.

"Business. You wanted to talk."

"Right." She swigs another drink. "Mick."

"Aye."

"He has to go."

"Not within my authority, Jackie."

"Rooney, get rid of him or we will."

"And you'll have a war on your hands. You won't want that."

"No," she says, dropping her head. "Can Mick be persuaded? Davy was 'persuadable'."

"Not this time, sweetie."

From her pause, I can see my words hit home.

"That's too bad," she says, after a bit.

"It's bad for business." I know the special relationship the Family has with the authorities is under threat, and that is bad for business.

I look at her face. It looks pained. I don't doubt that her injuries are causing her agony. "Jackie –"

"Fuck it, I need to go," she slurs. "I should get a fucking bag fitted."

She is halfway through the second bottle and has clearly passed the point of decency as she collides with a couple of tables on the way to the toilet, knocking glasses and a plate of food onto the floor. "Sorry, disabled," she says to the diners, getting a sympathetic response. Her visit to the toilet is extended and she falls over a table on the way back, her stick sliding along the floor. I rush to her, but a waiter gets to her first.

"You OK?" he asks, helping her up and handing her the stick.

"It's fine," she gasps. "Just a lady who's had a wee bitty too much."

"Oh right, take care." The waiter helps her to her feet.

I help her back to her seat. "Time for home, Jackie?"

This is the wrong thing to say. "Don't you tell me what I should or should not do Rooney, just don't you fucking dare." I see a sadness in the harsh stare. "I… just can't, I can't do this."

"We are not doing this, Jackie." I reach for her hand, which she pulls away.

"I don't mean this, us, I mean all of this." It becomes clear to me she is meaning her new role as Assistant Chief Constable.

"Jackie, I can help you."

"You?" She looks into my eyes from her tearful ones. "What about Mick?"

"I have already said he'll not do it."

She leans across the table with a seriously sharp and manicured nail pointing out from a hand clutching a glass.

"Rooney?" She wipes her eyes and nose. "I'll make it so hard for you bastards to score a ten-pound bag on Argyle Street, never mind renew your licenses for your casinos. Punters, rich or poor, will go elsewhere, understand?" She almost squeezes the last of the bottle into her glass.

"Jackie?"

"Aye."

"Us?"

"What 'us' Rooney?"

"No hard feelings?" I raise my glass to her.

"Fuck off Rooney, you and your holy fucking water. You said you'd help me."

I see the eyes, the glazed look, and I know the recriminations will come: the boozing, the affairs, the lies. It is time to go. I don my coat. "Bye, Jackie." She doesn't answer. I leave her clutching the empty bottle in both hands, her trying to decide whether to have another one.

PCs McCourt and Barry are out at a domestic. They have developed a particular reputation for dealing with partner disputes that were previously called domestic's, or in my day as a clinical psychologist 'domestic abuse', or way back as 'family problems'. They approach the close in Hill Street in Garnethill, an area where the Chinese community has resided for decades. They mount the short stair to the tenement flats and study the door access panel.

"Three one, third floor, first flat. Always the third floor," Joan says. The call had been made by the downstairs neighbour, Mrs

McLuckie, at two one. They would check in on her on the way up the stair. Barry presses the button. "Hello," comes back. Not a normal hello; this is a scared, shocked hello. "Hello," the woman answers again, this time with a sob.

"It's the police, we've had a report –"

"You had better come up." She releases the door.

They move up the stair, deciding not to talk to the neighbour. The voice on the intercom indicated a need to get up there quick.

Barry reads from the nameplate on the door. "Mrs… Tully. We had a –"

"A report, I know, come in." They do, gingerly. "He's in there, he's deid," she sobs. Although a very small proportion of domestics resulted in one of the partners being killed, mostly those with drugs or drink involved, this is different and they sense it, as is confirmed as they entered the living room. There, in the corner of the room, slumped in his armchair, is Mr Tully, his throat cut from end to end, his blood flowing onto the floor. "He didnae pay up," she says, flopping down on the sofa.

"What do you mean, hen?" Barry says.

McCourt checks out the body. "Dead, no doubt. Couple of hours, I would say," he says, from many years of checking stiffs.

"They came for the money," she says. "He didnae hae it. They cut his throat. I tried tae stop them. I was screaming at them."

I can see why the neighbours thought it was a domestic, Barry thinks.

"Then they left."

"Who did it, hen?" McCourt moves over to her, not expecting an answer.

"The McGing bastards. I don't care if they kill me for saying that. I've nothing tae live for now." She begins a sob that goes all the way to her heart.

I get home from the Chip, pleased to have escaped my rental flat in Ruthven Street, which, given it was on the third floor, was a real hike, especially with shopping. It was a Family flat and so rent was zero, which was necessary until I got some money in the bank. It has been two months since I found the Cathedral House and four since Davy took me under his wing.

Through this time, my 'salary' had grown commensurately

with the increasing joint Family income streams. I had no idea how much money the Family was taking collectively, because the Family accountants ensured the money was salted into an extensive and untraceable range of activities. The large houses obtained by the bosses were purchased through the Family solicitors, through mortgage fraud, using the buy-to-let market. Mine is no different and I don't mind; I know the house will never be mine and before long it will be foreclosed by the finance company or taken under the Proceeds of Crime Act; in the meantime, I'll enjoy it.

The new house, on Sydenham Road, is perfect, having excellent security through controlled gates and a penthouse building perspective offering a 360-degree view. This is a large Victorian flat in the fashionable Dowanhill area of the West End, a far cry from my old hovel in Partick. This house would have contained my last flat three times over. I bedeck it with paintings, this time oils, not posters. I began collecting them when I became familiar with the trappings of the wealth the Family had given me. Appropriately, I feel, I name the house 'The Cathedral'. It will mark my greatest work in the name of God.

I prepare some coffee from the Dolce Gusto coffee machine, which carefully makes an Americano. I press play on my CD player, set at a heady volume with *Requiem for the Gods* set up to go at a touch. I settle myself down on my chesterfield wingback chair, lift my glasses from a side table, and pick up *The Herald*. I pan the room with satisfaction. I have a Mutter, a Vettriano, and Howson's *Transfiguration*, and a smattering of unknown others I had collected as investments. I recall my miserable existence in my Partick flat, where I would sit with a bottle of whisky with only a voice for company, kept at bay by medication. Knowing alcohol and medication don't combine, I sip the Americano. "Ah, to come home to a nice house, sober."

Aye, the forty-nine-year-old, divorced, used-to-be professional man, living in a shitty Partick pied-à-terre, with only me for company and a bigger friend with the sauce?

"Back to torment me, bastard?"

Just reminding you of where you've come from, and where you'll eventually return.

There's a bottle of malt on my coffee table, untouched since I came out of hospital. To open it – pour from it – would mean the end of everything I had overcome recently, everything I had gained by not using it. It stands as a threat to my very life, saying "Come on son, you can have one drink, then another". It is saying "You or me, pal." I study the bottle with contempt, like a jakie would a bottle of milk. "I rule you, you don't rule me," I say to it.

And who rules you?

I rise and move to Peter Howson's painting *Transfiguration*, which I purchased at a local auction. I study the transformation of Christ from dead man to the divine son of god. "I will resurrect," I say. "I will be the Father. My ascension from a normal man will be complete. Then I will do the work of God."

And Shepherds we shall be, for thee, my Lord, for thee. In nomine Patris, et Filii, et Spiritus Sancti –

Brrr, my mobile just about buzzes off the coffee table. I lift it up. "Hello?"

"Your, the Family, agreement is over. You got that," issues from an unknown voice.

Across Glasgow that night, twelve people are killed and twenty-three faces are tramlined.

Hakim Ahmed, Imam of the Al-Furqan Mosque, is edgy. There are men in his mosque not normally there. They are wearing Kufi skullcaps and are talking in accents not known in these parts. There is tension in the air, not normally felt. These voices are severe. They talk of the secularisers who are trying to weaken the teachings of the prophet Mohammed. How local Muslims have become too westernised, taking on British values and behaviours. The Mosque has also become concerned over groups of hooded Asian youths, many from middle-class backgrounds, prowling the streets until the early hours fighting each other and rival white gangs. Many residents, too scared of reprisals to report crimes, fear for their safety and have sought advice in the mosque. They talk of being intimidated by gangs that vandalise cars, slash tyres, set fires, and commit house break ins. Others loiter on street corners intimidating passers-by or cruise the streets in souped-up cars. These men say they will "by Allah" improve matters.

"All the mosques in this country are against terrorism," Ahmed says to them. "In Islam there is no place for terrorism."

"You asked me to phone you," Mick says. "Can you no' talk to me, face-to-face?"

"I've been trying to reach you for days, Mick."

"Why?"

"We need a conference."

"Meetings, meetings, and more fucking meetings, Rooney. Everything's fine," Mick replies. "Meetings, meetings, and more fucking meetings, you dickhead."

"Everything is not fine, Mick. People are being killed. We have – had – an agreement. No public will be harmed. That's the policy. The McGings have crossed a line."

"You keep to your business, pal, and I'll keep to mine. No more liberty to no cunt no' going to pay up."

"Mick, the public and Police Scotland are bloody well getting edgy."

"Our fucking business, Rooney. You get on with your bible thumping and let me get on with sorting these cunts out."

"The Family need to consider this, Mick. They'll expect it. They'll expect you to show some… leadership."

He knows I'm correct. If he wants to consolidate himself as Father, he has to take the Family with him in any change of tactic. Not to do so would threaten not only his position, but also the McGings as lead family.

CHAPTER NINE

Are you ready for this?

"I have to be, bastard. It's my calling, my day of reckoning," I say into the bathroom mirror, meticulously brushing my hair and giving my teeth particular attention. "Today, I will be judged."

The Family meets at Gracelands. I arrive for the conference to find a line of cars waiting to go through the gate. I get out of the car and pass cars with blacked out windows. I know the inhabitants of the cars, the heads of the individual families. I also know they will see me approaching the gate.

"What's the problem here, John?" I ask the man at the gate. "Why don't you let them in?"

"Mick says they have to wait there until he is ready for them."

I take his mobile. "Mick, in the name of God, what is happening?"

"I'm boss and I'm exercising authority, It'll get me respect."

"They'll respect you more if you don't mess them around. These are important men."

The gates part and one by one John waves each car through. I return to the car and my driver takes me through the gates. I see black coated men patrolling the grounds. Cars approach the entrance to the house one by one. From each a gang leader and associate exit to be frisked by what only could be described as nightclub bouncers at the door. I can see the leaders are not happy to be treated with this degree of disrespect.

I move inside and even I'm searched. On a bureau in the hall, I observe a line of armaments taken from each guest as they pass through this security. I move inside the large boardroom. This was Davy's domain. His walls used to be lined by paintings of fly-fishing, his favourite hobby, where he would head to the river Tay when he could indulge. They have been removed. Guests were normally greeted with drinks; not this time. Normally a convivial atmosphere, igniting chat and banter; not this time, there's sombre silence.

Davy would normally take his seat at the top of the table ready to address the meeting, to invite me to talk for most items. This time my place is at the end of the table near the door, the place of least importance. Far from professional place cards, each guest has a piece of A4, giving the name in bold black, in what looks to me to be crude marker writing.

Mick arrives in the room and moves to the head of the table. The only place without a place marker. "Rooney called this meeting," he bellows. "I didn't think it was necessary, but I agreed it, and here we are. I am sure there are places we would all rather be so we had best get fucking on with it. Rooney?"

I get to my feet, feeling somewhat uncomfortably placed at the end of the table and out of the view of many men around the table. "Thank you, gentlemen." I clear my throat and take a sip from a glass of water. "There are crucial matters which I think we need to discuss."

"Well, get the fuck on with it," growls Mick. "Jesus, what's this man about?" He turns to those around the table. No one locks eyes with him though. Their gaze remains on me.

"Indeed, Mick," I say. "The Family is at risk."

This ignites a communal fidgeting in seats.

"At risk? We're no' at risk." Mick also gets to his feet. "The McGings have never been stronger. We're taking in a hundred grand each week, expanding our turf, taking on more players."

"I am referring to the Family, Mick, the Collective, this… congregation." I wave my hand like a minister from a pulpit.

"Aye right, on you go then." Mick sits down.

"The situation, our… business environment, is worsening."

"Shite, we have never been stronger."

"Running at twenty-odd murders a week, Mick. It's out of order. Our agreement –"

"The McGings are out of order," Bingham adds. He's held his breath too long.

"You, cunt, you know fuck all about what we are doing," Mick snaps at Bingham. "And fuck you and your fucking agreement," he directs at me.

"The unilateral and unwarranted actions will not be tolerated. They'll affect business."

"You are a fucking crazy horse, Mick," Bingham adds. "This will fuck us all up."

Mick retains a quiet, eerie, calm. He is about to explode. I need to keep them together, to resolve this. "And there are other threats," I say, seeking respite.

"And what threats are you talking about, Rooney?" Mick asks.

"Mick, for fuck's sake, shut up," says Alex Frame.

Mick jumps to his feet. "Listen pal, if you want trouble you'll get it. Fucking jumped up motor thief."

Frame also gets to his feet.

"Alex, sit the fuck down," snaps Bingham. "Mick, let Rooney speak,"

"Aye, Mick, come on," Alan Taylor, Mick's closest ally there, says. "Sit the fuck down and let him say what he is going to say, then we can get on with it." Bingham won't trump him.

"Thanks."

Mick sits down, knowing he has to. He cannot fight the collective might of these men and their teams. Individually maybe, but not en masse.

"The threats, Rooney?" Bingham asks.

I clear my throat. "International crime families have moved into Glasgow big style."

"Aye, the Romanians," Charlie Campbell says.

"And a Somali drug syndicate supplying 75 per cent pure crack cocaine," George Montgomery adds. "Addicts are queuing up for it. They're feeding them to the tune of twenty grand a year. These guys are now into a million a year."

"We'll fuck them," Mick says.

"The fuckers carry bayonets," Bingham says.

"Shiteing it, Bill?" laughs Alan Taylor.

Bingham gives a look to say "You are going too far, pal."

"The Russian Mafia are dangerous tae," John Fullerton adds. "And the Muslims –"

"The Muslims are pussycats," Mick says.

"The Russians are getting bigger and stronger and the Muslims are way out of order," Fullerton says.

"Some are going to Syria and returning as soldiers."

"Aye, the soldiers of Allah," Charlie Campbell quips.

"We'll batter them, we have in the past," says Mick.

"They may pass the point where we'll be limited in what we can do."

"Well, you seem to have the answers, Rooney," Taylor says.

"We have been asked to… cooperate with the authorities."

That's it, Mick's back on his feet. "Right, you all know what my father's position was on the Muslims. This is not our fight."

"We'll soon be fighting them on the streets, Mick," Bingham says.

"Well, bring it on pal," Mick says, pulling out the only handgun in the room and placing it on the table. "I'm ready."

"Right, Mick, you're out of order." Bingham stands to face Mick.

"You," Mick says. "I'll put one between your eyes pal. You always were a cunt."

Bingham moves to round the table, his lieutenant at his side. Taylor steps up to support Mick.

Charlie Campbell intervenes, halting Bingham's approach. "Right, Bill, enough, this is not the way. Not the way business is, has been, done here."

"Right, come on, Mick." Taylor hands Mick the gun back. Bingham and Taylor sit down. Mick ensures he is last to sit, scowling at Bingham.

"Rooney!" Bingham snaps, demanding order.

"These guys are a serious threat. Absolutely crazy men and rogue killers. They'll attack anywhere. Offices, restaurants, hotels, pubs –"

"Does that make them any different from us?" Taylor asks.

"Not much, given what is going on just now," Bingham says.

"Aye, right; what the fuck is different?" Mick asks.

"Our code," I say, "that your father agreed, Mick, is now at risk." All there know what I mean: the agreement that no members of the public or police officers would be harmed has been blown apart by the McGings' recent killings.

"These guys are into airports, bombings, beheadings," Campbell says. "What's that got to do with us?"

"They'll hit anywhere, anytime, anything."

"We protect our taxis, the drugs, casinos, our security firms," Bingham says.

"Absolutely; it's in our interests to maintain the status quo."

"Fuck's sake, Rooney, we're no' the bizzies," Mick says. "And they're fucking terrorists."

"They establish themselves right here in Glasgow and terror will be out on those streets." I point out of the window. "Apart from the damage to our business, the authorities will bring in the troops; no one will be able to move."

"A total fucking exaggeration, Rooney," Mick says. "Get your facts right." He pulls out an A4 sheet from a folder. "Listen to this, it's from a… Richard Jackson… from the Internet. "The chances of you dying in a terrorist attack are about the same as being killed by a meteor. Dozens of people drown in their bathtubs and toilets every year, presumably after bouts of alcohol.""

People look around at each other in disbelief, some snigger, drawing a scowl from Mick.

"We need to be together," I say. "We need to be in control, organised, to fight them. And we need to stop killing the public, Mick."

Mick refuses to listen. He's holding up the paper. "Look, 'Hundreds are killed every year and thousands are injured in DIY accidents. Thousands of people every year die in motor accidents. Thousands of people commit suicide every year.'" He looks around. "You get my point; there's no issue, this threat of terrorism is shite. So, as far as I am concerned, we do nothing. This is no' our fight, that's what ma da' said. The meeting is over, so let's get back to making money and kicking the shite out of the punters." He moves back from the table. No one responds. "Listen, I'm my father's son. I'm –"

"Mick!" I cut across his diatribe.

"What?"

"Great men are not born great, they grow great."

He hesitates, trying to absorb this, to understand it. But it is too late for his response, everyone there knows exactly what I mean.

Then, "I move Rooney is appointed Father," comes from Bingham, prompting a hush in the room.

"Whit!" Mick spits.

"You heard me Mick," Bingham says. "You can't fucking do this. You're no' up to it. You are going to fuck us all, everything, up."

"I can't fucking do this? I can't fucking do this?" Mick rounds the table towards him. He's stopped by a number of the men, which is just as well; Bingham was an amateur boxer in his youth and a renowned street fighter, and would have dropped Mick there and then.

Charlie Campbell steps up. "Come on Mick, get a grip, there's never been violence here," he says, grabbing Mick's arm. Taylor moves forward in support of Mick.

"Well, get the fuck out, the lot o' ye." Mick releases himself from Campbell's grip. "I'll do my own fucking thing."

"OK, Mick." I take to the floor. "Do we have a seconder?"

"Me, and me, and me," resounds around the table.

"Then I accept," I say.

At this Mick barges out, barking orders to his men. "Get the old cunts out. Time they were in a fucking nursing home. Anyone who refuses to leave, shoot the cunt."

"Shoot the cunt," Taylor repeats, pointing a finger like a gun barrel towards me. "I know what you are doing, you devious bastard. "Shoot all the cunts. You're all fucking dinosaurs: extinct, or soon will be."

The men rush to collect their guns to find they've been removed. They are all at risk. Mick is not beyond shooting them all dead there and then. They make a hasty retreat, into their cars and through the gates. Bill Bingham and I remain. "It's OK, Bill, I need to talk to this man."

Bingham looks at me, as if to say 'I'll do him now if you want', but instead says, "OK, but watch your back." He leaves slowly, emphasising defiance in the face of Mick's threats.

Mick returns to the room snarling. "Well, well, well, Mr fucking Father. Got what you wanted, eh?"

I sit down and look out into the garden. I appreciate my life is at serious risk. Only my skill over Mick's raw anger will get me out of this place alive.

"I should shoot you dead right here, man. You fucked me proper and you'll account for it."

Like Richard Attenborough would a gorilla, I remain seated, not staring Mick in the eye, which would prompt an attack.

"The Family rule is not to hit a made man. That would bring a vendetta on you and all the McGings."

Nice one.

"Fucking mafia shite; get real, crazy man. Anyway, we're heavier than any of them. Time we had a war anyway. Things have got too cosy."

"Collectively, they would destroy you, Mick."

"I have friends too. I'll set up my own family syndicate."

This is a serious threat. I know there had been rumblings in the Family. Some of them, the Taylors in particular, would support the McGings, who'd been alongside them since the turf wars.

The inseparability of power and money enters my head. "You kill me and your account'll close overnight."

"What are you saying you sly cunt?"

"I'm power of attorney for every head, granted by each and every one of them."

"No' for ma dad, he's deid."

"He said it in his will, you check it. Should he die unexpectedly, I would continue to manage his estate."

You are winging this; you know Mick would have no understanding of executory law.

Mick knows I manage the accounts of the Family and our 'investments' had brought them rich rewards. I had learned a long time ago since the Johnston days, that to have authority was to be in control of the finances. The leaders had allowed this, remembering the only way to bring a gangster to book, as in Capone's case, would be to get access to accounts: do them for tax evasion, send them away for a long holiday courtesy of Her Majesty. My managing their finances through a trusted firm of accountants gave them distance. "Nothing to do with me, he handles all the cash," they would say, if required.

"I'll have my accountants, solicitors, and every fucking bank manager I know onto the case. Then I'll deal with you and the rest of those cunts. We will have a war."

I pick up my coat at the door and turn to face him. "War is always the result of sin, Mick." He looks at me strangely. "Don't wage war with God, you'll lose." This is me, emboldened, assertive in the employ of the Lord. No longer subservient, I had prepared for this moment –

Of truth!

"If you don't get the fuck out now, I'll shoot you dead where you stand."

"And you'll be dead before the end of this day." He studies my face. He knows this is no idle threat. "God will smite the heads of his enemies." I turn and open the door, warily; closing it slowly behind me as I leave.

Power is being in control of one's destiny.

My heart pounds in my chest and sweat runs down my back. I move cautiously to the car, like a diplomat leaving the G8. I don't look back. I know Mick is at the window behind the net curtains, questioning himself as to whether he should do me in there and then.

I get into my car. "Go, driver," I say. "In the name of..."

God, the father, the all-powerful.

"He is powerful, powerful in mercy, justice and strength. He is my rock, my foundation."

OK, Rooney, I get it!

"Drop me off in Glasgow city centre."

"That's not advisable," my driver says.

"The Lord will protect me."

I get out of the car on Argyle Street and make my way along towards the Trongate. I pass a blind beggar sitting in Marks and Spencer's doorway. "Recover your sight; your faith has made you well," I say, as I pass. The beggar gets up, laughs and walks away. I come across a paralytic man, trying to get to his feet at the railings on Glassford Street. "Get up and walk," I say, as I help him to his feet and send him on his way. A drug-crazed man rushes at me as I turn at the Trongate. I grab him roughly and push him against a wall. "I command unclean spirits to leave you. Demons obey me and leave this man." The man is stunned and, pacified, turns and calmly walks away.

"The Lord is in me."

You're off it, pal.

I walk into the Trongate. I know I am a target, but not for neds; they know my power, but this is McGing territory, and one of their street players taking me out would mean immediate promotion and a big bonus.

I pause at the door of the Saracen Head Pub across from the Barrowland dance hall, where Bible John, a notorious Glasgow serial killer, met and later murdered three women in the late sixties, still unsolved.

A bit near to the bone?

Bible John was noted to have frequently quoted from the Bible, and was reported to have said he didn't drink at Hogmanay, he prayed, referring to Moses and his father's belief that dance halls were dens of iniquity.

A bit like you!

I move into the pub. I have arranged to see Ben there. I'm not comfortable with his formal role as my named person, but something holds me to my old pal. I have another reason to be there, however.

The original Saracen Head was built in 1755, and lays claim to being one of the oldest bars in Glasgow. Contained in a case on the wall is the skull of Maggie Wall, the last woman to be burned as a witch. The bar is known for paranormal activity.

I'm hit with the sound of bagpipes. The Saracen Head is not normally know for highland music, but this is the weekend of the annual world piping championship on Glasgow Green. It is nearby, and the pipers had been playing in the rain all day; time for some dry clothes and some wet refreshments. I find Ben in the booth in the corner as I come in the door to the right. He's trying to protect himself from the din farther into the pub. He sees me and gets up. "Hello, Rooney, not a night for saving souls is it?"

"No, hardly. I didn't know you were into the devil's music."

"Oh shut up, just enjoy it. I mind when you used to have a sense of humour and liked a laugh."

I cast a glance around the bar. "More serious matters at play now, social worker."

"Drink?"

"Water."

"Get it yourself." This was not a bar used to serving water. "You used to be a more pleasant man when you were drinking."

"Where did pleasant or drinking ever get me?" I move to the bar. "Water, please." Contrary to Ben's view it is delivered with pleasure and ice. "Could I see the skull?" This is a common request for this bar, which is on the tourist trail and where many a selfie is taken with skull in hand.

"No problem." The barman comes round the bar and moves to the case. Opening it, he passes me the old brown skull polished by hands that had stroked it for 350 years. He passes it to me, not leaving my side for fear I would steal this important part of the pub's history. I look at the skull, its eye pits facing me. Ben is looking my way and shaking his head. "I absolve you of all of your sins, ye daughter of the devil," I say. The barman looks at me quizzically.

"Rest in peace now, Maggie Wall, you are no longer held to this place." I kiss the skull and hand it back to the barman, who is now also shaking his head as he returns the skull to the case. "She will rest now, sir, and your pub will be free of her roaming."

"Now into exorcism, this is a new one," Ben says, on my return to the booth.

"I could not allow her to be owned by the devil."

"Oh right. I think I will request a review of your treatment plan."

"Thank you." I recognise his authority to do this, but I have no intention of attending such a review.

"I believe you are now the Father. Rooney, the Father. It's got a funny sound to it."

"Indeed."

"And what do you intend doing in that role? Seems a bit worrying for me, and I am sure for the mental health tribunal, that a man with a florid mental illness is in charge of the city's biggest crime syndicate."

"I will do God's work, Ben. Whatever else would a Father do?"

"I'm watching you, Rooney. I have to." I acknowledge he has the ability to return me to Hairmyres mental health unit.

Within two days, I have a meeting with the Family at the Grand Central, and all, bar two, families appear. The McGings and the Taylors are absent.

The Family came to be known as the Twelve Apostles. Even though it was eleven families, the double act of the McStay twin brothers, Robert and Peter, heading the McStays conjointly, made twelve. The remaining group is made up of the McGraws, headed by Jim McGraw, who are in drug trafficking; the Binghams, led by Bill Bingham, into extortion, prostitution, and drugs; the Frames, boss Alex Frame, into illegal scrap dealing and exclusive car stealing to order; the Campbells, led by Charlie Campbell, into car theft and selling off to continental customs, salting their money into taxi businesses in Glasgow; the Devlins, headed by Patrick Devlin, running security and bouncers throughout Glasgow and the West of Scotland; the Moffats, run by Paul Moffat, running a Rachman-esque flat rental business for students and foreign nationalists, extortion, and loan sharking; the Sighthill Mafia, managed by Ian Simpson, trafficking weapons across Glasgow and wider afield; the Hammie, governed by Andy Hamilton, who ran an extortion racket and sex trafficking; the Fullerton, led by John Fullerton, mixing nightclubs and drugs; and the Monty, bossed by Geordie Montgomery, who made his fortune from extortion, protection scams, security, and bouncers.

The Twelve are mature heads, leaders of significant gangs, well established over many years, and consolidated in organised family groups. Not like the young teams such as the Tongs or Fleeto, neighbourhood teenage gangs rather than established businesses, with nowhere near the maturity or strength of the family gangs. The young teams know their limits; they would never cross a Family team.

Under my watch, this becomes a new situation for the Family. Previously, Johnston brought them together and gave them the kind of strength they never had before. Davy was the strongest leader of the group and had been through the wars, as had all of them. I had been a good consigliore, but I had to prove myself as a leader. If not, I would be out as quickly as I had gone in. However, no leader of the syndicate would survive for long. I needed to both in-build my survival and determine they would do my bidding. A double bind is what I need. "God, give me strength." I say quietly to myself, as I rise to address the Twelve. "Friends you need me." I look around. "You and I know this. I offer stability in your lives and in your businesses." I am encouraged by Alex Fraser's nodding, but the rest of their faces belie interest. "I will act as the catalyst. I will hold you together as the most feared syndicate in Scotland, if not the UK, by which you will achieve great things and make more money that you will have ever known, which will be shared equally." They appear more interested. "Your power base will be consolidated, your future secured, and, in particular, your families will be safeguarded. Everything up to now none of you could have ever ensured or guaranteed. So yes, you need me."

I am relieved by a collective slapping on the table.

Campbell offers a sobering thought. "We will be fighting the McGings *and* the Taylors."

"If they have the stupidity to fight us we will fuck them," Bingham replies. "We'll have to."

"We will be... collectively strong," I say. "Well led, well

99

prepared, ready to defend ourselves against all old and emerging threats."

"And undo the fucking damage Mick caused," Bingham adds.

"We will… renew our relationship and our agreement with the authorities."

"You do it, you'll lead, Rooney. We've agreed," Bingham says.

They will kill you, someday. Power never lasts forever. Davy said that.

"Yes, but I will need an… insurance policy."

"Fuck off, Rooney, you don't need any insurance with us," Bill Bingham says. "We are your insurance."

"I don't mean that, Bill. Without a guarantee of my survival in this context, I am a dead man, and this will die as well." I wave my hand over the Twelve like a roman emperor, then leave my comment hanging in the air. They know I am right. "I need an insurance policy and that's the only way I will do it."

Paul Moffat speaks up. "OK, Rooney, a signed contract with us, as a syndicate, that no individual partner in this… consortium will do you harm?"

"Yes."

"What if things go wrong and it becomes necessary to… remove you?" Bill Bingham asks.

"Well, Bill, you need to know something." There is a clear sense of anticipation. I need to be judicious with my words, but as sure as death they know something significant is coming. "I know something about you all, individually."

You fox.

I look each of them one-by-one in the eye and I can see in each of them they know I am right. They know they have divulged something so important, entrusted in me. Recently, when meeting them individually, I had asked them their secret fears, something I could guarantee them as Father would never happen under the Family. I mustered all my persuasive powers, learned at Johnston's hand, and courted their belief that I, as an individual man, could not threaten this. They opened up; examples being, mistresses, illegitimate sons and daughters, parents, where they are salting their money, etc., etc.

"You all know I have information that, should I die, it'll be divulged."

There is nervous fidgeting around the room.

"I have given instructions to my… associates, that should I… *be retired* in unexpected circumstances, an email will be sent to multiple addresses. For example, *The Herald*, the BBC, the authorities, Police Scotland, etc. In saying this I know I have not only temporarily secured my life, but I have also sealed my eventual death.

"No fucking way, Rooney," Paul Moffat says, his hat down over his head. "We'll do this ourselves."

"Haud on, Bunnet," Bingham says, "This ensures all our survival, including mine. It's fair enough."

"And," Moffat says, "I'll guess if we don't accept these terms and shoot him now the email will be sent anyway. He's got us over a barrel, the savvy bastard."

I don't answer.

Gives the right impression.

"Kill the cunt," the McStays say together.

"The email goes," I reply.

"Don't agree to it," the Bunnet says.

"The email goes," Bingham says.

I gird myself, pushing back my shoulders for presence. "As Samson did the pillars of the temple, my untimely death will knock away the pillars that support this family. One, the joint account is in my name. It will crash. Two, the business contract, the same. Three, the guarantees from other families not to infiltrate into our territories, the same. The fourth pillar, the agreement with Police Scotland, the deal, i.e. we manage organised crime, they leave us alone, the same. Hubert will bring our house down."

I let them stew and go off to the toilet. Bill Bingham follows me in. I had a feeling he would. "You are one cunning bastard, Rooney," he says.

"I only do what the Lord would do in similar circumstances," I say. "These days enticing the money lenders requires more than a whip, Bill." I face the urinal wall.

"I speak for myself when I say this," he says, "but you know every one of those men in there thinks the same. If you say a word about our secret then you are a dead man."

"You know I won't, Bill, and they all know that."

"You are not only a cunning bastard, Rooney, you are one clever bastard." He dries his hands.

"Ecclesiastes, the protection of wisdom is the protection of money, and wisdom preserves the life of him who has it."

"Aye, very good, Rooney," he laughs. "And whoever has the gold makes the rules, Murphy." We leave the toilet like old pals sharing stories of past girlfriends.

There is a standoff in the Mosque. The most vociferous of the new group is challenging the Imam.

"Hakim, my name is Al-Jamal Saddam Al-Jamal. I will intervene, impose order. I will bring your young men back to the teachings of the prophet."

"You," Hakim says, "will not radicalise our people."

"The communities are scared of them and their... behaviour. We need to act, Inshallah."

"We will not be drawn into something which is not our concern."

"We need to... talk to your community."

"We know of how this talking goes." Hakim says. "Aqsa Mahmood, the young Glasgow woman who dropped out of university, she travelled to Syria –"

"I am aware of her."

"She urged Muslims in Britain to carry out "another Woolwich", a reference to the murder of Lee Rigby, the soldier. ISIS are killing in the name of our religion and claiming to defend the weak. Our young people are deluded and helping those engaged in genocide."

"She went off the rails, but Inshallah she is now in our arms."

"She has been seen carrying a picture of the black flag. She is saying to follow the examples of her... brothers from Woolwich, Boston, and Paris. She says if you cannot make it to the battlefields then bring it to yourself."

"We can bring these battlefields to Glasgow."

"What do you want me to do?"

"Muslims cannot be at peace in the West. The West is at war with Muslim lands. We must resort to violence because there is no security. We must protect them and their people here."

Hakim holds his hands on his head in despair.

Baird shows me into Jackie's office. She is deep in her computer surrounded by files. Everything is covered in files; even the desk chair I have to clear to sit down is covered in files.

"Well, *Mr* Father," Jackie says. "I am not sure congratulations are in order, or should I offer commiserations. From a forensic psychologist with an interest in the minds of criminals, to the head of the biggest criminal fraternity in the land; quite a jump. Not so much poacher come gamekeeper, more like gamekeeper come lord of the manor."

"Beats being a mad, bad, sad shrink, Jackie." I pull my coat off, take a seat and steeple my fingers together upwards over my face.

"Guess so." She gets up and moves towards me. "Slightly grandiose I would say, Rooney, don't you think. Do you need more medication?" I don't answer, just bringing the steeple over my face, leaving only my eyes exposed. "Being boss, does this mean we are back in business?"

"We'll see," I say, with as much authority as I can muster. "Mick is gone and the Family wish me to reinstate… mutual cooperation."

"That comes at a price, Father." She is now engaging in ridicule. Good, I like it.

"How much?"

"ISIS?"

"They're killing Christians."

"You know that's not what I mean, Rooney."

I rise. "Christians are being crucified for their faith," I say.

"Listen, you imperious, deranged cunt. Just find the fuckers, then we'll see if we can… cooperate."

CHAPTER TEN

John McCourt has had a quiet shift. A knifing of a drunk in Sauchiehall Street, a car driving over a biker at Charing Cross, and an altercation with some Asian men. If every day is like this, he'll happily go home to Mary and wee Jamie at the end of each shift.

He dwells on this day as he packs his uniform away in his locker. Sitting down on the bench in the locker room, he recalls the incident with the Asian men and it troubles him. He doesn't feel satisfied he did his duty well there, and this has got to him a bit.

It was Saturday afternoon and today was the annual Orange rally. He and other officers were lined up to observe the crowds streaming out of Glasgow Central railway station heading for George Square. Young men in green and white had been lining the Square since morning and other young men in blue, red, and white weaved their way between the mounted officers in the middle of the road, heading for the Square.

The authorities feared trouble at such a meeting of opposites in the sectarian divide; however, there are rumours that the SDL had planned to turn up at the Al-Furqan Mosque to coincide with the rally. At the same time, Mission Dawah, an Islamic proselytising group, had set up outside Debenhams on Buchanan Street handing out flyers to passers-by. This was also its Global Messenger Day, when thousands of Muslims from around the world call people to get to know and love the Prophet Muhammad.

The Council had been criticised for granting permission to both groups. Several Dawah members, a group of six jihadists, had travelled to Syria to fight for ISIL. They were back.

McCourt walked over to the Dawah members to warn them about the Orange rally and the SDL. "Our role is non-political," one said. "We are here only to preach the message of Islam." McCourt knew there would be arrests that day, arrests of hate crime. He knew from briefings that there had been hundreds of such counterterrorism arrests in England, Wales and Scotland over the past year; a 33 per cent increase on the previous year. Aside from the SDL demonstrations in the city, there had been pig heads left outside the Al-Furqan Islamic School, Glasgow and anti-Islamic "no-sharia" graffiti had been daubed on the new Glasgow Central Gurdwara whose opening had been heavily contested by far right groups in the city.

WPC Barry joined him as one of the group approached. This man's English was perfect, but southern; Birmingham maybe, she thought. Roughly, he said, "Why don't you get off our land and leave us alone."

"You should go home, sir," WPC Barry said. "There's going to be trouble here today."

"What do you mean go back to my home," he said. "This is my home. My land is invaded by your soldiers. Here I stay."

"Look son," McCourt said. "It's all done here, it's time to go home."

"What you mean 'done here, go home'. With Sharia law, we have order. You stay away from us. You hear me British policeman, stay away." He appeared satisfied to say this, becoming calm, and moving back towards the group.

"Just as well," McCourt said to Barry. "I was about to do him for breach."

"I wouldn't advise it," she said, nodding to across the street where a group of men had gathered. McCourt turned to see around a dozen men. They made no moves to approach them, but there was one, taller and more striking than the rest, standing erect, glowering at him in the centre of the men. He was wearing a white skullcap and a long hooded gallabiyah. The man they had previously talked to moved into their midst and stood beside him.

"It's OK, just go back to your homes and communities," McCourt called over. There was no response.

"Let's go, John," Barry said. "I think our presence here isn't... welcome."

"Isn't welcome? These are our streets," McCourt said. "We go where we want. You stay here."

McCourt walked over to the men. "Now you guys break up and move away or I'll bring a squad in." The men looked on impassively. "Hear me, move!" McCourt moved closer to the tall man, who appeared to have presence in the group. His eyes bored into his.

"Now go," he growled.

Barry arrived at his side. "John, we either leave here or we bring in the troops. I suggest we leave them to their business. Good community relations, you know what we've been told."

"Right, Joan," McCourt said. "Good community relations. Right, OK."

They turned away and walked along the pavement towards Sauchiehall Street, turning occasionally. As they did, they notice this man's eyes had not budged from them.

"He's a strange guy, John," Barry said, "but we can't arrest people for being strange."

"Seems a good idea to me," McCourt said. They laugh and head back to the station at Stewart Street.

McCourt closes the door of his locker, says cheerio to the staff coming on shift and heads home, determined not to take his work home with him. Recent briefings say no uniforms off shift and he has to be cautious. He feels OK, though. These are his streets and he knows every inch of them. He moves into Dunblane Street, where he parked this morning, not being able to get into Stewart Street car park as advised. The street was quiet at 7.30 a.m., when he arrived for his shift. It is quiet now. He clicks open the boot, throws his bag inside and moves to the driver's door. Just then, he becomes aware of a presence behind him. He turns quickly to see the man he saw in Buchanan Street earlier. Honed policing automatically kicks in. He looks around to see if anyone is around, and immediately catches sight of a street CCTV. He brings his eyes down. There is another man to the side of him: the smaller guy he had talked to earlier. What to do? He needs to stay cool.

"Can I help you guys?" They don't answer. He notices a crazed look in the big guy's eyes; fervent, staring. His mind says stay calm, his instincts say react. The smaller man is at his side. "Stay back." McCourt pushes the man back, to gain some space. The big man pulls a handgun. McCourt is a small arms geek and can see this is a Makarov pistol, favoured by Glasgow hoods after flooding the black market from Eastern Europe. This is serious. He looks at the camera. "For fuck's sake, someone see this," he whispers to himself.

"Give me your key," the big guy orders.

McCourt knows to obey. Immediately he knows what this is

and what to do; that is, go along with it, they'll get nowhere with him before the troops arrive.

"Get in." The guy pushes McCourt into the back seat and himself in beside him, all the while pressing the gun into McCourt's side. The other man takes the key and gets into the driver seat. In minutes, they are out of the street and heading along Great Western Road. McCourt looks out of the window hoping to catch sight of a patrol car, a traffic cop, anyone to indicate something was going on there, but the street is going about its business as usual, boozers moving from pub to pub, others heading out for something to eat. His child locks are on because of Jamie, so no chance of spilling out onto the street. He feels the nuzzle of the gun pushing into his side. There is no way of fighting this guy here, without the chance he would let one off into him. He has to go along with this.

Mary will be expecting him with his dinner, he thinks. If he's late, she'll phone to check on traffic, to ask him when he'll be in. He feels his phone inside his jacket. It'll buzz before long. He keeps his finger on it ready to open it and shout to her that something's going on. The guys will trace his GPS, find his car on satellite and cameras, set up a road block, stop the car. In the back of his mind though is the idea these guys would kill him and themselves in a flash. The car is now heading past the Oran Mor at the top of Byres Road. He needs to stay calm, observe everything, and wait for the right moment. Then, however, he feels a jab in his right arm. Turning, he notices a syringe being removed and dropped to the floor. The gun is pushed harder into his side making him catch his breath. *Fuck's sake, Mary, buzz,* he says to himself. He is losing consciousness,. The last act before he goes under is to press his mobile.

Mary is flustered, wee Jamie's been acting up. She looks forward to John coming in to take over, to give her some respite. The dinner is in the oven. His favourite: mince and tatties. He is late. She phones him, knowing he won't respond right away, unless he is in a traffic jam, even then only if he pulls over. There is no answer, not immediately. Then a voice she doesn't recognise, says, "Allahu akbar."

"John, is that you?" She knows it isn't him, but she has to ask. The phone goes dead.

It is after 9.00 p.m. when Jackie gets the call to say John McCourt has been taken. She is ensconced at home, glass of wine in hand, dressing gown on, feet up, ready to watch *The Fall*.

"Jesus, right, where, how, fuck. Right, I'll be there in half an hour. You've informed Armed Response. Good." She finishes her glass. "Fuck's sake. This is all we fucking need."

She hears the story on the way to French Street. Radio Scotland broadcasts has it as breaking news. *How the fuck did it get out?* she asks herself as she approaches French Street car park. She gets through security into the car park and feels the tension as she enters reception. There is always an energy when she enters French Street, but this is a different atmosphere, the tension is palpable. Voices are raised, people are swearing, moving at a frantic pace.

Being a police officer carries risks, she accepts that, but this is different, this shatters something secure, safe. Leaving your shift to head home to your family is always a transition to a safety zone, a place of normality – but now?

"Right, Euan, detail, please?" Jackie marches into her office, pulls out a hip flask in her desk drawer and takes a swallow.

Baird, as always, ignores it. "Not much to say at this time that isn't out there, ma'am."

"Aye, and how did that happen?"

"They've made a statement."

"Fuck, where is it?"

"We uploaded a recording, social media."

"Let me see it?" She moves across the room to the meeting room table followed by Baird. The wall mounted smart screen is on, the video on pause, ready for that inevitable question. She half sits on the edge of the table, her hands gripping it, securing her.

Baird touches play. Immediately there is a scene reminiscent of those from Syria. A man sits cross-legged on the floor, the indicative black flag with white Arabic wording and circle in the background, his face covered by a black hood, a man with an AK45 standing behind him.

"The Shahada," Baird says. "There is no God but God. Muhammad is the messenger of God."

"Thanks, Euan."

"We have taken a disbeliever," the figure in the video says. "An enemy of Islam. We have a crusader. Every Muslim should get out of his house and take a crusader. The Islamic State will fly its flag in

London, Glasgow, and Rome." The video ends.

"Is that it?"

"Yes, ma'am. We are searching all sites, Twitter, Facebook –"

"Twitter and Facebook. Is this what we've become?"

She checks her face in the wall mirror. No time to replenish the makeup, she moves into the boardroom. Hubert is there with the executive team and he's in full flow.

"Good, Jackie, have you seen it?"

"I've seen it."

"You and OCCT will lead in the apprehension of PC McCourt."

"Me?"

"Yes, you, ACC."

"I would expect to be involved – it is operational," Millar adds.

"*I'll* do it," Jackie snaps. "A kidnapping?" she adds, without lifting her head as she pores over a file placed in front of her.

"MI5?" Hubert asks.

"On board," Millar replies.

"Two objectives of the operation," Hubert says. "One, save PC McCourt and two, bring these men in. I'll deal with the media."

Jackie looks up. If she was leading the investigation, she should be the face of it. This was a chance to show in everyone's eyes, in particular her father, she is up to this.

"I'll save him. I'll bloody well save him… dammit," she says, the final phrase breaking with her voice. "And I'll do the media." All look at her. Millar is looking at Hubert.

"Jackie, come with me." Hubert beckons her into an adjacent room and closes the door behind them. "Are you OK, Jackie?"

"Aye, I'm fine. It's just…"

"Just?"

"I'm…"

"You'll be fine. Just do this."

"The media?"

"Just get McCourt."

I'm at home when I hear the news of McCourt's kidnapping. I know this means a total security clamp down, a game changer, and Jackie will be in touch. As expected, my mobile vibrates in my drawer. I know it is her, but I'll finish my prayers.

"I didn't think you were going to answer?"

"I was… busy, Jackie."

"We have a situation here."

"Yes, you have."

"Look, I have asked for your… support here. Now, I'm telling you, we are not fucking around here. Unless you assist us in this, I will make sure your players are picked up for sneezing in public. I will render your operation out-of-order, you got that?"

"Jackie –"

"Rooney?"

"I'm worried about you."

"Just… help me."

Jackie is still looking at her mobile wondering why, in her call to me, she expressed such vulnerability. I wonder too, settling on her labile state just now, from a mixture of substances, pain, and stress. Just then it buzzes in her hand with 'Jean' displayed on the screen.

Do I really need this? She wonders if she should ignore it, but the mobile prevails. *Best to answer the bitch.* She presses answer. "Hello, Jean."

"Well, it's happened, Jackie," Jean says, smugly. "Just what we wanted to prevent,"

"Prevent, Jean? MI5 prevent something?"

"Jackie!"

"Is this call being recorded? I thought all communications had to be in person."

"Jackie, I'm talking from home and I *need* to talk to you." Jackie can hear Jean panting. *Exercise bike or fucking*, she wonders. *She wouldn't, would she?*

"What; not rejoicing? They are active, Jean?"

"Apparently," Jean puffs. "You got Rooney on the case yet?"

"I am… working on it."

"Jackie, we have a situation."

"Sure, but no longer a situation of intelligence, of infiltration, it's now an exercise of recovery. I just bloody hope it's not to recover a body."

"We'll save him, get them."

"Oh yes, and what is MI5 doing, done, here?"

"You know we work… covertly."

"Oh, fine, less exposure that way. Well, we work *overtly* miss spook. We are out there in the full gaze of the public, in the way of the traffic, putting ourselves on the firing line. The public –"

"Would expect it's the Assistant Chief Constable's job to act decisively, especially in this matter, especially on the streets of Glasgow."

"We –"

"We, Jackie?"

"What you on, Jean, an exercise bike or a toy boy?"

"Jackie, just do your job."

CHAPTER ELEVEN

We meet at 7.30 p.m. in the Grandroom of the Central Hotel. This is now a familiar setting for the Family, the Twelve, and me. Always vary the time, sometimes early afternoon, sometimes late evening. It is my responsibility to ensure the safety of these people. Not that they can't do that themselves, however; but if one of them were to be popped as they arrive it would come back on me. Dinner has been provided and wine. Next time, no wine, I think; wine can be volatile in these circumstances. I hear the hubbub as I move through the door: "McCourt... ISIS... Hubert... the Muslims."

"Now we *have* to assist the authorities," I say, opening. "We just have to."

"We have our own problems, Rooney," Bingham says. "The Albanians are getting above themselves."

"Tell them to go to hell," Andy Hamilton says.

"The ground has shifted," I say. "This is a scenario we have to manage."

"What... scenario?" Charlie Campbell says. "The Albanians or ISIS?"

"The McCourt kidnapping. It's a gamer changer."

"He's a polis, Rooney," Campbell says.

"He's more than a polis, Charlie, he's a sign of things to come, a confirmation they are here and they mean business. Nothing will ever be the same again, believe me."

Alex Frame agrees. "If they can take a polis on the streets of Glasgow, they can do anything."

"We need to sort out our own stall, Rooney," Campbell says. "Why –"

"Set out our own stall, Charlie?" I correct.

"We *sort* our house out first, Rooney," Bingham snaps.

"Bill," I say. "In case you haven't noticed, the Muslims are growing in strength and confidence."

"Aye, man," Robert McStay says, "the Asian gangs are taking over in some areas. Look at Govanhill, Woodlands Road, Albert Drive."

Peter McStay adds, "Aye, try to score a bag there, get a prossie, open a tanning booth; you've no chance."

Bingham shakes his head. "Rooney, our... agreement with Hubert only goes so far."

"Well, it's about to be tested, Bill. Like I say, McCourt changes things." I look around. I can see thinking going on. "Look where we are, where we have reached, what we have achieved. We have structure, organisation, co-operation; and what is more, we are not killing each other. Anyone wanting to go back to the old way?"

"We can't fight the Muslims *and* the bizzies," Bingham says.

"Right, Bill. We fight the incoming teams and we help the authorities. That's the smart move. It goes hand in hand. We help the authorities and they turn a blind eye to us sorting the migrant gangs."

Frame says, "Ten percent of the gang leaders in Scotland come from minority ethnic backgrounds."

"Where did you get that from?" asks Bingham.

"The Daily Record," Frame replies.

They all laugh.

"It's true, seriously," says Fraser.

"They *are* moving in big time," Campbell says. "Human trafficking, DVDs, cigs, drugs. They have sources we don't have, even in Afghanistan. These Islamic state guys have sources of funds we can only dream about."

"They *are* a real threat," Moffat adds.

"The Pakis are OK," Patrick Devlin says. "We get on well with them."

"We are not talking about the Asian communities, Patrick," I say. "We are talking about these new firms and we are talking about Islamic terrorists."

"And what can we do, about these... terrorists?" Devlin asks.

"We have soldiers, players, informants, and downright eyes and ears on the street; we always have. These guys must have support. Where did they get their safe house from, who's giving them information, who's feeding them, taking in their halal carry-outs? These guys have kidnapped a police officer, they're holding him, and quite possibly they are going to take his head off. We know the score, we've done this stuff, we are serious experts in kidnapping, and we can find this man."

"And what do we get if we do?" Devlin asks.

"We get to do what we do without PC Murdoch breathing down our necks."

"No payment?"

"No payment. But if we do nothing, I can tell you, you will feel it in your bank balances."

"These guys are dangerous. What if they fight us?" Moffat asks.

"Then we destroy them," Bingham says.

I return to my flat feeling satisfied. I have the Family where I want. I will give thanks to God. I will lead his crusade and enjoy the penance for my sins in his service. I will give thanks and penance through self-flagellation. I kneel in front of his altar and whack my back with a leather thong.

No pain, no gain, Rooney.

"I purify my body and soul to redeem me from unholy thoughts." I whip the belt over my shoulder, connecting with the flesh of my back.

I want Jackie, but I want Jean even more. She brings out the devil; she is the devil. She brings out my base desires. I need them out in the open where I can understand them. She needs to harm me, abuse me. I need to feel the pain of Jesus. In doing so, I will take a step closer to God.

Or to being God, Rooney?

Jackie meets Millar in the boardroom at French Street. She pours from a flask, refusing to use the water cooler in the room. Baird brings in two cups of coffee. This is only one of the many meetings she'll have this day. Although she is in charge of the exercise, Millar and his DIs and DCIs are her operational arm. "Where do you think they have taken him?" She already knows some of the answer to that. "What are the options?"

"Well, love." Millar quips, accepting the coffee from Baird. Baird turns to look at Jackie.

Jackie snaps back. "Ma'am, ACC, QPM, Kaminski, or Jackie. I am not your love, Millar."

"Oh, right, Jackie, ma'am. It was a term of endearment in the Met." Millar winks at Baird, who doesn't respond. "Women didn't mind it there."

"Well, women here do, Martin. Just remember I'm your equal here, not your friend. You got that? And here, in Glasgow, 'love' will get you a slap on the mouth."

Jackie's diminutive frame is eclipsed by the bulk of Millar, but she is determined to match the presence of this man, who may have his say in the executive team, but not out here.

"Fine, ACC." Millar drops into a chair.

"That's worse, just Jackie."

"Fine," Millar growls.

"You were saying, love!"

"McCourt. They would have got him off the street as quickly as possible, dumped the car, the main identifier, to be found burnt out somewhere. Most likely, they had another car. We threw up a cordon around Glasgow in a flash. No way would they have gone on to the motorway. Two Muslim guys with a bundle in the boot or the back seat, no chance. He's in Glasgow, he must be."

"And where in Glasgow do you think they could they hold him?"

"They'll be in the Muslim communities. There, they have anonymity, support, eyes and ears on the streets."

"Just you mind I'm leading the civil liberties board."

"I remember."

"Aye, 'ACC Kaminski has good experience in community relations,' you said, thank you very much."

"Well, you do have... skills."

"Don't patronise me, Martin." She pours another glass from the flask.

"McCourt had an encounter earlier in the day," Baird says, sensitive to the need for a welcome intervention.

"Where?"

"On Buchanan Street," Millar says. "Some men in their PJs, annoyed at being told to clear off."

"Did we get them on camera?"

"Well, there are CCTVs on the street."

"We need that material, Baird, now! And you, Martin?"

"Yes."

"I want door to doors everywhere, including the Muslim communities."

Millar growls something about wishing Jackie wouldn't take her hangover out on him and, having had enough, leaves the room.

"Arsehole," she says, slurping from her flask.

"Ma'am?" Baird asks.

"What?"

"I need to tell you."

"What?"

"It's obvious."

"What's obvious, Euan?"

"The flask, ma'am."

"Right, you get the fuck out as well." In her reiteration, she emphasises she is getting seriously pissed off with misogynists, megalomaniacs, purists, and "fucking holier than thou bastards".

I meet Ben in Tennent's, in our usual corner. "They say a million a year from the Family, a nice salary Rooney."

"I work for God, Ben, not money."

"It's a lucrative business, crime."

He is referring to the substantial direct debit from the Family account to mine, commensurate with my new status. From my 'investments', I am indeed a rich man.

I allow myself a moment of imperiousness. "I am a steward of the Lord's wealth. Anyway, each of them will get their contributions back tenfold."

"I suppose the Chip would offer a better dinner than this." He tucks into steak pie and chips. "And you can afford it, but I suppose you can't do your missionary work there."

"No." I eye a group of students in the far corner. "I'll be back in a minute." I move over to them and hand out a variety of Christian leaflets, one of which is to invite them to a talk I am giving for the Glasgow Church of Christ the following evening.

"And I thought you were a pape?" Ben says, as I return to his seat.

"I am a Christian."

"I remember the struggles you had with your religion following your abuse."

"Please."

"No, but if you ever want to –"

"Talk about it, no thanks, social worker. I've got my own way of dealing with my past experiences."

"Aye." He notices the bible peeping out of my coat pocket. "How's the bipolar, your delusions, the voice?"

I'm fine!

"It's fine, I'm fine. Just keep your nose out of my business."

"Aye, just mind, I'm your named person. You appointed me. When you became ill. I've a watching brief on you."

"I can disappoint you."

He often does.

"You can, but I don't think you will."

He will.

"OK, if you… need to know, I was at my GP this afternoon and the news is good. My antipsychotic medication is to be reviewed. As long as I stay clear of the booze, he said I shouldn't have any more relapses."

"Any… residual symptoms you mentioned, Father?"

Delusions, oral hallucinations?

"I am fine, social worker. Now go back to saving children."

From Catholic priests, back in St Mary's, you as an altar boy –

"Shush."

Lying naked on the altar.

"You hearing something, Rooney? Did I trigger anything?"

"No. Please!"

Father Healey approaches you and pours sacramental wine over you. He says "In nomine patris" and he puts his penis in your mouth. It feels spiritual, powerful, enjoyable. Then he gives you a bag of sweets and sends you home. When you get home, your father asks you where you got the sweets. You tell him from

Father Healey, for eating his willie. He hits you hard on the face and sends you to bed, saying never to blaspheme a priest again.

Ben sees the vacant look on my face. "Rooney?"

"What?"

"Where were you?"

In here, social worker, where you can't reach him.

"God will save me, as he does all of his children." I pull out my bible.

"And who'll protect you, Rooney?" Ben asks. "And who'll

support *you?*"

"I have my guardian angels." I nod towards McDuff and O'Hara, standing like bookends at the bar, focused on the plasma screens. I had taken to employing a couple of street players to be my bodyguards. "James and John, the sons of thunder."

"Serious men, Rooney," Ben says. "Frighteners, no doubt." Ben understands that 'frighteners' are men who would threaten those witnesses who feel determined enough to raise a complaint against the Family. They create fear and alarm and most people would back down on the threat of being filled full of holes.

Some had been made examples, to maintain the order needed by the Family to do business without fear of being snitched to the cops. "Your two arms for hitting people with."

"Time you were leaving, Ben. I have had enough of your… counselling for one day."

"Right, I'm away." He knows he has pushed his interference in my life to the limit. He'll be back to continue, though. He has no intention in leaving me to the ravages of mental illness, nor the criminal fraternity.

On Ben's departure, John and James join me. We continue to talk for a while and get up to leave. Then, "Right, to Jinty's," I say, loudly, and head to the gents. We leave the bar on my return to a palpable relief, a noticeable positive change in the mood, and an increase in the hubbub and banter.

These three men head up the Byres Road, acutely aware of a four-by-four black BMW crawling alongside. Boldly they cross in front of it and head into Ashton Lane. Ashton lane is mostly quiet; but this night, Friday, is not a quiet night.

The BMW moves to block the end of the lane and five men get out. "Rooney," bellows out from the entrance to the lane. The men turn to see Mick standing there about ten feet away. As people crush to get out of the lane to the side of Mick, the five gunmen pull sawn-off shotguns from beneath their coats. "Kill him," Mick calls. This is the order to execute the man who has demeaned him in the eyes of the Family, the man who has taken his throne, the man that stands in his way of supremacy in Glasgow.

The three men turn square on towards those who would assassinate them. Shotguns blast shot out towards the men, but they stay on their feet.

From the smoke, Mick strains his eyes to see the man in the middle, the man he identifies as me, Rooney, as he walks towards the lane. This is not me, however, this is a favoured hitman of the Family; and, as he swings open his coat, what he can't see is that, like McDuff and O'Hara, he is wearing a stylish Garrison bespoke bulletproof suit.

Peppered by shot, some of which caught them on the neck and arms, the men are slow to react.

Not that this matters; from their side, coming out of the sub lane at the Wee Chip, at the entrance to William Hill bookies, three men arrive carrying AK-47s, Kalashnikov assault rifles. These men proceed to empty thirty round magazines each into Mick and his men as they try to reload. They are left dying and dead on the cobbles of the lane as their assailants casually walk up and out of the lane to enter cars in the car park at the back of the lane.

One of these cars contains me.

"Job done, boss," says my doppelganger, Gary Steele, who has a striking resemblance to me. He switched roles with me in the toilets of Tennent's Bar in anticipation of Mick's attack in the lane. A success for the Family's intelligence obtained easily by a McGing street player still loyal to Davy and his favoured man, myself, and a well-orchestrated counter hit. Mick is gone and no one cares, let alone the authorities, who I presume will be pleased to see his demise.

"I take vengeance on my adversaries and repay those who hate me. Deuteronomy 32:41."

"Aye, sure boss, sure," Steele replies.

At the same time, across Glasgow, similar counter hits are enacted. The McGings were intent in hitting the majority of the Family crime bosses, on a night where Mick and the McGings would take control and become the most powerful crime family in the country. The result, however, would leave the McGings without their leader or the cream of their street players.

Bill Bingham used the same tactic leaving Milngavie Golf Club, as did John Fullerton leaving his casino on the Broomilaw and Charlie Campbell in the car park of his taxi firm premises in Pollokshaws. He, however, wasn't as lucky as the rest. As he approached his assassin, who was on the ground to administer the coup-de-grace, he took a bullet in the stomach from one who carried a leg holster with enough life in him to have one last go. He would survive, however, and following surgery recover completely.

The McGings were finished as a firm in Glasgow and I had just consolidated myself as the most powerful man in Glasgow, if not Scotland. The Taylors, however, while not involved in Mick McGing's attempt at taking over Glasgow, remained out of the frame, a rogue team. Within days, George Taylor, from his operational centre in Shotts Prison, declares a vendetta on the Family.

"Right, Rooney, what the fuck is going on?" Jackie says, marching into my front room.

I get up from my afternoon prayers. "Jackie, my dear, the language is not necessary here. This is my –"

"Aye, I know, your personal chapel. I've heard all about it."

"And how did you get in?"

"James and John, your Muppets, were at the door. They let me in."

"Of course, they would have no reason to stop you. You are not here to harm me."

"No, and I will fucking crucify you, Rooney; no, on second thoughts." She observes the large wooden cross bearing a Christ-like figure, not unlike me since I had donned a Christ-like beard. "Not a good choice of words. What the fuck were you playing at? And you had better make it good because arrests are pending here."

"No member of the public was harmed, Jackie. That is our code."

"You left a number of men dead and dying on the streets of Glasgow, Rooney. Don't you think that was… harmful to the public? Not something you would like to encounter when out shopping with your kids on the Byres Road or going for a curry in Ashton Lane."

"It was evening and the streets were quiet. We chose our spots carefully."

"Rooney, you are admitting to murder here. There'll be an investigation. We'll take you all in."

"We were controlling pestilence."

"You were killing people, Rooney. Glasgow has erupted into violence."

I remove my cassock and place it over the back of a chair. Jackie scans the room, reminiscent of a priest's vestry she remembers from her youth.

"Jackie, it was the McGings. Since Davy died, they have been out of control, deadly. They were out to wipe us out. It was them or us. Coffee?" I place an Americano capsule into the coffee machine.

"Not sure which I would have preferred, Rooney. No, no coffee. Maybe we would have got more cooperation from them."

I drop slowly into the chesterfield, my coffee in my hands. "Please, Jackie." I beckon her to sit next to me. "Mick was a sinner."

"Sinner? So you played God?"

"I did the good thing."

"An eye for an eye?"

"Makes all the world blind, Jackie. They broke the code. They attacked the public."

She looks at me. She knows they did. Will this get her off my back?

"And McCourt?"

"Nothing, yet."

"We're working on it."

"Rooney, the only reason I am not having you arrested right now is because I believe you can give... us something."

I slide closer to her on the sofa, as if I am about to put my arm around her.

"No, Rooney. I'm not ready... not for you." There's discernible pain in her eyes.

I stand up and, leaning over her, lift my right hand, almost like a priest about to bless a congregant. "I... just wanted to –"

"Don't you dare try the 'in the name of' stuff with me. I had that before when you were standing over me on the street, after the bomb."

"Comfort you, Jackie."

She rises and moves to the window, covered in individual stained glass panes of Jesus in various biblical scenes. She notices one of Jesus and Mary Magdalene.

"It's from Magdalene's grotto in the Basilica Sainte-Marie-Madeleine," I say, moving closer to her. "I was there with you, Jackie... in God."

"God! I needed more than... God! I was dying, Rooney."

"I know, Jackie, but I couldn't treat your wounds. I could

only… look to your soul."

"Rooney, you have become obsessed, dominated by… God. What about human beings? What about the pain of the people? Will your god help them?"

"Through God, I will help them; and, by God, I'll help you too."

I move towards her.

"Oh, you will." She moves away. "You'll help me, Rooney?"

"I will, but you worked with Johnston, against me, to destroy me. I don't know if I can –"

"Trust me?"

Trust no one.

"Trust you."

"And who said I was trying to destroy you?"

"Someone… said you were trying to kill me."

"Is that why you did it, Rooney? Who triggered my bomb, Rooney? You were there. Who –"

"Jean was there too, Jackie."

She drops into a seat. "Oh, Jean, shite, now that makes sense."

"What did she tell you?"

"She said I was to be… assassinated that night. I was to be blown up… in a taxi."

"Oh, what a coincidence?"

One of those pauses occurs which indicate this is dangerous ground.

"I made a call."

"To who, Rooney?"

"Whom."

"Listen, pedant, tell me?"

"I thought I could stop you killing me. I called Davy. I didn't think –"

"You didn't think he would kill me, Rooney, is that what you're saying. Now it's starting to fit."

"Just perfect, with my frame of mind at the time."

"At the time!"

"Why did she want to kill you?"

"Oh, a number of things."

"We can turn her in."

"No, we can't."

"Why not?"

"We just can't…"

"You're fallen, Jackie."

"We had it all, Rooney… fallen? What do you mean fallen?"

"You killed Archie."

"He said he could save Gray. I needed Gray to ensure you killed Johnston. And that's why I can't turn her in. She knows I killed Archie."

"You were a fallen woman, like Magdalene, Jackie." I look to the glass pane of Jesus and Mary Magdalene.

"And you were a good man, Rooney. Now look at you."

"I am… repentant, Jackie. I will –"

"Abuse yourself, Rooney?" She sees the leather thong hanging over the church kneeler. "One abuse heals another? Get real."

I grab her. "Jackie, we can heal each other." I pull her down onto the kneeler. "We can get God's forgiveness."

"You crazy religious pervert, get the fuck off me, let me out of here."

I hold her fast. "God, forgive –"

She screams, bringing James and John into the room, then gets up and rushes out of the door, pushing James and John apart.

"Jackie, I am –"

Sorry?

"I would like to thank you all for allowing me to speak to you tonight," I say to the ensemble. To be in this building I had admired many times as I went to and from the bars of Byres Road thrills me. Kelvinside Hillhead Parish Church, on Observatory Road in Hillhead, is an incredible church, modelled on Sainte Chapelle in Paris and completed in 1876, "in this truly magnificence temple to our lord." I turn to the fine stained glass windows, one showing Jesus on trial before Pilate. "Like our lord, I feel on trial. I have sinned, but now I am saved." There is a rapturous applause. "Thank you," I say. "You'll know my… background, but also how my faith bears upon my… vocation." There's more applause. "I thought about giving a speech here today, but decided against this, but I do wish to stimulate a discussion." There's less applause now that the audience appreciate they will soon be participants, they will also have to talk; it is their time to think about a clever question.

Brian Cuthbertson sits in the front row, always the worst place; he would get his question in first and then sit back, best to get the most controversial out first. "What do you think about killing people in the service of God?" There is a deep collective groan. No, not that, not here, just too controversial for comfort. Brian would be spoken to later about this.

"Ah hah, not a shy retiring type, sir. OK, you asked it outright and many more here will be asking it in their head, so it deserves an answer." All sit back in anticipation. The organiser of the event, John Hume, standing at the back, holds his head in trepidation, not knowing where this would go. "Is it a sin to smite those who would harm the church, to defend the believers, to thrash the moneylenders, the unbelievers who would push down the pillars of the church; who would harm the weak, sick, disabled; rape our women; swamp the houses of the righteous and drown the children of the church with a dark flood of badness, bringing a swarm of locusts to feast on the flesh of good children, exerting pestilence on the community of God. If this is sin, I am a sinner and I will be judged by God on the Day of Judgement. Am I to be judged here, before you all, in this place of God?"

Where did you get that from?

A hush descends. John Hume is first to react. "Mr Rooney, we are not here to condemn you." He starts to clap and the hall erupts with applause. He waits for a follow-up question or response, but neither come. I know it is time to leave – point made.

CHAPTER TWELVE

"Thank you for coming today," Hubert says, "Mrs –"

"Mary, Mary McCourt."

"Mary, we really appreciate it, thank you. May I introduce Assistant Chief Constable Jacqueline Kaminski. She is leading the investigation."

"Keeping it in the family, eh?"

Jackie reaches over and offers her hand. "I'm pleased to meet you Mrs McCourt, your husband –"

"Has been kidnapped, Miss Kaminski."

Jackie withdraws her hand. "Yes, of course."

"We wanted to express our disgust over the kidnapping of John, and to assure you of our determination to bring him safely home to you and your wee son –"

"Jamie."

"Yes, Jamie. How is he, by the way?"

"He's fine. He doesn't understand much of it. He thinks it is a bit of a game his daddy's involved with. It is best that way."

"Indeed, and you?"

"Bearing up, what do you think? What's happening? Will you get him home soon? These bastards –"

"We are doing everything possible," Jackie says.

"Everything possible, they're going to kill my man, in ten days. You need to meet their demands. They are not fucking about."

"No, no they are not… messing about," Hubert says.

"So, you're in charge of the… investigation?" Mary asks Jackie.

"I am."

"But you're a woman."

Jackie opens her eyes wide. "I am."

"And you'll save him?"

"I'll do my best."

"Again, your best, everything possible." Mary rises to her feet. "Well, you's two need to listen. If my man dies, I will hold you two personally responsible. He's one of yours for fuck's sake." She begins to sob.

"We know." Jackie hands Mary a napkin. "We want him home as much as –"

"No, you fucking well don't and don't ever fucking say that again. He doesn't matter as much to you two as he does to me, to Jamie. Just get him fucking home." Mary pushes between them and out.

"She's upset," Jackie says.

"She's right," Hubert replies, "but she doesn't understand the… political context."

Jackie sighs. "Maclean won't do it, you mean."

"No way will he give into terrorist demands."

Jackie grips her leg as a cramp takes hold. "We need to find him then."

"You need to find him. And Jackie?"

"Yes, Dad?"

"You're under a lot of pressure, and on a lot of painkillers no doubt."

"Aye, Dad, painkillers."

"You'll tell me if it gets –"

"A wee bit too much? Aye, Dad, I'll tell you."

Jackie gets in her bath using the motorised hoist, which lifts her up, swings her around and slowly eases her into the warm and soothing bath. "I'm not moving from here." She rubs essential oils into her right leg. On a table at the side of the bath, alongside a bottle of white and a glass, she has placed two phones: one, the normal one and two, the secure line. She calls Jean on the secure one. "I do not intend doing your job, darling," she says, as she sinks deep into the warm soapy water, only the glass of wine, the phone and her head above it. "I've enough on my own plate."

"It's all our jobs, Jackie," Jean replies. Jackie hears an echo as if Jean is on hands-free. She wonders if someone else is there. "We are a conjoined service. It is the only way we can defeat terrorism." Jean sounds more polite and official than normal, confirming she is not alone.

"You fucking defeat… terrorism." Jackie hiccups. "I've a fucking officer to save."

"Jackie, I'll take this above you. I will."

"You fucking go ahead and I'll blow the gaff on –"

The echo stops, like Jean had clicked it off and is now talking directly into the phone.

"You'll blow the gaff, Jackie, really?"

"I'll squeal like a baby." Jackie hesitates. "On the spooks links with the mob."

"Oh, that. Listen, dear," Jean, says, clearly this time. "I'll roar like a bull on the make about you and Rooney. I will. You two, and your little… secret."

"The woman who knows things, Rooney called you."

"He was right."

"The secret?"

In the background, Jackie is sure she hears Jean say, "Can you give me a minute, darling?" Jean's voice rises. "Archie, DCI Archie Paterson," she says. "You killed him because he knew you lied in the Birelli case; the case that led to your promotion as DCI."

"What if I tell all on you, bitch? You were there when I was bombed. You told Rooney he was to be assassinated. What the fuck do you know?"

Click.

"Bastard." Jackie whacks the receiver back and takes a large gulp of wine. She would have a long think about this, but another call arrives from me on the normal line.

"Your… adjutant Baird asked me to call you."

"He's my assistant, and he's a DCI, not –"

"Jackie, earlier…"

"I need the information, and I need it now!"

"We've made contact with… certain groups and we await information."

"You're cutting it fine. You will help me, Rooney, you have to." The pain travels up her right leg. "You bastard."

"I am penitent, Jackie." She hears a whish and a thwack, and then my moan.

"We are both in pain, you crazy man, I suppose it's what drives us."

"I'll do what I can."

Jean and I meet in the Lismore Bar on Dumbarton Road. It's Thursday night and the place is full of early weekend boozers. I leave

John and James in the car outside on Mansfield Street at the side entrance of the bar. John leaves the car to watch the front entrance. It is an open mic night and a big chance for an old guy to perform his version of Alex Harvey's Delilah. We find a seat in the lounge, just off the bar, not so far from the music that would make any difference to the din.

"Just like old times, Jean." I get a whiff of the perfume I recall so vividly.

Perfume attack, watch yourself.

"Indeed, Rooney. We need to stop meeting like this."

"Why do you want to see me?"

"We always retained a… contact with Glasgow's… business community, Rooney, you know that." She moves closure than I would prefer.

"Oh, the mob working with the state?"

"Rooney, darlin', we've had links from the days of the Troubles in Northern Ireland."

Darlin'!

"When Davy McGing was an informant, in payment for being allowed to traffic drugs into the UK?"

"We got him a license to deal in drugs without prosecution."

"I'm not Davy, Jean."

"No, but we can offer the same… immunity." Her voice is husky and provocative.

"I don't need… immunity. Are you still tapping my phone?"

"You must have the safest phone in Glasgow."

"Thanks, that assures me no end."

"Jackie has asked for the Family's cooperation. I need it too."

I know what she needs.

"Oh?"

"But not in an… active, practical sense, I need *you, your* cooperation."

Co-op-er-ation, Mister Presi… dent.

"Just like Taylor, Jean, an informer."

"Not quite, Rooney. We have known each other for some time."

She's play-ing ga…mes.

I am uneasy about this woman, but intrigued by her just the same. She is dangerous. I recall the first time we had met, when she introduced me to the McGings in their safe house in Gardner Street.

I look at my finger, the end of it taken off with a chopper as a sign of their authority.

Sore one that.

"The McGings, Jean?"

"Indeed, the McGings, Rooney. With Davy and the Taylors, we had a very close handle on business for some time. However, with your elevation to within its ranks, its consigliere, we need to renew our…" She moves closer to me. "Relationship." Her perfume sets my head spinning.

The perfume attack, again!

"You said I was to be assassinated that night. That Jackie was behind it."

She slides closer to me. "You were to be blown up… in a taxi."

I slide back a bit, but I'm trapped in the corner between her and the two women. "I made the call, Jean, because you said that. And I bloody well believed you."

"I was protecting you." She is almost in my face.

"Jackie was hit."

"It could have been you."

Delilah is given full blast by the open-micer.

She was my woman…

"She was my –"

And as she betrayed me I watched and went out of my mind…

"She betrayed you."

Why, why, why, Delilah…

"Why?"

"She had her own agenda."

And just like a slave I was lost and no man could free…

"I… loved her."

She stood there, laughing.

"And you tried to kill her."

And I felt the knife in my hand and she laughed no more…

"I was scared, confused."

Forgive me, Delilah, I just couldn't take anymore.

"Can I rely on you now?" Her face is close enough to mine to kiss. Her perfume fills my nostrils and my head. Her eyes soften and smile. Her lips glisten with blood red lipstick framing pure white teeth, clearly whitened since I last saw her. I hadn't been with a woman since Jackie. I want one. I want her. There is danger in this, especially when the request is being delivered like a Mata Hari seduction.

"I presume you mean ISIS and McCourt?"

"We are extremely concerned, Rooney, Jackie has explained."

"A good polis. Shame. A family man."

"He is only the first, Rooney. There will be more."

"I have raised it with… my associates."

"Good, Rooney. They, you, have much to gain from our… cooperation."

"You will… advise us. The migrant gangs, international threats to our businesses, new opportunities, etcetera."

"And you too, Rooney, you too will gain, from our –"

"Relationship, Jean?"

"Yes, relationship, Rooney."

"My relationship is with God, Jean, God." By this time, some of the words we are saying are caught by the women and they are up and off through to the bar realising some heavy stuff is going on here. I push along the seat to gain more space.

"Yes." She follows me along the seat. "Your… spiritual relationship, Rooney; but you have… more earthly needs I can meet."

Get in there, Rooney.

"I need to go, Jean." I free myself. "I have… somewhere to go."

"Indeed, Rooney. St Peters, no doubt. Just remember, I am here for you."

Another open-micer takes up position. As I leave, I hear her begin *Mac the Knife*.

Oh, the shark has pretty teeth dear, and he shows 'em, pearly white…

I get in the car and we head up Hyndland Street, passing St Peters on the way. "Not today, Jean," I say, as I pass, heading for home.

A home befitting a "Father" status, Rooney? A HQ, a home… a church?

We travel up Sydenham Road reaching my house. Many times, I had passed this place, almost crawling home from drinking sessions on the Byres Road. I used to look through its large ornate iron electric gates. Now, this is mine, my sumptuous mansion. My 'cathedral' reflects my new status, my newly determined stature. The house was originally built in 1861, a top floor penthouse with views over the roofs of Glasgow, with an outdoor patio, covering the perimeter of the flat. This not only offers a place to sit, to grow plants, to observe God's city, but also an excellent view of the streets surrounding the house, in particular the entrance.

I kneel down to pray.

You want Jean. You want an abusive woman. You want to be controlled.

I reach for the leather thong. The first few whacks make me feel better.

Punish yourself, sinner-man.

I phone Jackie. It is late but, for this information, I know she won't mind. She reaches for the mobile on the adjacent pillow on her double bed. "The Family is committed to assisting… the authorities."

"Did you have much trouble persuading them?" I haven't persuaded them, but I know they will. "I knew they would. They couldn't not do it." I know. "Though, did you need the spooks to persuade you?" She pulls herself up on the bed.

"Jean explained things."

"Oh, it took her to persuade you; nothing I could do or say could do that?"

"I saw the broadcast."

"This is serious shit, Rooney."

"Apparently, these guys intend killing him."

"There's no doubt."

"Campbell?"

"He won't talk to them. It would open the door to more kidnapping. We have ten days."

I hear her breath deepening. I remember how she would fall asleep halfway through a sentence. "Dinner, Jackie, my place. Tomorrow?" I ask, before the snoring starts.

"Your place? I hear you've moved up the housing ladder. Stately mansion in the West End?"

"God has been good."

"Be careful, Rooney. The Proceeds of Crime Act. Time?"

"Seven. Your favourite, Shepherd's Pie?"

She's too tired to argue that she no longer eats Shepherd's Pie.

"Sounds good, formal?"

"Just as you are, Jackie."

"In my PJs?"

"That'll do."

Time for prayers, reflection, penance, then bed.

Ten hail Marys, ten whip-whacks?

"Hello, Mr Rooney, thank you for seeing me." Levan Meskhi enters my office. The morning light bathes the room in sunshine and pours through the stained glass windows, illuminating the room in surreal colour, not unlike a church with stained windows facing south.

I am pleased to receive him in my study, my vestry office. Apart from Davy's collection of Howson's and Mutter's that now bedeck the walls, having acquired them from an auction after Gracelands was sold, they hang beside masters of biblical scenes.

"Mr Meskhi, how can I help you?" I take his hand firmly and invite him to take up the seat adjacent from me at the other side of the desk.

"My daughter has been raped, sir."

"You need to go to the police."

"The police won't help me."

"Why do you think I can help?"

"I have nowhere else to go."

"So you come to me?"

"I hoped our God can help."

"Our God?"

"I am a Christian, Mr Rooney."

"You are Asian."

"I am from Georgia, sir, we are Christians forced from our lands. The Jihad."

Brush up on your Asian Christianity, man.

"Go on."

"My daughter was raped by an Asian man in front of his fellow gang members. They recorded the attack on their mobile phones. She was too scared to tell us, her parents, about the rape, and in the coming months the man prostituted her to over sixty men."

"This is a police matter."

"The police are… reluctant. They are afraid to intervene. They fear –"

"I know, of being branded racists. But is it OK for us to be seen in that light?"

"No, I don't mean that, but the police refuse to act." Ahmed slaps his palms on the desk. "This is an outrage, Mr Rooney."

"OK, calm down, my son. Tell me?"

He starts to recite what for him is an uncomfortable story. "She started a relationship with the man when she was fourteen. He said he loved her. She was young, stupid, naïve. She had no idea that he was part of a gang. This gang operates with impunity in Glasgow, Mr Rooney. It needs to be brought to book. You control the gangs, Father."

He has given me this respect, I like this. "I don't control this one."

"He supplies Glasgow's sex trade."

"He is a sinner."

Later that evening, Jackie arrives in a taxi. "Sure is a nice place, Rooney." John takes her coat.

"Yes, God is gracious." I invite her into my lounge.

"Sure beats your pied-à-terre in Partick, Rooney." She takes a wide view of my reception area. "You would have got your whole flat into this hall."

I show her into the lounge. "You got me out of my gutter, Jackie?"

"Mental, physical or practical?"

"I'm grateful, you know that."

I hold her hand and guide her to the sofa. She starts to sob.

"What is it?"

"Nothing, it's just work – get me a drink."

I head into the kitchen. "I'll turn the oven on."

"An invite for dinner, Rooney. People may talk," she calls.

"Well," I cry from the kitchen, "I knew you wouldn't come before. I needed a place I could be, I could –"

"Entertain in, Rooney. Only me, I hope."

"White, Jackie?" I crack open the top then smell the wine.

"Aye, what's keeping you?" She brings her legs up onto the sofa, laying her stick down along it. I pour wine into a crystal wine glass and bring it and the bottle through to her. "Italian Rioja white, chilled, you remembered."

"I try."

"None for you?"

"No, water's fine."

"Won't change it to wine, will you?"

"Funny, Jackie. If you'll excuse me."

"Again?" This time she follows me through. "Wow, Rooney, splen…deed." She examines the kitchen.

I slide the shepherd's pie into the oven. "Be about an hour." Just enough time to talk about our changing lives, though, for her, after sufficient drink she won't feel like shepherd's pie.

"We have come a long way." We arrive back in the sitting room. She reaches to slide the patio doors open. I go to help her. "No need; I can hold a glass in one hand and lean on my stick with the other. I'm getting used to it."

"Indeed."

"We have travelled on different paths."

"I suppose; myself on a path to redemption and you to glory and success."

"I didn't mean that. I meant one path good and one path bad."

"The old paths, where the good way is and where ye shall find rest for the soul."

"Sure, Rooney, rest for your soul; yet the path you chose is the path of crime."

"And your path, Jackie? We both chose the path of crime, but from a slightly different perspective."

"Aye, different perspectives, Rooney." She looks intently, but sadly, at me. "Mind if I go outside?" I slide the glass doors out onto the roof garden. She moves out through them and takes a 180-degree scan of the vista, of the rows of mansions up and down Sydenham Street. "I guess crime pays, Rooney." She pulls out her Rizla Tin and prepares a rollup.

"I invest the proceeds of sin, into more… godly pursuits." I join her there, refusing a smoke.

She finishes her cigarette and returns to the room, to follow the row of paintings along the wall. "Indeed, quite a collector of Christian art, I would presume." She tightens her eyes to see the nameplates. "*The Adoration of the Magi, Christ in the Wilderness, The Crucifixion,*" she says, as she moves along. "Tintoretto, *Magdalena penitente,* 1598. The penitent Mary Magdalene, not the original, Rooney?"

"As if, but a pretty good oil copy. Rewards for –"

"I know, as you say godly work with sinners. Ten percent on all the Family profits. You ever heard of the Proceeds of –"

"Crime Act. Yes, you told me. Do you think I am an international drug dealer?"

"No, but you look after some."

"I… facilitate."

"So you don't see the damage they do to lives?"

"They are businessmen."

"Businessmen. I could take all of this from you."

"Would you?"

"Who knows? Just don't get above yourself, Rooney."

"I live a frugal life."

"I know, a life of a hermit. And yet you are developing… a presence."

"A presence."

"Yes, with the media, the council, mixing with the great and good."

"Just like yourself, Jackie." She swigs the wine like a child would blackcurrant juice. "I hear you are doing a lot of nest feathering yourself. Exclusive health clubs, socialite parties, weekends in spa hotels."

"Fuck off. Stress and fighting bad guys out there in the streets." She points towards town, "And there, where it shouldn't fucking happen." She pulls out her ID card. "I need the fucking therapy." She sits up reaching for the bottle; a split in her dress reveals the scar on her right leg.

"Oh, you do!" I top up her glass.

"Any more wine?" She notices the emptying bottle.

I get another, then another, until it is clear the Shepherd's Pie is not going to be eaten. I go for another bottle and gesture to John for him and James to have the food.

"Jackie?" I arrive with a fresh bottle, the fourth.

"Yes?"

"The Muslim paedophile gang, grooming and raping white girls?"

"Yes."

"You guys won't act."

"No."

"Why not."

"You know why not. And don't think you fuckers are getting away with the McGings hit. Millar'll be pursuing that. The bastard been in touch yet?"

"We have the communities to consider."

She moves from the table taking the bottle with her. "Oh really, you fuckers take brutal action and we foster community relations. A bit cockeyed that, don't you think?"

"There are vulnerable people out there."

"You just leave that to us. Just keep the fuck out of police business."

"Jackie, the SCDEF say twenty-five foreign mafia gangs are now in Glasgow. We can't stand by and allow this. *This* is our business."

"Rooney, it's an exaggeration."

"The Albanian mafia, an ultra-violent team, has moved into our drugs and vice markets over the last year. They've links to world trade routes for heroin, guns and women. Their control of vice and heroin supply networks pose a major threat not just to you guys but to us, and our interests."

"We know them."

"Good, and you'll know other foreign gangs like the Chinese Triads, responsible for everything from cannabis farms to bootleg DVDs? Garnethill has become a battle ground for the Wo Sing Wo Triad and the Big Circle Gang."

"We are working with the Chinese communities over this."

"And people traffickers from Bangladesh and the former Czechoslovakia, as well as Yardies from the Caribbean, incorporating criminals from West Africa, peddling crack and prostitutes."

"Rooney, we are aware of this. Fuck's sake, give me peace."

"Jackie, you are doing nothing. They are moving in big style, and *we* can't allow it."

"You can't allow it? No more street wars in Glasgow. Remember the Family agreed this, one of the key constitutional matters. Davy agreed it."

"We will act, Jackie."

"Oh, you think you can move into my territory, Rooney. You think you are now big enough for that, Mr fucking Father. You think you are in control in Glasgow."

She gets up and nearly falls over the coffee table. I reach for her.

"I think someone has to be in control, Jackie."

As you wish.

She looks at me for a minute through bleary eyes.

"Rooney, come here."

"Why?"

"Just do as I say."

I move tentatively in her direction.

"Push the door over. I don't want your heavies to see this." I close the door hard and move to her. "I'll show you who is in control, your god's not here to help you now." She pulls me to her by the tie and pulls down the zip in her dress revealing flesh, perfect breasts, nipples erect, and a pair of knickers and nothing else. "I know you, Rooney. I know what you need."

I drop my eyes down over her body reaching the area of her injuries, the ravages and scars from the explosive device, now eight months on, red scarring, crisscrossing her abdomen, her nether regions, her thighs. "Jackie?"

"Shut up." She takes my hands and nestles her breasts in them. "Please."

"I may not look the same or be able to do the things we used to do, Rooney; but, I'll show you who is in charge." She undoes my trousers and releases my penis. I reach to remove her knickers. "No, Rooney." She takes my penis into her mouth.

She draws my hardening cock into her mouth. "God save me," I moan.

She pulls out. "No, God damn you, Rooney. Damn you, you fucking sinner."

I have no ability to resist. She grips the stem of my cock in her hands as her lips grip its glans, with an expert slow and deliberate up and down rhythm, releasing and tightening the grip as she does. By this time, I am hers, all the while gazing up at Mary Magdalene.

"For god's sake, I'll, I'll, I'll!" I grip her head as she grips my cock.

"You pathetic bastard, Rooney," she says, from the side of her mouth. "Do your God's work now, you fucking…"

I wonder how much her mouth grip would hold out before she tightens her teeth on me to bring me to a halt. She wouldn't have too much longer, however, to wait. "Jesus, I'm cumming, Jesus, Mary and Joseph. Jesus, Mary…"

Magdalene…

"In the name of…"

"The Father, Rooney, The fucking Father!"

"Argh," I cry, as she falls to the side, both of us whimpering, sobbing.

Who fucked whom, Father?

The congregation of Hillhead Church invite me back for a further talk. I title it, 'To Sin is to Repent." There is an energetic discussion over the balance Christians need to find in today's world, where both sin and redemption is inevitable. They were extremely interested in my presentation, along the lines of man is weak, man will do, man will take, man will use, man will need. I finish my speech with, "God made man in his own image, man is God, God is man. God can be bad to be good, man can be bad to be good. God can be good, man can be good. But only God can forgive, only God can save man. Man must repent. He must carry the burden of his desires, bear the responsibility for it. He must accept God's punishment, he must punish himself. Man being man will need, then man being man must repent, then man must thrash the desire that seeks to control him. He must feel the weight of God's crook and flail on his back." There is an almighty applause. I thank them and take my leave.

"Well done, Father." Ben appears, approaching me from behind as I leave the church. I turn to face him. "Let's go to Jinty's. We need to talk."

James and John follow us down the Byres Road until we turn into Great George Lane and then into the adjoining Ashton Lane. We avoid the part of Ashton Lane, which leads to Byres Road, still cordoned with police tape after the McGing shootings. The four of us go into Jintys where James and John take up positions at the bar, back to it, facing down through the pub. I order a pint of Guinness and an orange juice and move along the booths, finding Ben in the last. I squeeze in. Ben is focused on a screen on the wall before them showing the All-Ireland Football Final, between Dublin and Mayo at Croke Park, Dublin, another reason Ben recommended there. Although Ben is a big Partick Thistle fan, he'll watch anything that involves a ball getting shunted up and down a park. He's also aware this would be an antidote to some of the heavy stuff he knows will come from meeting me. He accepts the pint. Dry from my presentation, I take a long drink of the orange juice.

"Do you mind if I watch this?" Ben asks.

"If you must."

We take in the game. By half-time, Mayo are ahead.

"How you feeling now, Rooney?"

"I'm fine, how are you?"

"So, all of that in the church was… appropriate."

"And how are you, Ben?"

"I'm good, working my buns off for bureaucrats who don't give a shite, but I'm OK."

"Good."

"Rooney, who are you, really?"

"I'm the Father."

"And how are you?"

"I'm good, God has saved me from my demons."

"Guess you're not there yet."

"I'm getting there, Ben."

"That's good." He doesn't take his eyes from the screen. "And how's the Family?"

"Good, how's yours?"

"I'm talking about *the* Family, Rooney."

"I know Ben. Business is good."

"You're killing people. Even the Christians are talking about it."

"Only bad people, Ben; not good Christian folk."

"Bad people bleed too, Rooney."

"I sharpen my flashing sword, grasping it in judgment."

"Oh." Dublin take the lead. "Shite, there's a change on."

"We all change, Ben."

"You have become a bad man, Rooney," he says not talking his eyes from the screen. "You killed the McGings, Mick."

"Was God bad when he killed the firstborns of Egypt?"

"It had to be done, is that what you are saying?"

"Was he bad when he burnt to death by fire, raining burning sulphur on the people of Sodom and Gomorrah?"

"Bad is bad, Rooney."

"When he killed the Israelites by plague?"

"You sat with me over there," Ben says, pointing in the direction of Tennent's. "In Tennent's, then out there on Ashton Lane. Rooney, I watched your eyes when we passed the very place your guys hit the

McGings; there was nothing, no emotion, nothing."

"I wasn't there."

"No, but you orchestrated it. Just as culpable as those, your men, who shot the McGings."

"They were out to kill me. They would have killed you too if you were with me."

Ben looks at John and James, almost for reassurance. "You will kill those who seek to harm you?"

"God will protect his own and smite the wrongdoers."

"You really do think you are doing good."

"I have been asked to… assist the authorities… with McCourt, the policeman."

"ISIS, what are you doing about them?"

"ISIS are killing Christians, Ben."

"ISIS will kill anyone, Rooney."

"I pray they may see Jesus and accept his offer of salvation. If not, God will destroy them and their land."

"Christ, you are bad, you really are bad."

"It is God's way, it is his work."

"People are calling you lot Jesus and his twelve disciples."

"I like that."

"And I am calling you ill, delusional."

"Oh ye without sin cast the first stone, social worker," I say, as I get up to leave.

"Aye, right," Ben says, settling in to enjoy the rest of the match. "I'll see you… Father."

God bless you, my son.

CHAPTER THIRTEEN

John McCourt opens his eyes. The room is dark. He is in an orange jumpsuit, like a Guantanamo Bay detainee. He tries to get up, but he is chained to a cast iron radiator, his hands, arms and feet shackled. He scans the room; there are no windows, only a camp bed, a table, a portaloo, a small stair to a shut, and, presumably locked, door. He could be anywhere, he thinks. He remembers being dragged in here from a car, dropped on the bed, the light being switched off, and the door slammed. Then he sees it, a black flag on the adjacent wall with white foreign letters. Arabic, he thinks.

"Kidnapped," comes quietly to his lips. He tries to compose himself. He knows Police Scotland will be looking for him. It is just a matter of time before he is found.

"Indeed, crusader, you have been taken prisoner."

He strains his eyes. Turning his head, he sees a figure in a darkened corner, sitting on a chair facing him. The man was so quiet he thought he was alone.

"Who are you?"

"I am Al-Jamal Saddam Al-Jamal. He, who will deliver you, and you will honour me."

This sends shivers down McCourt's spine. "And why would you want to do that?"

"To kill the person who abuses the Prophet and whip the one who abuses his companions."

McCourt knows immediately he is dealing with serious Islamic fundamentalism here.

"Oh." McCourt knows not to irritate this man. Brian Keenan, John McCarthy, and Terry Waite come to mind. The feigned Stockholm Syndrome: make it hard for your captors to harm you. "My friend, what have I done to harm you?"

"You are an infidel soldier at war with Islam; killing our children en masse; slaughtering our people on the streets. You hit us with your drones and missiles, and you don't have the courage to face us, to fight us soldier to soldier."

"But I am not a… soldier."

"You are a crusader and you will be a martyr. Your family will be proud of you, a hero. They will put up a statue in your name, but first you will assist us."

"When we are here, death is not. When death is here, we are not. So why worry? Epicurus."

"What?"

"You will do what you will do."

"Just say a few words to your… people," Al-Jamal says, standing over McCourt. Having been in the dark until this point, the 250-watt lamp makes his eyes water. "Halid, Mohammed," Al-Jamal calls out. Two men come into the room and grab McCourt roughly, pulling him over to the adjacent wall and positioning him on his knees under the flag.

One of them pulls out a portable DVD camcorder. Al-Jamal moves around him and stands over him at his back. Nasheed music is switched on in the background.

Al-Jamal talks into the camera. "Oh soldiers of the Islamic State, be ready for the war against the crusaders," he says. "By Allah's will, it will be the final one. By the permission of Allah, the exalted, we will conquer your Rome, break your crosses, and enslave your women. Oh Britain and America, oh allies of Britain and its crusaders, understand that the matter is more dangerous than you have imagined and greater than you have envisioned."

Al-Jamal pulls McCourt's head back. McCourt believes he is going to be killed there and then. Al-Jamal looks for fear in McCourt's eyes. He sees none from this Glasgow cop.

"Tell them infidel, what is your dying wish?"

McCourt's not prepared to yield. "If I am to die then so be it. But find these people and bring them to justice."

"We… wish to talk to Mr Maclean, your First Minister."

McCourt sees a man to the side pass a ceremonial sword to Al-Jamal. "Don't give in to these animals," he says.

"You have ten days." Al-Jamal reveals the sword. "Then we will remove his head, Inshallah."

McCourt will have no truck with this. "Don't," he gasps, as gaffer tape is stuck across his mouth, preventing any more words. Al-Jamal moves behind him removing a dagger from his belt. McCourt's eyes follow him until they scream with shock, tears running down his face, the pain of losing the little finger of his right hand firing up his arm like a lightning bolt into his brain.

Al-Jamal returns to the side of McCourt, holding out the finger. He takes a rag, cleans the blood from the dagger, and puts it back in his belt. "Of the unbelievers, smite ye above their necks and smite all their finger-tips off them," he says. "On each day, within the ten days mentioned, we will remove one of this man's fingers. This will show the resolve of the children of Allah to the world. It is in your power to prevent your soldier's suffering and respond to our demand."

The man with the camera moves away. McCourt is helped to the bed. He is given Ibuprofen with a glass of water and his wound clinically dressed by a skilful hand. *This man is a health professional*, McCourt thinks, parking this.

"Your finger has been removed. In nine days it will be your head." Al-Jamal checks the chains on McCourt's chest. "Say your prayers, infidel soldier."

With that, they leave the room, turning the light off and leaving McCourt in the dark. Only then do the tears arrive in his eyes, driven by the pain in his heart that he may not see his son or wife again. He wonders what they would be thinking at this time.

A strange message is received by telephone in Hillhead Library. "You will check the Quran, in the Islamic section, where inside the cover you will find an envelope. You will call the police and advise them of this. In the Quran, the library assistant finds the envelope containing a polybag and a DVD. There is blood on the envelope. Two police officers are dispatched to take them to Stewart Street.

CHAPTER FOURTEEN

Ali Ameen is standing at the corner of Albert Drive. His date is Mary Kilpatrick, a young girl he met on Interracial Passions, an interracial chat room. She is due in five minutes. She is sixteen. He has told her he is twenty-one and has a business on Pollokshaws Road, a restaurant. He said he wants to take her out, take her to expensive places and spend money on her. He is intending to rape her. He'll take a video of the act. Then he'll threaten to put this about social media, and tell everyone she is a slut. He'll get her into drugs, then share her with his gang. Then, depending on how it goes, he'll get her into prostitution and into the gang's sex trafficking business.

I meet Paul Moffat, head of the Moffats and one of the Family. I know he has concerns about the Asian gangs. I say I need him to do something for me. I arrange to see him in an appropriate place: St Peters in Partick.

"You wanted to see me, Mr Rooney," Moffat says, from the pew behind me.

"I did, Paul." I get up from my knees to sit. I talk to him without turning around. The church is empty, but our voices are carried by the excellent acoustics. "I want you to act… on my behalf."

"Oh, and what about the sanction of the Twelve, the Family?"

"We need to act affirmatively and early. I will agree it."

"What do you want us to do?"

I whisper the scenario and add "The man who seizes her lies with her, and the man who lies with her shall die."

"Fucking hell, Rooney."

I tell him to shush and over my shoulder pass him details on a folded A4. He accepts it, knowing it contains the details of the hit. "He will not die, but he will not lie with her or anyone else for some time. Don't tell me what you'll do to him, but make sure he is off the streets for a while. Send a message that the Family will not allow this on the streets of Glasgow. That this stops now."

"It'll be my pleasure, boss."

I get to my feet. He is gone and I am alone. "My Lord, forgive me." I splay my arms out. "We must protect our children."

Ameen is anxious. She is late. A black four by four draws up. "Ali Ameen?"

"Yes."

"We have a message from Mary." Ameen is suspicious. This isn't part of the plan. "She wants to meet you in town. We'll take you to her."

Ameen starts to move away. Too late. A cosh from behind drops him to the pavement. He is bundled into the car. Thirty minutes later, he wakes to find himself tied to a chair, twine digging into his wrists and ankles. He looks around to see what appears to be a large warehouse. Two large heavyset men are there standing directly behind him. He turns to see a camera on a tripod about six feet from him. Two other men, not quite as imposing as the others, are at each side of the camera. One of the men steps forward and clicks the camera. He can see a small red light indicating it is recording.

The other man steps forward towards him. "Mr Ameen, we are informed of your activities in Glasgow. On behalf of the Glasgow people, we are sending a message to your group that we, the Family, will not tolerate the abuse and assault of young Glasgow girls. Let this be a lesson to you and to it that we are on the streets and we will hunt you down and... remove you."

Paul Moffat moves towards Ameen. The two men behind move too. One of them has a large, long-handled mallet. Ameen looks at him and then the mallet. "Please... no," comes from his mouth, but the "no" is followed immediately by a swhish as the mallet swings from the man's shoulders, taking a long arc towards Ameen's right knee. It makes a 'crack' sound as it collides with the bone of his knee, shattering it into pieces. He screams and sobs with the pain just as he sees the mallet, almost in one movement, arc through the air again with a whoosh and another 'crack' as it collides with his left knee. This time not only does the bone shatter, but the leg bends under the chair in a gruesome way. The weight of the swing nearly takes his leg off. Ameen is delirious by this time, hoping he would pass out with the pain, but no. Moffat moves forward and grasps Ameen's hair, pulling his head back, then takes a knife down the right side of Ameen's face and then the left. The blood spills onto the floor. Ameen knows he is a whisker away from death. "Please, please, it won't happen again."

"No, it won't." Moffat moves to Ameen's side to be in the frame of the video. "Please understand this; this man is only an example, and there will be more. Throughout the city, your players are suffering the same fate. Before the night is out, twenty of your men will find it very difficult to walk again and with two lines down their faces will be forever known as the men who abuse the young girls of Glasgow. So be warned, this is only the start. Leave Glasgow or you, the senior members of your group, will suffer similar fates. Next time we will take your heads." 'Click', the video is complete, to be sent by courier to the BBC at Pacific Quay.

The rain hammers off the car as Jackie arrives in my drive. John is there with an umbrella to keep her dry and to assist her into the house. I am at the door to receive her. "Jackie, please come in, a bloody awful evening."

"Shitty, I would say, Rooney."

"Aye, as you say; this is an unexpected surprise." I take her coat and hat and pass them to John. James goes out to check the gate and locks the door on the way back in.

She shakes her hair free. "What are you up to, Rooney?"

"You came onto me, Jackie."

"I didn't mean that. I was –"

"Drunk?"

"What are you doing?"

"I am not –"

"Don't insult my intelligence."

"No, you're right. We were being… proactive."

"Proactive, Rooney? I would say. The story is on BBC Scotland, a Horizon programme coming up. Look at this." She pulls the *Evening Times* from her bag. "The Glasgow mob have become vigilantes. The Family exacts justice on a rogue gang of rapists. Where was Police Scotland? Yes, I would say that was proactive, Rooney."

"We… had to take action."

"Oh, action? The mob cripple and rip twenty guys –"

"It was in our interests to control this… threat."

"You had no right, Rooney. You and your… Family have

overstepped the mark. Do you understand me? You, the Family, have gone too far."

"God's work has been done, Jackie. Now we can all get back to our... normal activity."

"It's not what we, you, or your fucking God, do, Rooney. Not in my patch."

"We were helping the community."

"The community! Give me a break. This is a show of strength. You said it yourself. The influx of external gangs moving into Glasgow. You decided to act. This is a message to all of them that the Family rule here. Well, you fucking well don't. We, Police Scotland, rule here, and you haven't heard the last of this." She sits and controls her breath and her temper, wondering whether to leave there and then.

"I guess the civic gratitude will have to wait."

"Guess so, you, you –"

"Jackie." I stop her short and reach for her. She doesn't pull away. Her eyes soften, almost to tears. I take her head in my hands and kiss her squarely on the lips.

She relaxes into my arms. "You, you bastard, Rooney."

I lift her off her feet and carry her to the bedroom where I despatch her onto the bed. "My darling, we are together in God." I remove her clothes. "I will deify you."

"Just do it, Rooney. But please, I am not... healed."

"God will heal you."

I reach for water, blessed at Lourdes, and sprinkle her pale body with it. "I bless and purify you, and pray for your miraculous recovery."

She pulls me to her. "Shut up, Rooney."

CHAPTER FIFTEEN

I take my seat in the BBC studios. Jackie arrives and sits next to me. She refuses to acknowledge my presence, staring in the opposite direction.

Mark Stevens takes his seat. He is anchor of this, the BBC2's *Rough Justice*, a current affairs programme. He turns to Jackie; then, before he has a chance to say anything, he realises he is on air.

"Good evening. We are here tonight to discuss the growth of what is being described colloquially as 'vigilante activity'. Our guests are Ms Jacqueline Kaminski, Assistant Chief Constable, organised crime and counter terrorism and safe communities. Welcome Jacqueline, quite a mouthful."

"Yes, indeed. Jackie'll do."

"Sorry, Jackie. We also have, interestingly, Mr Sean Rooney, who is the... representative of a group called the Family, as some people are calling it. Welcome, Mr Rooney."

"Sean."

"Sean, thank you. OK, to start, can I ask you, Sean... for the benefit of those, let me say, unfamiliar with the Family, to describe it?"

In my previous life as a forensic psychologist, I had appeared on TV and I know not to engage the camera, to relax and concentrate on a crisp, clear, and short answer. "People call our... collective many things." I loosen my tie. "We are businessmen, and yes, I represent them."

"Some say you lead them," Stevens says. "A kind of godfather figure, the Father... Some people say you —"

Jackie interrupts. "Some people say a lot of things." She pauses. "I need some water. Do you have any water?"

"Could you please get Ms Kaminski some water," Stevens asks. Jackie fills her glass from a pitcher and downs the glass in one gulp. "Can I ask you, Mr Rooney," he says, returning his concentration to me, "the attacks on the Asian gangs, can you confirm this was *the*, your, Family?"

I refuse to fall into this trap. "As I say, we are business people."

"In the business of crippling rapists?"

"We support the Christian and Muslim communities and we do not condone rape."

"Indeed, Sean." Stevens turns to Jackie, who is filling a third glass of water. She dips a hankie in it and mops her sweating brow and neck. "Ms Kaminski, as Assistant Chief Constable, organised crime, etcetera, were you pleased the bad guys were... punished?"

"They were about to be... apprehended. There was an investiga _"

"But were you pleased?"

"*We* were about to mount an operation."

"But the Family beat you to it." Looking increasingly uncomfortable, she doesn't answer, wringing her hands up over her chest. Turning to me, Stevens says, "Mr Rooney, sorry, Sean. It is said the Family is now stronger than Police Scotland."

I look to Jackie. "What the fuck is going on here?" she says, getting to her feet. "I agreed to appear on this programme to have a balanced discussion over the kidnapping of our officer, John McCourt, not to sit here and hear Police Scotland being referred to in this way." She pulls out her mic. "That's it, I won't take part in this... interview anymore."

"My apologies, Ms Kaminski," Stevens says. "Of course, I will come to PC McCourt's kidnapping in due course. Please, could you take your seat?" At that, Jackie storms out of the studio. "Miss Kaminski has been called away to urgent police business," he says to the camera, then, turning to me, "Sean, I am sorry. Are you happy to continue?"

"Yes, go on."

"Sean," Stevens says, "There is a lot of... talk going on, you know, in pubs, in homes, on social media, on the streets across Glasgow. People are saying only the Family could have... tackled this gang."

"Some men were injured."

"Some people are saying that it was good, that it needed doing. It saved a lot of young girls and stopped the bad guys."

"My... people, adhere to the laws of God, Mr Stevens."

"Whose laws, Mr Rooney?"

"We cooperate with the police."

"They say you apply 'God's law', that you are a –"

"I apply the law which is just."

"So I hear, anyway, we are not here to vilify the Family. Indeed, the people are holding you guys in high regard."

"We will do what we can for the brethren of Glasgow."

"I am sure you will, Sean, or should I say Father?"

"You can say what you will, but it doesn't confirm anything. I merely... facilitate."

"Thank you, Sean." Stevens realises that's as much as he is going to get from me. "We appreciate you appearing on our show today."

"Thank you."

Then, just as I'm taking off my mic. "Oh one more small thing, Sean. Can I ask?" I anticipate this. "Why did a good man, a forensic psychologist decide to become head of the country's biggest crime syndicate?"

I study him for a minute before answering. "It's a greater vocation." I remove my mic.

"You are an interesting man, Sean. I think we will be hearing more about you."

"God willing, Mr Stevens." I head off the set.

"Indeed, Mr Rooney, God willing."

I leave the BBC studios, onto Pacific Quay and into the visitors' car park, feeling pleased I had made an impact.

God's message delivered?

"I spoke his words."

John appears in the car to collect me, opening the door from the inside. However, just as I'm about to enter the car, Jackie appears from between the cars. "Remember me, Mr Father?" I indicate to John and James to remain in the car.

"Jackie, I –"

"Aye, me, who did you think, an ISIS solider out to cut your throat? Chance'll be a fine thing."

"Jackie, I didn't expect it to go –"

"The way you expected. What fucking game are you playing?"

"You know the way these things go."

"You won't fuck me, Rooney, publically or... privately. Jesus!"

"I think I should go. I have a busy –"

"Schedule of TV appearances, eh?"

"Lots of people seem to want to talk to me."

"I'll tell you why."

"Go on."

She comes close enough to stab my chest with a seriously sharp manicured forefinger. "You're riding on a wave of public interest. The mob is acting as… vigilantes. What were the police doing? What is the police doing?"

"What are you doing, Jackie? Calm down."

"Don't you fucking tell me to calm down. I know what you are doing and it'll not work. You got that?"

"Yes, Jackie."

"And, you are playing me like a rag fucking puppet. You know I'm –"

"Vulnerable?"

"You know what I mean. My job is on the rack here. I need to find McCourt. I need this, Rooney, and you said you would help me."

"Of course, I will."

She starts to sob. "Well fucking help me then." She turns to walk away, but trips on her stick, falling to the tarmac. I reach out to help her. "Don't, Rooney, not this time." She gets on her knees. "No blessing me this time, not like on Sauchiehall Street."

"I just wanted to –"

"Rooney, I can manage." She struggles to her feet. "I'm fine, thanks."

"Jackie?"

"Don't. I know what you're thinking. No, I haven't been using. I just… tripped."

"I just wanted to say, I –"

"Don't again, Rooney. Just call me a taxi."

"I'll drop you."

"A taxi, Rooney. I wouldn't want to be seen on TV in a Family car, with three… criminals."

"Thanks for seeing me, Jean." I invite her in. "Six on the dot. Can I take your jacket?" She passes me a long black coat, revealing a black satin dress underneath. "Cold out, winter coming in."

"Rooney, *you* are seeing *me*. Rooney's cathedral, they say. My office not good enough for you?"

"I was seeking some privacy, Jean. Your offices, don't quite feel quite right."

Careful, son.

"I wanted to see you too, Rooney." I invite her to take a seat at my dining table, bedecked with religious artefacts, a crucifix in the middle of it. "But no prayers, Rooney, please?"

"That comes after." I smile and take up a seat at the other end of the table. "Only joking, Jean. Don't worry, this meeting is more practical in nature."

"Oh." She moves round the table towards me. Becoming a bit of a habit, I think. "Not personal, Rooney. Don't you do personal?" She leans over the table showing ample cleavage from a split down her dress that goes all the way to her waist.

After your cock, Rooney.

"Personal, Jean?" I create some space between us.

"How can I help you? You invited me over here."

"I need information."

"*You* need information?"

She moves close again. Her perfume is making my head swim. I move farther along the table.

"The Albanians are harming our business."

She pulls herself up to sit on the edge of the dining table. "You are out of your league, Rooney."

"Let me, us, worry about that."

She tilts her head and looks at me quizzically. "I can't provide that kind of information, not just like that Rooney."

"OK, Jean. We'll let them build an empire and the kind of army even the SCDEA, MI5 and Police Scotland won't be able to control."

She opens her legs, provocatively; not by much, but enough to confirm to me what she intends. "I mean, not quite like that. You know how I work."

She'll eat you alive.

"And how do you work?"

"I fuck you, you fuck me, I get you the information."

"Just like that, Jean. What about your... ethics?"

"Fuck that; gave up on ethics a long time ago, gets you nowhere in my business."

"Seduction, foreplay, taking things slowly?"

"Fuck that, as well. I won't beg you." She stands up and straightens her clothes. "Anyway not here. I wouldn't fuck in a church."

"Did you marry… in a church?"

"What?"

Jesus, now I have to explain. "Martin and you?"

"Martin understands; he has to."

"You shall not covet your neighbour's wife. Deuteronomy 5:21."

"What if your neighbour doesn't mind his wife being… coveted, Rooney?"

"He is OK about you –"

"He actively encourages it, Rooney."

"I suppose it is OK, then."

"No, it's not a sin, Rooney. I'll arrange something." With that, she leaves, leaving only the faint smell of perfume to inhabit her place at the table and the room. I look to the Ascension for guidance, but I know I'll receive a file by courier the next day.

James shows Bill Bingham in as I finish my prayers.

"Sorry for keeping you waiting, Bill. I was –"

"You don't need to explain to me, Rooney. I need to talk to you."

I invite him to sit down. "I'm happy to see you, Bill. However, is it something we can discuss in a Family meeting?"

"I need to talk to you, in private." He looks at James. "I believe you hold private consultations here."

"I can see more people that way." I nod towards James to leave the room. "What's wrong Bill?"

"The Asian gang, don't remember that being agreed?"

"I authorised it."

"Rooney!"

"I had to take early and affirmative action. I hold a mandate on behalf of you all."

He looks at me. There's no dissension. I knew he would have no truck with a gang of outsiders coming in and raping Glasgow girls. Traditional gangs always had a 'policing role' over such activities in the tenement and scheme areas. I was confident they would applaud my action. He holds his look long enough to say "Don't get above yourself."

It is clear I can now act… unilaterally.

Power corrupts?

There's a pause indicating we had moved on.

"The Albanian bastards, they're moving in big style."

"I know, they intend controlling the drug trade."

"We need to fuck them."

"I am… monitoring them."

"They're mafia, Rooney, mafia *shqiptare*, fucking violent Albanian mafia bastards. They've taken over the sex trade in Soho. Now they're here."

"Prostitution, trafficking, arms, drugs?"

"This is our turf, Rooney."

"They came in as asylum seekers initially, then –"

"They've crossed a line."

"Let them have their pubs, restaurants, security; all within limits of course."

"They're selling drugs in the city centre, Rooney. We're in the city-fucking-centre!"

"I know, Bill. I'll get you some tea, relax." I try to manage his rising exasperation.

"Look, they're smuggling hundreds of pounds of heroin into the city every year. They've gone through Europe, London, and now they are here. And they say they'll shoot any cunt who tries to stop them. They *will* attack us."

"They are planning to attack our street players on all fronts: taxis, clubs, hotels, casinos. They intend sending out a message that they have arrived in Glasgow and are in control."

"And where did you get that from, Rooney?"

"A source, a wee bird."

"A wee burd? Don't tell me, Jackie or Jean? What other wee burds do you know?" I say nothing. "Can we fuck them, and I mean the Albanians?"

"I know what you mean, Bill. We have to respond… appropriately."

"If we don't, they'll take over. They *will* fucking dominate us."

I get up and wander around the room. This man has natural power, he exudes it, and he doesn't need my permission to hit the Albanians. The fact he has come to me means respect. I can't undermine this.

"You're right, Bill. We need to stop them in their tracks."

"Thank fuck, Rooney. I thought you might disagree, you being a holy wullie and all."

I smile. "But, they're organised; you hit their soldiers, they'll bring in more; you hit their bosses, they'll send up more; like a flat worm, they'll grow new heads."

He looks on curiously. I half expect him to say, "Let's just fuck them and see." I call upon Johnston's tactics. "We need to understand them, their strengths, weaknesses, vulnerability."

"I like it, Rooney. They're stupid and that's their weakness. I've been over there for guns. They don't know the difference between violence and bravery. They are stupid, but dangerous cunts."

"Stupid *is* vulnerability."

"They'll kill for two hundred quid, they are not afraid of it, they fear no one."

"How do they compare with the Italian Mafia?"

He moves closer to me. Close enough for me to see into his eyes. I can see he fears no one. "They say if you want a hundred Italians to be quiet, shoot one. If you want a hundred Albanians to be quiet, you shoot ninety-nine."

"Are you suggesting we shoot 99 percent of them?"

"Something like that."

"Not sure if I like that, Bill, but we do need to know where they operate, where they relax, where they keep their money, where they keep their families."

"Done, happy to do that."

"I'll be doing some… research of my own."

"We'll need the Family, they are one big fucking concern."

"We'll raise it."

"And then we will do them."

"We'll see."

"I suppose God'll guide us." He points to a picture of the Ascension.

"He will, and we'll send a clear statement to their leaders in Tirana. Leave Glasgow; this is not a place to live nor thrive."

"Or in common every day Glasgow parlance, Rooney, 'Get the fuck out of Glesca, this is not a place to have your babies, because we will fucking boil them up and eat them with chips and curry sauce.'"

"Right, Bill."

CHAPTER SIXTEEN

Jackie returns to her office in French Street, just as Baird arrives to place a blood stained notepad sheet contained in an A4 poly-pocket on her desk.

He reads it aloud. "The soldiers of the caliphate will kill the infidel soldier in nine days unless our demands are met."

"Another finger?"

Baird nods. "To the medics?"

"Forensics first, Euan, then the medics. How was it delivered?"

"A junkie. Twenty pounds to hand it in. He got it from another junkie. We're trying to trace him."

"Forget it, it's pass the parcel time."

"Ma'am, SGoRR has been activated." He hands her a memo. "A three-line whip email from the Chief, ma'am. SGoRR. 3.00 p.m., today."

"Great, bring the car round at two." Since McCourt's abduction, all personal cars were to be parked in the internal car park.

Jackie arrives at SGoRR, coordination facility of the Scottish Government, activated in cases of national emergency or crisis. Jackie takes her seat to the right of Hubert, indicated by a place card. She smiles nervously at him. She gives scant attention to Martin Millar, sitting to her right.

Alasdair Charlton, Justice Secretary, convenes and opens the meeting. "We are here to discuss the kidnapping of PC McCourt by ISIS in Glasgow. Before we begin, the First Minister has conveyed his position – it is this." He pauses and takes some water and reads from a prepared statement. "John Maclean says, 'The Scottish Government and I as First Minister will not bow to the threats of terrorism; to do so would open the door to terrorist threat across the land, which would put all our forces and the general public at incalculable risk.' This is the Scottish Government's position." Charlton awaits the inevitable hiatus, not expecting a response, before turning to Hubert. "So PC McCourt, Chief, your officer."

Hubert replies. "Yes, Justice Secretary, we have identified the man in the video as Al-Jamal Saddam Al-Jamal. He was a once a Free Syrian Army commander."

"Now with ISIS," Charlton adds.

DCC Cher comes in. "He has announced his repentance for membership in the battalion and the FSA, dubbing them apostates."

"Pledged allegiance to ISIS and is now one of their fighters," Hubert adds.

Cher continues. "They have designated Al-Jamal as a commander."

"Can I ask, ma'am, how did he get in here?" Jackie asks.

"*That*, we need to establish," Hubert says.

"We have to do everything in our power to save McCourt, Ms Kaminski," Charlton says.

"With respect, cabinet secretary," Hubert says, "we should deal with this."

"We understand your concerns, Chief," Charlton says, "and your ability to manage the situation locally, but this has implications for the UK in general and our parliament specifically. It implicates the First Minister." Hubert does not respond as he observes the nods around the table from the cabal of Cabinet Secretaries. "Ms Kaminski, an update please?"

"Yes, sir." Jackie attempts unsuccessfully to open a bottle of spring water. Hubert takes it from her and opens it, pouring a glass and passing it to her. "Thank you." She turns to Charlton. "We believe he's held by an ISIS cell in the Glasgow area, most probably in the city somewhere. The statement giving their terms was delivered yesterday, along with... the first finger." She stops. "McCourt's finger, Cabinet Secretary."

"Indeed, Ms Kaminski."

"And the second arrived today."

There's a deathly silence around the table.

"The... bastards."

"Indeed, sir. We now have eight days to accede to their demands."

"And eight fingers. But we don't... accede to terrorist demands, DCC Kaminski. You know our policy on this."

"Then they will kill him."

"Remind us please, ACC, the demands?"

"They're not specific, sir. Simply, they wish to talk to the First Minister. We believe they will make their demands known then."

"Free prisoners, leave Syria and Iraq alone to develop their state, give the Palestinians a homeland, desist in supporting Israel, etcetera, etcetera, no doubt," Hubert says.

"We can only speculate, Chief. Continue, Ms Kaminski."

"Thank you, though there is not much more to say, apart from…"

"Yes, Ms Kaminski?"

"They *do* intend to kill McCourt. The fingers are to confirm their resolve."

Millar realises it is time to get into the discussion. "*We* need to stop them."

"OK, this is now Operation Save McCourt," Charlton says. "This is the emphasis and our plan is this. A, we do, you do, everything in your powers to find McCourt and bring this group to book. Anything, resources, whatever you need in this task, will be provided, anything. B, the Scottish and UK Governments and intelligence agencies will do everything possible to… inform the operation and apply diplomatic and strategic pressure to have McCourt released. Thank you, ladies and gentlemen." With that, Charlton and the other Cabinet Secretaries gather their papers and get up and leave. The meeting is over.

"What are you doing with the fingers, Jackie?" Hubert asks.

"Deep freeze, the medics hope to reattach them, should we –"

"Should, Jackie? When we… find him."

"When, Dad, when."

"Let's travel back together, Jackie. My driver will go back with Baird. We need to talk."

"Yes, dad, sorry, Chief, that'd be good."

Hubert and Jackie travel along the M8 heading back to Glasgow. He drives. For most of the way, there is a peaceful joint contemplation. It's for Hubert to talk first, as always.

"Jackie, where is the… Family in this?"

Jackie understands this is not 'their family', but *the* Family. She resists the urges to use this as an opener to *their* family. "I have asked for their support, Dad."

"I'd do more than ask, Jackie." Jackie knows her father: he doesn't ask and his demands are generally backed up with action.

"Just tell Rooney that I'll kick the shit out of him if he doesn't cooperate."

"OK, Dad, I'll tell him."

"And you *will* liaise with Dempsie and MI5."

"I will."

"Good, come for dinner on Sunday, Mother is doing a roast."

The sound of 'mother' makes her feel sick. Hubert had left her own mother for this 'mother', Deirdre Hamilton-Brown, something for which Jackie had never forgiven him.

"I'll see, Dad, a lot going on just now, you know."

"Aye, I know." He knows Jackie never visits anymore. He feels he has to ask, however; but there's more to his need for some private time with her. "Jackie?"

"Yes, Dad."

"People are noticing."

"Noticing what?"

"They are… saying you are not yourself, since your injuries."

"Well, I'll never be without this." She pats her stick. "And these." She pulls out a blister pack of painkillers. "And this." She pulls out her Rizla Tin and opens it. Hubert immediately gets the waft of cannabis.

"Jesus, Jackie, you're in the Chief Constable's car."

"I know and I am the Chief Constable's daughter. What's wrong, your new wife disapprove? You used to use it."

"In the past, Jackie, you know that. Now put it away."

She puts the tin away, reluctantly.

"I know you're struggling, Jackie, suffering because of your injuries. But, there's more, and you know what I am going to say."

"I do?"

"I think you do."

"Tell me?"

"Your smoking, drinking, you're on edge."

She delays her response. "My smoking is fine, my drinking is in proportion. I am on edge, sure. Wouldn't you be, with what I have had to deal with?"

"It comes with the turf, Jackie. It's what you bought into. What you wanted." She feels a lecture on the reality of the job coming so she stays quiet. "Rooney, Jackie?"

"Yes, he's gone too far."

"He did us a favour."

"A favour?"

"He did nothing I wouldn't have done myself. They were raping young women."

"He, they, went too far."

"Interesting times, Jackie. In my day, we fought the mob head on, face to face, physically, and there could only be one winner. In your day, the mob fight for us, with us. This is no bad thing."

"And what do we do with the criticism, and the… approval of them from the streets? Police Scotland is not doing its job? They are –"

"We roll with it."

"We roll with it, great. That will instil public confidence?"

"We will say it was, is a… joint operation."

"Joint operation. The mob doing our dirty work."

"The public will accept that."

"Well, I won't, Dad. I can't have Rooney –"

"Rooney, Jackie. Is this about Rooney or the Family?"

"Both."

"Right, get this, darlin'." He turns to face her, with one eye on the road. "No innocent person was killed. It was a successful operation. Our position is there was full cooperation between us. Official. Us, and the Family's, unofficial, forces. That's it. And Jackie?"

"Yes?"

"Be there on Sunday. A roast."

"Bingham" appears on my mobile. I pick up. "Bill?"

"Rooney, I need to talk to you, safe like."

"St Simons, Partick, be there in an hour."

"Jesus, Rooney. This place gives me the creeps." Bingham slides in beside me on the front pew. "If my orange pals find out about this, my tea's oot."

"There's a side door out to the back road. You wanted to talk to me."

"Aye, one of our prossies agreed to mole into the Albanian setup."

"Oh." I indicate to him to keep his voice down.

"She was about to be sex trafficked and we got her out just in time. She says their base is a multiple occupancy in Maxwell Road."

"I know."

"Oh, the wee burd, Rooney."

"Tell me, what more do you know?"

"Lekë Zaharia, an Albanian businessman, groomed her and shared her with his compatriots. She said she was about to be sent to Paris to work in an Albanian sex club. They were feeding her heroin, but she managed to text us and we got her out."

"Maxwell Road. There's about forty soldiers there."

"We can deal with that."

"What do you want to do?"

"We go in and shoot the bastards, no quarter."

"Bill, we are in God's house."

"Well, what do you suggest, in God's house?"

I take a minute to remind myself of my research via Google. "The Albanians had a yellow house, a bloody yellow house, so called. We will have a red house. We will have a red sandstone tenement dripping with blood. The blood of Jesus will redeem us." I look up at Jesus on the cross.

"Rooney, you really are sick."

"It was the house the Albanian Mafia used to remove the internal organs of prisoners in the war in Kosovo. Then they trafficked them for big money, all over the world."

"I think I am following your thinking. God, you are weird."

"He moves in mysterious ways."

"Aye, suppose he does." Bingham looks up at the altar. "You papes really are mental."

"In knowing them, we defeat them. We will give them a taste of their own... medicine. God's justice will be upon them."

"And we... I nearly said 'fuck' there."

"The Lord's sword will be bathed in blood." I too look towards the altar.

"Right, Rooney, leave it to me. I'll deliver it. Now, I'm out of here."

I stay to pray for the success of God's battles ahead. I stand up to look upon Jesus's all-guiding face. I bow my head as I call upon the prayer of General George Patton in France, in December 1944, before the Battle of the Bulge. "God, graciously hearken to us as soldiers who call upon thee that, armed with Thy power, we may advance from victory to victory, and crush the oppression and wickedness of our enemies, and establish Thy justice among men and nations. Amen."

PC Stephen Hughes and WPC Alice Spence move gingerly towards the tenement door. "Check out 10 Maxwell Road, reported disturbance. A 'domestic' it was said." On previous occasions, they had been called to this address after neighbours reported loud music from the flats. They knew this house as multiple occupancy, ten to a flat, where suspected migrant workers were paying exorbitant rents to unscrupulous landlords. Neighbours had reported a succession of women coming and going. The Police suspected prostitution and drugs, but had no real evidence. Organised Crime and Counter Terrorism (OCCT) was about to mount a search; however, any information from the uniformed officers would help. Hughes and Spence approach the controlled access at the close entrance. It's nearly evening and getting dim, but something doesn't square. The door is slightly open; normally it would be solidly locked and only opened after a number of buzzes. Should he call in support? *Christ, this is his patch*, he reminds himself. He knew everyone in this area, but this house was always known to be strange. "Police Scotland," he calls, entering the close. Spence follows him in. A clinical smell takes him by surprise, completely contrary to the stench that normally comes from this place. "Ndihmë! Ndihmë," comes from an open door of the first flat on the ground floor. Cautiously they move into the flat to be confronted by a sight they will never forget and one they will never see again. As they move into the living space, a bizarre scene enfolds. Laid out in two neat rows are four hospital beds holding four men, each covered in bloodstained hospital sheets, drips fed into arms and each man strapped into the beds; not that these men needed restrained, they were heavily sedated.

"Call in, Alice: back up and paramedics," Hughes says, as he moves up the stairs to find similar scenes in each flat, then on a bloodstained wall a daubed message, 'Welcome to The Red Hoose', is clear for all to see.

"Cost effective, Jackie. The mobs fighting the mobs." Jean barges into Jackie's office, whips off her jacket, and drops heavily into a seat.

"Aye, very good, Jean. Excuse me while I get my calculator out." Jackie delves into her drawer. "Please have a seat, why don't you, this shouldn't take long." Jean stretches her arms upwards showing well-honed muscles. "Let's see," Jackie says, tapping her calculator. "Police response, fifty grand; NHS response, fifty grand…"

Jean coughs into a hankie. "An inestimable cost of policing these bastards, taking them through the courts, twenty-four-hour care in custody, resettlement programmes; oh, and what about the victims, the families, *and* the communities?"

"Police Scotland cannot condone acts of violence in Glasgow. Whether it be criminal or… benevolent actions."

"What *are* you doing, Jackie?"

"*We* are making enquiries and *we* will be arresting those responsible."

"The Family hit a gang of groomers and rapists *and* the Albanian Mafia."

"Oh, and that makes it OK."

"Successful military level operations, Jackie. Better get these guys signed up. I can see it now: 'Private SWAT teams augment local forces. The private and public sector come together to fight new wave of organised crime in Glasgow.' Catchy that. As I see it, no bad thing."

"As you see it, Ms MI5. As you see it. As I see it, the Glasgow mobs have moved way out of their fucking comfort zones. What the fuck are we saying here?"

Jean gets to her feet and makes a few air punches. "It's good to be fit, isn't it, Jackie?"

"If you say so, Digger Dempsie." Jackie looks down at her damaged leg.

"Jackie, let's be sensible about this. These were bad guys –"

"Bad guys hitting bad guys, and this is OK?"

Jean throws more air punches. "Bad guys hitting bad guys who export rape, drugs, sex trafficking; groom our young women. They got what was coming to them. The bad guys have been punished."

"We, us. *We* do the punishing, Jean, not the Family."

Jean gestures an invitation to fight. "Come ahead –"

"Shut it, act like MI5 might expect of you."

"Jackie, lighten up. Glasgow is no longer a comfortable place for international gangsters moving in. They'll get fucked."

"No, but it is OK for those here already? And where was… intelligence with this, Jean?"

"We had a watching brief."

"You didn't watch very fucking well, did you?"

"And what did you do, Jackie?"

"What we can't do is allow mob rule in Glasgow. They would take over."

Jean starts to pace the office floor, side to side. "The mob saved your arse, Jackie. They saved your job. The end justified the means."

Jackie grabs her stick and gets to her feet. "Oh. The spooks condone killing by bad men. Nothing new there."

"We work in the public interest." Jean crashes back onto the chair, putting her hands behind her head, flexing her arm muscles.

"Oh aye, indeed." Jackie rounds the desk towards her. "From covert *political* operations to ensuring certain threats to the state disappear, should this be required. No arrest, no charge, no court case to mess up your objectives. Just rub the fuckers out. MI5 has a rich history in that."

"No one was killed here, Jackie; and a solid message was sent out."

"Oh aye. Legs broken, faces marked, fucking kidneys removed, some message that."

"All done carefully, surgically."

"Mallets, razors?"

"Scalpels."

"Why the bloody kidneys?"

"Read the report, Jackie. A shipment of 'animal foodstuffs' destined for 'Albanian Mafia, Tirana' was opened by Port Health Authorities at Glasgow Airport. In the crate were forty-two kidneys. An A4 sheet says 'A gift from the Twelve to the Fifteen. Next time we send the rest of the bodies.' Absolutely fucking dramatic, Jackie. Kafkaesque. Wonderful!"

"The… rest we found in the Red Hoose, Jean. The walls of the tenement were smeared in their fucking blood. These are fucking psychopaths. What are we dealing with here?"

"Just the Family fucking bad guys, Jackie, that's all."

"That's what Police Scotland do, what I'm supposed to do."

"Fucking bad guys? You would have a problem fucking good guys?"

"I would manage."

A pause confirms both of their thoughts.

"You'd manage, Jackie? From what I hear you're struggling to manage on that score."

Jackie looks into Jean's eyes; what did she know about her disability, her difficulties?

"I…" Jackie struggles with the words. "I don't know what to say. That is completely –"

"Below the belt?"

"Inappropriate, unprofessional, fucking rude, warranting a good whack with my stick? Take your pick, Jean."

"Guess, it's hard for a… disabled woman, Jackie, you know, meeting the demands of a man."

"Won't be hard for you, Jean, from what I hear."

"We all have our needs, Jackie."

"Aye, we have. And your need is for… control."

"Control?"

"This is about Rooney, Jean; why don't you admit it?"

"And, *this* is about you and Rooney, Jackie."

"Oh?"

"You are not doing *this* for Police Scotland, nor for the public, Jackie."

"Sorry?"

"You think he is undermining you, your position. He is a big threat to you."

"And he is a big… need for you."

Jean moves closer to Jackie, who can see how much of a cougar she could be. "When I want Rooney, I'll have him, fully, completely, satisfactorily. When he has you, he'll have you partially, unsatisfactorily, dispassionately."

"I can…"

"Jackie, you know he has needs and… particular demands that need to be met."

Both know what Jean means. Jackie knows Jean can and will pursue this, and she knows she can't compete, not in the sex stakes; but maybe in other ways…

"Rooney is –"

"My ex-husband, my love, my crutch, my –"

"He's –"

"Doing your job, your job."

"And your job?"

"I can cope with that if it brings results."

"Well, I fucking can't."

"Stole your thunder, darlin'?"

"What?" Jackie is now hovering over Jean.

"Your turf." Jean stands up to face Jackie. "A big achievement lost. You had a chance to act, to consolidate your position; your... standing in the eyes of the public is affected, i.e. to protect Glasgow girls, prevent mob incursion."

"Organised crime and counter terrorism *is* my fucking brief, Jean, i-fucking-e, *my* fucking responsibility." Jackie's launch carries a serious amount of spit in Jean's direction.

Jean takes a hankie from her pocket and wipes her face. "Jackie, you are becoming, no you are, seriously neurotic."

"Fuck off, bitch, you and your fucking MI-fucking-5." Jackie moves back to her chair at the other end of the desk.

"Jackie." Jean also sits down. "I have to say this, but your... behaviour is becoming apparent."

"What?"

"Are you OK, Jackie? I mean seriously OK? These days, you seem overly –"

"I am seriously fucking angry, Ms MI5, you can see that." Jackie becomes aware of Jean studying her. "And don't you be thinking that I'm using anything."

"Jackie, are you saying to me you are?"

"I am saying nothing of the sort. I'm not using... not. I'm just upset." Jackie's tears dislodge her mascara, creating black tributaries down her face.

"You have to get yourself together, Jackie. This is not a way to act. There are greater threats in Glasgow than the Family."

"Just go, Jean, go."

Jean leans over the desk and holds out her hankie towards Jackie. "Here, take this, wipe your eyes, don't let your public see you like this."

Jackie refuses it. "Fuck off. Euan!" she calls.

"Yes, ma'am?" Baird says, arriving.

"Get this... thing out of my office."

Jean grabs her jacket and has one last swipe at Jackie. "Jackie?"

"What, bitch?"

"You really have problems getting your leg over?"

"Euan?"

Baird grabs Jean's arm.

"Get your hands off me, little boy." She pushes him aside. Although Baird is a fit man, he feels her strength. Jean marches out, slamming the door behind her.

"It's getting bloody, Rooney." Ben leads me to a table in the corner of Tennent's Bar. James and John take up positions at the bar keeping me in clear sight. They are aware of my being at the top of many hit lists in Glasgow. Ben places the drinks on the table: a pint of IPA for Ben and mineral water for me.

Changed days, no vices.

"We will shepherd the weak through the evils brought forth by evil men." I almost gesture to the group of inveterate drinking gamblers watching the racing on one of the multiple screens. "The souls of the wicked shall be purified by blood and sent back to their maker."

Ben shakes his head and takes his seat, looking around for any reaction. "In the name of the Father, and..."

"Shepherds we shall be, for Thee, my Lord, for Thee."

"Straight from the Boondock Saints, my deluded friend."

"We are not saints."

"And we are not all sinners."

"Power hath descended forth from thy hand that our feet may swiftly carry out thy command."

"Was that necessary?"

"*We,* the Family, will act."

"I meant the religious diatribe, Rooney. It's becoming... wearing."

"God's words."

"And you fucking well glorify in them."

"I was given the mandate."

"Who from, God?"

"From his Family."

"So, what's next in your godly campaign?"

The gamblers raise their voices in response to their horses heading for the finishing line.

I do likewise. "We defend our business, our patch, against all ungodly attacks."

I see I've been heard by one of the gamblers, who gestures to the others to move towards the screens on the other side of the bar. My presence among them makes for an uneasy atmosphere, especially since the recent hit on the McGings, only metres away on Ashton Lane.

"OK, Rooney. I do like to drink here… with others, not in an empty bar."

I look around and see the faces square on towards me.

Keep your sermons to yourself. This is not a holy place.

"Doing good in your terms doesn't make you a good man."

A good man bad or a bad man good?

"Who wants to be a good man? A good man doing good things gets nothing. A bad man doing good things gets something."

"A bad man doing bad things gets locked up, Rooney. A good man gets his rewards in heaven."

"Ah well, Ben, a sinner repents and gets more praise than the righteous person who has always done good. What's that about, social worker?"

"Well you are, were, the psychologist, you tell me."

"Better the devil you know?"

"Eh."

"I am the public face of the Family; people feel more comfortable with a face."

Not in here they don't.

"A face of a bad man?"

"A face they trust."

"You are more than a bad man, Rooney. You exploit their fears to build an empire."

"An empire of God."

"I know what you are doing, Rooney. Johnston did the same. Power, Rooney, power."

Power hath descended forth from thy hand.

"Live by the power of God's hand, Ben."

"I live by the power of man, Rooney. And if you are not careful you will die by the same hand."

Ben, surprisingly for him, doesn't reply, but stares at Rooney, like a psychiatrist would a mad man.

Just then a broadcast cuts across the racing on the television screen. "There has been an explosion on Gordon Street, outside Glasgow Central Station. It's thought a car bomb has gone off. Early reports are that there have been casualties. We will update you as information comes in."

Ben gets to his feet and positions himself under the screen. "Hear that, Rooney. Jesus, look at that." He sees a shot of Gordon Street. "A fucking disaster zone."

"Not us, Ben."

"No, not you, Rooney. It doesn't look like the work of God."

I get up. James and John move quickly to my side. We shoulder out through the people pushing in from the street to see the screens.

CHAPTER SEVENTEEN

Mary and her pal Sandra have just left the Horseshoe Bar. It is close to four in the afternoon and it is time to go home. They had been friends since school and had been in there imbibing for three hours after their traditional Saturday shopping trip to Argyle Street and up onto Buchanan Street, to finish in there for their roast beef and potatoes, as they had done for years.

This day is Sandra's sixty-sixth birthday and Mary is celebrating being a grandmother again. Her daughter, also Mary, had a wee daughter, also Mary earlier that week. Mary's are well represented in the Gallagher family. Consequently, they had one or two sherries more than normal. They say their "cheerios" just around the corner from the pub at the bus stop outside Glasgow Central on Hope Street. The 6 or the 6A would take Mary to Drumchapel; Sandra would get off at St George's Cross. They are well sozzled and revelling in discussion over the merits of their bus passes. They'll see each other, same place same time, next Saturday to do it all again. A 6A arrives. They are just about to get on the bus, but just then there is an almighty bang and all the windows shatter, showering them with glass.

"Jesus, you alright, hen?" Mary says to Sandra.

"I can hardly hear you, hen. You?"

"Aye, I'm the same, but OK," Sandra says, brushing shattered glass from her shoulders with her bus pass.

"Everyone stay calm," the driver says, as people are screaming and pushing past them to get off the bus onto the street. Everyone on the bus is well, however, albeit shaken. The bus saved many at the bus stop that day. Mary takes Sandra's arm and they move around the bus.

"Do we really want to go there, hen?" Sandra says.

"We just have to, hen," Mary replies. She knows there's a story here and they like a story; but more than that, she knows her forty years as a nurse in Glasgow Royal Infirmary before she retired will be needed there this day. Sandra's too, given they worked there in the same ward for the same amount of time.

What they encounter would more than make up for a lifetime of stories and a lifetime of nursing, however. People are lying everywhere. The sound from car and shop alarms is deafening. People are holding their ears, deafened by the blast. People are holding each other too, crying, and children are screaming. Some people are moaning, lying prostrate on the street. A car, or bits of a car, is lying on its side, debris all around. Mary and Sandra separate as they find casualties. Mary tends to a woman with a large gash on her head, blood pouring from it. A bandage and compression is needed there to stem the blood. Sandra treats a man who has shards of bone, bits of flesh, and blackened skin for a leg. A tourniquet is needed there. They set to work, underpinned with forty years of experience in Casualty at the GRI. Within minutes, the first responders are on the scene and ambulances fill both ends of Gordon Street.

"I heard it, Euan," Jackie says, entering the briefing room. "Tell me, casualties first."

"Incredible as it may seem, ma'am," Baird says, "no one was killed, but four are in the GRI with life-threatening injuries and two are critical."

"Who are we talking about here?"

"IS have claimed responsibility, but we have a report, Alan Taylor, the Taylors –"

"I know the Taylors."

"Last night he made four late-night phone calls to 999 claiming there were bombs planted at Glasgow Central Station. Taylor had used two SIM cards to make the calls from his mobile phone and was tracked down and arrested before any disruption was caused to commuters. No explosive devices were found after an extensive search of the station by the British Transport Police officers."

"Then today, a car bomb explodes in Gordon Street, just outside the station entrance. Where were our people? Why wasn't I... informed?"

"I tried to reach you ma'am, but you weren't available."

"No, I was... sleeping. I was sound. I'm taking sleeping tablets just now."

"I took an executive decision, ma'am. Things appeared to be

fine, there didn't appear to be any need to cordon off the station or surrounding area."

"No, you were right."

"Then today, this car arrives into the street, a guy gets out, and the bomb goes off; just like that, that quick. We didn't have time to react."

"No. ISIS?"

"We believe so."

"Taylor knew something?"

"More than coincidence, I would say."

"Bring him in."

"Yet again, we are here to discuss matters of national security," Charlton says in SGoRR. "The incident in Glasgow." He casts a glance towards Hubert, Jackie, and Millar, arriving into the room en masse. They had been held up in traffic. Charlton had decided to start.

"Indeed, Justice Secretary." Hubert takes his seat.

"There's more, Chief," Charlton says. Hubert looks to Jackie. She shrugs her shoulders. "Just minutes ago, we received this." Charlton places a bloodied sheet of paper contained in a plastic pocket on the table. "It's as you would expect." The poly-pocket is passed around the table, until it reaches Hubert. "Read it, Chief?"

Hubert lifts the sheet up adjacent to his eyes. Some of the font is covered in blood, but he can make it out. "OK, it says, 'We have redoubled our efforts to confirm our resolve.'" Hubert clears his throat. "'Please find your soldier's third finger. He has seven left and seven days to live. Now, we have bombed your city centre to confirm we can. This was a fifty-pound bomb, a fraction of the size of device we will use the next time. Do you need more persuasion, infidels? Why does your cowardly First Minister hide indoors while his people die on the streets? Why will he not talk to us?' That's it."

"Jackie, an update on the attack, please?" Charlton says.

"Indeed, Justice Secretary." Jackie pulls her notes from her bag and places them on the table, bringing out her glasses.

"Twenty-three casualties," Jackie informs. "Three serious: one lost an eye, one a leg, one an arm. The rest, flesh wounds, burns, cuts, grazes, bruises. We were…lucky."

"Thank you," Charlton says. "Hubert, Save McCourt?"

"Still pursuing leads. Nothing so far. These guys are dug in deep."

"We have to dig deeper, Chief."

"I agree, Justice Secretary."

"This Taylor guy?"

"Not sure," Jackie says. "There was a breakdown with some factions of the Family; the McGings and the Taylors went their own way. The McGings were hit in Ashton Lane. Mick, Davy's son, and some soldiers were killed. Family infighting."

Charlton remains stony-faced. "Why would Taylor call in to say he knew bombs had been planted, then the IS bomb goes off the following day? Doesn't make sense. Any connection there?"

"No idea, Justice Secretary," Jackie says. "We have him in custody and we're questioning him."

"OK, keep us informed. Threat level is now raised to critical, OK?"

"Justice Secretary," Jackie says. Hubert turns to face her, fearing something inappropriate will come. She doesn't disappoint him. "The First Minister?"

"Yes, Jackie?" Charlton asks.

"Why doesn't he meet with them?"

While all gaze at Jackie, Charlton looks to Hubert.

"Thank you, ladies and gentlemen," Charlton says, ending the meeting. "Hubert?" he adds, indicating he should follow him. Jackie makes her way out.

"I'll see you in the car, Jackie," Hubert says to her, pointedly.

After a few minutes, Hubert joins her in the car. "And why would you say that, Jackie, completely out of the blue?"

"It just came out, Dad."

"It just came out!"

"Maybe that's all they want. Then we get McCourt, and that's that."

"Jesus, Jackie, you know better than that. You, of all people, know what these people are capable of."

"I just thought –"

"You just thought nothing, Jackie. Get a grip, darling. This is your first big challenge. Don't mess it up."

"Yes, Dad."

Jackie is shaking like a lamb in the snow and at the same time sweating like a pig in the sun.

"Jackie, you don't look well. What's happening to you, are you ill? Are you –"

"No, I am fucking not, Dad. I know what you are thinking. You think I am using something."

"Jackie?"

"Aye?"

"Shush, get some help, treatment, sleep, whatever."

"OK."

"And Jackie."

"Yes, Dad."

"You have to work with MI5 Glasgow, Jean, on this. Charlton demands it."

Jackie thinks about this. "Yes, Dad."

"Doesn't mean you have to like it, darling, but your career…"

"Depends on it, Dad?"

The Taylors meet in the conference room of the Oran Mor, a large church bar conversion at the top of Byres Road. I have some people there on the staff. I am aware they have much to discuss. I am also aware George Taylor, the father and boss of the Taylors, after our hit on the McGings, has given instructions from Shotts Prison to attack the Family. Alan is now on remand in the Bar-L. The three remaining Taylor brothers, Jim, John and Bob, are there in the Oran Mor. They need to decide who will lead until Alan returns and how to follow their father's orders. The natural brother to lead would be Jim; next to Alan, he is the oldest, but he favours a shared responsibility across the three brothers. Alongside them are around fifteen of their lieutenants. These men lead an army of over 300 soldiers. God knows the Taylors are a formidable team.

"The phone calls?" Jim pours the wine. "What the fuck was Alan up to?"

"Fuck knows," Bob replies. "The only thing I can think of is he's trying to lay the blame on the Family. Seems a good idea."

"Alan's no' daft. There's something else," John says. "Dad wants Mick's death avenged. The McGings would have done the same for us. We have a vendetta with the Family on our hands."

"We are fucked then. We can't fight the Family. Individual teams maybe, but not altogether."

"They're baiting us," says Bob.

"Maxwell Road was one of ours," Jim says. "We need to respond."

"Not yet," John says. "We hold things together until Alan comes back, then we decide."

The brothers advise the lieutenants to instruct the street players to be "extremely careful", and that they would meet again when Alan returns to the fold.

"Fine, to the grub," Bob says. The food arrives into the room on large trays. The waiters and waitresses filter in to serve the hungry men. Plates are placed before them and the trays are placed on the tables to share. Salmon, roast beef, prawns, dishes of coleslaw, chips, and salad. Bottles of red and white are there already. The men dig in. The waiters and waitresses filter back out, leaving the men alone. Then, around ten minutes into their food, there's a knock at the door. Two street players are placed out outside the door for obvious reasons. They will be hungry too. This will be their knock to ensure some is left for them. One enters.

Bob opens the door. "Don't worry guys, there's plenty for you."

"No problem, boss," one outside says. "It's this, this has been delivered." He hands in a large plastic bag with Cicero on the side. The Taylors love Cicero's Ice Cream. They are hesitant, however, and study the bag carefully, casting curious looks around the room. "I've checked it out, boss. It looks OK. Four half litres of double cream vanilla. All the lids were solid on. We opened them, the ice cream's undisturbed. A bag of wafers. It looks OK. A guy with a Cicero ID delivered it. He said "Enjoy, you know your friends." Do you want me to test it?" he laughs.

"Ciceros?" John is already salivating at the thought of his favourite vanilla flavour.

"Fuck sake, Ciceros, boss; down the Byres Road."

All there know there has always been an affinity between the Cicero family from Largs and the Taylors; Southside men who piled down there in numbers for weekends away from the city, as lots of Glasgow patrons did for many years. They tear open the cartons and heap ice cream onto plates.

"Hold on," John says. "Do you think it might be –"

"Poisoned, John?" Jim says. "Don't be fucking daft. This is not Chicago. Ice cream is ice cream and this is Cicero's ice cream."

It is clear their liking of Cicero's ice cream is trumping their fears.

"Right, who's for a wafer?"

Phone call one arrives as I open file one: The Family Agenda. "I need to talk to you, Rooney," Jackie says into her mobile as she prepares her bath.

"Oh?"

"Hold on." I hear a thundering flow slow as a tap is turned off.

"You having a bath, Jackie?"

"I am. It happens."

"Enjoy, you need to relax. What's up?"

"I've been told to lay off, no arrests, no charges on the… Asian gangs' incident."

"The powers that be decide it is best to leave alone, perhaps?"

"Something like that." I hear the whirl of her hoist. "But if you and your… crew so much as piss in the wrong direction we'll come down on you like a ton of your dodgy DVDs."

I expect she's in, the water covering her breasts.

"Business as usual?"

"As usual."

Then as she expects me to say "Good, pleased about that, we have some license going forward," I ask her if she wish I were there.

"You fucker, don't push it."

"Enjoying your bath, Jackie?" She doesn't say she isn't, confirming she is. "I could scrub your back."

"And I could kick your balls."

"Talk soon, Jackie."

Phone call two arrives directly after phone call one, just as I open file two: the Family Constitution. Finding the number engaged, Jean had pressed 5 for ring-back. "Jackie is very annoyed, Rooney," she says, deep in her armchair at home, her mobile snuggled into her shoulder. Martin is preparing dinner in the kitchen.

"Oh." I push the files to the side to make way for my elbows.

"She's angry at you, Rooney."

"Really?"

"Better watch, she'll knock you off your pedestal, your throne, your pulpit."

"She'll do what she'll do."

"Rooney, you can't be a Robin Hood, Rob Roy, or Charles Bronson. It's all been done."

"I'll do what *I* need to do."

"God's work, Rooney?"

"Whatever." I pull my Bible centre desk, to within my sight.

"Not to say we condone what you did with the Asians and the Albanians."

"We did what we had to do."

"They should have been brought to justice, that's why she is annoyed, Rooney."

"We –"

"Fuck it, Rooney, we know. Just to say, you did take affirmative action that removed a threat to the city. We in this service are obliged."

"We…"

"You are not under scrutiny here, Rooney." She turns to receive a glass of red from Martin. "Thank you darling." She accepts it. "We… I want you to do something else… for me."

"For you?"

Jean snuggles into the chair once more. Martin returns to the kitchen.

"For us."

"Us?"

Her voice deepens. I try not to, but I imagine her lips just about touching the mobile, close enough to kiss; her perfume: alluring, provocative, demanding.

"We want you to build a ring of steel around Glasgow. There are many radicalised people in Glasgow. Your hitting IS will create… anger, instability, insurgency, and risk."

"With risk comes excitement, Jean."

"Oh, you pathetic boy, you want to play." Then, when I think she may 'play', "Work first boy, then we play," she says.

"What do you want me to do?"

"We want you to root out the extremists and take them out."

"Is this official?"

"Is anything… official, Rooney?"

"The Family and MI5 working together."

"You and I together… working, boy, then –"

"It's been done before, Jean. Davy McGing."

"You know this?"

"I make it my business to know it."

"Yeah, sure you do." She takes a large slurp of wine. I hear it.

"Enjoying a glass or two?"

She ignores me. "He gave us inside information, numbers and types of guns to Northern Ireland, the makeup of UDA brigades, their key players."

"Risky business."

"It's the biz, Rooney. You pays your money –"

"He… took his chances."

She detects my hesitation. "Don't worry, Rooney, no one is overhearing this call, you can say what you like."

"It caught up with him."

"It did."

"Malky Fraser, open razor, shot to the head, terrible amount of blood I hear."

"We will talk about this, some other time."

"Yes."

"Rooney, we have the power to destroy."

"Jackie?"

"Too far, Rooney, but –"

"But?"

"Work with me, fuck with me, and someday I'll let you into a secret about her."

"You told me she would harm me. I spoke to Davy on that day, that call. Davy hit Jackie."

"Rooney, you triggered the call, that's *our* secret. Jackie never needs to know. Now work against me, and you'll never know the full story. Jackie will always wonder about you. You will always wonder about you, whether you are responsible for your lovely ex-wife's injuries. Play ball and she'll never to need to know about your phone call."

"You are a Machiavellian, devious cow."

"And you are a pathetic boy, who needs to be punished, just like your…"

This is getting dangerous. "Leave it, Jean."

"Alright, child, but if you would like to come over here, I will whip your bollocks like a bad boy."

Time to switch tack. "You will provide us with information, strengthen our position?"

"Indeed, but work against us and we will open the gates of hell."

I get up and move to the window. Now approaching dusk, I can see the twinkle of lights down towards Partick over Hyndland Road, and beyond. This is both an opportunity and a threat. She continues without waiting for my reply.

"However…"

"However?"

"However, we, us, work together, and everything else will take care of itself, that's it."

"Dinner's ready, darling," comes from the back of the phone.

"I need to go. Rooney, there's one more important thing."

"Yes."

"I'm going to have you, you know that. I know what you need." From her volume, this was not meant for only my ears.

"The woman who knows things."

"Got it."

CHAPTER EIGHTEEN

Early next morning, Baird calls. "Good morning Mr Rooney. ACC Kaminski would like to see you in her office, 9 a.m. prompt."

"Jawohl der führer."

I arrive fifteen minutes late, on purpose. Baird shows me in. "What, no… personal setting, Jackie. Your house, your bath, your bed!"

"Sit there, Rooney." She orders me to take to a seat at the side of her desk. "Well, Rooney. Mr fuck the Albanians. Mr fuck the Asian rapists, Mr fucking Fa –"

"Mr fuck the ACC?"

"No deal Rooney, no can do; wish I could, but I can't." She turns to Baird, wondering if he had heard that. "That'll be all Euan, and close the door, thank you." Then, getting on her feet, she turns to me. "Listen Sean, what happened, happened. I would have preferred it hadn't, but it did, but you don't need to broadcast it to the world."

"The way I remember it, you initiated it."

I half expect her to say it was to do with drink, or lust, or something. "What are you doing to help find McCourt?" She keeps it practical.

"We will do what we can."

"Well, I guess your… high profile, aggressive activity will not go down well in the ethnic communities, by way of getting the information we need on McCourt."

"No, well, we have had… much praise from the –"

Her phone buzzes. She picks up. "Yes, Euan. Jesus. Where? Right. Shut the place. Get forensics in. Check everything, especially for poisons."

"Staff canteen?"

"What do you know about the Taylors, Rooney?"

"Quite a lot, you know I do."

"Last night, every one of them was taken to the Western. Food poisoning, seriously ill, critical even. Well, Rooney?"

"Ironic, given George is at Her Majesty's Pleasure, savouring the food there."

"There's something here, Rooney. I know there is. What did you put in it, Rooney, rat poison?"

"I didn't think you were a lover of the Taylors?"

"Alan Taylor made calls the night before the IS bomb. What the fuck is going on?"

"Maybe he knew something."

"What the fuck do you know about them, the Taylors?"

"*You* have Alan Taylor, what do you know, Jackie?"

"We think he was trying to raise the alarm on the Central Station bomb."

"He knew about ISIS?"

"Possibly."

"Links?"

"Maybe he knew something about McCourt, Rooney?"

"Well, why don't you find out, Jackie?"

"What do we have now, Rooney? The Taylors have been hit, Alan Taylor is in custody. Though, with no charges and no indication he has anything to do with the IS bomb, he'll walk soon. What is going on?" I remain stony quiet. "We will make our enquires, and if they point to you and the Family, we *will* make arrests. We will be making an… official visit to your place, you got it, Rooney?" No answer. "You got it, Rooney?"

"God's silence is louder than words, Jackie." I get up and leave.

Almost immediately, Jackie's phone goes again. "I have Ms Dempsie on Line 1," Baird says.

"Fantastic, put her through."

"You've to work with me, Charlton says," Jean growls. "ISIS, McCourt, the bombing, it's all of national importance. This is no longer local, ACC."

"Police Scotland is national, Jean; we *are* fucking national."

"National security, seamless links, cooperation between *all* services."

"You fucking grassed me, didn't you, with Charlton?"

"I have a duty to report on… local relationships."

"You, are a back stabbing bastard. You fucking him: Charlton?"

"Jackie!" The tenor of Jean's voice drops. "Try not to think of this as… personal, it's more serious than that."

"Sure Jean, not personal."

"We will work together, or I'll work around you, over you, but more importantly – and you make sure you understand this – against you."

"Charlton's girl in Glasgow?"

"Jackie, we have a critical threat level. We have Daesh, McCourt, the bombing, and more likely –"

"There's more to come. I fucking well know that."

"Where are we with McCourt?"

"Tight as a drum. And what about you, in the *intelligence* service?"

"Local information. Rooney?"

"He's with the bad guys."

"The bad guys are doing your job."

"Not above the fucking law, Jean, no way."

"They can help find McCourt."

"They can help themselves."

"We are not unhappy about this."

"Just go away, spook!" Jackie slams the phone down.

Baird arrives. "Ma'am, we have just received the fourth finger, PC McCourt."

Jackie puts her head in her hands. "I just knew this day was going to be a humdinger," she says.

"And ma'am, the *Evening Times* called. Matt Hurley is covering it, front page."

"Fantastic, where is it?"

"Forensics' freezer."

"Where was it?"

"In a postbox, next to Churchill's on Great Western Road."

"Christ, I know it."

"It was just sitting there on top of the mail with the usual note. Ma'am?"

"Get some DIs over there."

"Done. Ma'am?"

"Aye?"

"We have a… situation developing… outside."

She goes to the window. "What the…"

"About fifty people, ma'am," Baird says, joining her. "It's Mrs McCourt; the McCourt campaign."

Jackie opens the window slightly to hear, "Save John McCourt, save John McCourt," from a loudhailer directed toward the building.

"Best to keep out of sight, ma'am."

"You're right." She peers from behind the curtain to see the demonstrators. "What are they saying?"

"I can tell you ma'am, I've been out there. They are saying that Police Scotland is doing nothing to save their own. That John Maclean and Police Scotland are scared of ISIS. How many fingers will they take before they take his life? Why won't you act? He is one of your own. Will you let him die? Also –"

"That'll do."

"One more thing, ma'am."

"Oh go on, make my day."

"Jim Taylor just died."

"Guess good things come in threes." She shakes her head and returns to her seat.

"Suspected poison in the ice cream. We talked to Cicero's, the ice cream folk. They said they had no knowledge of any delivery by them to the Oran Mor."

"No, I don't think they have rat poison flavour on their ice cream menu."

"I'll keep you informed, ma'am."

"Aye, thanks Euan."

Jackie phones my mobile. I'm almost home, having picked up some croissants from Churchills.

"Rooney?"

"Yes, Jackie." I take the call as John pulls the car into the car park outside the house. "I had to go, things to do."

"I know, God's work."

"A lot of polis at Churchills, Jackie."

"The fourth finger, in the postbox."

"I'll use Hyndland Road next time."

"Now listen, Jim Taylor's dead. Poisoned."

"So I hear. Radio Scotland's running it."

"A Family hit, Rooney. I know it and you know it. Now, you need to tell me."

I signal to John to exit the car.

"The Taylors were planning a hit on the Family. It was self-protection. George Taylor –"

"George Taylor is in Shotts Prison."

"George Taylor runs his family from there."

"I know that. Why did you keep this quiet from me?"

"You said you would arrest me, Jackie."

"Expect a visit, Rooney."

"I'll put the wine on chill."

"Funny man."

"Jackie, the Taylors and ISIS?"

"The Family is consolidating its power base, Rooney. You know it. I know it. Everyone fucking well knows it."

"The Taylors were gun running with the Albanian mafia. They intended getting together with the Albanians to hammer us."

"You said ISIS."

"ISIS are paying them to protect their Glasgow operation."

"You know this."

"I don't know everything."

"If you are lying to me."

"We have some… information. I need to meet with you."

"Where?"

"The Rio on Hyndland Road."

"I'll see you there in twenty."

Jackie switches off. "Euan," she says, holding the console button.

"Yes, ma'am."

"Arrange a briefing. All the team. We need to make arrests."

"Who, ma'am?"

"I'll think of some people. In two hours. The briefing room at Stewart Street. And Euan."

"Yes, ma'am?"

"Get some undercover officers to the Rio Café on Hyndland Road, in fifteen. They may be needed."

"Yes, ma'am."

I'm in the Rio, ahead of her as she arrives. "Coffee?"

"Please. Latte."

"Tunnock's Caramel Wafer?"

"No, thanks. Well, Rooney?"

I get the coffee. "Shame, best place to get your Tunnock's; also do a whole range of cakes, sweets, wine; not bad for a café bar."

"Rooney?"

"Yes?"

"Shut up." I shut up. "The information… you mentioned. And before you tell me, you really need to know this. I am building a case against you. You are seriously close to waking up in the Bar-L." She checks out the only other couple there. A glance in her direction confirms their plain-clothes police status.

"The Taylors."

"Yes, and ISIS, if this is a red herring, Rooney."

"One of the Albanians talked."

"One of the guys who is now missing a kidney?"

"I am not admitting anything… however."

"However?"

"He was willing to talk."

"As he was having his belly opened?"

"He was willing to talk about their links in Glasgow. It was in our interests to know this."

"Yes, I imagine you would. Tell me."

"He explained that the Taylors were key allies in Glasgow, that they run drug cartels together. They also hold a massive property portfolio in Glasgow, hundreds of flats, multiple occupancy, mostly migrants, DWP benefits. 10 Maxwell Road is one of theirs."

"Indeed."

"They were playing for both sides at the same time. Being part of our collective and part of the Albanian mafia.

"But they dropped out of the Family."

"They knew we were on to them. You'll remember us interviewing George Taylor in London Road police station after the Taylors brought the roof on Lord Owen and the others in the Grosvenor?"

"I remember."

"When the SAS… executed –"

"Took out."

"Took out fifteen of their players."

"Right, we know, they deserved it, now get on with it."

"He hated the Asians, remember?"

"I remember; a confirmed racist, dabbled with the BNP, hated all non-whites, Eastern Europeans, in particular Asians, south and east."

"Now doing three life sentences."

"Indeed, Rooney."

"When George Taylor took over he established links with the Albanians to force out Asian landlords from multiple occupancy, so establishing the Taylor dominance in the property sphere of influence."

"And ISIS?"

"The Albanians' links with ISIS are well known. Syria's insurgent militias have become enmeshed with organized crime. ISIS has, in their ranks, crime syndicates and insurgent leaders who are racketeers. A Kosovo Albanian leads the ISIS Army in Fallujah. Hundreds of Kosovos are fighting alongside militants in Syria and Iraq. Kosovo ranks eighth overall and first per capita among the twenty-two Western states with citizens fighting in Syria and Iraq. Many of these ISIS men are Albanian mafia and they maintain the links."

"And fund their operations through bank heists, extortion… kidnappings?"

"And other tactics more commonly associated with the mob than Islamist extremists."

"ISIS, the ISIS cell. Al-Jamal?"

"Al-Jamal has the mentality of a Mafioso. This is not someone with the mind of an ideological fighter."

"We know he is suspected of advancing his criminal enterprises, including –"

"The kidnapping of foreigners for ransom."

"Shite."

"ISIS is the Mafia of the Middle East, Jackie. It's a business, a bloody and illegal business."

"Like the Mafia."

"They are after money, Jackie." She stays quiet. "You said you wanted to bore into the hive of bees."

"I didn't say that, Rooney. It was Jean that said that, and what she said was we have to *delve* into this hive of bees. You got it wrong."

"Oh sorry, I thought you said –"

"I said fuck all. You've been talking to your… friend." Jackie's voices rises increasingly with every phrase, prompting her plain-clothes colleagues to get out of their seats. "Your fucking colleague, your fucking friend, and no doubt fucking lover."

"You OK, ma'am?" One of the undercover officers approaches the table.

"Oh, fantastic, you arrive with the cavalry. You really did intend to arrest me. Just great."

Trust no one, Rooney.

"Don't be so… dramatic. Back off DC. Rooney, what you said was –"

"Valuable, interesting, upsetting, what you wanted to hear?"

"Is… interesting."

At that, I pick up my coat to leave. The two officers move forward. James and John appear from nowhere to get between me and them.

"Ma'am?" The officer turns to Jackie.

"I said back off DC. Rooney, call off your dogs. Rooney –"

"I wanted to help, Jackie."

"Rooney?"

I turn and leave, James and John follow. All there know what each of this pair was carrying and that they would have opened fire had the circumstances required it.

"Get me Dempsie, Euan," Jackie barks as she arrives in her office. "And a coffee, please."

Baird delivers both.

"Afternoon, Assistant Chief Constable, and how can we help you today?" Jean replies, like a BT operator.

"You been talking to Rooney?"

"I do, Jackie, you know I do."

"He said a funny thing."

"And what is that, Jackie?"

"He mentioned boring into the hive of bees. You said that to me. But you said delving, not boring."

"Delving, boring. Jackie, let's not get paranoid."

"ISIS is after money. They have links with the Albanian Mafia and with the Taylors."

"Now poisoned, I hear. Rooney has been busy."

"You know all this."

"MI5 knows many things, Jackie."

"I know there is more to this than you're telling me, Jean."

"We are getting extremely worried about McCourt, Jackie. The ISIS bomb ups the ante."

"You know this is about money?" Jean doesn't answer. "I guess our friend in common told you that ISIS wants cash to fund their operation. That's why Al-Jamal wants to see Maclean. He wants a massive payday from the Scottish Government."

"Rooney says that, but it's bigger than that Jackie."

"Bigger than cash? Pay the bastards and let McCourt live and let us all get on with our lives."

"What, and let them win?"

"If they lose, McCourt dies."

"If they win, McCourt dies, Jackie. They'll never let him go. You need to find him."

"This is not about McCourt or the money, this is about face, and I fucking know it, Jean. This is about you, MI5 and Charlton, your cabinet secretary. We do the dirty work and you guys get all the credit."

"Your job is also riding on it, don't you forget that, Jackie; your first big challenge. The public are getting extremely edgy, Assistant Chief Constable. They don't like car bombs on the streets of Glasgow."

"Fuck off, bitch," just precedes the phone being slammed down.

"Can I have a few words?" Matt Hurley corners Jackie as she leaves her office to head onto French Street. She looks around for any other police officers for support with annoying reporters, especially this one who has been particularly critical of her in the *Evening Times*.

"Sorry, I am very busy," she tries to push by him, "as you will expect."

"Yes, so we believe." Hurley moves aside. "Can we have a statement… about the Family?"

"Another time. The Family?"

"Yes, the Family. They have been busy. They hit the Albanian Mafia, the Taylors, *and* the Asian gangs. What is happening, Assistant Chief Constable?"

"We have a kidnapped police officer and we have had a car bomb in the city centre. Don't you think *we* haven't been busy?"

"Seems the Family have been… more active."

"I have nothing more to say to you, Mr Hurley. Now if you'll excuse me." Jackie gets to her car and opens the door.

Hurley prevents it being closed. "People are saying at least the Family is doing something."

Jackie gets onto her mobile. "We have a situation here in the car park on French Street, send a unit please?"

"OK, Assistant Chief Constable. I'll leave it there, but if you ever want to talk, here's my card." Hurley releases the door and hands Jackie his card. She drives off, dropping it out of the window.

Jackie calls me by hands-free in her car. "We need McCourt, Rooney. He is there somewhere. We are doing house-to-house searches and picking up everyone with a known affiliation with the Islamic groups. We don't have much time. You need to help us."

"We are doing what we can, Jackie. Are you following our thoughts about the Albanians and ISIS with Jean?"

"Oh, Miss MI5 knows about all of that stuff and is making her own enquires, but it is for us to save McCourt. It's in the title, Operation Save McCourt, you got it?"

"Operation Save Kaminski's job?"

"Rooney, please, I don't need this."

"OK, you need our help."

"I need your help. Rooney?"

"Yes,"

"You fucking well owe me."

"What was wrong with your office, Jean?" I approach her in the lounge bar of One Devonshire Gardens where she is taking up a good proportion of a sofa. Her legs are tucked up under her, her breasts pushing through the thin silk of her blouse, drawing glances from around the bar. I thought about looking at her for a while before I talked to her, but presumed the manager would have asked me to leave.

"I thought it best to meet in a more… relaxed setting." She waves her hand around the lounge, pointing out the fine furnishings and paintings. "Wine?" She lifts the bottle. "An excellent Côtes du Rhone. I was hoping you would like it."

I shake my head. "Why here? It's very public, the kind of people who will prattle: the spook and the crook."

"Very good, Rooney, kind-of rhymes." She pushes the wine in my direction.

"Sorry, you know I don't. I can't."

"No, no vices."

I settle on the sofa next to her, leaving little space, then the perfume reaches me, again.

"And you don't fuck in church," she says. I stay quiet, unsure of where is this leading. I was soon to find out. "Come with me.". I hesitate for a minute and then follow her through the lounge and up the grand staircase, where she opens a solid wooden door into a suite. "In there." She points towards the bedroom, as she disappears into the bathroom. I wander into the bedroom.

Walk into my parlour, said the Spider to the Fly.

"I know not what I do, Jesus." I sit on the bed, but I know what is going on. I hear a spray from the bathroom, the perfume again. This has been coming and I know it. I shouldn't have come, but it's inevitable. I get on my knees and start to pray, my elbows sinking into the bed. "Show me the right path, O' Lord. Point out the road for me to follow."

Fuck her, my son.

"I am only a child, O' Lord."

She arrives from the bathroom naked. I always wondered what she would look like out of her clothes and she doesn't disappoint me. She is small, but completely and solidly athletic. Her arms, shoulders and legs reflect a strict workout regime. Yet her breasts, hips and buttocks hold the sexuality of a glamour model, but taut, firm, proud.

"Nothing on but Chanel Number 5, Jean?"

"Just for you, Sean. Pleased you are on your knees, sinner."

"Does Martin know you are here?"

"Oh, yes."

I just knew he would have. "I am with the wife of a man who condones it. I do not covet my neighbour's wife? This is not a sin."

"Rooney, just take off your clothes off and get back on your knees."

I remove my clothes and fold them over a chair. I return to the kneeling position at the bed. She opens the bedside drawer and pulls out a flail whip. I catch sight of it.

"You will drive out the devil?" She moves behind me.

"I will show a dog who is its master."

"I will be free of sin?"

"You will be punished."

'Whack', the flail sounds as it thrashes against my back. I respond with a dull moan. 'Whack' it goes again. I feel a deep sting, like the skin has been lifted from my back. I just know a welt has risen, crossing the first one.

Just like your father did, Rooney, with his leather belt.

I crawl onto the bed and lie face down, waiting for the inevitable more to come. I wonder how many. I hope it hasn't stopped. Then she climbs on me and, putting the whip around my neck, pulls it until I struggle to breathe. I feel like I am about to expire, then she removes it.

"Turn around, dog."

Of course, I have to obey. She is strong and forceful, but wet and ready for me, not like….

Jackie?

She slides down me, so deep she is crushing me into the bed. Although her slide becomes easy, her grip tightens, drawing me with her with every upward movement. I syncopate my thrusts, matching hers one for one. Then she is up, turns, and is on her knees. "Fuck me, dog."

In an instant I am in her and pounding her incessantly. Then she grabs the whip and, holding her shape with one hand, she uses the other hand to whip the flail over her shoulder and, in an arc over my shoulder, whacks my back. The pain is excruciating, yet this is the most powerful thing I have felt since I was a child.

"Ride me, holy man, ride your mistress; fuck the goodness out of her and ram the badness into her." 'Whack', the flail collides with my skin again.

I'll no' do it again, Dad. Please…

I erupt into her, sobbing loudly. "Punish me, oh Lord, for I have sinned." I collapse backwards onto the bed.

"I will fuck the devil out of you, holy man." She straddles me once more, this time working her way up until my face is smothered by her vulva, pushing into me, up and down, harder, harder, as she rides my face; until, in convulsions, she cums, covering me with vaginal fluid, until she expires and falls panting, moaning, shuddering beside me on the bed.

"You will absolve me, holy man," she says, after a while.

"I cannot, for we are both sinners." I sit up. "We are both damned."

"Then, I will see you in hell. Now get the fuck out."

CHAPTER NINETEEN

John McCourt fixes his eyes on the ceiling. His hands are on fire. The Ibuprofen is doing nothing more than dulling the pain. His increased temperature is telling him his body isn't dealing well with the massive assault on it. He has lost two fingers from each hand and he knows there is more to come, or go. *Why aren't they coming, my body won't take much more of this.* He looks towards the ceiling. *My mind will though; 'pain is a perception of the soul,' Descartes said.*

The door opens. Three possibilities go through his mind each time it does. One, they are coming to kill him, so get it over with, but he cautions himself against this thought, thinking about wee Jamie and Mary. Two, they are coming to feed and water him and empty his toilet bucket, which they also do once a day. Or three, they are coming to take another finger, which they also do once a day. He hopes it is number two, but he knows number three is inevitable this day, and so is number one at some point over the next few days, it may even be today. He tries to keep himself amused by the thought that if they run out of fingers they will start on his toes, and then where will they go, he wonders, musing that his willie will go then. *Mary certainly wouldn't like that*, he thinks, enjoying the levity of it.

As Al-Jamal walks in with Halid, he knows it is one or three. Halid alone feeds him and empties his bucket. McCourt fixes his stare solidly on the ceiling. If ever his mediation sessions were needed, this is the time. He knew of countless examples where people in pain managed to block it out by the power of the mind. This would be another he was determined to prove, mainly to himself.

"Good day, infidel solider," Al-Jamal says. "Your leaders have deserted you and we have to convince them of our resolve." He has used these same words for the last four days. McCourt digs his hands under him, but Al-Jamal roughly pulls out his left hand. "Let me see, infidel, what is it they say in the West: this little piggy went to market, this little…?"

Keep focused on the ceiling, take your mind to that happy place where no pain can reach, McCourt says to himself. Halid, holding the rest of him down, roughly grasps his hand. His thumb is pulled outwards by his strong hand, his arm follows. *Focus on the ceiling*, he thinks; *think about that time you and Jamie went kayaking in Arisaig, the blue sea, going through the skerries, the seaweed*. A 'snap' sound immediately precedes the knowledge the thumb of his left hand has been taken off with a twist of a sharp knife. It is gone and his hand drops to the bed. He represses the scream and the pain, which reverberates around his mind like an echo diminishing in intensity with every lap of his mind. Halid takes his hand and wraps it tightly in a bandage, stemming the blood.

"Take these infidel," Halid says, putting three Ibuprofen into his mouth, followed by water. McCourt takes them willingly, knowing it will control his temperature; however, more than anything, he needs to stave off any infection. He knows this would kill him before the loss of blood or the pain. "I will deliver this," Al-Jamal says, holding out the thumb. "It will go to your leaders in your police force. They who have deserted you." Al-Jamal leaves, leaving Halid in the room. He moves closer to McCourt. "Do you wish your… medicine?" McCourt nods. Halid pulls out a half bottle of whisky from a drawer next to the bed, pouring a thimbleful into a plastic beaker and handing it to McCourt. He waits. McCourt puts the beaker to his mouth and takes the whisky. Halid leaves. McCourt removes the bandage and puts the stump of his thumb in his mouth where the whisky is held, as he did with the other fingers. He cleans the stump with his tongue, sloshing the whisky around it. Then wraps it back up in the bandage, relieved it is clean.

Jackie is deep in thought as she leaves French Street. She'll pick up a bottle in Oddbins on Woodlands Road on the way home, maybe something else from a contact she'll meet in the car park at Kelvinbridge Subway. She heads up into Park Quadrant and finds a space for her Porsche outside her house, the closer the better for obvious reasons. She wonders whether it is worth the discomfort and pain for a disabled woman to reside in these flats, but she loves the view into Kelvingrove Park. She pulls herself out of the car and, as she reaches into the back seat for the Oddbins bag, she hears a familiar voice, last heard through a loud hailer.

"Hello, Jackie Kaminski." She turns to see Mary McCourt standing next to her car. "I thought it best I talk to you face to face."

"Mary, John's wife."

"Correct."

"You were outside our offices yesterday, with a crowd of people."

"We were demonstrating about my husband."

"Yes, I am very sorr –"

"Yes, I'm sure. Maybe you'd like this." At that, Mary throws a half litre of red paint over Jackie, much of it covering the car. "Maybe this'll mind you of the colour of my husband's blood."

"Mary…" Jackie looks down to see the paint drip from her clothes into the gutter.

"Don't Mary me. You don't give a damn. Five fingers down and five to go. Five days to his death, because you bastards have no intention of doing anything to save him," Mary starts to sob. "He is my husband, my husband, and he is only a name and number to you and all you bastards."

"Mary…"

"No, don't say anything, don't say… anything!" Mary walks away crying, leaving Jackie trying to wipe some of the paint off her head and face.

Her upstairs neighbour sees this happen from his window and rushes out to help her. "Your lovely car," he says, helping her in to her flat.

"Aye, multi-coloured, John, not unlike me."

"Will I contact your colleagues?"

"No, please leave it."

"I need to see you, Rooney." Jackie gets out of the shower having applied a liberal amount of shampoo. Thankfully, the paint is a water-based emulsion and comes off easily.

"You sound upset, Jackie." I tuck into a plate of spaghetti bolognaise.

"I am upset, extremely upset. You need to come here."

"I will, in an hour."

"Half an hour."

I finish the spaghetti and head to Jackie's apartment, a spacious Victorian flat. I am pleased to be here; surely this is a sign of her warming to me.

Any hope of this is dashed as she greets me. "Don't get any fucking ideas, Rooney. I need to talk to you." She is standing there in her robe, tightly fastened around her, leaning on her stick. "Come in." She takes me through to her sitting room, tells me to sit down, and explains the incident with Mary and the paint. "Bloody red paint. Mary McCourt."

"Bloody red, Jackie?"

"I said 'bloody' red paint, shithead. Mary is right, though, and that is the thing, she's right. The poor woman can only do what she can do. She can do nothing to save her husband, but we can. You can Rooney, and you will."

"I said I wanted to help, Jackie. I gave what we know… ISIS being after cash and all that, the Albanian mafia, the Taylors."

"We need locations, Rooney. We need to know where he is. We need information that will take us to him, rescue him. You have sources. You can put pressure on, in the way you know how, get those sources to find something. That's what we need, you bastard."

She pushes me out of the way, rushing into the bathroom.

"Jackie…"

I wander around her sitting room, taking in the fabulous view over the park and Glasgow University. I notice a few zip lock plastic bags with hearts containing fine, white powder, which I recognise from my days as a forensic psychologist as powdered cocaine. After a few minutes, she returns. I reach for her.

"Easy, Rooney, please."

"Jackie, you need…"

"I need… help, Rooney, help."

"You need, me." I know she does. I am the only person in the world that can help her. She needs me, she needs what I can give her. I reach for her, my hands pinning her shoulders to the sofa. She submits. I open her robe to find her naked as I hope or even expect. There are spots of red paint on her neck. I lick them.

"Rooney, please don't."

"Don't?"

"Please don't hurt me."

Mohammed, nicknamed Moh, is standing in the entrance of the Arlington Bar on Woodside Road. He is one of the G-Star gang, after a popular brand of designer clothing.

Steve McGraw approaches him. "Any crack, pal?"

"How much my friend?" Moh says, in broken English, then gestures over to a black Vauxhall Insignia car containing three heavyset men.

"Two rocks, class A."

"Over there. Forty pounds for the two, to me."

McGraw passes over the forty and makes his way to the car. The passenger window is already down as he gets there, where a hand stretches out holding the two rocks.

"Thanks pal." McGraw reaches for the drugs, at the same time, reaching inside his jacket to pull out a snub-nosed 38 revolver.

"What the –"

McGraw shoots the man in the face and indiscriminately sends another five bullets into the car as it screeches away. It gets about thirty metres along Woodlands Road before it mounts the pavement and runs into the railing outside the Drake Bar on Lynedoch Street. McGraw runs after it and, reaching it, opens the driver's door to shoot him dead. Then he opens each door to make sure of the two men in the back seat. By then Moh is running towards him with a bayonet like a cavalry man. Calmly, McGraw turns and shoots him twice in the chest and, as he lies on the road, puts another into his head. Then he walks up towards Park Circus, where there is a car waiting to whisk him down onto Argyle Street. Out of sight, near the Park, he pulls up a drain cover and drops the gun into it along with the clear plastic glove used to conceal his prints.

Jackie gets the information from Baird via her mobile as we are getting ready to leave her flat. "Rooney, explain. The Somalis have been hit. Now, fucking well tell me."

I knew it was to happen, but not where, when or how. When she said it was the Somalis, then I knew. We move back inside the reception hall.

"Jackie, Somali gangsters are flooding Scotland's streets with deadly crack cocaine. You'll know that well." She looks at me. "They are a violent mob, touting misery to addicts desperate for a fix." She avoids my eyes. "Many of them are carrying sharpened bayonets in case they're robbed by rivals."

"Oh, the vigilante stuff again."

"Actually, it's a separate hit, Jackie. It was the McGraws."

"And a member of the Twelve. So, it was sanctioned by you."

I avoided saying anything incriminating.

Wise.

"Jackie, this is a million-a-year drug empire. They deliver all over the city twenty-four hours per day. Addicts are giving them twenty thousand a year. They've got so many buying from them, you can multiply that by at least a hundred. We know dozens of addicts –"

"Referring to me, Rooney?" She drops down onto a chair in the hall.

"Jackie, I know you use this stuff. We both know I do."

"What I do, Rooney, is my business."

"Addicts used to buy from the McGraws, Jackie. Now they get it from the Somalis every day. They're specialising in selling highly-addictive crack cocaine, a freebase form of cocaine smoked by users."

"The SCDEA are battling for control of the drugs trade. Three Somali drug dealers were jailed for a machine gun killing of a rival in Edinburgh."

"We did what was necessary."

"We?"

"The McGraws."

"We'll be making arrests. We know where the McGraws are."

"Jackie."

"Yes?"

"I would prefer if you would leave it."

"You are asking me to leave the murder of five men on Woodside Road, not a hundred metres from where I live?"

"Aye." She looks at me, like she is trying to muster up a scream. "We've sent a message to the Somalis."

"Fuck's sake, Rooney. The Albanian mafia, the Somalis, ISIS; what the fuck is going on?"

"We've said we will wipe them out if they don't give us information about the ISIS cells. It may lead to McCourt."

"Fucking brilliant. I'll –"

"Jackie?"

"What?"

Her voice drops. "Just leave it. It could come back on you."

"Back on me? You can't use or hold any moral or operational high ground in this, Jackie."

"A bit of contradiction, Rooney?" She does up her coat and dons her hat. "Is that what you are saying? A conflicted high ranking police officer using –"

"Wouldn't look good, Jackie."

"Wouldn't look good being seen with you, Rooney." She looks out onto the street before pushing me out of the door, then to follow me when I had reached my car.

Colin Moore arrives as usual that Thursday evening at the Clarkes. Anne and Joe pick up their benefits on a Thursday, also as usual. He gave them £250 six years ago and they have now paid him over £40,000. He takes £100 tonight, leaving them with £15 to live on until next week, then he'll be back. Joe has a mental illness and Anne, multiple sclerosis. Last week, after the couple could only give him £50 after paying a large electricity bill, he jabbed his car keys into Joe's eye, almost blinding him, as a reminder of what would happen if they didn't pay up weekly. "My payment comes before your electric, you got that." He leaves the couple's house and makes his way down Partickhill Street heading to his flat in Broomhill. He has another hundred like the Clarke's. Tonight they were the last in his collection. A good night with around £1,500 brought in. He is also a drug dealer, funding his drugs stashes, getting his drugs from a Zultan Mohammed, a Romanian drug trafficker.

As he approaches his close, he notices two men hot on his heels. He accelerates into the close. He is armed but he has a handy sawn-off shotgun inside his door just in case. *Just get in there and he'll be safe*, he thinks. He fumbles with the keys to his house. He has a number of mortises on the reinforced door to get through. Ironically, if he had a normal door he would have been in.

He hears a voice behind him and reaches for his piece tucked in his belt at the back. "Colin Moore, mind me?" Patsy Hughes from the Sighthill Mafia is out of his patch here, but Moore knows him. Everyone knows Hughes and the Sighthill Mafia.

"Hello, Patsy, didn't expect to see you around here."

"No, just doing a favour to a made man."

Moore knows immediately what this is, and he is to be hit: a whack. "I just need to get…" He spins around, his gun in hand, but he is slow to the men who are ready for anything from him. Patsy's accomplice, Gerry Burns thumps Moore's arm with a jemmy bar and puts a knife to his neck. Moore's gun arm is disabled immediately, dropping the gun.

"Finish getting the door open, Colin, let's go in, it's cauld the night." Moore fumbles with the keys and, opening the remaining locks, they are in.

Inside, he is pushed into the sitting room and onto the couch. By this time, Burns is covering him with his own gun. "You have a wee rest Colin, I'll have a wee look around." Patsy leaves him in the control of Burns. He knows where he is going, he has been tipped off, he knows where Moore keeps his stash box. Pulling out his bed and the bric-a-brac under there, he uses the jemmy to pull up the floorboards, where he finds six large plastic boxes full of money and drugs. He puts them on the bed and takes one through to the sitting room.

"Nice stash, Colin." He enters the sitting room. Moore knows he is a dead man.

"Take it all, Patsy. It's all yours and I can get more if you gie's a break. Ave goat weans, Patsy," he pleads.

"OK, take out your mobile, Colin," Hughes says. Moore obeys. "Phone your supplier."

Moore does what he is told. "What do you want me to say to him? He's a bad bastard, Patsy. He'll do me and my weans."

"So will I, you bastard, if you don't do it."

Moore awaits the reply. "Hello, Zultan, it's Colin Moore," he says after a few seconds. "Aye, Colin Moore. Aye, hold on. What will I say to him, Patsy?"

"Gies the phone," Hughes demands. Moore complies, he has no choice. "Hello Mr Mohammed," he says into the phone. There's a deathly silence from the other end of the phone. "I know you are there, fucker. I want you to listen, very carefully. Get the fuck out of Glasgow or we are coming for you," he roars into the phone. "And listen to this tae. Colin, tell Mr Mohammed something, anything."

"Whit Patsy, whit will I say."

"Tell him a nursery rhyme."

"Whit, OK. Ba, Ba, Black Sheep, ha –" Bang, a shot is fired into Moore's head, the sound reverberating around the room and into the phone. Hughes takes the mobile from Moore's dead hand. There is no one on the other end of the phone, but he knows the shot was heard and the point made. *Job done, contract completed*, he thinks.

CHAPTER TWENTY

The door opens. McCourt's eyes are fixed on the ceiling, again. *Switch off body, retreat into mind,* he says to himself.

"Good morning, Mr McCourt," Al-Jamal says, entering the room. *Jeez,* McCourt thinks, *he's using my name.*

"Good morning, are you here to take another?"

"Your people have deserted you; we need to mark this in our usual way."

"Get on with it then."

"Do you wish to say anything to your leaders?"

"Yes, I am resigned to die for Allah."

This off-foots Al-Jamal. "You wish to die for Allah, infidel, this is not possible for a Christian."

"I wish to become a son of the Prophet, just like you."

This is a magnanimous decision by you, albeit not a truthful one, but I believe you are trying to manipulate us."

"And how would I convince you?"

"You would martyr yourself for Allah."

McCourt decides the loss of another finger would do for then. The index finger of his left hand is taken.

"Will you come to a press conference with me?" Jackie asks.

"Why?" I ask.

"I need you there. Just that. Surely you can do that for me."

Go with her, should be fun.

"I'll pick you up."

Jackie and I arrive at the press conference in Police HQ in French Street. Jackie goes to the podium. I take a seat at the back.

"Good afternoon, ladies and gentlemen," Jackie says. "We have no additional information to add regarding PC McCourt's abduction. Enquiries continue. If we have any news, we will report it through the normal channels. Thank you. Questions?" She half hopes there'd be a few seconds pause, when she could say, "Thank you," and leave.

However, "Aye, I have a question," comes from Mary McCourt, standing at the back of the room in a group along the back wall. "Why is Police Scotland doing nothing to find my husband?"

This creates a hush, and all await Jackie's response. She plays with her hair, almost checking for any red paint she didn't manage to remove. "Good to see you again, Mrs McCourt," she says, preventing herself saying something controversial, like "Not like the last time when you threw a bucket of paint over me, you bastard," but knows this needs to be a show of support. "I assure you that everything is being done to find your husband, our colleague," she says.

"You should be ashamed of yourselves," Mary says. "He's one of yours and he's mine." She starts to cry; her friends move to her and console her.

"I am sorry, Mrs McCourt, but there is nothing I can say to convince you of our determination to bring your husband home safe and well."

"Aye, minus his head," Mary says.

There's a hush.

"Can I ask another, kind of unrelated question?" asks Matt Hurley, this time reporting for *The Herald*.

"Yes, Mr Hurley, go ahead."

"Thank you, Assistant Chief Constable," Hurley says. "We have been running a theme in our paper on the Family." *Here we go*, Jackie thinks, as I slide further into my coat and down my seat, pulling the lapels of my coat further up around my face.

"This isn't exactly why I am here, Matt," Jackie says.

"I know, but it's an opportun –"

"I know, but I'd prefer if –"

"Go on Assistant Chief Constable," Mary McCourt says from the back. "We are all interested in hearing what you have to say about this." I hear her words whizz over my head, worried she will see me sitting a couple of rows from her.

"Aye go on," comes from another member of the audience.

Jackie doesn't want to go there, but to back out and retreat would only leave Police Scotland open to more criticism.

"OK, what do you want to ask?" Jackie says, trying to see if I am still in the room.

"We are getting letters," Hurley says, pulling out a batch held together with a rubber band. "Some say the Family are out of control, they are taking revenge, attacking with impunity, and with no police response against the mob in Glasgow."

"The –"

"Sorry, and others are saying that the Family are doing what Police Scotland are not, taking on the bad guys, policing the streets. What is Police Scotland's position vis-a-vis the Family, Assistant Chief Constable?"

"We don't have a… position, Mr Hurley, on the Family. However, you can ask their representative yourselves. Mr Rooney is sitting at the back of the room." Everyone turns to me.

"Christ," I murmur under my coat. Everyone is now looking my way. I can see the daggers being drawn.

"Mr Rooney, would you like to say something?" Hurley asks.

I pop my head out of my coat. "Thanks." I draw my own daggers at Jackie. "I would however prefer not to say. We –"

"We, in the Family?"

"Yes, we, don't like –"

"We know what you don't like to do, Mr Rooney," Hurley says. "But it is what the Family is doing, is more to the point, Mr Rooney." I stay quiet. I know the man is on a mission. "*It* is… breaking legs, tramlining faces."

"They were rapists."

"Hitting Somalis."

"Drug dealers."

"Removing the kidneys of Albanians."

Lovely in steak pie.

"They are the Mafia."

"The Family is above the law, Mr Rooney."

"We are protecting our businesses."

"I think that will do," Jackie says loudly over the discourse.

"Well, Assistant Chief Constable, are you saying it is not?" Hurley says. "What are you saying about the Family? What is Police Scotland's position on the Family?"

"Aye, what is Police Scotland's position, Assistant Chief Constable?" Mary echoes.

"You have had your say, asked your questions. This conference is over," Jackie says, abruptly. I slip out of the back.

Jean arrives in Jackie's office. "What, Jackie, you invite Rooney to a public press conference, Je… sus. I'll have one of those too, if you don't mind." She nods to the coffee machine in the corner of the office. "Nice of you to ask." Jackie spins huffily around in her chair to make another Cappuccino.

Jackie passes the drink. "Here," she says. "It's my *personal* machine."

Jean takes it. "I'll think myself lucky."

They eye each other for a few seconds, then Jean puts her feet up on Jackie's desk. "Jesus, taking a chance are you not?"

"Well, time the public had a chance to ask him some questions for a change."

"Took the focus off you, Jackie."

"Rooney is getting above himself, you know that." Jackie pushes Jean's feet off the desk.

"He's getting things done, Jackie." Jean gets up. "They're bad guys hitting bad guys."

"That's our job, you know that too."

"Come on, roll with it, Jackie, and follow the party line."

"Right from Holyrood itself, Jean, Charlton and Maclean? Take the heat off them and put it on us."

"McCourt?"

"I knew you'd get to that."

"Anything?"

"Do I really need to account to you, Jean? It's bad enough dealing with the press."

"Yes, dear, you have to." Jean leans forward over the desk and pushes out a stare designed to reach inside Jackie's head.

Jackie tries to bat it back, but there's no competition. "Nothing. House to house searches, bringing in all known contacts, working with community groups, getting nowhere. Four days –"

"And four fingers –"

"In four days they will take his head." Jean sits back arms folded. "And what are the spooks doing?"

Jean leans forward, once more. "We are stepping up our efforts nationally and internationally. There are links between these groups."

"Eh?"

"Islamic State, the Albanians, the Somalis; there are links."

"Oh, Rooney said you had been providing information.

Something about ISIS allying with Somali terror groups, originally tied to al-Qaeda."

"I gave him data. *My* remit, Jackie, mine."

"Cute, Jean. Doesn't find McCourt."

"It links, Jackie, can you not see that?"

"What I can see is you, Rooney, the Family, and…"

"We all have to work together, Jackie."

"Yes, work together with the Family, Jean; you guys have form in that respect."

"Go on, we both know you will."

"George Taylor and Davy McGing, Glasgow Godfathers. Their links with the UDA in Northern Ireland and the London firms."

"If it's in the interests of the state."

"If it's in your interests, Jean?"

"What *do you* mean?"

"You know what I mean, it's well known you like fucking powerful men. Charlton?"

Jean gets to her feet. "Jackie, you are getting seriously close."

Jackie pushes herself up in her seat to face her. "And what will you do, Miss Whiplash, hit a cripple?"

Grabbing her coat from the back of her chair Jean barges out, leaving the door open. Baird comes in. "You alright, ma'am?"

"Fine." Jackie's voice is shaking. "Cancel all my appointments for today."

John takes Jackie's coat as he escorts her into my flat. "She's bad news, Rooney," she says, dropping onto my sofa. "You know that, but what does that matter if you're getting into her knickers."

"And what are you doing?" I am sorting out a pile of A4 folders and laying them square on across my desk. I see Jackie noticing 'ISIS' and 'Romanians' on two of them. In the dim light she strains her eyes to see the others behind a block of hardback books. "Do you know, four in ten British Muslims believe that the police and MI5 are responsible for the radicalisation of young people who support the extremists?"

"You know fine well, Rooney. The government have stated categorically *we* are not responsible for radicalisation."

"Everyone knows fine well that the police and security services are partly to blame for the actions of those who travelled to Syria to join terror groups."

"Jesus, Rooney, what the fuck are you reading?" She notices a book, 'Friction: How Radicalization Happens to Them and Us'.

"Just trying to educate myself, Jackie. I need to keep up to speed with the Islamic stuff if I am going to be on telly."

"Aye, you don't want to damage your image."

"But it's not that, Jackie. I got my information from a survation poll. Do you not read the papers?" I hand Jackie the Telegraph. "Read it, take it away with you."

"I read what is important to read. You stay real, Rooney."

"Harassment by the security services contributed to the radicalisation of Mohammed Emwazi, the London student identified as 'Jihadi John', the killer from the Islamic State."

"We are trying to build bridges between communities, plonker."

"The Glasgow folk respect us for taking action."

"And you build your reputation at the same time. I know what you are up to pal."

"The poll… let's see." I take *The Telegraph* from her and open it. "'The missed opportunity of law enforcement authorities in working closely with British Muslim communities, especially in relation to counter-terrorism'," I quote.

"If we go in heavy handed we create tensions, build barriers. We are getting nowhere on McCourt, but you can. You can do more."

"Oh, we are a resource then, not a blight on the community?"

"The hits, Rooney. You are really pushing our patience. We can't condone them."

"We, you, Jackie. No one else seems to mind."

She launches a barrage that brings John into the room. "Me, I'm Police Scotland, Rooney. We *don't* condone it. You fucking got that?"

"It's fine, John. Leave and close the door behind you. What's your dad saying?"

"Never you mind what he's saying. It's what I am saying that counts and I am relying on you to deliver."

"The Family want quid pro quo."

"Quid pro quo?"

"We do your dirty work for you and we get to do our business."

"Don't even go there, Rooney. Our agreement doesn't go that far. No fucking deals on mass fucking murder. Get above yourselves and we will fuck you proper, you got that?"

I move deliberately towards her. "And what if we fuck, proper, Jackie?"

She recoils. "Just don't go there either, Rooney. You know I can't… proper." She pulls away. I reach for her again. This time she submits. "You bastard, Rooney."

"Together, Jackie, in God." I guide her hand to my crotch.

"We need a meeting, Rooney," Bill Bingham says, by text.

"I expect it," I return.

We meet in the Central Hotel.

"Some of us want to know what's happening, Rooney," Charlie Campbell says. "We give you a mandate and you take action. We provide the troops like the united-fuckin'-nations and we hit Albanians, Somalis, and the Asians."

"They were… a threat."

"We're losing too many men," Patrick Devlin says.

Bill Bingham intervenes. "We need to do it."

"Hitting loan sharks?"

"They had links with Romanian drug traffickers. Their soldier ants are migrating through Glasgow, Patrick."

"It needed done," Bingham says.

"Good, then we hit the Ubercabs," Campbell says. "They are fucking destroying my business."

"No," I say.

"And why not?"

"They are legit. The public wouldn't stand for it. It's our policy. We don't hit legit business nor the public, just the –"

"Aye, I know, the bad guys," Devlin says. "The bad guys hit the bad guys."

"It works," I say. "Never have we had the profits that are coming in now."

"I support it," Bingham says

"Me too," Alex Frame says. "We need to fuck these guys and protect our patch."

"Show of hands," Bingham says. Eleven hands are raised, his own included; one is missing.

"OK," Campbell says, raising the final hand. "But, you work

for us and you mind that."

I stare on impassively and wonder how long I will be able to control these men.

"Hear you're becoming a bit of a saint in Glasgow, Rooney," Ben says, bringing the drinks over. We are in our usual booth in Jintys. James and John take up their positions as sentinels at the bar.

"Saint and a sinner, Ben. I like it."

"More of a sinner, Rooney."

"Being a bad man pays the bills."

Ben takes a long look at me as he drinks. "Didn't think you would kill, though."

"Kill, I don't kill."

Where have I heard this before?

"No you don't, not directly, but like your forebear you get others to do it for you. You don't get your hands dirty."

It is clear that Ben is referring to Johnston, the previous Father, the proxy killer. "I provide a… service."

"You are killing people, Rooney."

"The Family is taking these guys off the streets."

"They are leaving these guys dead on the streets." On this, I decide it is best to remain quiet. "The papers are full of pictures of dead guys, blood pouring into the gutters."

"The newspapers sensationalise things. We are working for the people of Glasgow."

"You, the killer. You, the psychologist, the man I worked with on numerous major incidents, holding hands, words of comfort, counselling relatives, the first responders. Now?" He stuns me with his words. "You *were* a good man, Rooney."

This is an extremely uncomfortable discussion. I am pleased we are in a booth where no one can overhear us. "I do God's work, Ben, in the way I know best. It is my vocation."

"Your religious vocation or your religious delusion, Rooney?"

He is not hearing me. "When was it delusional to love God, Ben?"

"You know I don't mean that, Rooney, there's appropriate god fearing and there's –"

"Inappropriate?"

"Yes, you are not acting… appropriately."

"I feel sorry for you, Ben, you just don't understand."

"I understand that you have a mental illness and happen to be the head of the biggest crime syndicate in the land and you are killing people. For me and your consultant that's grounds to have you recalled to hospital."

Jesus, he is threatening me with being detained again. "Have you any evidence I am killing people?"

"No, you know I don't."

"You'll remember Abraham, who was commanded by God to sacrifice his son, Isaac?"

I am impressed by Ben's biblical knowledge. "Yes."

"'Abraham,' God called. 'Yes,' he replied. 'Here I am.' 'Take your son, your only son – yes, Isaac, whom you love so much – and go to the land of Moriah. Go and sacrifice him as a burnt offering on one of the mountains, which I will show you.'"

"He was hearing voices from God compelling him to commit a heinous act of violence. What're your thoughts on that, Rooney?"

"He was doing God's will, as from his own words."

"Thought so, no insight. You are going to see Dr Melville, Rooney. I'll arrange it."

Guess you're heading back in, son.

"Well, go ahead then, you and Doctor Melville, try to readmit me. I'll take it to the Court of Session."

"At least agree to a review of your medication and your treatment plan."

"I'll do what I need to do. Now is that our consultation over for today, social worker?"

"It'll do, for now."

I blank him long enough to make him realise he's not welcome there. He leaves.

God is guiding you, Rooney.

CHAPTER TWENTY-ONE

"Can you get me the Quran, Halid?" McCourt asks.

"I will have to ask Al-Jamal."

"Please. I want to know what drives you folk to do these things."

Halid leans over him. "Islam has never condoned the killing of non-Muslims simply for being non-Muslims, there needs to be… other things."

"Other things?"

"If non-Muslims are attacking Muslims, then in the presence of a qualified leader, a Khalifa, Muslims may step in and fight the non-Muslims to prevent oppression."

"I, we, are not –"

"The Khalifah is representative of Allah on earth, and he will unite all Islamic lands and people and subjugate the rest of the world."

"This appears wrong, but I need to understand, to achieve basic human knowledge on this matter. Descartes says that the senses can be deceived. We can be led to believe anything by greater beings."

"Believe this, my friend, you are a murderer of children, a soldier of an army at war with Islam."

"I need to understand this…. Islam."

"I'll see what I can do."

Later Halid drops a Quran on McCourt's bed.

"Jesus, it's three o'clock in the morning, Bill." I almost fall out of my bed to reach the phone on my bedroom table.

"Charlie Campbell has had a taxi blown up."

"Sweet Jesus, when, where?"

"Twenty minutes ago, Tradeston, in his compound. Fucking bomb blew it into the fucking air."

"Anyone –"

"One of his key players just got into the cab for a hire, switched on the engine, and it went up. Lost his fucking legs, bled to death before the responders got there."

"Jesus, the Taylors, the McGings?"

"ISIS, Rooney. Your fucking friends made a call to the taxi service. 'You wage war with Islam and Islam wages war with you. Al-Jamal Saddam Al-Jamal.' They are now fighting us, Rooney. You have fucking drawn us in to this. We had no quarrel with them before all of this."

I need to compose myself. "I thought they might do something like this. It confirms things, the links."

"Eh?"

"The Albanians, Somalis, Romanians, they are all –"

"Linked, the links as you said. We hit the migrants and ISIS hits us. We are now at war with ISIS, are we?"

"Inadvertently."

"Oh, inadvertently. Rooney we need to talk about this… this fucking war, this fucking man."

"He's dangerous. Who knows what he'll do next."

"Well you can give us your thoughts on this… dangerous man at the meeting. Seven tonight, location half an hour before." He doesn't need to tell me the rules, no forward information about location: too dangerous.

"OK, see you there." I get up for to pray for Campbell's man. "Eternal rest grant unto him, O Lord…, rest in peace. Amen." I get on my computer to arrange a wreath for him and flowers for his wife.

"I want to know about Islamic philosophy, Halid?" McCourt asks.

"And why? I gave you the Quran."

Sitting on the edge of the bed, McCourt leans forward towards him. "Yes, and I am reading it intently. But it is helpful to discuss Islamic beliefs and how they are… expressed."

"What do you want to know?"

"The Quran does not condone the taking of life."

Halid pulls in a chair, getting closer to McCourt than he normally would. "Yes. You have been reading."

"I just want to understand why things are happening here, to me."

"Six one five one, here, check it out," McCourt says, passing the Quran. Halid opens it on page 390. "Look." He passes it back to

McCourt. "God said 'Take not life, which Allah hath made sacred, except by way of justice and law'."

"Yes, take not life."

"Except by way of justice and law."

"So, to kill me is justice and law."

Halid gets back to his feet and moves back to the door. "We have to give a dedicatory statement 'in the name of Allah' which has to be employed to make it lawful."

"So you will say 'in the name of Allah' when you remove my head?"

"We will."

"How can you say this is lawful; that this is justice and law?"

"You have taken Muslim lives."

McCourt stands. "I have taken no lives."

"You soldier brothers are steeped in the blood of the sons of Allah. You are them, they are you, your life is their life, and it is justice and law therefore to take your life."

"This, Halid, is a cockeyed representation of what is said in the Quran, an interpretation to justify your... wrong actions."

Halid studies him for a minute. "I need to dress your wounds."

"You are a doctor, Halid?" Halid remains quiet. "I think you are, and a doctor has taken the Hippocratic Oath. 'I will utterly reject harm and mischief,' it says. You will do me no harm." Halid remains quiet and leaves.

I head into Glasgow by Subway. I have an engagement at Waterstones Book Shop on Argyle Street. A local author, Donald McKay, a true crime author, has written a book on the unique crime context in Glasgow. I have agreed to be his guest. He would do readings from his book and ask me about the developing role of organised crime in Glasgow. I am nervous about this and look anxiously around the carriage. James and John have taken up opposite seats at each end. I position myself in the middle of it. Public transport has obvious risks, but so has driving into Glasgow and parking a black four by four on Argyle Street. No, the Subway will do.

I move out from St Enoch's subway station and am about to cross Argyle Street to Waterstones. It is 7.45 p.m. and the book launch will be well underway. I will arrive by Q and A, which is fine. I have the questions in my mind: "Mr Rooney, do you think the Family is stronger than the official forces in Glasgow?" My answer: "No, but we aim to augment and support the authorities in managing crime," etcetera, etcetera. I may even put in a good word for Jackie.

Crossing the road, I hear the throng at George Square; the Halloween festival is well underway. Lasers crisscross the sky, the Phantom of the Opera is blasting out across the city from massive PAs, people are heading there dressed as the undead.

Then, as we are about to go through the door of the bookshop, a massive bang stops us in our tracks. James and John react immediately. John steps out into the path of a taxi turning into Argyle Street, halting it.

James bundles me into the back of it. "Sydenham Road, Dowanhill," he orders the cabbie, "and fast, get us out of here."

"No problem, son," the cabbie replies. "I'm going nowhere near George Square. Did you hear that bang? Something big has happened up there."

He turns on the radio. "We have an announcement," sounds out. "There has been an explosion on George Square during the Halloween festival. We are unaware of casualties at this stage, but we will keep you informed as information arrives. Police Scotland say to stay indoors and not to go into the city centre. If you are there at present, make your way home as quickly, safely, and orderly as you can. We will provide updates as we receive them."

No more was said on that journey. We arrive back at my flat. James and John arrange for additional soldiers to be there, just in case. Like others that day, we tune into BBC Scotland and establish throughout the course of the day that a pressure cooker bomb had gone off at the Square, killing two and injuring sixty-seven.

"I hear you are reading the Quran," Al-Jamal says. "I am heartened by this."

"I want to understand," McCourt replies.

"Good, it will help you to prepare for death."

"I want to understand why you will kill me."

"It is important to understand what you have done."

"What *I* have done?"

"It is said, on page nine two five, at twenty one thirty five, please look." McCourt tries to open the Quran, but has difficulty due to his bandages.

"Halid?"

Halid opens the Quran, saying, "It says: 'Every soul shall taste death, and Allah will test you by evil and by good by way of trial. The actions, your actions, which have led to your death will be appraised'."

"I have not," McCourt says. "I am not…"

"You *are* responsible," Al-Jamal says. "Sign this." He hands McCourt a paper with a statement. "At the bottom, it will indicate your support of Allah. It will protect your wife and family."

McCourt signs it.

"Now, let me have your hand?"

"No, please." McCourt cries as Halid holds him fast, his left hand held out.

Jackie, Hubert, Millar, and Baird are in conference.

Baird starts. "Pressure cooker bomb, simple design, left in a rucksack next to the cordon barrier which was round the square during the festival. People were crowded around it. No one noticed the man leaving it there nor it being there until it exploded. It killed two young men instantly and injured nearly one hundred people, many seriously. Given it was left at ground level, many had leg wounds." Jackie runs her hand down her thigh and drops her head.

"Clearly evocative for yourself, Jackie," Millar says.

Jackie gives him a stony stare. "Aye."

"More, Baird," Hubert says.

"Right Chief, we have released photographs and a surveillance video of two suspects. They were identified later that day as two Chechen brothers. We have declared them suspects in the bombing and have released images of them."

Hubert coughs. "Good, keep us informed. Jackie?"

"Yes, sir?"

"McCourt, ISIS, this is all connected."

"Indeed, sir."

"Tell me?"

"They have sent a statement," Baird says. "And a polybag."

"Give it to us."

"It's with the medics, into the freezer, as usual."

"I meant the statement."

"Oh, sorry sir. It's the same as the car bomb on Gordon Street." Baird puts his glasses on and lifts the paper to his eyes. "It says, 'We have redoubled our efforts to confirm our Jihad'." Baird coughs. "'Please find your soldier's seventh finger. He has three left and three days to live. Once again, we have bombed your city centre to confirm we can – a larger bomb this time. Do you need more persuasion, infidels? Your cowardly First Minister insults the Caliphate, and allows his people to die on the streets of Glasgow. If he will not talk to us, we will unleash a thousand soldiers and a thousand swords on the heads of the people of this city.' That's it," Baird says.

"Not good, sir," Millar says.

"There's something else, sir."

"Go on."

"We have a statement… from McCourt."

"How do you know it's from McCourt, Euan?" Jackie asks.

"It's signed by him, ma'am, we have had it verified. It has his blood on it and it was in the polybag with his finger.

"Jackie!" Hubert says, meaning "it was McCourt's statement".

"What did it say?" she asks.

"OK," he says, putting his glasses back on. "'Our leaders are cowards', he says, 'they refuse to meet the men holding me. They refuse to take action to protect you or me. They want blood on the streets of Glasgow. They want me to die. They want you to die. Your family, my family are at risk if our leaders refuse them. Me, I will die in three days, Inshallah. Signed John McCourt.'"

"Al-Jamal?"

"Undoubtedly."

"Keep me informed," Hubert says. "I need to see the Justice Minister."

The Family meet, this time in John Fullerton's casino on the Clyde.

"Rooney," Bill Bingham starts. "We are now in a war with the Muslims."

"We are indeed, Bill," I say. "At war with the Muslim gangs who seek to take over our territory as they have up and down the length and breadth of the UK. We have to fight them. And, collectively, we can fight them."

"They fucking bombed us," Devlin says. "One of Campbell's soldiers, ours, is fucking dead, Rooney."

Charlie Campbell acknowledges this with a dispassionate nod.

"It was a response to scare us off. We need to keep our nerve. We are stronger than they are in Glasgow. They know this. We –"

"*We* lost a good fucking man," Campbell says.

"I… accept that."

Bingham comes in. "We lose soldiers in wars."

"The bastards need to be stopped," Devlin says.

"I want… compensated, the taxi, and my man," Campbell says.

"I'll see to it," I say.

"What the fuck is this really about, Rooney?" Devlin asks.

"Sorry?"

"All of this, the Muslims, hitting loan sharks, doing the polis's dirty work. What the fuck is it all about? We, you, are getting way out of our league, pal."

"This needs to be our mission, a new crusade. Our crusade will not be a secular war, but a Holy War. Christendom is divinely destined by God to fight and destroy the armies of the Antichrist, and illuminate the world with the Holy Faith."

I can see my words have evoked an interesting silence as the men look around at each other.

Has he flipped, they are thinking?

"So, we have had some success?" Jean says, as Jackie is shown in. "Thank you, Margaret."

"And hello to you too, Jean." Jackie slumps down on a seat adjacent to the table covered in files. "We released the CCTV footage of the bombers. Some worshipers of the Al-Furqan Mosque recognised the men from the television. The Iman called us, Hakim Ahmed, we brought him in. He said he had been concerned about rising radicalisation in the mosque from a small group of young men, of which these two men were a part. They appear to be governed, influenced, by a particular worshiper."

"Al-Jamal Saddam Al-Jamal?"

"Indeed, but it took serious questioning to reveal him."

"Why didn't he come forward?"

"Same as the others in the mosque, he knew he would be a dead man if he did."

"Christ, do these people –"

"These people?"

"I mean those people in there, in the Muslim communities. They need to be part of the fight against *these people*. They need to stand up and be counted."

"There are lots of people in Glasgow who are against what ISIS is doing in the Middle East. They have relatives there who are being murdered and under threat by ISIS if they say a word against them."

"So, no location, no address?"

"Nothing. Al-Jamal turned up at the same time every day to worship and to talk, then left. No one asked him his business."

"Is he still attending?"

"No way."

"Jackie, this is not good. We could have put some operatives in there, followed him, bugged him, traced him to his place."

Jackie takes a big breath. "Listen, we have bombers on the streets of Glasgow and we have brought in officers from all over the country, concentrating our efforts."

"Have to be seen to be doing something, Jackie?"

Jackie groans. "Think what you like spook, I am doing my job."

"What about Rooney?"

"Rooney, what about him?"

"Anything?"

"I thought you were the one giving Rooney information. Not reciprocated, eh?"

"He has been somewhat forthcoming in some respects, Jackie. She looks mischievously at Jackie. "And how are *you* getting on with him?"

"He was my partner, Jean, you know that. I am still –"

"Fond of him, Jackie." Jean moves around behind her.

"Maybe slightly less partial to him than yourself, Jean, eh?" Jackie says, stabbing into the back of Jean's head. "Like you would use anything to feather your own... bed."

"Well, I have a good model in you, Jackie. By the way, how's your... wee addiction? You getting enough these days?"

Jackie smashes her stick across the files on Jean's desk. "Just you keep out of my private life, you got that?"

"If you don't take your stick off my desk now ACC, you'll find yourself in front of the Police Complaints Authority, if not Alasdair Charlton." Jackie removes her stick and gets up to leave. "Al-Jamal, the mosque?" This stops Jackie in her tracks.

"He was promoting Islamic thought, Jihad, encouraging grievance against the West, distrust of law enforcement and opposition to Western forms of government, dress, and social values. All the bloody stuff that MI5 and MI6 should be concerned with."

"Sounds like a nice guy." Jean ignores Jackie's jibe. "The bombers?"

"Muslims from Chechnya. They travelled to Syria to join ISIS. ISIS Chechen militants who managed to inculcate themselves into the local Muslim community."

"Fuck's sake, Jackie, what are we doing?"

"We, Jean? You sound like Rooney. A fair number of British Muslims believe that you, MI5, and I, we, the police, are responsible for the radicalisation of young people who support extremists."

"Well, it's clear you guys are not working with the Muslim communities, to counter radicalisation, terrorism. What's your title, Jackie? Something about... Assistant Chief Constable, organised crime... counter terrorism... eh, safe communities. Not doing well on any of these core job descriptors, are you, Jackie?"

"And what is your remit, Jean? Something about national security, a focus on terrorism, both Muslim and also Northern Irish."

"You bloody well know that we are a civilian agency without formal executive powers and only become involved in criminal investigations when tasked to do so by Police Scotland, or any other law enforcement agency. Are you asking us to become directly involved in something you guys are both responsible for and reluctant to do?"

"You bastard, you know if we go into the Asian communities all guns blazing we will create tensions and build barriers."

"So Rooney said, you said."

"Are you fuckers talking about me?"

"The bombers, Jackie, let's get to something... tangible."

"I'll give you something... tangible."

"The bombers?"

"Asylum seekers. Sent up from London under the government's dispersal programme. Moved to a thirteenth-floor flat on the Red Road. Their asylum application was rejected and they were about to be moved on. Then they disappeared off the map until they turned up here making pressure cooker bombs."

"Now dead, no evidence, no links."

"They opened fire on us."

"Shots to the head."

"We made sure. Now look, I know where this is going, spook, and I don't like it. Get off my tits, you got it."

"Sure, that's Rooney's place… I believe."

With a "Fuck off," Jackie is out of there.

CHAPTER TWENTY-TWO

McCourt is in meditation as Halid arrives with his food and water.

"La ilaha illa Allah, Muhammadur Rasulullah," McCourt chants. "There is no God but Allah and Muhammad is the messenger of Allah."

"That is good my friend." Halid passes the food. "But to be a Muslim, you also have to believe that the Holy Quran is the word of God, revealed by him, that you believe that the day of judgment is true and will come, as God promised in the Quran. You have to accept Islam as your religion and you will not worship anything or anyone except God."

"I can do that." McCourt reiterates Halid's words. "The Holy Quran is the literal word of God. I believe that the day of judgment is true and will come, as God promised in the Quran. I accept Islam as my religion and I will not worship anything nor anyone except God."

"Ah, if I could truly believe you, you will soon be ready for God."

"I have to be ready for God. I have no religion. I was a protestant, but it didn't offer anything to me. I dabbled with Catholicism, and it too wasn't for me. Then I thought about Buddhism, because it related well to my philosophies and mediation." McCourt places his bandaged hand on the Quran. "But only Islam, having read Allah's words, meets my... needs, to have a good death."

"Every soul shall taste death, my friend. Only on the day of resurrection shall you receive anything in return."

"I don't want anything in return. Please believe me." McCourt reaches for Halid's hand.

Halid pulls back. "The Prophet said, 'When a person tells a lie, the bad smell that comes out of the lie keep the angels one mile away.'"

"I will show you."

"I do not understand."

220

"Give me the knife."

"You have nothing to hold a knife my friend."

"I have my thumb and index finger on my right hand to grip the knife and a ring finger on my left hand to remove with it. Please give me the knife, Halid?"

Halid passes the knife. McCourt goes back into his meditation for two or three minutes. Then, as Halid looks on aghast, he watches McCourt grip the knife in what is left of his right hand and remove the ring finger of his left hand. He grunts slightly as he does and tears come to his eyes. Not so much for the pain that rages up his arm but for the removal of the ring finger, still wearing the wedding ring he has worn since he was married years ago. But if this pains his heart he is determined not to show it. "I give you this as a token," he says, as he passes the finger to Halid. "You will see this is my ring finger. The wedding ring remains attached. "This is for the family I once had before I found Allah. My friends are now my family." Halid takes the finger and passes McCourt a surgical wipe and a fresh bandage.

"I have Mrs McCourt on the line, boss," John says.

"What the… Put her through," I say.

"Ms Kaminski gave me your number. I need to see you, Mr Rooney," Mary says.

"Why, Mrs McCourt, we are not the police?"

"Exactly why I need to see you."

"Come here this afternoon."

"I need to see you now."

"Come now."

Mary McCourt arrives within ten minutes. John escorts her into my study.

"You are keen to see me, Mrs McCourt."

"I was. That is ten thousand pounds, Mr Rooney, in used bills." She slaps a full A4 envelope on my desk. "That's all I have."

"Please sit down."

"No, I want you to save my husband."

"That's a police job, Mrs McCourt. We are businessmen."

"The police don't give a fuck. He'll die before they get anywhere near him."

"And what do you think we can do?"

"More than anyone else."

"I'll think about it." I put the envelope into my desk drawer.

She turns to leave the room. "Thank you."

"Mrs McCourt?"

"Yes?"

"What if I need to contact you?"

"I'll contact you, give me your mobile number."

"No, I'll take yours, best that way." She provides it reluctantly, turns and leaves.

"You want some?" Jackie is scoring a line from my glass top table. I wander through with a tray containing a pot of tea, a jug of milk, and two cups. She arrived there in a state twenty minutes earlier. She needed to talk to me, badly. "Sorry, Rooney, I need this."

"No thanks, I don't do drugs, and please go easy with my table."

"Rooney, I am not shooting up in a fucking alley with all the druggies. This isn't…. drugs."

"It's drugs, Jackie."

"You fucking her, Rooney?"

"Who?"

"Jean, you know… who."

"She came onto me."

"Oh, before you came onto me."

"I was weak."

"I know you're a slave to sin."

"It's not –"

"Why are you fucking her, of all people; you know how much she hates me?"

"For reasons known only to myself and to God."

"Mmm, she is… benefitting you, though, Rooney. You are getting something from it, her."

"She is, has been… helpful."

"She can fuck you properly?"

"It's not a competition."

"No, well let's make it one."

"Jackie, you are… irrational."

My robe opens easily. She finds my cock. I am dispassionate, never taking my gaze from the stained glass pane of Jesus and Mary Magdalene. I cum and pull my robe around me. I pour two more cups of tea, handing Jackie one, but she is back on the table scoring another line.

"Jackie. I need to tell you."

"Aye."

"Your drugs."

"Leave me alone."

I meet with the heads of three of the Asian gangs in Balbirs on Church Street. I make sure I am late. Neki Sumal, Balbirs' manager, greets me.

"So good to see you, Mr Rooney," Sumal says. "Please be assured that anything you and your guests have tonight is on me, enjoy."

"Thank you, Sumal, it is appreciated."

I remember Sumal being threatened by a Southside hood for protection money. The Family sorted it.

I approach the table. No one gets up to meet me, no greetings here. "Good evening gentlemen, thank you for coming."

Dabir Maan and Bashir Anwar grunt something indiscernible. Jamilah Ahmed looks on, interested. "You wanted to see us Mr Rooney?"

"I did."

"Business?"

"Not exactly. The police officer and ISIS."

"Our communities are very upset at what is going on, Mr Rooney. We have had… repercussions."

"Oh?"

"Windows smashed, graffiti on the walls of our mosque, threats made. Why did you wish to see us?"

"It's in our shared interests to fight ISIS."

"The Family assisting the police, that's new," Mann says. "We knew you were cosy, but that cosy?"

"I mean our… respective responsibilities."

"Us?" Ahmed says. "We have no such 'respective responsibilities'."

"Indeed," I say. "I think you have and as we speak we are… apprehending a good number of your players, taking them off the street for a while."

The men's phones start to light up. "Right, right," comes from each of them.

"We have hundreds of men, Mr Rooney, we can cope with

this," Ahmed says. "You can't hold them for long."

"We have selected your front line players, those involved in trafficking, drugs, DVDs. You'll lose big money in no time."

"Why is the Family doing this?"

"You need to do something for us."

"And what is that?"

"We need information on ISIS, safe houses, sleeper cells, soldiers, everything you have."

"We will see Allah before we can do that," Anwar says.

"Your men will see the virgins if you don't," I say.

The food arrives, no one eats, they are drinking water only.

I leave, but before I do I place a listening device under the tablecloth on the table. Outside, I find a doorway and ring the bug number on my phone and listen to them talking.

"We will fight the Family," Dabir Maan says.

"Don't be stupid," Bashir Anwar says. "They'll destroy us."

"Good evening ladies and gentlemen. Thank you for coming." Justice Secretary Alasdair Charlton is addressing the meeting of SGoRR. "In particular, given these matters of national security, I would like to welcome Ms Dempsie, section chief security services, Glasgow office." Jean smiles warmly at him, then turns to Jackie with a glance. "The current position is this," he says. "One, Police Scotland have received PC McCourt's eighth finger; two, we have had a second bomb in Glasgow; and three, we have the Glasgow families taking action against migrant gangs. What are we doing and where are we in all of this?" He removes his glasses to look directly at Hubert. "Chief?"

"We are continuing our enquiries on McCourt, Cabinet Secretary."

"Ms Dempsie," Charlton says, "Jean."

"Yes, sir?"

"You are working closely with Police Scotland in this?"

"Indeed sir, I am attempting to do this, despite resistance in… some quarters." Jean casts a deliberate look towards Jackie.

"Jackie?" Charlton asks.

"We are cooperating," Jackie says, "but they… are withholding information." All turn to look towards Jean. "We believe MI5 is supplying the Family with information."

Jean stays quiet.

"MI5 has to work in a variety of ways, Assistant Chief Constable, you know this," Charlton says. "We sanction anything and everything they do, and we receive regular reviews from Ms Dempsie."

Jackie is being side-lined and she knows it. She looks to Hubert who does not offer any support. She storms out.

"I am sorry Cabinet Secretary," Hubert says. "My daughter, the Assistant Chief Constable, is under extreme stress at this time, she is —"

"I leave her with you, Chief, she is your responsibility; you will manage this."

"Yes, Cabinet Secretary. I intend to."

"Good. Ms Dempsie?"

"Yes."

"I am authorising your direct involvement in these matters."

Jean smiles.

Jackie's distress is apparent as she leaves St Andrews House. Reporters are waiting at the entrance. Baird pulls up in the car. She is about to climb into the passenger seat when "The Family is taking action against ISIS, they are doing Police Scotland's job," is fired into the back of her head as a reporter pushes a microphone at her. "Comment please, ACC Kaminski?" She grabs the microphone and smashes it on the roof of the car. Cameras are trained on her to deliver the pictures across social and public media in minutes.

"Why the fuck do you not leave me be?"

The reporter turns to his camera. "This is the Assistant Chief Constable's response to our... interview with her."

At our notified address, the inhabitants are awaiting their dinner of halal chicken, pulao rice, and paratha. For the previous couple of days the house had been watched, the time of delivery of the food and typical containers noted, how the deliveryman approached the door, his dress and manner, no words ever spoken: just hand it in and go quietly about his business.

This time, the door opens, the deliveryman hands in the food, and the door closes. His knock is heard through a projector mic from a listening device fed quietly through the wall from the close the day earlier. It hears four voices. One says, "We will eat and then we will kill." Contrary to Al Jamal's plans for John McCourt, this is a celebration meal in the name of Allah in anticipation of a hit on a Subway station, the listening device has ascertained. They had prepared suicide belts full of explosives to be detonated in Buchanan Street Subway Inner circle, at 4.45 p.m., the busiest time of day, where commuters are pushing on to the platform for trains to the west end and home.

Just then, a stun grenade device in the bag is detonated by a remote transmitter and Family soldiers crash the door in, shooting dead four stunned men with accurate shots to their heads. This is no SAS in full assault gear, however; these are six men in jeans and black jackets with balaclavas. These men are more like a mob that would do a bank and leave the scene in much the same way without any identifying evidence that they were there at all.

"You bastards, Rooney," Jackie says, arriving into my house. "I am being publicly pilloried for not taking action against ISIS over McCourt and you fuckers hit a cell. The whole fucking world has gone topsy-fucking-turvy, you sanctimonious bastard." She disappears into the toilet.

I punch some words into my laptop. "Ah, nice to see you too, Jackie."

She returns five minutes later. "I am writing a post on The Family Facebook page." I read aloud as Jackie comes into the room. "God's family is all powerful."

"Oh, you fucking think so, nothing but fucking mental vigilantes, just bloody criminals."

"What's on my mind?" I say, referring to the Facebook post.

"Why don't you tell the world that you guys killed four ISIS soldiers?"

"We don't reveal… covert actions on behalf of the people of Glasgow."

She looks at me askance. "I can't believe you? What the fuck you on?"

I resist the opportunity of poring more scorn on her use of substances. "Sweet Jesus. I am aligning the physical strength of the Family with the resources of Police Scotland; this is joint working, Jackie."

"Joint working, bastard, you are working against us, over us, under us, undermining us, jeopardising everything we have been trying to do as an official force." Time to stay shtum, I think. "Where did you get the information on the cell?"

"We have been developing our sources. I can't tell you yet. We are getting close to McCourt. If we tell you we may lose him."

"You are getting information from your lover, Jean, aren't you? You don't fucking trust me, you bastard."

"We don't reveal our sources, not yet, Jackie, we can't. You have to trust us."

Then, just to indicate the lability of Jackie, she starts to cry. "I don't know what to do Rooney, this is all getting too much."

I move towards her. "I am here with you, Jackie." I put my arm around her.

"I wish I could trust you, Rooney. What is this? Sympathy, lust, or... You don't know how hard it is to…"

I kiss her and the tension, pain, rage, and blame all flow from her body into my arms.

CHAPTER TWENTY-THREE

Halid pulls out a portable DVD camcorder. Al-Jamal moves around McCourt and stands over him at his back. He removes the index finger of McCourt's right hand.

"By the permission of Allah, the Exalted, we will kill this man by twelve noon tomorrow. Please find another token of our... determination."

"Can I talk?" McCourt asks.

"Talk, infidel."

McCourt looks into the camera. "Listen everyone, the authorities, my colleagues, my family. Please know that I support ISIS and their Jihad on the western forces which kill their children."

Al-Jamal moves into camera shot. "You will see our preaching has brought your soldier to Allah. He will be happy to die tomorrow, unless your First Minister, the great dictator, sits down with us to discuss our terms."

"Inshallah," McCourt adds.

"And to you the great criminals of the Glasgow underworld, who are now in Jihad with us, we give you this statement. We will find your wives and sons and kill them."

"They are going to kill our sons, Rooney," Jim McGraw says. I had received a letter at home with no more than 'The Family kill sons of Allah. The sons of Allah kill the sons of the Family.' I have to pull the Family together to discuss this threat. We meet in the Grandroom.

"I have made arrangements for your sons and your families to be safeguarded until after this.... war is over."

Charlie Campbell speaks up. "This is not our war, Rooney," he says, "I've lost a good man, I'm not going to lose my son."

"This is a war we can win, Charlie. We are in a war we will win."

"This is your fucking war," McGraw spits.

"These killers are in our midst and they are not going to go away. We allow them to remain in Glasgow and they will eventually find a way to reach us. They will get us if we don't get them first. I need a mandate from you all to find them."

They know I am right.

"We need to cut off the arm of ISIS, which reaches all the way from Syria into Scotland and here into Glasgow."

"First it was the migrant gangs, now it's ISIS," Campbell says.

"Both have been forced upon us, Charlie. We have no option."

"He is right, Charlie. No one can rule Glasgow, but us," Bill Bingham says. "A vote," he demands.

I take a vote. "A show of hands for the fight against ISIS." Bingham is first to show, then Robert and Peter McStay, then Alex Fraser, Patrick Devlin, Paul Moffat, Andy Hamilton, and John Fullerton.

It is a majority and carried, but it is not unanimous.

"Against?"

McGraw and Campbell show their hands

"Abstentions?"

Ian Simpson and Geordie Montgomery show. I knew they would. Simpson's taxis are extremely vulnerable to attack and Montgomery bouncers are exposed on the doors of bars, clubs, and the restaurants.

Bill Bingham is not happy with this.

"Not good enough for me," he says. "If for one minute it gets out that we are not completely united in this, we are fucked. These people will see it as a sign of weakness and fuck us proper."

He's right and all there know it. Ian Simpson and Geordie Montgomery are the first to show their hands, followed by McGraw and Campbell.

I get home and call Mary McCourt. She had heard the statement from her husband; so had I.

"They are going to kill him by twelve noon tomorrow, Mr Rooney. Tomorrow."

"I heard it on the radio, Mary. It is said he supports ISIS."

"No way."

"They brainwashed him. He's a Christian."

"Have they fuck, Rooney. I know our John and he would not do that. He is playing them along. You have to find him."

"We are getting close."

"You have one day, Mr Rooney."

"We have one day, Rooney." Jackie pulls off her coat and hat, as she sets off to my kitchen to return with a glass of Sauvignon Blanc. "One day to save McCourt and my –"

"Reputation, Jackie?" We move into the sitting room.

"My bloody career, Rooney." She sinks into the sofa. "You know what's at stake here."

"We are at war with ISIS. The Christians are at war with the Muslims."

"Rooney, normal peace loving Christians and Muslims are not at war."

"Christians all over the world are rising against the Islamic Jihadists. They brought the war to us. We are fighting a Christian war at home."

"You are at war with everyone, Rooney. And you'll be at war with us if you don't help."

"We are doing what we can, Jackie."

"Well, you need to do more, I am desperate. Please, Rooney."

I reach for her and she pulls me to her. "Rooney, please have me. I need the... physical security."

I kiss her. She struggles to remove our clothes. "But you... can't." I try to enter her, but it's not possible.

"Please, Rooney, fuck me, fuck me, please."

I try, but I just... can't.

Turn her around, that'll do it, you won't see her face, you can imagine it's Mary.

I try to turn her, but she can't get on her knees. I help her, but time after time she just can't take the weight on her knees. She keeps falling to the side. Then I also fall to the side on the bed.

"Just fuck me, Rooney. I need it. I need you to. Please, you on top."

I fail and drop to her side.

She pulls herself up, grabbing my dressing gown to cover herself. "Do you have a problem with my disability, Rooney?" She sobs. "No problem with Jean on that respect, eh. Miss Whiplash, super-fit, super-sexed, super-ride. You'd get it up her, no problem there, eh? Hard as a fucking rock with her as she whacks you stupid. Me, I –"

"Jackie, I just need –"

"Shusht." She reaches for my cock and applies simultaneous fellatio and masturbation. She removes my cock from her mouth.

"You are fucking your Mary Magdalene and she is whacking your back so hard the blood is running down your arse." She is chanting now. "Fuck her hard, fatherman. Take the belt, sinnerman."

On each stroke, I am getting hard, and harder. I can only take so much of this before I... I shudder and whimper, "Jackie, I –"

"Don't Rooney, please don't."

According to Margaret, Jean has been "uncontactable" for days. "You tell her to get back to me or I go to the newspapers," Jackie says to Margaret.

"Do you want to leave a message on her voicemail?"

"Aye, go on," Jackie says. "You are fucking me through Rooney," Jackie says into the voicemail and almost immediately, "Jean" appears on her mobile.

"That sounds seriously profound, Jackie," Jean says. "Proxy fucking. Brilliant, I can fuck all the people I hate just by fucking their lovers, husbands, and partners."

"Just like Johnston, who killed through proxies, you are fucking me through him."

"Well, I hope you are enjoying it, because I certainly am."

"Enjoy it because it won't last forever. The poor bastard will see sense soon, and then it'll be him that'll do the fucking. You wait, you have his balls in your grip just now, but I know him better than anyone."

"How's the sex, Jackie? Need a wee hand on that score? I'll do it for you. Proxy as you say. I'll tell you how good it is. I'll enjoy it for you."

"Fuck off and die, you bloody pervert."

"We know where he is, Jean?"

"Tell me?"

"We are about to go in."

"Where, Rooney?"

"Why should I trust you, Jean?"

Trust no one.

"Because you have to. I own you, you bastard."

"Maclean?"

"He won't do it."

"He'll let McCourt die?"

"It'd open the door to many more."

"It's all about money, Jean."

"Eh?"

"ISIS is all about money. They want to extract millions from the government to fund their war in Syria, but more to line their own pockets."

"They are no different than you people, Rooney. Just gangsters."

"Correct."

"You have the address, Rooney? We'll let you guys go in, to get the credit."

"And Police Scotland, and Jackie?"

"They get egg on their faces."

"You really hate her, don't you?"

"You have the address?"

"We have the address."

"We will allow you to do it, Rooney. However, if you aren't up to the job…"

Trust no one.

"We are up to the job, you know that."

"We will… coordinate our efforts."

"But we save him?"

"You save him."

"Good."

"When will you go in?"

"Tomorrow morning."

"Cutting it fine."

"We will strike at the optimum time."

"I'll strike you at the optimum time, Rooney," she says, taking out her whip. "Take your clothes and bend over. You need a dose of this." She puts the whip underneath my chin and lifts my head back.

"God, forgive me, for I have sinned," I say, pulling my trousers down.

CHAPTER TWENTY-FOUR

John McCourt rises early. This is the day of his death. They normally come in around seven with breakfast. He is up by five, not that he had any sleep last night. He read the Quran all night, meditated and chanted the rest. He is prepared.

Halid comes in at 7.00 a.m., dead on time.

McCourt is reading the Quran. "Chapter seventy eight, thirty one… for the righteous there will be an achievement. This is true salvation. The attainment of the final goal. The supreme achievement. The fulfilment of the highest in human nature. The satisfaction of the true and pure desires of the heart."

"Prayer is better than sleep, my friend, for today you will suffer Shahada, a death for Allah."

"Inshallah," McCourt says.

Halid puts a prayer mat on the floor and presents McCourt with a white dishdasha and pyjama bottoms. He leaves and returns with a porcelain basin and a jug of warm water and a face cloth.

"Today you will be in paradise with houris, seventy-two virgins with eyes like pearls, splendid, voluptuous, large-breasted."

"Inshallah."

Halid helps McCourt to remove his clothes, then washes him from head to toe, drying him with a warm towel. "It is sunrise," he says. "We will face towards Makkah and pray."

They kneel together and begin the act of prayer, saying "Allahu Akbar," while raising their hands to their shoulders, well, for McCourt what was left of his hands.

"Allahu Akbar," is said four times, then "Ash-hadu an laa ilaaha illallaah," twice. McCourt adds in English, "I bear witness that there is no God but Allah." They both add, "Ash-hadu anna Muhammadan-rasulullaah," twice. McCourt says, "I bear witness that Muhammad is the messenger of Allah." Then they both say, "Hayya 'alas-salaah," twice. McCourt says, "Come to prayer." They

233

both say, "Hayya 'alal falaah," twice. McCourt recites, "Come to the good." They both say, "Allahu Akbar," twice. "Allah is most great," McCourt says. "Laa ilaaha illallaah," is said once by them both. "There is no God but Allah," McCourt repeats.

"Peace on you and the mercy of Allah." Halid leaves and returns with the video camera and places it on the bed.

"Thank you."

"You are a brave man, John McCourt."

"Why you doing this, Halid?"

Halid looks dumbfounded, as if he has never been asked this question, even if he had asked it of himself.

"For the Caliphate, Islam, Allah."

"Where are you from, Halid?"

"I am... not able to say."

"I am going to die soon, at least tell me who you are."

Halid looks at him for a minute and sits on the bed. Looking occasionally at the door, he is uneasy, but then he starts to talk.

"I am twenty-six and the eldest of seventeen children from two mothers."

"Two mothers?"

"My father had two wives at the same time. I come from Kirkuk in Iraq. I completed sixth grade, meaning I am literate. I am married with two children, a boy named Rasuul, which means Prophet, and a girl named Rusil, which is the plural of Prophet. Islam is central to my life. I was working as a labourer to support my family when I lost my job. Then a friend from the same tribe, but only distantly related, approached me with the offer to work for ISIS." Halid looks at the door again. "You must not say this to Al-Jamal or my life is over," he says. "Life under the Islamic State was just terror. I only fought because I was terrorised. Others may have done it from belief, but I did not. My family needed the money, and this was the only opportunity to provide for them."

"This is hard for you, Halid, in another country with the threat of death hanging over you."

"It is, even more so knowing my family will be thrown into poverty."

"Tell me more."

"We are children of the American occupation; we are filled with rage against America."

"But you are not fuelled by the idea of an Islamic Caliphate without borders?"

"No. Only ISIS, since Al Qaeda, has offered us a way to defend our dignity, family, and tribe."

"So this is not radicalization to the ISIS way of life, but the promise of a way out of insecure and undignified lives?"

"It is the promise of living in pride as Iraqi Sunni Arabs, which is not just a religious identity, but cultural and tribal, and based on the land we live on, too."

"I understand." McCourt allows the pause. "You will die, Halid, and go to heaven, is that what you believe?"

"I do not want to go to heaven. I want to be with my family. Now you must promise not to share my... thoughts."

"I will, Halid."

"Good, and now you must prepare to die."

"Halid, Al Jamal, what kind of man is he?"

Halid is now increasingly uneasy. "I cannot..."

"You would not allow me to understand the man who will take my head?"

He looks around.

"He is a clever man, with great ambitions for the Caliphate."

"Is he a moral man?"

"He has no morals, he is a commander, and he will kill every disbeliever or Christian he can, especially if they are American or British."

"He is a bad man?"

"He killed a family of five because their father refused to marry off his daughter to him. He ordered the execution of the family members. Three of them were children. Al-Jamal proposed to marry the fourteen-year-old girl, but her father declined the offer, not wanting to marry off his daughter to a terrorist. He ordered the family's execution, kidnapped the girl, and took her to an undisclosed location. He has executed dozens of people for his own interests."

"What is his background?"

"He is a former drug dealer and Free Syrian Army commander from Georgia near the border with Chechnya. He joined ISIS purely for business. He killed the family of a Syrian businessman and beheaded all of his sons and made both the parents watch the execution."

"What drives him?"

Halid is increasingly anxious, watching the door. "Personal gain."

"I want to know everything about him. I have a right to know about the man who will end my life."

Over the next ten minutes, Halid gives McCourt a detailed description of Al-Jamal.

"What does ISIS want?"

"Money, support, arms, recognition."

"What will suffocate ISIS?"

"The lack of these."

"Halid, I have one request."

"And what is that my friend?"

"I want to leave a message, a personal message to my wife and son."

"I doubt if Al-Jamal would allow that, but I will ask him."

McCourt puts up his bandaged hands. "I would prefer if this remains between us, as friends. As I protect your secrets, you will protect mine."

Halid looks at him. "I would have no way to deliver the message without it being known to Al-Jamal and the others. I cannot do anything over what is required of me."

"It will not be attributable to you."

"And how could this be done?"

"I do not know."

"I will leave you to compose yourself. Al-Jamal will be with us shortly and then you will meet Allah."

Five minutes later Halid returns with a camera and puts in a DVD. "On this DVD you will leave your message," he says. "I will respect your right to say goodbye in privacy. There will be two discs: one a DVD, which you will do just before you die, and two, this CD which I will deliver after you are dead and buried, and are then not a threat to the... operation."

"Thank you, my friend."

"And you will say nothing to Al-Jamal about this. If you do, your family will never receive your words."

Halid presses record and leaves.

McCourt straightens himself and talks into the CD machine. "Mary and Jamie, my wife and my wee boy. My Mary, I have to say goodbye to you. I love you and hope you will find peace. My son, Jamie, I love you and hope you will live a long and happy life, and achieve everything you are able to achieve. I will be with you every step of the way. Try not to grieve too much. I have had a good life with you both. But I need to tell you, because what I have to say can have an important effect on this fight against these madmen. First, I have not converted to Islam, although I do share some of its philosophies. I have used this to gain the trust of one of these men, Halid. He is a good man who is not committed to ISIS. It is important to understand these men to fight them and to fight the twisted organisation that controls them. Al Jamal, however, is a crazed killer who is in ISIS for personal gain. ISIS is no more than a power hungry, cash-fuelled organisation intent on domination. It is not dominated by Islam, Allah, or the Prophet Mohammed. It is dominated by power and money, not religion or dogma. ISIS obtains its revenues from criminal and terrorist activities. Challenge this and you will destroy ISIS."

McCourt reiterates all Halid had said about Al Jamal and presses Stop with his thumb.

Halid returns. "Are you finished?"

"I am."

"Prepare for death, my friend."

Halid takes the CD and leaves.

I'm at home awaiting Hamilton's call. We hit the house. We had no time to watch it to be sure. We had to trust the information and go in. A selected team of street players went in under Andy Hamilton, boss of the Hammie. He wanted to lead it, sure of his team's ability to carry it through. The Family agreed the plan.

My mobile buzzes on my desk, AH on the screen.

"Hello... how did it go?" I ask Andy, terrified of the possibility of failure. I can't contemplate it.

"No so good, Rooney, no McCourt, no Al-Jamal," he says. Another sleeper cell of suicide bombers. We interrogated one; one we kept alive. We thought it would lead to McCourt. He said they were set to enter Hillhead, Partick, Buchanan Street, and St Enoch's subways at 5.00 p.m., at the height of the rush hour. He said they were planning to kill hundreds of commuters heading home from city centre offices. They were planning to set off devices and kill as many of the infidels as they could and to martyr themselves for Mohammed. What will we do with him?"

"Follow the plan."

They sit him down under the flag. Hamilton's men gather behind him.

"We are killing your fighters to show the strength of the Family," Hamilton says, from under his balaclava. "No force is greater than us in Glasgow. This man will be with his ancestors today." Then a large street player man takes the man's head from behind; and then, as if he was cutting the throat of a sheep, he cuts the ISIS fighter's throat from end to end; then with a further cut and a snap he removes the man's head from his body. "We know of your intentions in Glasgow and you will not, I repeat, you will not prevail here." The disc is removed, downloaded, and sent to BBC Scotland.

McCourt puts the DVD in and positions the camera on the bed facing him, ensuring he's in shot. He kneels on the floor. He takes the porcelain basin, covers it with the towel to conceal the sound and the pieces, as he smashes it against the bedpost. He takes a large shard of porcelain in his hand, his thumb gripping it against the stump of his index finger now gone, and faces the camera. He presses Record with his thumb, then the final finger is put to the last and fatal task of his life. "I give my life to Allah." He draws the shard across his throat. "Allahu Akbar." His blood runs down the white dishdasha and onto the floor.

Al-Jamal and Halid enter the room to find McCourt's dead body in a prayer position with his head slumped on his chest. Al-Jamal lays his knife on the bed, the one he intended removing McCourt's head with.

"He has given himself to God," Halid says.

"He has martyred himself, so it is good, it is best," Al-Jamal says. "It shows the strength of Allah."

He lifts the camera and hands it to Halid. "The infidel has become a believer. He has given himself to Allah and has rejected the way of the sinner. He is an example to all of the power of God." Al-Jamal takes the DVD from the camera and places it in a DVD pocket. He marks "Allahu Akbar" on the front with a marker and places in in McCourt's hand, removing the shard. "In the name of Allah the avenger, it is done," he says.

"Report, Baird," Jackie says, getting into his car. Her leg is playing up making driving difficult and she has an obvious aversion to travelling in taxis. She gets a roll-up out. Baird makes a face. "It's only a wee one," she says. "I'll keep the window down."

"OK, ma'am," Baird says.

"The hit?" she says, lighting up.

"Not good, ma'am." Jesus, this is the last thing she wants to hear.

"Go on."

"OK, as planned, 56 Calder Street, flat zero one. Two hours ago, on the stroke of 11.00 a.m., Special Ops went in; stun grenades were delivered into the front room where Arabic voices were heard on a listening device. The guys chose their time carefully and went in when all the terrorists were in the same area. They sprayed the interior of that room with gunfire. They had no chance. Ma'am?"

"McCourt, tell me?" She puffs smoke his way. He tolerates it getting into his eyes and his nose for fear of an angry response.

"Ma'am?"

"McCourt?"

"It wasn't Al-Jamal, ma'am."

"McCourt, fuckit."

"Not there, ma'am."

"Not there, who the fuck was there... Baird?"

"A family."

"The mob?"

"No ma'am, a normal family."

"A normal family!"

"An Asian family. Mr and Mrs Ali and Misbah Hagg and their three children, Ali, Misbah, and Aamer, eight, six, and four."

"Fuck."

"Ma'am?"

"McCourt?"

"Yes?"

"He is dead ma'am."

"In the house?"

"No, ma'am, it wasn't the house."

"Jesus, it just gets worse."

"This has been handed in."

He passes her a pair of plastic gloves and a brown A4 envelope.

She dons the gloves and gingerly opens it to find a DVD, an A4 sheet, and a photograph of McCourt's dead body. She pulls out the sheet. "Your soldier is dead," she reads. "He died by his own hands. He martyred himself in the name of Allah. He will be buried in accordance with Sharia law, by sundown today, after his body has been washed and buried in a sheet. He will lie facing Makkah. There will be no headstone and we will not conceal the location of a child of Allah. Inshallah, he will be with the virgins today." She adds, "Allahu Akbar," as she reads the DVD pocket. She removes the gloves and returns the contents to the envelope, handing it back.

"The DVD, ma'am. I have a player in the back."

"No thanks, I know what will be on it. Get forensics on to it."

"Yes, ma'am."

"Al-Jamal and ISIS?"

"Still no location."

"Fuck."

Jackie's mobile goes. "It's the Chief," she says. "Great, just what I bloody well need." She drops her spent cigarette out of the window, much to Baird's relief. "Hello, Dad."

"Jackie, we have SGoRR, and you have to report."

"I know."

"What happened?"

"It'll be in my report, Dad."

"Jackie?"

"Make this good or this will come down on us, you, everyone of us, like a ton of bricks."

"I know, Dad." The call ends and she takes out another roll-up.

"Rooney?" Jackie voice sounds solemn down the line. "We need to talk."

"Yes, we do, Jackie." I switch on the bedside light. "But not tonight, it's ten past six." I hold up my watch to catch the light.

"And you are in bed?"

"I am, it's been a busy day."

"We fucked up, Rooney."

"Really?"

"We were given the wrong address and you went to the wrong place. We are both fucked."

"We hit ISIS, Jackie. You hit the public."

"Thanks for the supportive words, Rooney."

"You're welcome."

"You hit the wrong ISIS, Rooney. Where did you get your information? Why didn't you talk to us?"

"We received information through… our sources. We had no time to communicate, nor –"

"And, you had to act. But *we* could have acted."

"We couldn't take the chance."

"You couldn't take the chance."

"They were planning to hit the Subway, we found stuff to prove that."

"Jesus, fuck, fuck." Jackie throws her phone across the room.

"Jackie, Jackie?"

John Maclean, First Minister, arrives into a packed media centre at St Andrews House in Edinburgh. There is tension; no, there is aggression in the air, the kind of which he has never felt before on these occasions, while presenting the government's position on 'serious matters concerning the Scottish people'. He starts, "Today we mourn the death of a brave Glasgow Police Officer, we give tribute to a courageous man, and we give our sincere condolences to his wife and his family."

Aileen Clark is given precedence. As is protocol, BBC Scotland will have the first question. She is ready. "Mary McCourt has made a statement, First Minister," she says, boldly.

"We have heard her statement," Maclean says. "She asks that she and her son are given privacy in their time of grief."

"Yes, First Minister, but she is also saying that you and your government had no intention of saving him and Police Scotland had no ability to save him."

"She is… upset. I will say this. I give you my assurance that we will find the monsters that committed this crime."

"Did you try to save him?"

"Our… forces went to great efforts to save him."

"They didn't do very well did they?"

A pause confirms the expected affirmative, and allows John Stewart from STV to come in. "You would not meet with them," Stewart says. "You would not meet their demands."

"We could not accede to the demands of terrorists. It would –"

"Yes, we know, lead to many more, government policy, etcetera. We are informed that the Family tried to save him and destroyed an ISIS cell intent on creating mayhem in Glasgow's subway system. At least they tried."

"We tried," Maclean says with a faltering voice. "We also have to report on the family, Ali and Misbah Hagg and their three young children, Ali, Misbah and Aamer, who were unfortunately caught up in the... events," he clears his throat, "To save PC McCourt. We are... extremely sorry this happened and I will be meeting with representatives of the unfortunate family to give our condolences in person." It is clear to all there this is not a time to harangue the First Minister. "This was an everyday, normal family, about to have dinner, who have been killed." His voice drops at the end as he reaches for a hankie. He clears his voice and blows his nose. "We have no more information on this at this stage, but we will keep you informed of matters in the forthcoming days. Suffice to say we are extremely upset over these recent events."

"The police made a ballsed up attempt to save my husband," Mary McCourt shouts loudly, stepping into view from the back of the centre. "And you killed an innocent family. Disgraceful. Disgraceful," she says, breaking down.

"Look, I am sorry," Maclean says. "I can say no more at this time. Let's just take time to absorb this very sad day for Scotland. Just remember blood is on the hands of the so-called Islamic State today. Thank you." With that, he is off through the baying crowd of journalists to the safety of his chambers.

CHAPTER TWENTY-FIVE

I'm in Tennent's Bar. It's one o'clock and I've been here for over an hour. I need this time to think. Ben'll be here soon. I had arranged to see him here, but for now I need to be somewhere with a buzz, and there's certainly that in Tennent's on a Saturday afternoon. Short of quiet, however, people are nodding towards me as I coory into my usual corner. "That's Rooney over there, that's him, head of the Family, took out the Albanians, rapist gangs, and an ISIS cell," I hear them say. I keep my head in *The Herald*, trying to indicate to all to leave me alone. Then a familiar voice cuts through the peace.

"You wanted to talk to me, Rooney?" Ben pulls a seat into the table.

"I do, Ben. Thanks for coming."

Ben looks around and catches the sight of James and John observing us from the bar. "Worried you're going to get attacked?"

"Every chance of that."

"But your god will protect you, I guess."

"I'll protect me."

"Oh." For a couple of seconds he looks into my eyes. "You seem different, Rooney, more composed, relaxed even. How you feeling?"

"Just what I wanted to tell you. I'm feeling better. As you suggested, I have been back to Dr Melville and he's changed my medication. He started me on Clozapine and it… feels better."

"You sure Rooney, Clozapine takes time."

"Melville is happy with me."

"He told me. You've seen him three times in the last three weeks, since – ."

"I saw you last; since you said I was killing people, since you said that I had become a bad man."

"I'm pleased, Rooney."

"Me too, Ben, thanks." I hold up my hand and he slaps it. "You have been a good friend and –"

"You would have done the same with me."

"You stuck by me."

"Rooney?"

"Yes?"

"A lot has been going down."

"I know."

"You *are* at risk. Mick, migrant gangs, ISIS, etcetera."

"I am aware of that, Ben. I'll –"

"I know, you'll take precautions. Sure, but these guys."

"Let's say I am taking a very keen interest in any arms deals or shipments to Glasgow."

"Won't stop a hit in here, Rooney." Ben looks around. I doubt if he's even able to imagine the reality of his statement. "You just have to be –"

"I will be careful."

"God on your side, Rooney?"

"A clear head on my shoulders, Ben."

"Rooney, get out."

"What, Ben?"

"Get out of it. The whole Family thing. You and Jackie sort things out and get your lives back."

"I have things to do."

"God's work?"

"Doing good, Ben."

"Being bad, doing good?"

"Got it, pal."

Jackie arrives to see Jean. There'll be no barging in this time. Margaret makes her wait in the reception area. "Monday, Ms Kaminski, just catching up; she'll be with you directly." It is clear Jean's instructions to Margaret are to delay Jackie as she rifles through the magazines. Then, nearly an hour later, Margaret returns. "She'll see you now, Ms Kaminski." Her hand guides Jackie through the open door.

Jean is at the window overlooking the river, her back to Jackie as she enters. "Come in, Ms Kaminski," then, turning, "sit down," she adds, with an inevitably cool welcome.

Jackie positions herself at a hard back seat next to the desk, avoiding the comfort of the sofa. This is not a day to feel comfortable. "I need to talk to you, the operation –"

"The Haggs and their three children, an innocent family; seems you guys hit the wrong place." Jean returns to her desk. "Not good, Jackie, not good."

"Seems you gave us the wrong information, Jean."

Jean allows a power pause of a couple of seconds, while writing notes in her desk diary. "It was the information derived from our sources, Jackie."

"Your sources, Jean?" Jackie's voice rises from a hush to a yell.

"Now, Jackie." Jean waves through the office window to Margaret outside, indicating all was well. "You know we don't reveal our sources."

The silence returns as Jackie turns away to look towards the outside window, appreciating the enormity of this statement.

"They were wrong and we are getting it in the arse," Jackie says. "No, wrong again, I am getting it in the arse. There'll be a full investigation into our actions, the death of the family."

"Of course, Jackie, and I'll be happy to assist the investigation in any way I can."

Jean's smugness is only eclipsed by her lack of concern as she fills in her diary.

Jackie raises her voice. "Listen to me." Jean raises her eyes from the desk diary. "You will say that you gave us the wrong information?"

Jean stands to gain perspective. "What I say will be cleared at Whitehall, Jackie. MI5 will have immunity in this matter." She proceeds to tidy her desk.

"Oh really, so what you are saying is whatever you say or don't say, MI5 will not be viewed to be culpable in this matter."

"You know how it works, Jackie. It is in the interests of the country that MI5 is free to carry out its duties, for its sources to be protected, without –"

"You will have to report, to account."

"The only people I account to, Jackie, are the Director General and the Queen, and you will be assured I will be reporting as per my statutory obligations."

"And in the mean time we fry?"

Jean stands again. "I can do no more, officially, Jackie; however, if there is anything I can do, you know… personally, I would be only too happy to." She moves to the door, indicating the interview is over.

"Anything you can do, like fuck Rooney or fuck me, and fuck my career?" A shrill in Jackie's voice reverberates through the room. She gets up, straightening herself with her stick.

"Please, Jackie, you are becoming irrational again." Jean is in eye contact with Margaret through the glass.

"Irrational! You won't get away with this." Jackie's voice intersperses with sobs. "You bastard, you bastard you."

Jean hands Jackie a box of paper hankies. "Please, no hysterics or tears, dear. It is very unbecoming of an Assistant Chief Constable of a national police force."

Jackie takes the box and throws it at Jean, at the same time almost taking the hinges off the door as she flings it open. "This is not the end of this, you conniving, devious bastard you."

"Goodbye, ACC. Margaret, show her out."

"A reality check, Jackie?" I find Jackie where she said she would be. "Curlers Bar, 3.00 p.m.. Be there," she had said.

"Aye, a reality check, Rooney." Jackie pushes a chair out from beneath the table with her stick. "I believe you're starting to see things a bit clearer now?"

"Suppose."

"Well, Ben says you are."

"Ben, my guardian angel."

"Religious stuff?"

"No, just a joke."

"There's not much to laugh about, Rooney."

"Tell me about it?"

"It's all upside down, inside out, and the wrong way round. You guys are viewed to be the good guys, we are the bad guys; you get the credit and I get my arse kicked."

"I guess."

"They're all out to get me, Rooney."

"Who?"

"Jean, ISIS, the Mob, Millar, they are all on the same side."

"Jackie, I was the one with the paranoid delusions."

"They are all in it together."

"Eh?"

"It all creates a context."

"A context?"

"Why did she try to kill me, Rooney?"

"When, who?"

"You know who, Jean. My attack, Rooney; on Sauchiehall Street."

"Me, I –"

"Not you, Rooney; she made you think that."

"Eh?"

"OK, you made the call, but that did nothing. She ordered the hit that triggered the bomb, Rooney. She wanted you to think you made the call that triggered it."

"Why?"

"So she could manipulate you. You thought she knew something that would incriminate both you and –"

"Davy. It was Davy I phoned."

"I knew it was Davy."

"How?"

"I knew a lot about him, such as would have jailed him; but she also knew something about him that would have jailed him. He didn't want to hit me, but he had to. She wanted me dead."

"Jesus, Jackie, OTT!"

"And, you thought that if it got to me, it would destroy me and you would lose me. She set up a conspiracy of silence. She's MI5, Rooney, she does that stuff."

"She's bloody good at –"

"She wants you, Rooney, she's having you, and she has you exactly where she wants you."

"I…"

"No, Rooney. I never thought for a minute you would harm me."

"I made the call."

"You thought if you didn't you were a dead man. She lied. I had no intention of harming you."

"She said I was to be assassinated by you. To be blown up in a taxi."

"She used you."

"Don't trust –"

"Anyone, Rooney."

"I don't know if I can buy all of this, Jackie. You've been under a lot of stress, recently." Then, as if on cue, I receive a text: 'I want to see you Rooney, J x.' "I need to go, Jackie." I am on my feet and ready to leave.

"Rooney?" She reaches for me, grasping my hand.

"Yes?"

"We need to be together in all of this."

"Of course, Jackie."

Trust no one.

SGoRR is in full flow and Jackie is up next.

"And now we turn to ACC Kaminski to talk about the... McCourt incident," Charlton says.

"And the messed up attack," says Bill Grant, DCC, across the table, drawing scowls from Hubert.

"Indeed, now for the... important matter before us," Charlton says. "Ms Kaminski?"

"Thank you, Justice Secretary. You will excuse me if I do not stand." Charlton nods amiably. Jackie pulls her papers towards her, fixing her glasses solidly back on her nose. "OK." She clears her throat. "One, our position in the department is this." She looks at Hubert. "It would have been impossible to save PC McCourt. He was intent in not allowing them to kill him. We believe he did not wish to give them the success, the message, that they could kill an officer, our officer, that is."

"Go on, ACC," Charlton says. "We believe you had the wrong location."

"Yes, sir, we received... incorrect information." She looks along the table. MI5 did not normally attend these meetings, but she wanted to check. "We received incorrect information on the location, from –"

"Indeed, Ms Kaminski, but it is not necessary to reveal detail here. Why did you act on this information?"

"We acted on it because we were assured it was reliable. It was from –"

"I said, we do *not* need to know the source, Ms Kaminski," Charlton says. "Please go on."

Jackie looks forlornly at Hubert. He is looking at the table. "But, we –"

"Please move on, Ms Kaminski," Charlton prompts.

Jackie starts to sob. Hubert reaches over and gives her a paper hankie. "Jackie, get a grip."

She nods and gives a good blow into the hankie. "OK."

"Are you OK, Ms Kaminski?" Charlton asks.

"Yes, I'll be fine, sir."

"Please continue."

"Well, we received information. Information we believed, given its status, was correct." She looks back at Hubert. "We acted on it and yes, we... inadvertently, hit an innocent family." She puts her papers on the table and stands holding onto the table. "Listen, sir, and all here." She looks around the table. "We were set up. We believed we had Al-Jamal. We believed we had McCourt. But we were tricked... by –"

"That is fine, ACC," Charlton interrupts. "We will have to conduct an exercise –"

"In face saving," Hubert snaps.

"Chief!" Charlton says. "We will need to ride this out."

Hubert turns to see Jackie sitting with her hands in her head. "Indeed, Cabinet Secretary," he says, casting his eyes upwards towards the ceiling.

"We will return to the matter when we confirm the terms of the investigation," Charlton says. "However, we have news on the international front which presents a threat here at home, which we need to discuss." There had been rumours of hits on ISIS in Syria, but nothing official until then. "The Prime Minister is to clear air strikes of ISIS in an emergency debate in parliament. It is expected they will occur sometime later tonight."

"Fantastic," Hubert, murmurs. "That'll improve our situation no end."

"We must manage local matters in an international context, Chief," Charlton replies. "As we are expected to do."

I had to see Jean, I just had to. Compulsion, desire, penance, something basic inside me; whatever, before I knew it I was standing in her doorway.

"You wanted to see me, Ms Dempsie?" I say, as she opens the door. Without saying anything, she invites me in to her sitting room. She is wearing a black satin gown, open sufficiently to reveal nakedness underneath.

"Indeed, Rooney." She drops into the sofa. "A lot has been

happening recently. I thought it would be good to sustain, ensure our… relationship." She pulls me towards the sofa.

I hear the 'relationship' and feel her hand on my crotch.

"I wanted to talk to you to, Jean. I just –"

"You just need to fuck, Rooney; and so do I. An antidote to all of the stress going on at the moment. We can use it to… ride…," she pauses to release my cock, straddle me, then to slide herself deliberately down onto it, "the stormy waves."

"I had decided…"

"You had decided you would end this and support your ex-wife through this troubled period, while you take the credit for killing an ISIS cell and fucking a MI5 officer. Yes, you decided."

"I decided."

"But, you are a weak cunt."

"You set me up, making me think I had hit Jackie, that I had triggered the bomb attack. You fucking deceived me."

"Oh, Rooney," she says, pinning both of my shoulders into the sofa. "You poor deluded little boy."

She rides me hard, towards the inevitable point we both knew I would reach in seconds. I groan and she continues thumping down on me until I plead, "Please."

"Please?" She gets off me.

I fix myself and am about to get up to leave, my plan subverted by hers, when 'whack' she takes a riding crop across my back. "No!"

"I will punish you for your lack of loyalty." She delivers a few more strokes. "Your lack of trust in me; when, after all, I am your… master." Her voice breaks into a growl at the master. She pulls me from the sofa and through to the bedroom. I try to extricate myself from her, but I don't have the strength nor the will. I have no way to release myself from her psychological, sexual, and brutal grip.

Just then, I hear the outside door opening. "Home early, darling?" she asks, not taking her eyes from me. "Dinner in the oven, hon, I have something to do with this man before I join you.

I turn to see Millar standing inside the door. "Hello, Rooney," he says, nonchalantly. "OK, darling? Enjoy." He retreats to the kitchen. "I'll keep yours warm for you."

A BBC news release is emblazoned across television screens, including Jackie's as she nurses her hangover with a breakfast of orange juice. "ISIS cell in Glasgow and Al-Jamal still at large. He threatens to kill a Glasgow police officer for every drone sent into Syria that kills ISIS fighters."

"Shite." She grabs the juice and goes to dress.

Hubert takes the emergency meeting of the Executive Team at French Street. Jackie arrives to hear his opening comments. "You would have heard the headlines. ISIS is going to hit us for every drone strike."

Although Hubert says these words there are scowls towards Jackie as she settles in her chair. Millar's follow up speaks for all of them. "If we had got Al-Jamal this would not be happening."

"If Cameron hadn't ordered air strikes, this wouldn't be happening," Hubert returns. "This is a political matter which we have to manage."

"Fine, all our officers remain at base until the threat is over," Millar says.

"Be sensible and realistic, that's not bloody viable," Hubert replies.

"No, not viable." Millar looks at Jackie, who turns away.

Hubert reveals the security strategy to be employed by all uniformed officers. Then he draws the meeting to a close and moves quickly out of the room. Jackie makes her way out of the room followed by Millar. She waits for the lift, aware of his pungent smell behind her. The doors of the lift part and Millar moves inside as she enters the lift. She presses the button to head down towards her office. "You have some cheek, Jackie," he says, squeezing in.

"What?" She turns to him.

"You don't know what you have exposed our officers to. No officer will be safe on the streets tonight."

"Martin, just fuck off and get out of my face." She grabs the handrails to steady herself as the lift arrives at her floor. He reaches past her to close the doors. She tries to pass him to open the doors once again.

He grabs for her. "You could make this easier. I could make this easy for you. I could be your ally in this. We could work together rather than you doing this on your own." He is inches from her face and his pungent breath is nearly making her sick. He tries to kiss her and she turns away, his face colliding with the side of her head.

She pushes away from him, but without a grip she falls to her knees.

He reaches for her. "No, leave me alone, you bastard. I can get myself up." She drops her stick and reaches for the handrail with both hands to pull herself up. She fails. Millar see his chance. He pushes his groin into her face and tries to undo his trousers, grabbing her hair to pull her in. "Just do what is expected, Jackie. While my wife fucks the brains out of your man, I can fuck the brains out of you. It all fits. She fucks him, I fuck you."

Jackie reaches for her stick and swishes it in a long swoop across the floor to collide with his leg. "Aghh, you bastard," he cries out, just as the doors reopen and a group of office juniors pile in. "Dear me, Jackie," he says. "These lifts are difficult for those with... walking problems." She allows them to get her to her feet, out of the door, and into her office, to the sound of Millar moaning that the lifts were not suitable for disabled people, that he would "get admin onto it". "Hope you are OK, Jackie," he calls out. She turns away, giving him two fingers.

"We are here to discuss recent events." I get to my feet to open the Family conference. The heads of the constituent families sit back, not wishing to wade in, not yet. "We have received plaudits for our attempts to save the police officer and for our taking out the ISIS soldiers." All eyes are boring into mine.

Jim McGraw pipes up, breaking the silence. "They are definitely going to kill our wives and sons now, Rooney, for your fucking war with ISIS. They'll be well out to get us."

"As said in our meeting in October, Jim, we made security arrangements for your families to be safeguarded until after this war is over, and I would like to know how these arrangements are being delivered."

"And," McGraw adds, "as I said then, this is not our war, Rooney. This is your fucking war."

"We agreed," Bill Bingham says, pulling his six foot two frame to his feet. I sit down.

"Not unanimous, Bill. I didn't agree," Jim McGraw says.

"Nor did I," Paul Moffat says. "And there were abstentions."

"We made a majority decision. It was carried," Bingham says.

"Can I ask," McGraw says, "just what advantage to us, the Family, has this hit on ISIS been? Rooney?"

I get to my feet. "We… are, we were, at war with Muslim killers of Christians. We –"

Bingham steps in. "Ok, Rooney, you said all that shite, you and your crusade. Listen, I knew why we hit them, because we needed to, to send out a message that we are in control in Glasgow, no other fucker comes in and takes over, and that includes ISIS or any other of the migrant bastard team."

"Yes, thanks Bill, this has always been understood. A statement it is."

"And listen, gentlemen," Bingham says. "We are being held up as saviours by the Glasgow folk. These bastards were going to kill hundreds, create mayhem. As well as the effect on our business that would have caused, no fucker would have gone out, we're right in there with the punters."

McGraw says, "And how long do you think that'll last before they start saying it was in our interests to do them, it had nothing to do with civic responsibility."

I look at these men. Even the term 'civic responsibility' would not have been a term used by a boss of a firm in the past. These men had graduated with PHDs in crime from their experiences in and out of prison, and had become business executives to rival captains of industry and commerce. "We make the best of it, Jim."

"And we take advantage of it," McGraw adds.

"Eh?"

"We use the impetus, the climate to do any other cunting team out there that thinks they have a chance. And, incidentally, are we not missing a very important fact here?"

"What's that, Jim?" John Fullerton asks.

"Rooney got it wrong." McGraw says. "He sent our soldiers to the wrong place, we hit the wrong ISIS cell. We didn't get the intended target. We fucked it up." He turns to me. "Where did you get your information, Rooney? We need to know what the fuck happened. Why we hit the wrong team."

"I had information from the Asians," I say. "They thought they had the right cell, Jamal; only so happens it was another ISIS cell. How were they to know?"

"Maybe they were acting… against us, to protect Al Jamal," Fullerton says. "Maybe they knew they were dead men if ISIS found out."

I hadn't thought about that!

Clever!

"We hit ISIS," Bingham says. "Don't you think ISIS will be unhappy about that?"

"I promised the Asians, they would not be fingered," I say. "It was part of the deal. Apart from the fact we would have fucked them if they hadn't assisted."

Some faces turned to each other, not so much by my statement, but by my swearing. Is this the same Rooney they have before them, they wonder?

CHAPTER TWENTY-SIX

Ben is in his car, heading home from an incident. As leader of the major incident counselling service, he is on call twenty-four hours a day. This was a particularly difficult one. WPC Joan Barry, PC McCourt's operational partner had been killed while out for lunch with her friends in the city centre. He had been allocated to the Barry family, John Barry and their ten-year-old daughter, and had spent the last few hours letting them talk, giving them support; proper counselling would come later. Shock and disbelief comes first.

Tennent's is calling Ben in for a medicinal pint. He gets one, finds a seat, and opens the papers. The first opportunity he has had to have a read. He pores over them. It's too early for a full report on PC Barry, but he knows the circumstances. She left the restaurant to have a cigarette in the adjacent lane; then, while there, an unknown attacker sidled up and quietly and furtively stabbed her twice in the chest. Then, stealthily and easily, he walked down the lane and off into Buchanan Street, dropping the knife at the end of the lane. She stumbled back into the restaurant and collapsed in the foyer to die later in the GRI. The knife had gone through the side of her heart and she had bled to death.

Ben was aware of the context before most, as while he was there John Barry received a visit from Hubert who advised him that Police Scotland had received a call to say this was in response to the UK government drone strike in Syria against an ISIS target. Ben was eager to read the detail of the strike that happened late the previous evening, but it was in *The Herald* that morning. "Here we are," he whispers to himself, taking occasional gulps through the lush head of a pint of Guinness. "Cameron has advised Parliament that Reyaad Khan was killed in a targeted attack by a UK Royal Air Force drone as he was driving in a vehicle near the ISIS-controlled Syrian town of Raqqa." Gulp. "He was one of two other ISIS fighters killed in the strike. He said this was a legitimate attack because he was planning armed attacks on British soil." Gulp. "He said that the government would 'not hesitate' to repeat the action if there was no other way to prevent a terror attack in Britain." Gulp. "That these were terrorists who had been planning a series of attacks on the streets of our country, some involving public events, and that there are other terrorists making similar plans and we have to do what we can to keep our streets safe."

Ben takes a final and larger gulp as he realises the significance of this. "Al-Jamal has acted," he tells himself.

Jean agrees to meet Jackie in the Lismore. Jackie had arrived a few drinks before her. She finds her in the corner seat of the bar.

"You came." Jackie pulls a large glass of wine towards her. Jean notices another two empties.

Jean takes a seat. "I only agreed to see you outwith the office, Jackie, because here, in public, I hope there'll be less histrionics."

"And less chance of interruption from… Lurch." Jackie takes a large mouthful.

"Margaret does her job."

"She does what you tell her."

Jean goes to the bar and returns with an orange juice. She looks around as she sits across the table from Jackie. "It's a good idea, Jackie, I love the Lismore anyway. I've met Rooney here a few times."

Don't rise to it, Jackie thinks.

Jean takes a few sips of her juice. "OK, let's have it."

Jackie looks around. The bar is sparse and quiet. A few punters going back and forth from the bookies, some shoppers, those lining the bar, staring at themselves in the gantry mirror. Perfect, she thinks.

"You are not in the office now, bitch. Talk, I want the whole fucking story."

"Ah ha, a diplomatic start. Had a few drinks, no doubt." Jean nods towards the empties. "Ready to have a go." She gets up to leave. "Well, I don't –"

Jackie uses the hook end of her stick to grab her by the arm. "Don't have to stay here; yes you do, bitch." With her stick, Jackie pushes Jean back on her seat, then looks around to see if anyone had seen her.

Jean leans over the table and, in a slow drawl, says, "Jackie, touch me again and cripple or no cripple I'll kick you through those lovely stained-glass windows. It'd be a shame that."

Jackie puts the end of her stick close to Jean's face. "And I'll stick this so far up your arse it'll come out of your mouth."

Jean sits back. "Maybe you do need to say it, get it out," she says. "Then we can get on with our jobs, and our lives."

"Good, well let's start with this." Jackie looks at her glass to realise it is empty and goes off to replenish it. She returns with a large glass of Pinot Grigio. Jean is content with her juice, she is driving. So is Jackie, but she doesn't care. "Right, missy. I'll start, will I?"

"Go on, can't wait."

"Right. I'll tell you what I think, will I?"

"You will what you will."

"Right, this is what I think." Jean turns her head away. "You had me attacked. Davy, you had something on him. He did it. You made Rooney think he had done it."

"Interesting, go on."

"You knew about me lying about the Birelli case."

"And you getting the promotion from that and all your other lies."

"And Archie?" Jackie waits for a move of Jean's eyes, a flicker of her eyelids, a tightening of her lips, anything to indicate something, which doesn't appear on her stony face.

"Go on," Jean says, confirming something. "You tell me about Archie's death and your... role in it."

It is clear Jackie is about to say something, but she holds off. It is just too risky at this stage.

"Why are you out to fucking get me? I need to know why."

"I... I don't believe I need to –"

"You don't, but I do." Jackie screams and throws the contents of her drink into Jean's face. Jean gets up just as Jackie's stick rises in a swish to connect with the side of her face, knocking her on to the floor. Jackie gets to her feet and whacks Jean a further six times on her back before bar staff arrive to pin her to the seat and to get Jean to a safe place. Within minutes, they had called an ambulance for Jean to be taken to the Western Infirmary and a police unit for Jackie to be huckled to Partick Police Station.

Hubert reports to SGoRR. "Al-Jamal has killed PC Barry, as he said he would in response to a UK drone strike on ISIS. She died in hospital and we believe there will be others. We need to ask the UK government to desist in drone strikes immediately."

"Usual commiserations to the family, Chief; but on the drones, impossible," Charlton says, with equal measure of insensitivity. "Cameron is determined to hit them in Syria to prevent them hitting here."

"They are causing hits here. Bloody get him to stop."

"Please, Chief, you know he won't do it."

"If it was on the streets of London it would be a different matter. In Glasgow though, it doesn't matter there; bloody dying in the streets anyway, another PC won't matter that much, they've got plenty more."

"Chief, we know this is hard, but please… some composure."

"Fuck the composure." Hubert pushes back in his seat.

"We must find these men before they hit anymore of our people," Millar says.

"Guess your wife and the MI5 haven't come up with anything, Martin."

"Chief, let's keep the personal jibes out of this," Charlton says. "We need to step up the hunt for these guys and hope we get them –"

"Before they hit any more of our guys, you mean."

"Indeed Chief." Charlton prompts a pause. "We need to discuss the investigation into the McCourt affair, the… Family."

"I have to allocate it," Hubert says. "I think Jackie should do it." As he says this, Hubert realises why Jackie didn't get an invite for this meeting.

"We needed to move quickly on this," Charlton says.

"I'll talk to her later today."

"We… wonder if she is the right person, Chief? You know she has been, is, very close to the matter."

"She has strategic responsibility."

"She may be implicated, Chief," Millar says. "She was involved."

Hubert knows neither the Police Authority or the politicians will sanction Jackie conducting the investigation.

"Well, who would you suggest?" Hubert asks.

"Millar," Charlton says. "He has operational oversee of these matters and he was not privy to any strategic decisions regarding the matter. He can do it."

"I'll do it," Millar says.

There is no arguing this, Hubert knows this. It has been decided in the corridors of power that Jackie would not do it. He also knows she will not be happy about this.

"I believe you were attacked, Jean," I say. She is in tracksuit and trainers, sweating from an exercise session and out of breath.

"Superficial, nothing broken," she says, puffing. She removes her top to reveal the marks across her back from Jackie's stick, then turns to reveal her sweat covered breasts. "Kind of enjoyed it Rooney, not had a good whacking for a wee while." She pushes her breasts into my face. I smell her sweat, mixed with strong perfume. I take her left nipple in my mouth and put it between my teeth. I think about biting hard, but she withdraws it from me and puts her top on. "I do appreciate you coming." She invites me onto the chesterfield. "Rooney, your ex-wife is becoming more irrational. We'll have to do –"

"Jean, she is… vulnerable."

"Vulnerable? She is a nutcase, drunk, druggie, irrational, and losing it."

"I need to protect her."

"I'll protect her if you fuck me, not her, Rooney. I can give you what you want, she can't." She pushes me onto the floor, whips off her tracksuit bottoms, takes out my cock and straddles me. "Fuck me, you godforsaken sinner. She pounds me into the floor. "Fuck a woman, not a cripple."

"God save me."

Martin Millar arrives in the room to collect a book. "Hello, Rooney," he says, as he passes. "Have fun, darling," he says to Jean.

"I will darling, shame you can't fuck like Rooney."

"I have other… attributes, darling." Millar leaves the room.

"Are you trying to destroy her, Jean?"

"What, boy?" Jean says getting off me. "Of course I am."

I thought she would be less direct, more circumspect, but narcissist personality disorders aren't, normally.

"Please don't, Jean?"

"Please don't, sinner? I'll do what I think needs to be done. And you do what I tell you or Jackie will really get what is coming to her. Get on your knees… boy."

I can only submit. I kneel on the floor while leaning over the sofa. I hear Jean opening a drawer on her desk. I know what is coming. A whish and a thwack sounds, as the belt collides with my back, one, two, three times. "You are a bad boy, Rooney," she says. On the fourth stroke, I can't stop. It is close anyway from her humping of me. "Ahgh," I moan, as I cum.

"That's it boy." She whacks me three more times. "Did you cum when your father whacked you. Is that why you like it so much? Now get out – out." She leaves me in the sitting room, shaking like a leaf, as I try to compose myself. I hear Jean and Millar laughing in the sitting room. I get up and try to sort myself as best I can and get out of there.

"Fuck's sake Jackie, what the fuck is going on?" I hand her a mug of black coffee. "Here, with tons of sugar, you need it." She had arrived late the previous night totally drunk and just about fell through the door.

"See you are back to your usual foul mouthed state?"

"Sorry, I… I'm worried about you."

"Worried about me. What the fuck do you care?"

"Jean, you gave her a real doing."

She sobs. "She fucking deserved it." I pass the box of hankies. "Jesus, Rooney, I'm a fucking mess. Charged with assault of a MI5 senior officer, bailed out by Dad, and an investigation into the McCourt fuckup. I've been suspended pending the result of the investigation *and* an internal inquiry into my… conduct."

"Jesus, suspended, Jackie."

"Aye, Dad landed that on me on picking me up from Partick Polis Station. Apparently, a 'political decision in response to the McCourt affair and the death of the Haggs prompted by public pressure'."

"Mary McCourt is stirring up quite a wasp's nest. She's developing quite a profile."

"And getting the ear of Charlton, while Jean is getting his cock."

"Jesus, Jackie. This is –"

"Irrational, you bet it is."

"What you going to do?"

"Get fucking wasted and get fucked by a big brawny builder down the Gallowgate."

"You know that's not possible."

"So what's the alternative?"

"Me, I can be a builder." I put my arm around her.

"Bob, the fucking builder, you'll do. But first, any booze?"

I reach for the bottle of malt, untouched since I stopped drinking. The unopened bottle stood on my coffee table as a symbol of my abstinence and a sign I had control of my drinking, knowing to open it would be the end of control and the start of a path back to the decrepitude of my past life that nearly killed me. I look at it, seeing my image in the dark glass. I recall the last time I saw my image reflected in a bottle. The last time, when I saw the man I had become: a mental illness, an alcohol abuser, a destroyed man. I crack open the seal, pull out the cork, and pour two large glasses.

We finish the bottle in under an hour and fall into bed. We fumble more than fuck and fall asleep in each other's arms. She was first to rise the following morning. As she does, she looks at my body, thinner than she has ever known. The bones stick out of my back, the marks from the leather belt when I was flagellating myself, then some fresh, recent marks, red whelps, heightened, angry wounds.

"Rooney?" She shakes me.

"What?"

"Your back, where did you get those marks?"

"Something you don't need to know, Jackie."

"I know what that is. Jean. You are the plaything of Miss Spook. Jesus, on top of everything, she's your dominatrix. Fuck, Rooney."

"It's my punishment, my penance, Jackie."

"I don't fucking want to know, Rooney."

She gets up and, gathering her clothes, heads for the bathroom to get ready. Five minutes later, she's heading out of the door.

"Where you going, Jackie?"

"As I said, Rooney, to get pissed and to get fucked by a builder."

"Hello, Assistant Chief Constable."

"Eh!" Jackie spins her cart round in Waitrose upstairs car park to see Mary McCourt leaning against her car. "I'll call the cops. No paint, no more."

"See you're having a party." Mary gestures at the full bottle carrier.

"Aye, lots to party about." Jackie opens the boot of her car to store the bottles.

"Sure you should be driving in your state?"

"I'm fine, now if you'll –"

"Sure, you can go, but I need to tell you."

"What?"

Mary takes a breath and spews it out. "You killed my husband and you killed those folk in that house, and I'll see you burn in hell. But before that I'll see you in Court and I'll see you are never in charge of even a pair of traffic wardens in Glasgow. You're finished, Assistant Chief Constable."

"I am –"

"Too right you are."

"I –"

Just then, Mary McCourt's palm whacks off Jackie's face. Jackie quickly gets herself into her car, dropping her stick. Mary McCourt picks it up and throws it at the departing car.

Jackie screeches out of the car park, driving straight out onto Byres Road without stopping at the road end, only to collide with a taxi racing up the road trying to get through on the amber light at the top of Byres Road. The collision is minor, taking the front light from the taxi. The passengers of the taxi are safe and well, but the passing traffic cops see everything. Despite her protestations, her being an ACC, they breathalyse, arrest, and remove her to Partick Police Station, where she would spend the rest of the night in an austere police cell. As she is driven away, Jackie casts her eyes up to the car park above Waitrose to see Mary McCourt clapping her hands and waving down to her.

CHAPTER TWENTY-SEVEN

"We need to find Al-Jamal." I pass Bill Bingham a Guinness in Curlers. "The Family need to act decisively."

"They'll not be happy about the whole ISIS thing, Rooney."

"It's the only way to guarantee safety, Bill. Cut off the head."

"I agree, but they're split on it. There's a fear it'll only inflame things."

"I'll talk to them."

"Best leave it to me, Rooney."

"I'm Father, Bill."

"I know, Rooney, but they'll fuck you."

"I have my… guarantee, my insurance."

"Won't stop them having an EGM, and voting you out, Rooney. You know, you are not –"

"The same man?"

"You were great at bringing us all together and getting business moving in the same direction, but this ISIS stuff. It's not like fighting the local teams."

"What do you suggest?"

"Let me talk to them, individually."

"OK, but if they don't support me in this, I'm out."

"You'd be out anyway, Rooney. Let me talk to them."

"OK."

"I just wanted to discuss the brief on the investigation, Chief," Millar says, delivering two pints to their table in the Belle.

"Aye, a big job."

"Yes… a big job, Chief." It is Millar's hesitation that helps Hubert realise there is more to this. "I have been advised by the Scottish Police Authority, indeed by the Cabinet Secretary himself, that it would be best that you are not involved, Jackie being your daughter and all, being so close etcetera."

Hubert sits back on his seat like he's thinking of a word to finish his crossword. "And what do you think, Martin? Don't you think, as Chief, I should know what the terms are?"

"Chief, we are friends, but in this it's impossible. It would threaten the… integrity of the investigation."

Hubert studies Millar intently. "And how's Jean, Martin?"

Very sore, the bruises will take some time to heal, but she'll be OK."

"Pleased about that."

"Boss?"

"I won't apologise on behalf of my daughter, Martin."

"No, I didn't mean that."

"Oh."

"I wouldn't rock the boat just now. Just let me get on with this."

Hubert stands up, stares him in the face, finishes the dregs of the Guinness, and heads off before he says or does something he would regret later.

"Bye, boss."

Hubert doesn't respond, noticing his mobile lighting up. He moves outside to take the call.

"Mr Kaminski?" the caller says.

"Yes?"

"Your daughter, Jacqueline Kaminski?"

"Yes?"

"I'm Brian Crockett, Doctor, A&E at the Western Infirmary."

"Jackie?"

"She's fine, her condition is stable."

"What, how?"

"She was admitted by ambulance today. She was found in her home by her cleaner. She'd collapsed."

"Is she OK?"

"She had consumed a large amount of alcohol, hard to discern from the results of the stomach pump, possibly wine, whisky, maybe brandy, then she took a hefty handful of paracetamol tablets."

"Is she… in danger?"

"We removed the contents of her stomach; however, we remain concerned, the paracetamol…"

Hubert knows from his beat days that even a few days after taking paracetamol, kidney failure can occur. "Yes, I understand, the kidneys."

"Yes, Mr Kaminski, but the overdose. She is clearly at risk."

"I'll come right away."

"That would be helpful. She is being assessed by a psychiatrist and he may detain her. When she is fit he may wish to transfer her to the psychiatric unit."

"I'll look after her, don't worry I'll make sure she's OK. She's not going to any loony bin."

"Mr Kaminski!"

"I know, sorry, I shouldn't have said that. I'll be there soon."

Hubert calls a taxi on Byres Road at the same time texting his wife. "Jackie, OD'd, in hospital. Going there." In the taxi, he calls me.

I see "Hubert" appear on my mobile screen. I'm not used to Hubert calling me. Our relationship was strained after Jackie's attack, Hubert thinking I had some hand in it, contrary to Jackie defending me. "Rooney?"

"Hubert."

"Jackie."

"I know, OD'd. In the Western, I'm heading there."

"I'll see you there." Hubert is comfortable with this. He knows Jackie wouldn't listen to him on his own, but if I were there maybe she would.

I arrive at A&E reception, just shortly after Hubert's arrival. "Any news?" I ask him.

"Just spoke to the doctor," he says. "She's sedated, shaken up. Physically, we'll just have to see how she goes over the next few days."

"Jesus, what happened?"

"Thought you would know, Rooney. She said she had been... seeing you again. How was she the last time you saw her.?"

"She wasn't great, obviously upset about... things. She said she was going to... let's say get drunk and then get..."

"She was arrested for drink-driving. I bailed her from Partick Police Station twice."

"Aye, I know. She's been under a lot of pressure recently."

"Would you like to see her?" the charge nurse asks. "Only for a minute, though, she's –"

"I know, very tired," I say. "That's always said that in these situations."

"Aye," Hubert says. "You'd know all about that."

"My god, a fucking pincer attack," Jackie says, as we enter the room.

"What the hell, Jackie," Hubert starts.

"Just stop right there, Dad. I'm in no fucking mood for lectures. What's this then, father and ex son in law rallying round to support daughter, ex-wife?"

"I just thought –"

"Don't, Dad. You did fuck all to prevent my suspension."

"I had no control –"

"You are the Chief."

"I know. "

"How are you, Jackie?" I am aware of the need of a supportive question.

"Well, the consultant says I can't go home on my own. He threatened to section me. I said I would go home with you."

"Rooney," Hubert says. "Why not us, your –"

"I keep telling you, Dad, she's not my mother."

"She'd be happy to have you."

"It wouldn't work. I'll go to Rooney's. Is that OK with you, Rooney?"

"Yes, aye, fine, when?"

"When they let me out. I've to have tests tomorrow, then –"

"Jackie?" Hubert asks.

"Yes?"

"You need to –"

"Sort myself out. OK, that's it. Right, go," she orders. Both of us head for the door.

"Rooney?"

"Yes," I say. Hubert leaves, knowing she wants me to remain.

"You have to help me, Rooney," she says.

"I'll do anything."

"Good, then destroy Jean before she destroys me."

"Cameron has threatened more drone strikes," Ben says, arriving in Tennent's, en route from the Western.

"Fantastic," I say. "I wouldn't want to be a police officer in Glasgow tonight."

"No, not without a suit of armour and chain mail."

"Won't stop a bullet, Ben."

"A knife or a sword?"

"Nor a bomb."

"Jackie wants me to… destroy Jean, Ben."

"The Father of gangland Glasgow murders the MI5 chief intelligence officer wouldn't sound too good on the BBC news, Rooney."

"It's got a ring to it, Ben."

"Just you keep a keen heid on you. You've just got yourself sorted out."

"Aye, good reason to celebrate."

"Eh?"

"Time for you to pay back some of those pints I got in for you while I was tee-totalled."

He orders two pints of Deuchars, which is fine for a start, but then I am looking for something stronger. "Stella, barman," I ask, leaning across the bar.

James and John look over in unison from their side of the bar. I call them over. "Fuck off guys, I'm having a drink with my friend."

"OK, boss. You sure?" James asks.

"I'm sure." They are reluctant to leave the bar. "Ben, what'll you have?"

"Aye, go on, another Stella. It's nice to have a drink with my old pal, but only one, no more, you need to mind your meds."

Six drinks later we stagger out of there. Ben, to catch the bus home into Merchant City at the top of Byres Road. Me, to meander up through Dowanhill, up towards mine on Sydenham Road. I turn on to Victoria Circus, however, I notice a black four by four crawling along behind me. *Where are James and John now*, I think, remembering my lapse of concentration brought on by a need to get rat-arsed when I sent them home.

The car pulls up right by my side and the window opens like an upside down portcullis.

"Hello, Rooney, can I have a word with you?" I know immediately this is Alan Taylor, but something tells me if Taylor wanted me dead I would be lying on the pavement oozing blood from a number of bullet holes. "Please, get in?" Taylor asks, also acknowledging this reality.

"I'll just stay here, thanks." I keep my distance from the car. Being shot is one thing, being abducted and kneecapped to be dumped on the Byres Road, is another.

"Please yourself," Taylor says, from the car. "But I need to talk to you, it's important."

"Ice cream not your flavour of the month these days?"

"My brother Jim died, Rooney. But that's the life we lead, and we have lost some good men in fighting the Family, but that's the price we pay."

"What do you want to say, Alan?" I am sobering up at the reality of this event.

"Jean Dempsie, the information on McCourt given to Jackie."

"Aye."

"We gave Jean correct information on McCourt. We believe she passed wrong information to Jackie."

"And why would she do that?"

"Work it out, Rooney."

"Why?"

"You need to work it out."

"No, why are you telling me?"

"I need something… from you."

"You do nothing for nothing, Alan, what do you want for this… something?"

"I –"

"Better move along gentlemen," comes from behind me as James arrives. By then John is at the other side of the vehicle, where he is tapping the passenger door. "Aye, better move along," he says into the car. Both men have sawn-off shotguns trained into the interior of the car.

The cars windows go up as the car pulls away. "Cheerio lads," James says.

"We're to get you home, boss."

"Oh aye, who says."

"Mr Bingham."

CHAPTER TWENTY-EIGHT

I'm escorted home, refusing to accept any heavy lecture by John. As I enter the house, Ben texts. "Got home OK, Roon - hope you did too - without incident!" Little does he know! I read on. "Two more drone strikes, Rooney, lock up your coppers."

PCs Grant and Crawford are suited up: bulletproof vests and Glock 17 pistols holstered. Bicycle cops, they'll patrol the riverside walkway on the Clyde, from Trongate at the Clutha Vaults to the SSEC. They have been briefed. Any possibility of confrontation and they'd to bring in the ARUs. An ASU would patrol from above and all officers were to be monitored through Vauxhall Movano vans acting as mobile offices by GPRS as they travelled the city streets. All CCTVs across the city would be monitored by extra staff. Any indication of a potential attack would bring a combined response from all units.

There had been calls to take the PCs off the streets, but Hubert was determined they would remain high profile. The public needed to feel their presence, to know they were around.

This night is quiet along the Clydeside: the usual jakies drinking publicly against the law, but not worth filling in a charge sheet for, some druggies having a hit underneath the Caledonian Railway Bridge, and some prossies plying their trade along the Broomilaw. The PCs will stay on the move as advised and call in mobile units if necessary, and they will 'stay alert'.

I hear the Klaxons from the Central Hotel as I am about to address the Family. Some of us move to a window overlooking Gordon Street. We are informed, following two drone strikes, there has been an attack on two police officers policing the Clydeside. It gives me the opportunity to introduce my key business that day. We return to the Grandroom and I stand up to address the leaders of the respective teams.

"Out there," I start. "Out there, ISIS is attacking police officers, taking our turf, affecting our businesses. In here, we are prevaricating over what to do, what this Family stands for. We need to stand with the authorities on this matter. We need to fight ISIS."

The meeting is over with tacit approval of my proposals. Being the first out, Robert McStay is the first to be hit on leaving the hotel. His bodyguards are hit by the same gunman walking purposely towards the hotel. He sprays them with gun fire from a Croatian-made Agram sub-machine gun, putting four rounds into each of them. The rest of the Family are coming down the stairs, but their bodyguards are way ahead of them, bundling them back up the stairs with a few racing down, their own automatic weapons ready. The gunman, by then, is at the bottom of the stairs, having shot two of the reception staff as he walks past. He fires at one of the bodyguards hitting him on the leg, bringing him to his knees. The rest take cover only long enough for him to be up on the man and calling "Allahu Akbar." He puts two rounds into his head and continues up the stairs to be brought down with a hail of shots from the men there. He drops his arms, his gun falling to the stair, and collapses from his legs up, like a human World Trade Centre, until he is on a heap on the stairs. One of Bingham's bodyguards reaches him, puts a sure shot to his head and kicks him down the stairs where he rolls until he lands on the ground floor of the hotel. Three body guards move gingerly down the stairs to be met by a second gunman facing them there. He sprays them with bullets bringing three of them down. Then with another "Allahu Akbar", he opens his jacket to reveal an explosive device strapped to his body. He reaches for the detonator and the resultant explosion splatters blood and minute bits of flesh and bone everywhere in range, as well as destroying the reception area and killing two residents who had been cowering behind a sofa at the foot of the stair.

The sound is deafening to me and the members of the Family as we are hurried along the first level corridor towards the staff door out of the hotel; there, staff are trying to get out on to the street, followed by a good proportion of public in the hotel that day. Police cars heading to the Broomilaw are screeching to a turn heading for the hotel.

Mayhem is on the streets of Glasgow City Centre. People are running in every direction. Then, just as there appears to be sudden calm, like entering the middle of a hurricane, a further blast erupts at the entrance of Buchanan Street Subway, killing a suicide bomber and sixteen members of the public.

The first responders do not know which incident to race to. People are dazed, covered in dust, wandering about deafened by the blast. Mary McCourt and her demonstrators run from the Square to assist people. Meanwhile on the Squiggly Bridge at the predetermined time, the two gunmen who killed the policemen on cycles, kill their hostages and put their guns to their own heads before police marksman are allowed the opportunity to do the same, while saving the hostages. It's two bullets too late for the hostages, however, an elderly husband and wife out for a walk along the Clyde in the early evening before dinner.

Aileen Clark, BBC Scotland, starts, "These are unprecedented days for the City of Glasgow. A wave of terrorism has engulfed the city. Six citizens have died at the entrance of Buchanan Street Subway, two young police officers have been murdered on the riverside, two elderly residents have been murdered on Tradeston Bridge, four members of the public are killed in the Grand Central Hotel and an undisclosed number of businessmen and their... assistants have died." She pauses; no one is ready to follow her.

Hubert moves to the mic. "Thank you, Miss Clark. I am shocked, as this city is shocked. I offer my condolences to all those families who have today lost loved ones. I assure you." He moves closer to his mic. "I assure you, I will not rest until I bring these men to book, this organisation which has attacked our city. I –"

Clarks coughs. "You, Chief Constable, are losing officers, but the citizens of this city are being killed."

"We must stay calm at this time of great threat. Our officers will meet this threat, as did our brave PCs John Grant and William Crawford –"

"And my husband, John McCourt." Mary McCourt pushes through the crowd as the camera swings round to catch her face full frame. *"He* put himself in the firing line."

"Thank you, Mrs McCourt," Clark says. "Have you anything to say to the families of these brave policemen."

"I want to say this," she says. "My husband died due to a failure of leadership, he died because of a lack of political will, and he died because he didn't matter in the national scheme of things."

"Thank you, Mrs McCourt," Clark says, turning to the camera. "I am Aileen Clark and we will keep you informed of developments in this, without doubt the most shocking day in Glasgow's story. Please stay home, stay safe, and stay calm."

CHAPTER TWENTY-NINE

I get myself home and set to throwing a guard around the Family heads. Security protocol swings into action. All bodyguards have been given instructions. Bosses and their families have been taken off to safe locations, where security provided compares with that for heads of state. James and John are joined by a dozen armed men, two at the entrance to my gate, four patrolling the ground, four joining James and John inside. All mobiles have been removed; however, the mainline phone buzzes. I reach for it. John gets to it first. "No boss, your protocol has been implemented." I would be wrong to disregard the arrangements we drew up to ensure the safety of the Family heads. Security has taken over and bosses would defer to security until a collective decision is made, again by the Family security, that the threat is over. It's Bill Bingham. John hands me the phone.

"Robert McStay and six of his soldiers are dead, Rooney."

"I know, Bill. It could have been worse if they had managed to get up the stairs. I guess protocol kicked in."

"You may say that, Rooney, but I see it differently."

"Eh?"

"You put us in this position, Rooney, you. You and your perverse need to fight ISIS. The only thing you forgot is that ISIS fight dirty, even dirtier than us."

"What are you saying, Bill?"

"I'm saying you were wrong, Rooney, and I for one, alongside others, want you out. We can look after ourselves."

"Are you saying I am out or the Family is out?"

"Both."

"Great."

"The bosses are withdrawing the soldiers. They are looking to their own. Pass the phone to McDuff or O'Hara."

"James or John?"

"Just cut the religious bullshit as well, Rooney. Give the phone to McDuff or O'Hara, whoever."

"Bill."

"The phone, Rooney."

I hand John the phone. He receives Bingham's instructions.

"Sorry, boss," John says. "Hope you'll be OK," James says. They and the four soldiers join the others in the ground to enter three cars to speed down Sydenham Road and away.

For this first time in this house, I am alone.

I call Jackie on the main line. "Jackie?" She had been trying to call my mobile, now buzzing away in John's pocket.

"I've been trying to get you. Are you alright?"

"Aye, I guess. It's been a big day."

"You're telling me. Rooney, I'm home."

"You'll be pleased. Your liver?"

"I've passed the danger period. They think I'll be OK. The got the tablets out of my stomach in time."

"Good, and you weren't sectioned."

"No thanks to you, Rooney. I was supposed to come home to you. You said. I couldn't get you. You were… in conference."

"We had to meet. I was coming for you, until…"

"I guessed things had changed. I convinced them I would be OK. I promised I wouldn't do the same. As it happens, as soon as the sky fell in, Hubert sent two uniforms. The doctor was happy with that."

"You'll be arrested if you try to kill yourself. I like that."

"And I've a community psychiatric nurse coming in tomorrow to… counsel me."

"I could do that."

"Aye, right, Rooney. Are you safe?"

"They've gone."

"Who's gone?"

"James and John, and security."

"Jesus, Rooney. Lock your doors and don't move until I get someone over there."

I did what I was told and within ten minutes a PC is at the gate. Fifteen minutes later I am at Jackie's flat. Baird opens the door. "In there," he says. I pass Jackie in the hall in her robe and pyjamas. "I am talking to my father," she says, as I make my way to the sitting room.

"There's a SGoRR in the morning," she says, arriving from the hall. "Charlton wants to send in the army. Hubert is resisting it; he's determined to hold things together locally, to find and apprehend all the ISIS, in particular Al-Jamal."

"Al-Jamal?"

"He made a statement, Rooney. On Al Jazeera."

"What did he say?"

"That ISIS has triumphed. We have risen to defeat the British soldiers. We have killed the infidels in their own garden. We have shown we are in control of a major city of the UK, and we will now move to conquer other major cities of the UK in the same way."

"The Family have disbanded. Bingham called."

"I thought they would. The whole world has gone mad."

"Changes things."

"Sure does. What are you going to do now?"

"I could counsel you; attempted suicide is my forte. I'll give you a discount, twelve sessions are the normal programme. Initially, at least, then we can see where we go from there."

"You can start now if you like." She pulls me close, nodding at the police officer and then to Baird. "You can go home, Euan." Baird readily accepts, but only with the agreement that the uniform at the door stays. Baird hands him a chair and tells him to stay put until he is relieved the morning after. Then he tells the PC to call home, to assure his partner he is safe, on this night where police officer's wives, husbands, and partners, across the city are waiting for them to come off shift, fearing for those who are still on or are going on shift. Fear is on the lips and minds of police officer's partners. Anger is on the lips and minds of the police officers, however. Another two of their colleagues have been murdered on the streets they are charged with making safe.

I follow her through to her bedroom where we lie together. Then, as if in the need for a post-coital cigarette, she comes through from the kitchen with a bottle of white. "I thought we could have a wee drink."

"Jackie, you are just out of hospital, where your stomach was pumped, after consuming a cupful of tablets. Give your liver and brain a chance."

"I need it, Rooney."

I accede and we finish the bottle. The sedative the medics gave her mixes with the alcohol and she is asleep in my arms in no time.

Back in his favourite watering hole, the Belle, Hubert sips a large whisky through his teeth. "Jesus, Martin, has the world gone fucking mad?"

"Not like you to drink whisky, boss." Millar arrives from the bar with his own drink.

"I need it, far less a triple on a oner."

"Heavy, boss."

"What the fuck is going on, Martin?"

"Oh, ISIS have the upper-hand just now, but I –"

"You?"

"Well, in an operational sense, I have taken assertive steps to bring them to book. We, in the operations, that is, are going to get these bastards."

"Oh, fine. You *will* keep me informed."

"I will that, boss. I'll report at the next executive team meeting."

"You didn't answer my question."

"I think you are just voicing it out, boss; you know what is going on, ISIS is going on."

"So, sort ISIS and everything is sorted?"

"Definitely."

"That'll stop the calls for my resignation, remove Jackie's suspension, sort out the mob, kick the Lord Provost into touch, ban the terror-tourists, etcetera, etcetera?"

"It'll stop the killings, sir, that's a start."

"Suppose." Hubert finishes the drink.

"I'll get you another, large?"

"Aye, go for it. I'm getting pissed."

Millar brings back a large Grouse. "Here, boss, down the thrapple."

Hubert shakes his head. "You'll know the McCourt investigation'll have to hold." He finishes the drink. "The climate's changed, we need Jackie."

"Sorry, boss. I've been told to pursue it."

"What? Who?"

"The police authority and Charlton, sir. I don't have any control of the matter, it needs to be brought to a conclusion. So I've been told."

"A strategic matter, outwith the power of the Chief Constable, fucking great. What is going on just now? This is a total fucking war with an international power and they are intent in burning a local ACC, my daughter, and I'll be next, no doubt."

"Boss?"

"What?"

"You're right, and I'll do everything in my power to prevent that."

"So you will, Martin." Hubert lifts his glass to Martin as if to toast him. Millar puts his glass forward to receive it and Hubert withdraws it before the chink.

"I need to see you," I say to Jean by mobile while Jackie is in the shower.

"And I need to see you, Rooney. I need to fuck you. Where have you been?"

"Jean, we were hit by ISIS and the Family has disintegrated. Where do you think I've fucking been?"

"Just come over, Rooney. A good fuck'll sort you out. I'll get my stuff on." I look up to see Jackie arrive into the bedroom. "I'll be there as soon as I can," I say into the mobile.

"Where you going, Rooney?"

"Something to sort, Jackie."

"No bodyguards, Rooney."

"I'll keep my head down."

"Aye, and your lapels well up, hat on, head down. Got some love for me before you go?" I take her into my arms. "Is that it?"

"More later. I'll come back."

"Good; stay away from your house until things calm down,"

"Will do."

I get ready and head to Jean's flat. But not before I call Ben.

Ben arrives in Tennent's shortly after me.

"I guessed you would want to meet, Rooney, Lucky escape, pal?"

"Aye, lucky white heather."

"Might not be so lucky the next time, Rooney. Where's James

and John?" He looks around the bar.

"The Family's gone its own way, the teams that is."

"Inevitable, Rooney. You know that. No way could they survive forever. It was always in danger of imploding. These guys are motivated by money, Rooney, nothing else. They don't want to be involved in a war with ISIS."

"I know that, Ben, but I needed them, it."

He studies me. Is this delusional talk? Am I relapsing?"

"You needed them?"

"I needed them. I thought I could use them to sort things in Glasgow."

"Oh, like a citizen's army? They are the mob, Rooney."

"They are a powerful unit, together, invincible."

"Not that invincible against terror organisations, pal."

"They can fuck ISIS, no problem."

"They don't want the mess of it. The risk of it. They are fat businessmen, with fat bank accounts in Switzerland, big holiday homes in Marbella and Florida, kids at private school, wives in the Round Table. It's just not worth the risk, the hassle?"

"What?"

"You are not fucking Robin Hood, Rooney, and these are not your merry men."

"I thought I was God."

"That was before your recovery."

"From mental illness or alcoholism?"

"Mental illness."

"Sounds good, get them in."

Seven pints of Deuchars, four whiskies, and two vodkas later, I fall out of the bar, literally onto the street. Ben helps me into a taxi. "Get him home, driver," he says, handing the taxi driver ten pounds.

"Cleveden Gardens," I slur.

Jean opens the door and I fall in to land in her hall. "See you've had a few, Rooney. Thought you didn't drink… to excess anymore?"

"No, but just felt the need to get pissed."

"You thought you could arrive in my house in that state and I would let you in. You underestimate me, boy and you kept me waiting." She grabs me by the hair and using brawn, honed by hours on her weights in her personal gym, she drags me in. I submit, not that I had the strength not to.

"You said you needed to see me, boy." She lifts me onto the sofa and pulls off her housecoat to reveal a black leather catsuit with a full zip down the front, then drags me to my feet and roughly pulls off my clothes. Standing over me, she pulls out a thick leather belt and links it under my chin. "You've been a bad boy, Rooney. You need to be punished."

She lifts the belt over her right shoulder. I look at it with terror on my face. "No," I say, then, "Yes," I add, as it swishes towards my arse. I feel the sting of it and my cock gets hard. As I feel the sting of another, my cock gets harder.

"You told me of how your father used to use a belt on you, Rooney. Is this what you felt?" Another whiz, another whack, the sting is more pronounced, my cock gets even harder. She opens her catsuit slowly, the zip going down, down. I am salivating. Then she jumps on me, taking my breath away. She grabs my cock roughly and slides herself on me, straddling me on the sofa. She is nearly suffocating me with her breasts, the provocative smell of leather against sweat.

"Fuck me," I say, quietly.

"What boy?"

"Please fuck me, fuck me hard, ma'am."

"Ma'am, do you mean mammy, Rooney? You want your dad to belt you and your mammy to fuck you."

"Fuck me," I say, in a childlike voice.

"I'll do both, boy," she says, consecutively riding me, then whacking me. I cum uncontrollably, wildly, her releasing herself from me as I do. Then as my sperm erupts from my cock she whacks it with the belt, sending the sperm across the room, as my cock retreats to a red, sore, and spent piece of flesh.

"Got what you wanted, boy?"

"Yes."

"Want more?"

"No, but…"

"Yes, you mean." She lifts the belt above her head ready to bring it down on my flesh.

"No, not that."

"Then, what?"

"I need to talk to you."

"Oh, right." She gets off me and puts a satin housecoat on. I get back into my clothes. "Go on."

"Jackie."

"Jackie, what about Jackie? This is not about Jackie. This about you and your… needs."

"I care about her."

"I don't care about you caring about her. What do you want to say?"

"Why do you hate her?"

"You wouldn't want to know."

"I do bloody want to know." Sick of being subservient, I am standing over her. "You don't control my mind or my heart, Jean."

"I'll hit you again, do you want that?"

"And I'll wrap the belt around your throat and strangle you with it."

We face each other. Although Jean is smaller than me she is more than capable of giving me a real battering. I am recovering confidence, though, and relying on the skills I had developed as a forensic psychologist. I'm well able to stand my ground. She backs off.

"You'll submit to me once more, boy. I have no doubt of that. When your sap rises and you need your dose of this." She holds up the belt. "You'll be back for more, and then you'll get a double dose. Not get the fuck out!" She screams into my face as she pushes me towards the door.

"I need to ask you why, Jean. Why do you want to destroy her?"

She approaches me, her face within inches of mine. My eyes twitch in a nervous response.

"You wouldn't understand, you're just a pathetic wee boy."

A pathetic wee boy.

I feel a pathetic wee boy. The wee boy that was used by a priest and dominated by his father is a pathetic wee boy.

I have to get out of there. I need to think. I need to get back to Tennent's.

CHAPTER THIRTY

Next day, as usual for a Sunday morning, Ben is also in Tennent's, poring over the Sunday papers he consistently buys, *The Observer*, the *Sunday Herald*, and *The Sunday Times*. At one point, he lifts his eyes towards a TV screen above him and notices a live BBC news report. He moves to the bar to ask the barman to turn the sound up, much to the annoyance of a group of guys waiting for the Sunday football to start.

"Sorry, guys," he says. "Two minutes. I just want to catch the news, then I'll go happily back to my wee corner, to my papers." They groan something about him going to a fucking library if he wants to fucking read.

Ben moves back to underneath the screen. THE CHIEF RESIGNS runs along the bottom of the screen on a perpetual banner. "Jesus," he says, having difficulty hearing the reporter's words over the hum of the football punters. "The Chief resigns," he repeats.

He hears the BBC reporter add, "We are informed that Chief Constable Hubert Kaminski has resigned."

"Guess it was inevitable," Ben says to himself. "No way could he survive the calls for him to go."

He listens to the story that only confirms his thoughts. "The Chief, having protected Police Scotland's role in a botched attempt to save John McCourt and having failed to anticipate the attacks by ISIS on the Glasgow people and further attacks on his police officers, bows to the calls for his resignation, some significantly political led by McCourt's widow Mary McCourt, who now has the ear of top politicians." Then, far from thw happier poses from Hubert in the days of his launching the new national police force, arrives Martin Millar, Assistant Chief Constable, on the screen.

"Mr Millar, I believe you have been appointed as caretaker Chief," says the reporter.

"Bloody hell," Ben murmurs.

"Acting Chief Constable," Millar says, correcting the reporter.

"Indeed, Acting Chief Constable. Can you please give us, the public, an up to date position, from the Police Scotland perspective?"

"Mr Kaminski has resigned," Millar replies, sharply. "I have the Inquiry report. You will have received a copy," he says, opening the report and reading from it. "The Inquiry has highlighted serious failings in the management of Police Scotland."

"Yes, we understand this," the reporter says. "Could you… summarise for our viewers?"

"Well." Millar draws breath. Here we go, Ben thinks. "OK, simply put, Police Scotland, under Hubert Kaminski has failed."

"Bastard," Ben whispers.

"It failed to save PC McCourt from ISIS and it failed to apply proper procedure to protect the people of this city."

"Could you be a bit more explicit, Acting Chief Constable?"

"Jacqueline Kaminski failed to obtain proper authority for the attack on ISIS."

"Botched it up and PC McCourt died."

"Indeed."

"She didn't get proper authority and the Chief has to bear responsibility for the whole affair?"

"Yes. This is what the report says," Millar proclaims.

"Indeed, however, the other police officers, WPC Joan Barry, and PCs John Grant and William Crawford, they weren'tv… Ms Kaminski's fault, Mr Millar. ISIS is punishing Police Scotland and showing it has total power in Glasgow."

"Police Scotland has to protect its officers. So far, it has failed to do so. I intend changing that."

"Good to hear that, Mr Millar. ISIS cells *are* gaining control of Glasgow. And, since it was hit by ISIS and lost six of its men, and kicked out its boss, Mr Rooney, the mob has lost its battle with the migrant gangs."

"Migrant gangs," Ben utters.

"Migrant gangs, backed by ISIS," Millar reports, as if he had heard Ben.

"ISIS has defeated the Family and intend taking over the mob's turf to create –"

"Instability and mayhem, and we in Police Scotland cannot and will not allow this to occur."

"Indeed, Acting Chief Constable; instability, mayhem. More migrant groups are arriving, etcetera. They say five thousand ISIS fighters are arriving with the refugees Glasgow has agreed to take."

"Yes, Glasgow is a very dangerous place to be just now. We at Police Scotland will now be more assertive."

"Indeed," the reporter says, hesitating. "And what is Police Scotland's strategy regarding all of this?"

"Simply this." Millar looks into the camera. "I have given my officers the mandate to protect themselves," he says, coolly.

"Does that mean allowing them to shoot… to kill?"

"They will employ arms."

"This is radical, Mr Millar."

"Radical and practical. Now, if you'll –"

"Yes, of course, excuse you, you'll have a great deal to do," the reporter says, turning his back on Millar. "That is BBC Scotland's news report for now. We have more on our special report later on an extended six o'clock news, please join us again. Our thanks to Acting Chief Constable, Martin Millar."

"Jesus!" Ben sits back down to find me sitting across from him.

"Mr Rooney. Didn't expect to see you here on a Sunday. Thought you didn't do pubs on a Sunday."

"Sundays no longer have the same relevance for me."

"No. Sobered up?" I don't answer. "You look pale, shattered."

"Are you surprised?"

"You want a drink?"

"I want a lot to drink."

Ben returns from the bar with a pint of Deuchars and a double whisky. "Here," he says.

I take it, finish the whisky with a gulp, and start on the Deuchars.

"See you've heard about the Chief?" I say, observing the head-lines in the paper.

"Shooting to kill, Rooney?"

"Shoot to kill, Ben." I finish the pint and head to the bar for more.

"Need to keep your head down?"

"Aye, need to be on guard for polis with guns." I return with another double and a Guinness for him.

He looks around. "You missing James and John?"

"They came with the job, Ben. No job, no protection."

Makes you vulnerable?"

"Yup, guess so."

Ben goes back to his newspapers. "What the fuck is this?" He points to a piece in the *Sunday Herald*. "Apparently a rogue family is supporting ISIS."

The Taylors, always have been, right back to McCourt. We always knew they were. Supporting ISIS, getting arms and money, exclusive access to drugs from Afghanistan."

"Thought you took them out, poisoned them, I haven't eaten ice cream since."

"Jim Taylor died. It was a warning from the Family."

"Didn't stop them, though. In fact, it seems to have emboldened them. They are with ISIS."

"George Taylor is well known for playing for both sides at the same time."

"Watch them, Rooney. They are as a big a threat as anyone."

"They've had their chance and didn't take it, Ben."

"Oh?"

"After leaving you recently, heading up the road."

"Fuck's sake, you didn't tell me that."

"Alan gave me information on Jean, about the McCourt stuff. She gave Jackie the wrong information."

"Always wondered why they went to the wrong place."

"Well, now you know."

"Why would he, Alan, want to help?"

"That, I have yet to understand."

"And why didn't you get to McCourt? Why did you hit the wrong ISIS cell?"

"Again, wrong information, Ben."

"Eh?"

"My Asian contacts got it wrong. All they knew was it was an ISIS cell. Just so happened it was the wrong ISIS cell, not Al-Jamal, or the cell holding McCourt." A soothing silence arises like a warm bath towel on a cold night. "I need to think."

"Why not talk, Rooney?"

"As social workers say, Ben."

"Just trying to help."

"Of course you are."

"Mind we used to use the place, when we needed to chew the fat."

I recall how Ben and I would exorcise our feelings there, talk through some serious situations, dilemmas, conflicts. Why wouldn't he offer a vehicle to talk?

"Aye, it helped. Jackie?"

"Jackie."

"She thinks Jean is trying to kill her."

"Why would she think that?"

"I don't fucking know. Why do social workers always bat things back?"

"It's what we do."

"Alan Taylor said something about Jean giving Jackie wrong information."

"And why would she do that?"

"That's what I said. He said 'Work it out, Rooney'."

"Why?"

"Jesus, Ben!"

"All right, alright. Let's work it out. Jean and Jackie: bullet points."

I could have exploded right there, but I recognised Ben's way of getting things out, clarifying, confirming matters.

"Bullet point one," I say.

"Go on."

"The first time I met Jean she told me not to trust Jackie, this woman who knows everything I called her."

"Yes, two?"

"I made that call, the call I thought triggered the bomb in Jackie's taxi."

"You thought you triggered the bomb, but you didn't know that."

"I presumed I did. Jean said."

"Why did you make that call, Rooney?"

"Jean said Jackie was going to assassinate me. I had to make the call."

"Although Jean, albeit she would have known how to do it, wouldn't have done it, Rooney. If you know what I mean?"

"What?"

"She wouldn't have hit Jackie. Not directly. MI5 and the police, come on?"

"No, you're right."

"She has a secret… about both Jackie and me."

"You?"

"That I killed a man."

"Did you?"

"Well, I helped him on his way."

"Jackie?"

"That she killed Archie."

"Did she?"

"Well, she said she did."

"If Jackie killed Archie, and Jean wanted to destroy her, all Jean would have needed to do would have been to call the press. Jackie is right, she wants to kill her."

"But she is MI5 and Jackie is a police officer."

"Correct, she can't, won't do it, directly; she is not that stupid."

"How did Johnston, the Father work, Rooney?"

"He didn't kill directly."

"No, he didn't."

"Jackie tried to kill herself."

"Correct, but it didn't work."

"Jesus, she'll get someone else to kill her."

"Just like the taxi."

"Jackie didn't think I tried to kill her."

"She was right."

"Who did she think tried to kill her?"

"The mob, Davy."

"She was right."

"Jesus."

"Get out, Rooney. You and Jackie, get the fuck out of Glasgow, while you still can."

"Not yet, Ben. I have to sort this."

CHAPTER THIRTY-ONE

"Thought you said you would come to my place," Jackie says into my controlled access.

"Come on up, Jackie." I open the gate.

I go to the flat door and open it just as Jackie arrives, as she just about falls through the door.

"Jesus, Jackie, come in." I grab her to support her. I help her in and to a seat in the hall. "Can I get you something, a glass of water, maybe?"

"When did I ever drink water? Come to think of it when did you ever drink water, Rooney?"

"Yeah, I guess things have changed. Jesus, are you alright?" I get a look at her deteriorated state.

"You said you would come to my place. Where have you been?" She starts to cry, cupping her face in her hands. "I needed to talk to you, to see you."

"OK, OK, you're here." I hand her a box of paper hankies and put my arm around her. "You're upset."

"Please don't. Suspended, demoted to DC1, she's trying to kill me. I ended up in hospital, Rooney."

"Jackie, the secret she has over you. I need to know?"

"Yes, I guess you do." She moves out through the patio windows out onto the balcony. She lights up and takes a few draws, clearly intended to prepare her for this. "She knows I killed Archie." She takes another few draws. "It's simple. I needed you to kill Johnston. Johnston had you over a barrel. He had your friend and mentor Alistair Gray, and said he would kill him unless you did his bidding, to end his life. This was his last act of control to prove he could force a good man to kill. But Archie said he would save Gray, so I had to kill Archie. I know it was wrong, but it was the only way I could get you to kill Johnston, if you knew he would kill the person you revered most in the world."

"Shite."

"Indeed."

"There's more to do this, I know there is."

"Rooney, you have to help me, you just have to."

"We crack this, her hold over you, the Archie situation, we can bring her down"

"You expose her over Archie, you expose me too. Remember, I did try to kill him."

Mary McCourt is in Glasgow that day addressing a group of students at Caledonian University on the other side of the Square, next to the City Chambers. In December they would have had problems competing with the Christmas fairground, but today, for obvious reasons, George Square is an empty and somber place, just the atmosphere she needs. Especially so when she heard that Martin Millar would be meeting John Murphy, the Lord Provost, in the City Chambers directly in front of them. Perfect! She had stirred the students to the point of fervour. "Our streets are dominated by the mob, ISIS, migrant gangs, and gun-toting police officers. "Miller's Militia," she calls them, "is on the rampage." The loudhailer is pointed towards Murphy's office. Martin Millar and Murphy move to the window of the office. They had been aware of the planned demonstration, but wanted to hear what was being said of them.

"The people of Glasgow demand protection, but not this kind of protection," Mary McCourt calls out. Seeing an opportunity for some publicity, Millar and Murphy arrive outside the Chambers, to see Mary and the group of students marching towards them. Murphy looks to Millar for protection, although the Chamber's security and the police are there already. Recognizing her, Millar holds up his hand in a traffic policeman gesture, not a good idea given PC McCourt was a cop often directing traffic on Glasgow's streets.

"Hold on, Mrs McCourt, this is not a place for –" The words are nearly out when he is hit by her hat as she whacks him in the chest. He flinches and falls behind the police officers pilling into the students pushing them back onto the Square.

"Go on, fucking shoot us," Mary calls out. "You're good at shooting the public."

"We are protecting the public," Millar says, trying to get it out.

"Well, you and your militia are not doing very well are you?" She tries to whack him again, until she is lifted away bodily to be pinned against a street barrier. This is the trigger for the students to throw themselves into the fray. They launch themselves at the police officers, who are off-footed by this onslaught of young people; not briefed in fighting unarmed students, they retreat. The students push through them and reach Millar before they are repelled by additional police officers arriving at the scene. "Police brutality, the police turn on the people," Mary McCourt shouts.

The demonstrators move back into the Square where more students join them, and before long hundreds arrive. Mary takes up centre spot in the crowd. A student finds a milk crate to allow her to just about – because she is only five foot one – shout over the heads of the crowd. "Glasgow has been taken over by the thugs, official, unofficial, and the terrorists," she cries. "We have lost these streets." She pans George Square. "In this place nearly one hundred years ago where Maxton, Gallagher, and Shinwell fought the brutality of the establishment, we are here to fight the same madness here today." Millar and Murphy look on aghast.

CHAPTER THIRTY-TWO

"Thanks for coming, Sean." Martin Millar invites me into their home in Cleveden Gardens. *Sean*, I think. It had been a while since someone called me by my first name. I move inside to be greeted by Jean, who's wearing a revealing dinner gown.

"Hello, darling, thanks for coming," she says, embracing me. We move into the sitting room.

"We," Millar says, "need to talk." Here it comes: his wife's adulteress affair with the boss of the crime families and how we can't let it get out, how damaging it would be to "all of our careers", but no. "We have a common need." I catch Jean's eye tighten. Common need, I think, common for whom, them?

I settle on the sofa. As a psychologist I will enjoy observing these two psychopaths. "We need a… joint approach," Millar says.

I enquire, "A joint approach?"

"We have a mutual benefit in bringing the violence in Glasgow to an end."

"And with it the destruction of ISIS in Glasgow," Jean adds.

"And what is this… joint approach?" I ask.

"Police Scotland, the intelligence service, and the Family," Millar says. "We can't defeat ISIS alone."

Albeit this appears a sensible and necessary idea, I wonder to whose benefit is this intended.

"I agree you two and your official services can't defeat ISIS," I say. "When the intelligence services can't find them and the police services can't destroy them, because they are so deeply hidden in the recesses of subterranean Glasgow, you have to rely on those who understand the subculture they rely on to remain out of sight."

Millar and Jean look at each other.

"Aye, that's right," Millar says.

I ask, "And what is the… mutual benefit, personally?"

Again Millar and Jean look at each other.

"Darling," Jean says, moving onto the sofa next to me. I take a surreptitious glance at Millar. He isn't unhappy about this. "We can all benefit personally," Jean adds, putting her hand on my leg. She slides her hand up towards my crotch. "The three of us can be together in this," she says, beckoning Millar to join us on the sofa.

"Aye, joint benefit." I move off the sofa.

"You," she says to Millar, "will consolidate your position in Police Scotland, remove that 'acting' word, Martin. Chief Constable Martin Millar, nice ring to it, eh?"

Millar gets to his feet. "Defeating ISIS would secure that, no problem. And you, Jean. Playing your part in destroying ISIS would take you into MI6 and off to those parts of the world that you yearn for when you are standing looking down the Clyde from your office window." Jean's eyes glaze over at the thought of this. "Where you can exercise your needs, passions and… predilections."

Perversions, I think.

Jean moves towards me, again. Is there no escape? "And you, Rooney. Think of the kudos. Head of 'organised business' in Glasgow plays a major part in protecting the people from Glasgow from terrorism. You and your… cohorts will be free to do your business without interference from us, from the police, from the politicians. I could go on about the… personal benefits you yourself will obtain. You will become a very rich man indeed."

"And what about Jackie, Hubert, et al?"

Again, I catch Millar and Jean passing eye messages.

"We have to move on, darling," Jean says.

I make space for myself. "Yes, we do," I say.

"Yes, we do, Rooney," Millar adds. "After all, your needs are being met in this… relationship," he says, putting his arms around Jean and my shoulders. I smell his repugnant body odour, but it isn't that that makes me nauseous.

Time to get out of there, I think, backing off towards the door. "I'll get back to you, on your proposal." I take my leave.

I stop a taxi on Cleveden Drive and arrive at Partick Cross. I need a place to think and drink. The Three Judges bar would allow both; although Black Friday, the traditional last Friday before Christmas might not be the most suitable place to do any thinking. But drinking comes first, as I order a pint of Deuchars Ale, always perfect in this real ale mecca. I study the Ale Board of beers on the wall, then I settle for a seat at the elevated area with corner windows looking over Partick Cross, a great place to observe the world and take stock.

Groups of Christmas office party animals fill the Cross, heading in and out of the bars. But then, before I have a chance to turn my psychologist's brain to the Jean and Martin setup, my mobile buzzes, with "Bingham" heralded on the screen. "Hello Bill, you OK?" I ask.

"Six soldiers dead, Rooney; four hospitalized, not a good day."

"No, but you're OK?"

"I'll survive to fight another day. I need to talk to you."

Great, so much for solitude. "I'm in the Judges, Partick Cross."

"Be there in five."

Bingham arrives and the atmosphere in the bar changes. Two soldiers take up position at each of the two doors, hands deep in removed inside pockets, hands-on access to their guns. The bar empties of those who recognise Bingham, leaving those oblivious to work their way down the one to ten selection of beers.

"Drink?"

"I'm not here to drink," Bingham growls.

"OK."

"We need to get back together."

I know what he means and resist the urge to say something funny like "Come to my house for dinner, Bill," which would most likely prompt Bingham to throw a punch.

"The Hammie got a kicking, Bill, and you guys were lucky not to be annihilated," I say.

"Wouldn't have happened if we were organised, managed, and had the collective strength we had, just wouldn't have."

"I agree."

"I need you back."

"Not about you, Bill. They, the bosses, need to need that."

"I'll sort it. Keep your mobile on. I'll get back to you." And with that he is up and out of the bar, and with him his men, and with them the palpable tension in the bar. I observe a noticeable rise in the hubbub.

I settle down to a heavy session. Lots had happened, lots was likely to happen. I was at a crossroads. I needed to decide which way to go. Jean and Millar, or Jackie and Hubert? Easy one that. The Father of organised crime in Glasgow or plain old psychologist Rooney, the shrink with a drink? The love of Jackie or the lust of Jean?

By ten o'clock, I am heading for the bar for my seventh drink and number seven on the real ale list. I had decided to work my way up the strength indicators. Following the Deuchars, I move on to a Long Man, Long Blonde beer at 3.8% and am now on a Williams March of the Penguins at 4.9%. I enjoy the imaginary relief of these titles and I'll get to the Fyne Ales Zombier at 6.9% in due course. My knocking a table of drinks on the way back to my seat indicates to all, including myself, I am becoming severely pissed. "Sorry, guys," I slur to the guys around the table, pulling out a twenty. "Replacements all round," I add, staggering towards my seat. I briefly scold myself for this indulgence, but also for missing my medication for the last three weeks, while there was so much going on. Ben'll be after me, I ponder. By drink nine, the 6.5%, my stomach is aching. My being tee-total for some time had allowed my stomach to heal. I recall my ulcers, the threat of oesophageal varices, liver damage, blood vessel ruptures. I was prescribed Ondansetron to stop the vomiting. I recall a number of occasions where, in a variety of bars, I would unexpectedly and involuntarily spew the contents of my stomach out over the floor of the bar, then get out fast, to leave unfortunate barmen to clean it up.

I go to the toilet just in case. The sliding door with a drop hook gives some assurance that no none could fall in the door unexpected. I will sit there on this small toilet pan in this small, barren closet until it passes. If I'm going to be sick, in here is the best place to be.

Look at the state of you.

"What!"

Sean Rooney, shrink with a drink from Partick, back where you were.

"Fuck off, bastard."

"You awright in there," comes from outside the door.

"Aye, I'm fine, no problem." I nearly say, "Just hearing voices," but I resist, knowing the barman would have the police battering the door post-haste.

Ah here we are, Rooney, like old times. I've missed you.

"Well, I haven't missed you, the monkey on my fucking shoulder."

Well, if you had stayed on your meds, off the drink, you would've been rid of me.

"Go away, bastard."

I calm myself, forcing a spew into the toilet pan, and follow it with a wash in the sink. I gather as much decorum and stability as I have available and make my way into the bar, picking up a batch of crisps at the bar, to put a lining in my stomach. I settle on my seat, a high stool made all the more precarious by my inability to stop swaying. I find a seat against the wall near to the toilets, just in case. I pick up a bottle of Sweetheart Stout, thinking it would sit easier in my stomach than the Fyne Ales Zombier and set it between my hands and central to my vision. I think if I focus on it, it'll stop the dizziness and my head swimming.

What have you become, Rooney?

"Oh, fuck, no' you again." I thought I had rid myself of this infernal voice.

Like what you see?

Last time, I saw the man I had become: a drunk man looking at his reflection though a bottle.

What do you see? Last time you saw a mental illness, an alcohol abuser, a destroyed self?

Like before, I stare into the bottle. I see the dark liquid. Then my eyes pan outward to focus on my reflection. Last time, I liked what I saw. Like Narcissus who fell in love with his own image reflected in a pool of water, I saw a new man, a transformed man, a bad man.

You liked what you saw, Rooney? You were a made man; you became the cold, hard, bad bastard, you wanted to be. What are you now?

But then, similar to the last time, I saw the man I feared. I saw the face of my father; the bloody eyes, the blood vessels in his cheeks and nose, protruding like tributaries of a subterranean red river running just below the skin of his face. This is what I have become.

Big decision to make, fatherman. You can become the man you have always feared you would become, the failure, the drunk, the father.

"And what's the alternative?

You could become the Father, a bad man?

"Any others?"

You could become the man your mother always wanted you to be, a good man.

"And what did good ever do for me; bad gave me much more."

Well, it's up to you pal. Though another one is: do good by being bad.

I spend the next three days recovering. I attend my GP and see my CPN. I know to go back to where I was would kill me; however, although something of that appeals to me, I have work to do.

"We need to talk, Alan," I say into my mobile, finding Alan Taylor's number in there.

"I knew you would get back to me, Rooney. Curiosity?"

"Something like that."

"Fancy a curry?" he suggests, like he was arranging to meet a mate on a Friday night. As he says this, my stomach starts to ache, but such is my craving I would risk any possible or consequential damage to my stomach wall.

I arrive early in the Wee Curry Shop at the bottom of Byres Road, to find Alan Taylor already there and studying the menu. "They do a brilliant Lamb Saag here," he says.

"Aye, on another day. Chicken Korma for me, today, dicky tummy." I take my seat across from him. He'd selected a seat overlooking the Byres Road and the door entrance, where he could see his men sitting in the dark BMW at the pavement adjacent to the door.

We order food and avoid the drinks menu, favouring a jug of water.

I am nervous as we await the food, playing with a tumbler, tapping my ring off it. "Calm down, Rooney. I'm not going to kill you."

"Thanks Alan, that makes me feel so much more comfortable."

"Even though, you, the Family, killed Jim my younger brother, and were responsible for us becoming... estranged."

"Good description, Alan, estranged, I like that. As far as Jim and the Oran Mor was concerned that was a Family decision to hit you guys, you had become... a threat. Estranged? You did that yourselves when you aligned with Mick and took a vendetta against the Family."

"You were in charge of the Family at the time, Rooney."

"And just, as the McGings and the Taylors were to take yourselves out of the Family."

"I was following my father's orders." Taylor chinks his glass on mine. "Anyway, we need to move on."

"What do you want, Alan?"

"What do I want? What do *you* want, Rooney?"

"You said you wanted something from me, that time in Victoria Circus, in your car, before we were rudely interrupted by James and John."

"Aye, the flowerpot men. So I did, Rooney. And I told you something you didn't know. I wanted something in return."

"And what is that?"

"Easy. We want peace, we want back in."

"Not easy, Alan, you pissed off a lot of the Family."

"Oh, I know that. But…" He holds while two plates of food are placed in front of us followed by rice and naan bread. "But, we can either have a war." He tears off a piece of naan and dips into the Lamb Saag. "Or we all get together. We are still one of the heaviest teams in Glasgow."

"If you can't beat them, join them." I tear the naan and use it to scoop a lump of Chicken Korma with some sauce.

"Whatever, Rooney, but the Family would do better with us in than out."

"And so would you."

"And what about George, your father?"

"He's going nowhere, Rooney, he'll die in prison, he has had his day. I'm taking over. I'll say which way the Taylors will go."

His hesitation before he said his father would die in prison interested me. "The gun running, ISIS, working with MI5?"

"Things will change, Rooney, when I am boss."

I study him as I struggle with the curry, taking a large gulp of water and trying to force the naan down. He's looking at me too.

"You're no' too well, Rooney. I can see that."

"No, but I'm getting better, thanks. Anyway, I don't have the same influence, in the Family, I'm no' –"

"The Father, no more."

"No, but I know that'll change."

"Well, you know more than me."

"Bingham'll get you back."

"You know that."

"I know lots of things."

"Oh, you do. You are beginning to sound like the woman who

knows things."

"Jean?"

"Jean."

"We told her stuff, Rooney."

"So you said that night, in Victoria Circus."

"Don't trust her, Rooney."

"Where have I heard that before?"

"There's a rumour that you're fucking her."

"Really?" I push my plate away, this is too much for my stomach to cope with.

"We told her about ISIS, where they were."

"You took a chance there, Alan."

"She said she would… do things for us. Get our da' out."

"Trust no one, Alan. But I meant with ISIS, a dangerous lot."

"I know that too."

"One of the reasons to get back into the Family, safety in numbers."

"Maybe."

"What were your links with them?"

"They paid us big money. They wanted protection. We could give them it. They wanted safe houses. We have plenty of them."

"We hit the Red Hoose. That was one of yours."

"It cost us that."

"Showed you how fit the Family were."

"We could have hit back."

"You didn't, you couldn't have fought the Family." A pause confirms he agrees. "There's more, Alan, I know there is."

"Jackie."

"Yes."

"Davy hit her. My father told me."

"Oh?"

"You wanted him to stop Jackie. Jean said Jackie was trying to kill you, that she was going to assassinate you that night in a taxi, one of ours. Jean wanted Jackie dead, but she didn't want to do it herself, for obvious reasons."

"Davy and George agreed this?"

"Jean had things on them, the gun running, etcetera. She said she could do things for my father, privileges in prison, mobile phones, computers, meetings, everything which would allow him to continue his business in jail."

"Anything else?"

"Of course. She said she would get him out in five. Pull strings politically. A pardon for information –"

"Davy?"

"Ambitious man, MI5 promoting his links with the UDA, gun running to Northern Ireland."

"The Troubles are over, Alan."

"Don't believe it. MI5 certainly don't."

"The Good Friday agreement. Arms were given up. Amnesty."

"The supply routes are still there, Rooney. Jean has the links, sources, routes."

"Davy's dead."

"She had him killed by Malky. A contract hit."

"He knew too much?"

"Correct."

"Jackie."

"The same."

"I said to Davy to stop her, not kill her."

"It was made for her to think it was you, Rooney; as if you had triggered the attack."

"Why didn't Davy tell me?"

"Come on, Rooney, with what she had on him."

We wipe our plates with the remnants of the naan. I need to know. "The vendetta on the Family, does it still stand?"

"I'm not prepared to act on it. It would be suicide. We can't fight the Family."

"You want to fuck your father, Alan?"

"Just like you, Rooney?"

It's clear a change of theme is required. "You tried to warn the authorities. The ISIS bomb at Central Station."

"I did."

"Why?"

"Because I am not daft, Rooney. ISIS is too far. My father went too far by helping them. The mad man will destroy us."

"Do you know anything about Archie?"

"Sorry?" From his response it was clear he didn't.

"Archie, Jackie's dead sidekick, DCI Archie Paterson."

"What?"

"Jean had a secret on Jackie."

"She has another secret, Rooney."

"Oh?"

"Charlton."

"Jesus, she is having an affair with Alasdair Charlton, the Justice Secretary?"

Jealous, Rooney?

"Archie?"

"I'll see what I can do."

"Good, I'll support you with the Family."

The following evening the Family meet in the Grandroom.

"And what are they doing here?" Paul Moffat asks, from the other end of the grand table, referring to Alan, John, and Bob Taylor.

"I invited them," Bingham replies.

"And him?" Moffat nods towards me, sitting at the end of the table.

"We talked about it, Paul," Bingham says.

"Aye, we talked about it, Paul," Patrick Devlin adds.

"But we didn't talk about they bastards," Moffat says. Alan Taylor resists the urge to batter him there and then.

"No, but Rooney and I did."

"I think you need to explain, Bill," Charlie Campbell says.

"I'll let Rooney explain, Charlie, but first, do we endorse him or not? That is why we are here." They all know this and though not all of them are comfortable about me, they know I am the only impartial person there, that could hold them together as a group, and a group they had to be to meet the challenges they faced in Glasgow. There was a slap from Bingham on the table, followed by Campbell, then one after the other they all slap the table until there is a resounding thundering of the table.

I take the floor. "Thank you, Bill." I take a drink of water. They all settle back on their chairs to hear me, all except Alan Taylor, who sets his elbows hard on the table. "First, thank you for endorsing me once again as your Father, the Father of this Family." I see Bingham's look which says "Get on with it Rooney". "But enough of that, we have business to discuss and first I want to explain why the Taylors are here." I see sets of eyes deepen in concentration over this. "First, we need to prevent war within the ranks of Glasgow's teams, we have enough to contend with. The Taylors are a strong team and they are better with us than against us." There is a palpable note of acceptance of this.

"And what about the McGings?" Fullerton asks.

"They are seriously weakened," I say. "They do not constitute any threat at this time."

"Aye, but we need to watch them. They can still hurt us," Fullerton says.

"I give you my assurance, they will not cause you any problems," Alan Taylor says.

"Second," I say. "Alan has… sensitive information, which concerns us."

"We know where ISIS is," Alan Taylor says.

"Aye, we heard that before and we *and* the polis hit the wrong places," Campbell says.

"Aye, but I'll guarantee it and we'll be first in. If we don't, they'll kill us," Taylor says, "as they do all people who know where they are."

"It's not enough for me," Moffat says. "We can't trust the Taylors. Not while George is alive."

Bingham turns to look squarely into Alan Taylor's eyes. He turns to pass the same look upon his brothers. They know what they need to do.

A quiet contemplation descends on the room.

"Together, and now with the Taylors, we can defeat ISIS," I say, "and any of the migrant teams that support them, and we can rule Glasgow again. But it needs to be coordinated."

They look at Bingham

"He leads," Bingham says.

The table slapping returns until one by one we leave the hotel. I head down the stair to notice James and John there. "Hi boss," they say. "Good to see you guys."

I am certainly relieved to see them and to understand my status in the Family is regained.

Time for a pint, I think, heading out of the door, followed by James and John. I check my phone. A few texts have arrived when I was in conference. Interestingly, there is a text from Mary McCourt. I open it. "I need to see you. I have information, Mary."

I text her back "Horseshoe Bar, 9.30 p.m."

I enter the Horseshoe and go around the bar to the back, which offers the best position to observe all there. I order a pint of Deuchars. James and John take up their customary position adjacent to each of the doors. I nearly offer to buy them a pint, but drinking is not in their contract.

I see Mary arriving to the left. She catches sight of me and moves over to me.

"Hello, Mrs McCourt. It's good to see you."

I ask her to sit down. She declines.

"I have something for you." She takes an envelope from her bag and hands it to me.

I can feel it is a plastic CD container. As she hands it to me, I hand her an envelope, the one containing £10,000 she had given me. "I didn't think it right to keep it. I didn't save your husband."

"You tried, Mr Rooney. And for that I am grateful."

I hand her another envelope. It contains an A4 sheet with everything Alan Taylor had told me. She opens it and reads it. She looks at me for a few seconds, shakes my hand and leaves.

I get home and play the CD. The one prepared by John McCourt, sent to her personally by Halid. It tells me everything I need to know about Al Jamal.

CHAPTER THIRTY-THREE

Next morning Alan Taylor calls. "Rooney, I need to talk to you."

"Go on, Alan."

"I spoke to my dad about Archie, last night."

"Go on."

"He said Jean fabricated the whole Archie thing. He helped Archie to escape to France."

"Thanks, Alan."

"And Rooney?"

"Yes."

"My father died this morning."

"Oh." This did not surprise me. I did not push the Archie stuff any further, but I was to find out later that George Taylor died of "complications arising due to food poisoning". There was no PF enquiry.

I call Jackie.

"I am back, Jackie."

"Oh?"

"I am the Father again."

"Oh, just great, get yourself killed."

"I have information for you, about Jean."

Her interest is piqued. "Tell me, Rooney?"

"Jean, she set you up. The secret she has held over you, about Archie."

"Archie?"

"How did she do it, Jackie?"

"She wanted something on me. It was about control."

"No, I know that, it is her modus operandi. I am asking how she did it? How did she know about Archie? Jackie, she's not a clairvoyant."

"Well, how do you think she knows?"

"You tell me."

"Because she said she knew everything. She knows I shot Archie, it was in my report. She obviously got access to that, as she does."

"But that said you shot him in self-defence, not that you set it up or you intended killing him."

"She knew. That was the secret. That I intended killing him."

"What exactly happened, tell me, in detail?"

"Well, I took Archie into a side room. I said we needed complete privacy to talk, and a direct line. I fired two shots, one into Archie, then one into my arm to make it look like he had shot me. When they came in, I was slumped over the desk, blood oozing from my arm. Archie lay behind the desk, a blood pool around his head."

"Are you sure he was dead?"

"I saw the blood."

"Did you see the blood come from his head?"

"Jesus, Rooney, there was a blood pool on the floor."

"Did you see the bullet enter his head?"

"Well, I fired the bullet at his head, and I didn't wait to see the spurt of blood, like you see in the movies, I just dropped the gun."

"Jean set it up, that's why she knew."

"Eh?"

"She must have known you would have had to kill Archie."

Jackie takes time to answer this.

"OK, I'll tell you, Rooney. I haven't told you this."

"Go on."

"I had said to her that I had to stop Archie saving Gray, your friend and mentor. If Archie had saved Gray, you wouldn't have done it. Gray was Johnston's lever of control over you. You had to destroy Johnston or he would have killed Gray."

"But, I didn't –"

"Kill Johnston? But we didn't know at the time you had another plan, and she said I had to kill Archie, that was the only way to secure your commitment. She would arrange it to ensure it looked like self-defence. She arranged for me to have a procedure to look as if my arm had been shot. I was given warfarin and just had to remove the dressing on my arm and let the blood pour out."

"Did she give you the gun?"

"Yes, I had to shoot Archie, then put the gun beside him to show that, after he shot me, It had to look like I struggled to get it from him and the gun went off, killing him."

"It held blanks. You didn't kill Archie, Jackie. She set it up to make it look like it. Obviously she arranged it with Johnston who wanted me to kill him as a last act of control. He was a proxy killer after all; he knew how to exploit people. It did the trick and got me to finish Johnston, and it gave her a hold over you. She knew your secret, Jackie."

"So, if I didn't kill Archie, what happened to him?"

"To be continued, Jackie. But there is one thing you have to do."

"What's that?"

"You have to tell your father."

"Hello, Al-Jamal," I say to a nondescript Muslim man leaving the Glasgow City Mosque. I had received accurate information from Alan Taylor and, although I knew the key cell with Al-Jamal and Halid had moved after McCourt, I placed men at all the main mosques in Glasgow. I guessed Al-Jamal would have used one where he could have some anonymity and I wasn't surprised when we got a report.

"I do not know who you are referring to sir, my name is –"

"Al-Jamal." I take out a photograph of him as a Free Syrian Army commander.

He looks at it. "Sir, I can see the resemblance, but can't you see that I am not that man?"

I study this man's face and for a second wonder whether Alan Taylor is wrong in identifying him as Al-Jamal. This man has a slimmer shape, not bearded like the man in the photo, dressed in western clothes; but looking into his eyes, this is Al-Jamal, I know it. "You are Al-Jamal; some changes to your appearance, but you are Al-Jamal. I know you are."

He pushes to get past me. I step in his way. Then three heavyset men appear from the shadows. "Sir, if you do not allow me to pass, my friends will remove you."

"And if your men move a step towards him, we will remove them," Alan Taylor says, also arriving from the shadows with his brother Bob and six of his team.

Al-Jamal knows he is rumbled, but he doesn't believe he is compromised. "Sirs," he says. "If you believe I am who you say I am, you are at serious risk." He is right, and all standing there knows he

304

is. Al-Jamal would have a hundred soldiers to call upon should this be necessary.

"I need to talk to you, Al-Jamal."

Al-Jamal knows he could fight his way out of there, kill as many as possible, but if his alias was revealed, he would not retain his integrity in Glasgow. His operation there would be over.

"OK, but you and I only."

"You know who I am."

"I know who you are. We have been watching you."

I feel slightly uneasy about this.

"You killed our soldiers."

"And you killed ours."

"You would wish to destroy us?"

"You would wish to destroy us."

"What do you want from Glasgow?"

"To conquer it."

"We will not allow that."

"Then we will all die and you will all die too."

"And how will you do this?"

"In a great attack."

"There will be rivers of blood."

"It is inevitable."

"We will talk."

"Where?"

"This way."

We walk to One Carlton Place, only the site of Glasgow Sheriff Court, where by day the security at the door resembled airport security. I knew this area would be on CCTV and a group of serious men would evoke attention, bringing in the police. "Just us, Al-Jamal," I say. He agrees and we find a place by the wall overlooking the river out of view of CCTV. Not that we are out of sight of our respective teams, however, who would have been there in seconds from their vantage point on Albert Bridge. It is after court hours and quiet and, for anyone passing there, we are two men leaning over the wall looking onto the River Clyde having a chat.

I start. "I believe you have executed dozens of people for your own interests."

"You should not believe western blogs, Mr Rooney."

"You are a former drug dealer and Free Syrian Army commander who joined ISIS purely for business. You are a profiteer from death."

"And you are a gangster of a crime syndicate who sells prostitution and drugs on the street." We pause. I wonder whether we may break into small chat about the river or Glasgow. I nearly point out the cathedral where I lived before I moved in with Davy McGing, but no chance, I had to make every word count. I see him studying the array of litter and rubbish covering the bank of the river, the residue of an example of Western society: empty Buckie bottles, beer cans, cigarette stubs, used condoms.

"Should there be a war, our soldiers, through our associates, now know all of the locations of your cells, seven of them, and we are monitoring them." Al-Jamal looks dumbfounded, but it is clear he is aware we know the locations and the strength of his cells. "On my signal we will attack them," I say. "If you try to bring your men together into an army, we will hit them before you can do so. Do you want to respond?"

He does. "We have locations of the head of every family in your organisation, and their key lieutenants; we are aware of the schools of all of their children, their golf clubs, their wives' coffee shops. We are aware of their business suppliers. On my command, we will kill every head and his family and destroy their drugs and gun sources. Our soldiers are not just contained in sleeper cells ready to bomb your city and its people."

This is getting into serious territory. It is time to reveal the information received from Alan Taylor. "We know of a camp you are using outside Glasgow in the hills near Loch Lomond, in a disused farm. We are aware of the strength of ISIS there and believe you are using this both to train your men but also to teach new recruits in the ways of the Jihad. We are informed you have forty-five soldiers and thirty-four new recruits. We will move in on this camp at my orders and we will kill all there."

I see him look over in Alan Taylor's direction.

Trust no one.

"We have trained armed cells in place, ready to go to predetermined sites and kill everyone in these places. On my command I will set them off on their journeys now." He takes his mobile out and places it on the wall. "They will be in heaven tonight."

This is a very dangerous moment.

"The Quran does not condone killing."

"Mr Rooney, we do not discuss the teachings of Allah with an unbeliever. You are not... qualified to provide a perspective on the Quran."

"But McCourt did."

He looks at me in the way I expect him to.

"You are a Christian, Mr Rooney."

"Are you a holy man, Mr Al-Jamal?"

"You know I am. I follow the Prophet."

"And what does he say?"

For the first time he turns to face me. "There will be a great battle against Rome," he says, "and a final showdown with an anti-Messiah will occur before Jesus returns at the end of days."

"You are a fraud."

"How many Christian soldiers do you know who will martyr themselves for their faith?"

"McCourt, for his."

"McCourt died for Allah."

"He died for his belief in humanity. I can prove this to you." He looks perplexed at this. "We have on the one hand the indomitable spirit of humanity and on the other the irresistible power of money. Where do you stand?"

"We have no... humanity, while the Christians defile the Prophet."

"You cannot fight the human capacity for love with greed."

"We do not observe... normal love. It is the love of Allah we observe."

"It is the love of cash you mean. Why are you targeting Glasgow?"

"Your leader said, 'We will not bow to their false prophet'."

I remember Maclean, the First Minister, speaking out against ISIS after the London and Charles Hebdo attacks. "What he actually said was, "We will not be cowed by these... sons of a stupid prophet'."

I look at Al-Jamal, he is incensed. This is an even more dangerous moment. A shootout in front of Glasgow Sheriff Court is a very real possibility.

I had to defuse this situation. "Why Glasgow?"

He looked at me intently for a moment, then appeared to take on a more persuasive demeanour. "We are targeting the capital of prostitution and vice, to bring terror into the hearts of the crusaders in their very own homeland." I think about challenging his view of Glasgow being a capital of prostitution and vice, but decide I couldn't win that debate.

"Glasgow is his homeland," he says. Jesus, Maclean comes from Glasgow, born and bred in Dennistoun, moved through to Edinburgh, opened a law practice, got into Labour politics, became an MP, became leader of Labour in Scotland, then First Minister. "He blasphemed the Prophet and we are avenging his name."

I am pleased he has some control and composure, because I intend to go deeper into personal territory.

"You are adept at making videos."

"We are comfortable with this media. It gets our message across."

"I have one I would wish you to see."

"Why would I wish to see your video?"

"Because it concerns your family."

He looks even more perplexed as I open an iPad and press play. Immediately there is a look of horror on his face; there on the screen is his father, sitting under a black flag which says, 'THERE IS NO GOD BUT THE TRUE GOD. THE FATHER IS THE MESSENGER OF GOD." I press pause.

He moves back from the wall, but realises to attack me would not resolve the predicament which is before him.

"Through our… contacts, we found your father in his home in Georgia's Pankisi Gorge." I was aware that, like him, many of the Chechnya fighters were from the Pankisi Gorge on the border of Georgia between Russia, Iran and Turkey. It was easy to trace his father and from him his wife and children.

I press play.

"My son," his father says, "these men have your wife, your children, myself, and your mother. They will kill us all. Please do not bring this great disaster upon our family."

"We will all meet in paradise," Al-Jamal says.

"Allah, you would martyr your family for Allah?"

"I would."

"You would martyr your family for ISIS?"

"I would."

"What do you really want?"

"To smite the crusaders in their homeland."

"Rubbish, you want money and that is why you want to see the First Minister. Fuck your view that you're avenging the prophet or attacking Glasgow because it is the capital of vice. Give me a break. "

His face softens and he returns to the wall. "You are an interesting man, Mr Rooney."

"Do you know, I wondered about challenging you about your beliefs, why you kill in the word of Allah, misrepresenting the Quran's teaching, defying Sharia law, but it would be futile because you are not a moral man. Religion and creed is not your motivator, nor your motivation for travelling all the way here to attack us."

"Oh, and what is?"

"Money, simply that; you are as big a crook as me. Money motivates you. You are here for money. Killing and terror are only your vehicles to obtain this."

"Indeed, Mr Rooney."

"ISIS is no more than international Mafiosi, with no different value systems than us. You want the First Minister because you know he has access to the kind of resources you need: cash, fifty million, but he is not the only one who can access that kind of cash."

"Oh."

"He won't give you the money."

"He will, they always do."

"But what will you lose before he does?" He looks at me intently. "ISIS needs money, not kudos, nor revenge, nor your Jihad. Holy war is a front for extortion, kidnapping, to obtain the cash you need to fund your organisation and your caliphate." He doesn't answer. "I will make you an offer –"

"Ah, an old-fashioned mafia offer, the Godfather, I like it."

"To leave Glasgow."

"I don't understand."

"I will spare your family and I'll give them one million pounds, and I'll give you a way out."

"And what would that be?"

"Martyrdom; you will be with the virgins in heaven."

"What kind of pretext is that?"

"You blow yourself up and we'll give ISIS fifty million pounds."

"You are crazy."

"You die a hero and go to heaven, ISIS get fifty million, your family survive with a million to ensure your children go to fancy western schools, and ISIS disappear from Glasgow."

"The alternative?"

"You die a coward, having committed suicide in your bed, your family die, ISIS get nothing, and we wipe out all of your cells."

"And I unleash a wave of death across your city. My men are ready with assault rifles, explosive belts, and a thirst for death. I just need to send." He lifts the mobile.

"Go ahead, your choice." This is the moment of truth. "I said, go ahead."

He looks at his cell phone, then the iPad screen, then back.

"How do I know you will keep your word?"

"I am a Christian, I don't tell lies."

I knew he had no intention of keeping his, but I knew he would disappear just the same.

CHAPTER THIRTY-FOUR

"Hello, Martin, thanks for coming," Hubert says to Millar, as he pulls up a seat beside him in the Belle. "Or should I say Chief-in-waiting?"

"Acting Chief, Hubert."

It feels strange for Hubert to hear his previous Assistant Chief Constable call him by his first name.

"Acting Chief. Think you'll get my job?"

"I think so. I have the right credentials."

"Yes, square and compass, English public school education, trained in the Met."

"I have been here twenty years, sir. I know the –"

"Ropes, the way to get on, brownnose your way to the top?"

"I know what it takes, and I believe I have it."

"Ah, but have you the correct values, principles, values?"

"Values and principles?" These words seem incongruous coming from Millar's mouth.

"Yes, a womaniser, living with a dominatrix for a wife, who's prepared to stab his colleague in the back?"

"Seems a good background for a Chief Constable, sir." Good answer, Hubert thinks.

"What about you having knowledge that your wife tried to kill my daughter?"

Millar is struck quiet.

"I have… no knowledge of my wife's –"

"Affairs, the Justice Secretary; her using the mob to her own ends; her trying to kill my daughter; her setting up Archie Paterson to get Rooney to kill Johnston."

Hubert can see from Millar's darting eyes he understands; he has always known about his wife's activities. "My daughter, your colleague; you knew, you exploited her situation for your obsessive ambitions. It is over, Martin."

Millar looks into his beer and sees his demise.

I meet Jackie for lunch. She doesn't "do lunch", but when I said it was about Archie, she agreed. We meet in Curlers. Contrary to the last time we were there, she slides in beside me on a seat by the wall.

"I told Dad about Jean, he said we need rock solid evidence to have her brought to book."

"Aye, expected that."

"He confronted Millar; he must have known about Jean."

"He'll tell Jean, no doubt, that we know about the secret."

"Of course, won't change anything there. So, what really happened to Archie? He wasn't dead, so where was he?"

"Secreted away."

"Where?"

"Where do MI5 normally secret people away? Think about UDA and IRA informants."

"Marbella, Mexico?"

"Alan Taylor said MI5 Glasgow had Davy McGing hidden for a time in France."

"France?"

"A wee discreet island off the west coast. Îl De Ré, next to La Rochelle. Full of expatriated Brits. Alan said George helped Archie to move to France, that Jean was behind it."

"Can we prove this?"

"George died in jail."

"Great, so all we have is hearsay, from the mouths of crooks."

"Not exactly."

"What do you mean, not exactly?"

"I've got some hard evidence she was making payments to sustain his wee holiday on the state."

"What kind of evidence?"

"An Excel file from her desk computer, titled A. Paterson, with a record of payments to a bank in St Martin, in Îl De Ré, La Rochelle, payments made to an account titled Mr Archibald Paterson. It even gave the account number which we can link to MI5. This is a direct link from Jean to him."

"Jesus, how did you get that; don't tell me you broke into MI5 offices, that would have got you hung in the past, Rooney?"

"Might be a crook, but not into burglary, Jackie. I got it from Margaret Johnston."

"Get to fuck, Rooney, Jean's admin, no way."

"You'll remember saying she wasn't too happy in what she was doing."

"I did; didn't mean she would break the Official Secrets Act."

"Enough to detect some serious discontentment with her boss and enough for her to think it was in the public interest to finger her."

"Nothing to do with a very large transfer into her bank account."

"Not about money for her."

"A woman with morals."

"A woman who hates her boss so much she wants to destroy her."

"The information, on Archie?"

"An anonymous envelope sent to me with a USB flash drive with the Excel file on it."

"Anonymous; wise woman, no direct link to her. But more."

"Go on."

"I have Archie and he is prepared to blab."

"Jesus, where?

"La Rochelle, where the payments were being made. I went there."

"Oh a wee holiday in France?"

"I enjoyed it, gave me time to think, to reflect."

"A junket, Rooney?"

"I booked myself into a wee hotel, in St Martin, on the harbour and went out for a drink."

"Nice."

"Why do people in St Martin go out, Jackie?"

"Go on," she says. I lift the bread from the table, then the wine. "For bread and wine?" I nod. I open the menu. "For dinner?" I nod. I pull out a twenty. "And for money?" I nod. "OK Harpo," she laughs. "What happened?"

I enjoy making her laugh with my Harpo Marx impersonation. It is good to see her smile, not like the last time we were there, when we first met after she came out of hospital.

"What happened? Well, I positioned myself at a restaurant, adjacent to the bank and the bakery, and where everyone has to pass to go into the village for bread, for food, for money. I waited there for three days. On the third day, this guy came waddling along. I didn't recognise him at first due to his expanded waistline, but it was Archie; no one waddled like Archie. He took a seat a few tables away and ordered a Kronenbourg. I went over and took a seat at an adjoining table. I also ordered a Kronenbourg. I thought he would recognise me and make a run for it, but I reckoned he wouldn't get very far with his enlarged girth. We sat for a while overlooking the harbour as the sun set to the west. It was peaceful. I can understand why he would have wanted to stay there."

"Why didn't you go straight up to him?"

"I was enjoying the suspense."

"Pervert."

"He was about to pay his tab and leave, when I said, "I'll get that, Archie.""

"Shocker."

"Well, not really, he just looked at me. 'Rooney,' he said, warmly. 'How are you? Are you on holiday?' he asked."

"Strange."

"'I thought you were dead, Archie. Jackie,' I said."

"Christ!"

"He stood there for a minute or so, then started to cry, and then it all came out."

"Oh?"

"He said Jean had blackmailed him. He had been taking money from the Taylors. I said I knew, Alan Taylor told me. He said that Jean said she would kill you, me, and have him sacked and disgraced. She offered him a quiet retirement in a warm climate, where he could live out his life in the way he saw fit, eating French bread, drinking French wine, enjoying the peace and tranquillity of St Martin. How could he refuse?"

"I will make you an offer…"

"Is he prepared to make a statement, officially?"

"Yes."

"Jesus, this is amazing. I am so… obliged, Rooney."

"Are we OK, Jackie?"

"Yes, but there's something we need to put to bed." It was the provocative way she said "put to bed," that took me back to the sex games she used to play with me. "You wanted me 'stopped' and you called Davy."

Oh dear, I fear the serious stuff is coming out again. But, as she runs her hand up my arm, I relax. "I did," I say.

"You were paranoid, Rooney," she growls, as she allows her hand to drop under the table onto my thigh. I look around. No one is looking; good. "You thought I was planning to kill you." I nod. Her hand is travelling up towards my crotch. "Jean said I was going to assassinate you." For the first time since we were together, properly, this felt good, normal. "You thought if you didn't stop me, I would kill you, eventually." I nod again. Her hand is now gripping my cock through my trousers. I am getting hard. "I always knew you wouldn't harm me…" she says, as she grips my cock hard, "intentionally!"

I look into her eyes; the old mischievous Jackie is back and with it us, the way it was before the whole sordid Father thing.

"You deluded man, come here," she says, pulling me to her and kissing me squarely and deliciously on the lips. I turn around and everyone is looking.

"I need to see you, Jean," Jackie says, barging into her office. "And you move towards me and you'll get this," she says to Margaret, pointing her stick at her, while almost winking at her.

"It's fine, Margaret. Come in, Jackie." Jean says, approaching her. "I'll take that." She grabs Jackie's stick and hands it to Margaret. "Take this. If I need you, I'll call you." Margaret takes the stick and leaves.

"I am going to do you," Jackie says, quietly, as she enters Jean's office.

"Really, without your stick?" Jean moves around to her desk and resumes her writing in the desk diary. "Irrational, alcoholic, drug addict attacks intelligence officer in full public view, now exercising paranoid thoughts. Clearly meets criteria for detention. Signed, me." Jean turns to the phone using hands-free. "Margaret, please get me the EPT, tell them we have a deranged woman in our office threatening to destroy a senior officer of MI5 who needs sectioning."

"Go ahead, Jean. But, if you do, you need to know that I have been in touch with *The Herald* to say you gave me wrong information on Al-Jamal and McCourt."

"Margaret, hold that call."

"Why do you want to destroy me, Jean?"

"Don't blame me for your self-destruction, Jackie. Anyway, where would you get such stupid information? Time to go, Jackie, pick up your stick on the way out." Jean gets up and grabs Jackie's arm.

"The Taylors." This stops Jean in her tracks.

"And why would the Taylors say such a thing?"

"George Taylor said it. He and Davy, the taxi and the bomb, what do you say, Jean?"

"I can see the new inquiry into your conduct. Paranoid delusions against a government officer. The stress of the new job sent her over the edge. Her injuries and use of alcohol, painkillers, illegal drugs pushed her into psychosis. Bet we could have you detained for a very long time. Attempting to kill an intelligence agent. Mentally disordered offender. Let's see; I ordered this in just in case." Jean picks up a copy of the Mental Health Act. "Grounds: Mental disorder, yes, no problem; significant risk to self or others, yes, tick; medical treatment is required, yes, I would say so, tick; and is guilty of an offence punishable by imprisonment, absolutely, tick. The State Hospital awaits, darling." Jean moves to the door. "Margaret, could you come in here?"

Margaret arrives at the door, but Jackie gets in first. "Margaret, please record that I have information on Ms Dempsie, which will be provided in court at her trial, that she orchestrated an attack on me to my serious injury?"

"Margaret, will you alert security?"

Margaret nods and leaves.

"And you led Rooney to think he had triggered the bomb," Jackie says. "Why?"

"Delusional."

"I'll tell you why, because you need something on people. To control, you need information which will destroy them."

"Oh?"

"Rooney was under the impression he would be arrested. You forced him into hospital and then into the hands of the mob. You used him, you needed something on him, to control him, to abuse him."

"Oh, I think Rooney didn't need much… persuasion in that regard."

"Yes, he has his own needs and demands, that's for sure, but you exploited him. Why? To get to me. You wanted what was mine, it was part of your plan to destroy me, but it didn't work."

"Margaret, has security arrived as yet?" Jean asks by phone hands-free.

"Yes, Margaret, bring them in," Jackie says, "and look forward to *The Herald* headline tomorrow morning. The chief spook who set up the acting Chief Constable, to be followed by a story that goes all the way back to the Johnston Father situation, where you set me up, to make me think I had killed my colleague, DCI Archie –"

"Oh, come on, Jackie, why would I do that?"

"Same as Rooney; a secret. You needed something to have a hold on me. Something you could pull out of the bag when you needed it."

"You killed Archie and you lied about the Birelli case, which got you promotion. Then you got the credit for the Johnston case when Rooney killed Johnston."

"And Rooney is made an outlaw and I am held forever by your threat of destroying my career and having me charged with killing my colleague. Miss Machiavelli, you certainly learned from Johnston, the Father."

"You killed Archie, and yes, it is time to reveal this to the world. It is time indeed for you to atone for your sins. I have tried to protect you, in the interests of the state, but now it is clear you are dangerous and will kill again. The State Hospital beckons. I doubt if you'll ever leave there, until you leave in a box. You set it up."

"What did I set up?"

"Archie's supposed murder, to make me think I had killed him. Back then, to get me to ensure Rooney destroyed the Father, Johnston. You used this secret over me to control me and I am going to see you burn you in hell."

"Are there any more delusions, Jackie?" Jean presses her button. "Margaret, security... get them in here now, she is threatening to kill me." Jean moves closer to Jackie. "Jackie, mind the impunity which comes with my job. It doesn't matter what you say about me. Whatever allegation you make against me, I have state impunity. Nothing you can say can hurt me."

"No, Jean?"

"No, Jackie."

"Jean, I have Archie."

"What do you mean you have Archie?"

"I have Archie, and he said you blackmailed him into taking part in your plot to force me to put pressure on Rooney to kill Johnston. Such a clever plan, such a clever, but extremely dangerous, woman."

"Oh, you have spoken to Archie, a dead man."

"Archie is alive, and you and I both know it."

"Archie is dead and you killed him; you are now hallucinating, talking to dead people. Time to be incarcerated for the rest of your life for his murder and your threats to kill me."

"I said I wanted to destroy you, not kill you."

"Easily perceived to be the same. You attacked me recently and it is clear you mean to harm me. Through my contact with the Justice Secretary, I'll ensure you are never released from the State Hospital. That you are a threat to the state and the Scottish people."

"Archie is prepared to testify against you."

"Oh, from his grave?"

"I'll have the grave opened."

"Sorry, no way would you have the authority to do that. No court would sanction that, Jackie."

"He's prepared to testify, in person."

Jean is looking less confident now, more perplexed, more unsure about her ground, more worried about Jackie's.

"Dear me, you are getting worse. Time for security I think." Jean moves towards the door.

"You blackmailed him. You arranged for him to disappear. George Taylor's UDA sources, disappearing gun runners in Spain and France, the Caribbean. You sent him to France."

"France?"

"St Martin, near La Rochelle."

This stops Jean in her tracks.

"He's dead, Jackie. Stop thinking dead people are alive. It can only confirm your delusional and dangerous state."

"Jean, he is here."

"He is here?" Jean looks around. For the first time, Jackie sees both panic and fear in Jean's eyes.

Jackie nods through the floor to ceiling internal window. Jean turns to see Archie move into sight, peering through. Jean turns back towards Jackie. Jackie anticipates either an attack or a frenzied exercise in self-defence; she gets the latter.

"It's his word against mine, Jackie. As a police officer he was bought and sold by the mob; you're all in cahoots, you, Rooney, the

Family, Archie. Christ, will this be easy."

"I have hard evidence, Jean." Jean looks to her computer, then to Margaret standing at the other side of the glass wall looking at her. "And, one thing more, before I have you taken away."

"You have no authority."

"You obviously haven't heard."

"What's that?"

"I've been reinstated. I'm back to being Assistant Chief Constable and I have here a warrant for your arrest." Jackie hands Jean the warrant. Jean is speechless. "But one thing I need to know, Jean." Jane looks at her intently. "Why did you want Rooney?"

Jean regains her composure. "Because he was yours, Jackie, and because I could."

"I though as much, but Jean… your hold over him is now broken."

"Are we talking about the man who likes to be whacked with a belt to remind him of his father?"

"You are a horrible depraved woman, and you are going down. The woman who knows things. Trust no one, Jean."

Two police officers appear.

"Take her away," Jackie says.

"Margaret, call Alasdair Charlton."

"Ma'am, the Justice Minister has resigned."

"Do something, Margaret."

"I have, ma'am," Margaret says, passing Jackie her stick.

John Maclean, First Minister, takes to the podium at the media centre in French Street. "I would like to welcome you all today to this, my report on the recent events in the City of Glasgow." All push forward to get optimum positions for the statement and the après-statement interview, and to get the best vantage point for their cameras. "In particular, ladies and gentlemen, I would like to welcome the Chief Constable of Police Scotland, Hubert Kaminski, who, as you will know, has now been re-established in his the post. Welcome, Chief," Maclean says, starting an applause.

"What happened to Martin Millar, Cabinet Secretary?" says Matt Hurley of the *Evening Times*.

"Mr Millar has resigned."

"Resigned; shoved, more like."

"We are grateful to Mr Kaminski and his wonderful ... services for returning this great city to a state of order, stability, and safety. And to my left, I would like to welcome our new Chair of the Scottish Police Authority, Mary McCourt." More applause. "And to my right, Ms Jackie Kaminski, recently reinstated to her post as Assistant Chief Constable. Thank you all for joining me here today on this momentous day for the people of Glasgow."

"Sir, the Justice Secretary."

"I have accepted his resignation."

Hurley is satisfied, knowing Charlton's affair with Jean is already in the tabloids. He moves to more serious matters. "ISIS, First Minister?" he presses, keen to get his statement back to his editor immediately to meet that evening's papers.

"Yes, Mr Hurley, ISIS." Maclean enjoys voicing these words. Far from announcing a state of destruction and despair, he could now report on a positive outcome to the ISIS crises. He knew that no one would interrupt him at that very point. However, they would very soon into the statement. He would enjoy this pause. Then, "Like rats racing out of a house fire, ISIS has left this city," he starts. "We will pursue them, however, wherever they go until we bring them to justice for the bomb attacks, the deaths of citizens and our brave police officers, the fear and instability they have caused to the City of Glasgow. There will be no hiding place. We will work with our international partners in seeking this scum out and ending their campaign of terror for good."

"How do you know they have gone? They could have gone underground, planning more hits."

Maclean looks at Hubert. "We are assured that they have gone, Mr Hurley. We are confident of this."

"And what about the mob, they are just as dangerous. They'll just move in and get control back of the city."

"Mr Rooney?" Maclean prompts all there to spin round to search out me. "Could you please join us on this podium?" I come from behind a pillar to join them there. "Mr Rooney, could you provide the assurances Mr Hurley is seeking?"

"Interesting to see the head of organised crime in Glasgow sharing a platform with Police Scotland, First Minister," Hurley says.

I square myself up to the microphone. This is a new experience for me. To be alongside the forces of law and order and political power in Scotland. I will enjoy this.

"I am here to assure the people of this city that... organised business will work together with Police Scotland and the civic leaders to make this a city to be proud of once more."

"Oh, the mob is going legit?"

"Mr Rooney represents a new face of the business community in Glasgow," Hubert says, "and has been instrumental in making this city safe."

"It is being said he had more than a small role to play in... stabilising matters here."

"Indeed, sir, now if you'll –"

"Mr Millar, First Minister, we believe he has been arrested."

"Yes, there have been irregularities in Mr Millar's practice and there is to be an investigation."

"Oh, another investigation? What did he do apart from develop a shoot to kill policy?"

"We cannot –"

"Oh, you cannot discuss, prejudice the case, blah, blah, blah. And what about the rumours that there has been a breakdown in relationships between the intelligence services and Police Scotland, First Minister?"

"We have entered into new protocols and new agreements with the intelligence services. That is all I can say at the moment."

Ben and I have a wee celebratory drink in Tennent's Bar, before heading to the Chip for a particular Hogmanay dinner. "And what is happening in... Fatherland, Rooney?" Ben asks, as we hang over the bar.

"Bingham has taken over," I say. "I am providing a consultancy service, a business management service, and the heads are going legit."

"But are you going legit, Rooney, the bad man doing good, or the good man doing bad? What are you, Rooney?"

"I am free, Ben, free to be me again. I am returning to my job and the... clinic."

"Back to counselling, finding serial killers, major incident stuff, chewing the fat, putting things to bed here every night before heading home to a warm Jackie?"

"Sounds good to me."

"Boring."

"Happy New Year, Ben."

"When it comes, Rooney."

Jean has been bailed, pending investigation.

"Martin you do look silly." Jean looks up to her husband, hanging from handcuffs and stirrups from the ceiling. "With your eyes, tongue, and balls sticking out. Not often for you not to say anything when you're getting your arse whacked, your nipples crushed, your throat stuffed with a pair of my knickers. But hanging there kind of… makes me love you more." She looks on a pale, bloated, and very dead figure of her husband. "But for now, I'm going out to get pissed and find a man. I'll see you later."

CHAPTER THIRTY-FIVE

Bill Bingham is on his feet. "I would like to wish you all a happy Hogmanay and a guid New Year when it comes," he says. "To what will be a prosperous and fulfilling year for all of us." He raises his glass, followed by me, Hubert, Jackie, Ben, Archie Paterson, and Mary McCourt. "Happy New Year when it comes," is said in unison. "I would also like to raise a toast to Sean Rooney, who has been somewhat... influential in all of us being here today in friendship." He raises his glass once more. The chinks from our glasses sound out through the space of the garden area of the Chip restaurant. "This marks a major step forward for the management of business in this city, and –"

Additional claps interrupt their conviviality from a very drunk Jean Dempsie walking towards us from the bar. "Congratulations, and a happy New Year, when-it-comes, to the gang of thieves, liars, and killers," she says. Hubert scowls at his minders who had missed her for another pissed woman heading towards the toilet. "Well done, all of you, in particular you, Rooney, the man who likes to get whacked to remind him of his father, the man who likes to be punished. You'll be back. You can't do without your punishment. I'll be waiting for you with my leather belt."

I remain shtum behind my glass.

"Get her out," Hubert says, as his minders reach for her.

"Get your hands off me," she says. "Don't forget I have something on all of you."

"Take her away," Jackie roars.

"Oh, yes, Ms Kaminski, the woman who crashed through the glass ceiling by lying about cases, resorts to murder, deception; gets her father the chief to appoint her to a high-ranking post on a wave of sympathy."

"You are going down, Jean," Hubert says.

"Impunity, Chief. Impunity for intelligence officers, you know the score."

Pointing towards Archie, she says: "She… you –"

Jackie screams "I didn't."

Archie adds "She didn't."

Mary McCourt sits dumbfounded, wondering what the hell is going on and who she is sitting amongst.

"I'll get every one of you, don't you worry about that." Jean looks at each of us in turn. "Archie, you are finished when it comes out what you have done. Hubert, Maclean'll burn you, Chief, when I tell him about you. Bingham, your businesses will fail when I expose your shady dealings. Rooney, the tabloids will make mincemeat of you, pal, when I describe your perversions to them. Jackie, I deliberately kept you to the last. I'll save my coup de grâce for you. How about the Birelli lie and attempted murder of Archie; you are going south."

Then she addresses them as a group. "Do not worry, my friends in Whitehall are, as we speak, enquiring into your collective actions against the state. I will –" At that she is grabbed and lifted bodily down the stair to be delivered out onto Ashton Lane.

"More wine, son," Bingham demands of the waiter. "And champagne."

Mary McCourt is all the more serious now as the drink gets hold and the ensemble become more animated in their roles. First, she observed Bill Bingham, now with his tie off, his shirt coming over his trousers. He is bullying the waiter. She sees aggression on this man's face, the kind you wouldn't want to be on the wrong side of. "Businessman," she whispers to herself. Then, she observes Jackie, hardly able to stand, throwing the wine back as if there would be no tomorrow, who would literally have to be carried out and dispatched into a taxi. Hubert, only responsible for the biggest police force next to the Met and for the protection of his officers, and yet her husband is dead and her son is fatherless. She wonders why Archie is there, a man who had deceived the law and hid in France. What were his morals and professionalism as a cop? "John would have punched you," she says to herself. Only Ben seems kind of normal, she thinks. Then she turns to me: this enigma, she thinks. A psychologist caught up in all of this crap. She wonders what is going on in my mind as I fall deeper into alcohol-related brain damage, turning from time to time as if I was talking to an imaginary friend: what was going on in my mind? By then she has had enough. She gets up from the table and reaches for her coat hanging over the back of her chair. She thinks of taking a selfie with us all in the background, which she could upload to YouTube, Facebook, and Twitter immediately that evening. She does it anyway for her own records, of what she will face as Chair of the Police Authority in days, months, years to come.

I'll impose ethics and standards, Mary McCourt promises herself; but for then she'll retain her decorum and leave there without saying goodbye. We are all so deeply locked in our own pathological bubble anyway, we won't even notice she is gone.

I do though, as I catch Mary at the top of the stair. "Mary, I just wanted to say…"

"Nothing to say, Rooney. I only hope my husband died for something you – deep in there," she says, pointing into my chest " – care about."

I see the sincerity in her eyes, but I'm so pissed I can't find the words to say to her. I can only say, "It's been difficult."

"Aye, so it has, pal, but you have to do the right thing. Do you hear me?" she says, getting close.

"Aye, I hear you."

"Just don't trust –"

"You heading, Mary?" Jackie's arrival there curtails Mary's point being made.

"Aye, wee Jamie'll be waiting," Mary says, as she heads down the stair.

"What did she say to you, Rooney?"

"Nothing important. I need to go to the loo."

"Aye, me too, hon."

Just then, Ben also passes by. "I'm off Rooney, heavy boozing going on here," he says. "I'm going home to bring the bells in. You stay safe, pal." He gives me a big hug and heads down the stair.

"Aye, see you, Ben, thanks for coming."

Jackie and I retreat to the respective toilets and, washing my hands, I find myself staring into the face in the mirror.

What do you see, Rooney? A good man, doing bad? A bad man doing good? A bad man doing bad? A good man doing good? What are you? What have you become? Where are you going?

"Oh great, the bastard is back," I say into the mirror, causing only the same guy I encountered in there only weeks ago to spin in his tracks and to give me an effeminate twist of his head upwards as he leaves the toilet. Then he gives a "When will you leave me alone," and a slap on the door of the toilet in disgust as he leaves.

You are a good man ruined, Rooney.

"I am a good man ruined." I repeat. "A good man, ruined." I look deeply into my face, more bloated due to my serious return to the drink. My eyes are deep and bloodshot, my skin pale and almost translucent. I reach into my eyes, trying to see into my head. I see the face of my father appear, transmogrifying my face. "You will never be anything, son, so don't even try." Then I see the warm image of my mother coming through my father's profile." Aye, you will son, you'll do good things one day, good things." My face gradually returns, but this is a confused face, a seriously pained face.

I hesitate for a minute then reach inside my trouser pocket for my mobile. I find a text ready set up to send to the receiver. I look at the text and the name in the address bar, thinking for a few seconds.

Will you do it, pal?

I press Send.

Jean falls on her knees more than once as she makes her way out onto Byres Road. In her mind she knows all she now needs to achieve, after confronting her nemeses, would be to get in a taxi and utter her address to be dispatched at her gate. Martin will be hanging there. Normally he would have something to say if she came home with a man, woman, or a Chinese takeaway. That night, he can only look on through empty eyes, a deteriorating and increasingly smelly and stiffening body; so much so, the funeral directors will have difficulty getting him into a box.

The oncoming Police Authority investigation into his conduct would be coming up, but before that they would receive the report of an FAI. Suicide, it would say. She would say he became a sad and desperate man. Her reputation would survive, she knew this. MI5 would close ranks around her and create the kind of story which would see her through, but she could not work in Glasgow again. It would all get out to the papers, and he had no such protection. She'd be lucky to get his pension. It was time to disappear, but before she does, she would have one last swipe at all of her enemies and Jackie would be at the top of the list, then she would disappear. St Martin in France is appealing. She had thought about it after googling it as she signed off Archie's monthly payments. It was the kind of place to disappear to.

She reaches the end of the lane to see a car waiting. "Taxi?" a voice says from inside as the window of the car slides down. "Good," she slurs, "a private." She would brass it, knowing private cars weren't allowed to pick up on the street. This would avoid the queue. She opens the door and pulls herself into the seat. As she does, she recalls immediately Jackie's attack in the taxi; how she would have reacted as she felt her mobile start to heat, ready to trigger the filament that would ignite the bomb inside. She dispatches the thought as she pushes herself back into the seat. "Cleveden Gardens, please, driver," she slurs. She thinks she recognises the guy's eyes in the mirror as he pulls out onto Byres Road. She settles into observing the Hogmanay imbibers going up and down the road to and from their favourite watering holes, trying to get in somewhere before the bells.

They pull into Great Western Road, heading west. It is quiet, before all the pubs are out. Then they turn right onto Kirklee Road, at Churchill's shop, and then, rather than turning left at the end of the road onto Bellshaugh Road and towards Cleveden Gardens and the safety of her house, the car turns right, down towards the entrance of the Botanic Gardens' Arboretum. Darkness invades the car as they move out of the street lights. He is taking her off her route. *He can fuck me*, she thinks, wondering why the driver has taken her this way. *Martin won't mind. He's dead. Anyway, Martin never minded me fucking strangers*, she thinks.

She would ask anyway. "Excuse me…"

The driver turns. She sees his face; she recognises this man. "Trust no one, Jean," he says, as she hears a pop-pop of a sound. She feels a strange heaviness descend in her chest, a stabbing pain, like indigestion. The thought she was dying didn't occur to her as she was dispatched on the pavement next to the entrance into the Arboretum. She could be mistaken; she was severely drunk after all. She would get up and pull her way up the road by the help of the wrought iron railing along the side of the park, but she couldn't get up, and she couldn't have known she was dying.

I return to the group, just about the same time as Jackie returns from her extended visit to the toilets. She looks intently serious as she takes her seat. Then, I notice that the hubbub in the group has stalled momentarily and each of them is looking down at their mobile phones, Hubert, Bingham, Archie, and Ben.

They all look at me, as if they have something to say. I look back at them as if I have, too.

End